Cupid Comes to Little Valentine

The Venturesome Ladies of Little Valentine

Book 1

By Emma V. Leech

Published by Emma V. Leech.

Editing Services Magpie Literary Services

Cover Art: Victoria Cooper

Illustrations: Amanda Wood

ISBN No: 978-2-487015-56-2

About Me!

I started this incredible journey way back in 2010 with The Key to Erebus but didn't summon the courage to hit publish until October 2012. For anyone who's done it, you'll know publishing your first title is a terribly scary thing! I still get butterflies on the morning a new title releases, but the terror has subsided at least. Now I just live in dread of the day my kids are old enough to read them.

The horror! (On both sides I suspect.)

2017 marked the year that I made my first foray into Historical Romance and the world of the Regency Romance, and my word what a year! I was delighted by the response to this series and can't wait to add more titles. Paranormal Romance readers need not despair, however, as there is much more to come there too. Writing has become an addiction and as soon as one book is over I'm hugely excited to start the next so you can expect plenty more in the future.

As many of my works reflect, I am greatly influenced by the beautiful French countryside in which I live. I've been here in the South West since 1998, though I was born and raised in England. My three children are all bilingual and my husband Pat, myself, and our four cats consider ourselves very fortunate to have made such a lovely place our home.

KEEP READING TO DISCOVER MY OTHER BOOKS!

Other Works by Emma V. Leech

The Venturesome Ladies of Little Valentine

The Venturesome Ladies of Little Valentine

Girls Who Dare

Girls Who Dare Series

Daring Daughters

Daring Daughters Series

Wicked Sons

Wicked Sons Series

Rogues & Gentlemen

Rogues & Gentlemen Series

The Regency Romance Mysteries

The Regency Romance Mysteries Series

The French Vampire Legend

The French Vampire Legend Series

The French Fae Legend

The French Fae Legend Series

Stand Alone

The Book Lover (a paranormal novella)

The Girl is Not for Christmas (Regency Romance)

Audio Books

Don't have time to read but still need your romance fix? The wait is over…

By popular demand, get many of your favourite Emma V Leech Regency Romance books on audio as performed by the incomparable Philip Battley and Gerard Marzilli. Several titles available and more added each month!

Find them at your favourite audiobook retailer!

Acknowledgements

Thanks, of course, to my wonderful editor Kezia Cole with Magpie Literary Services

To Victoria Cooper for all your hard work, amazing artwork and above all your unending patience!!! Thank you so much. You are amazing!

To my BFF, PA, personal cheerleader and bringer of chocolate, Varsi Appel, for moral support, confidence boosting and for reading my work more times than I have. I love you loads!

A huge thank you to all of my beta readers and cheering section! You guys are the best!

I'm always so happy to hear from you so do email or message me :)

emmaleech@orange.fr

To my husband Pat and my family ... For always being proud of me.

Table of Contents

Little Valentine

Chapter 1

It was all the fault of that blasted mouse!

Little Valentine, South-East Coast of England. 1st June 1815

Clementine Honeywell stared down at the word square game she had drawn out with satisfaction. It was a perfect construction. None but her family knew that she was Mr Benedict Civil, the mysterious word game setter for Little Valentine's own newspaper. She varied the games, from riddles to anagrams and the occasional acrostic poems. To be fair, *newspaper* was a rather grandiose appellation for what truly amounted to a few pages of local news, adverts and the odd bit of scurrilous gossip. Still, the construction of a word square or a riddle was, to Clementine's orderly mind, the ideal blend of cleverness, creativity and just a little bit of diabolical slyness that had people tearing at their hair. The theme she had chosen for this latest offering to the Valentine Morning Star was the seasons. She already had Vivaldi's Winter, and Autumn by Samuel Johnson. Coming up with the clues was something she would enjoy setting her mind to later and wondered if she might somehow include Johnson's famous quote, *great works are performed not by strength, but by perseverance.*

She still had ages to work on it, as she always had a game or two in hand to give herself enough time. Gathering up her papers, she put them neatly away in the drawer of her father's desk which he had given over to her, seeing as she spent far more time at his desk than he did. Arranging the quills, ink, and pounce pot and straightening everything to her satisfaction, Clementine darted a pained look at the table to her right, where her father kept his correspondence, his books, invoices, and any sermons or papers he was working on. It was a masterpiece of chaos and made her twitch with the desire to tidy it. However, she knew better than to do so. Her papa, Reverend Honeywell, insisted he knew where everything was and refused to let her rearrange things. A lenient and doting father, it was the only thing he ever got tetchy about. So, resolutely turning her back on the unsettling mess, she closed the study door and made her way to the breakfast parlour, where the sound of the Honeywell family gathered together was as raucous as usual.

Breakfast in the Honeywell residence was a lively affair. It wasn't just the chatter, Clementine thought with a patient smile as she took her place, though there was plenty of that. Mrs Adie bustled in and out, setting dishes on the table and taking empty ones away, scolding Beatrice for not eating and Isabelle for bringing a book to the table. Their father was preaching to the family, practising his Sunday sermon and breaking off at intervals to scratch his head and glower because he couldn't read his own writing. The family divided their time between listening and making suggestions, sharing their plans for the day, eating and keeping the children entertained. Reverend Honeywell seemed to revel in the chaos, although the sermon would not come together properly until Clementine had helped her father by writing it out again in a legible hand.

Clementine smiled fondly at her papa, who was an absolute darling and a man with a keen understanding of human nature. Unfortunately, as his busy brain was always occupied with the problems of his parish and how to solve them, he could be a tad absentminded. Keeping him on schedule and in the right place at the right time was no small achievement.

"More jam, Clemmie?"

Clementine turned to her little cousin, four-year-old Caspar, and smiled. "What do you say?"

"*Pleee-ase!*" he exclaimed, drawing the word out and grinning at her.

Clementine laughed and obligingly gave him another piece of bread and jam as his little sister, Daisy, squealed and tried to take it from him.

"No! S'mine!" Caspar objected, stuffing it hurriedly into his mouth.

"All right, you too," Clementine said, finding a piece for Daisy, who bounced excitedly in her chair. She handed it over, delighting in the happiness something as simple as a bit of bread and jam could bring the child.

The Honeywell family had seen their fair share of tragedy, for their mama had died almost ten years ago when Clementine was fourteen years old. It had shattered their father, who had adored his wife, and the whole family had been shaken to the core by her loss. But Papa was too good-hearted and too optimistic to allow them to fall into gloom. Besides, he truly believed they would be reunited again in the next life, and that comforted him. More recently, their aunt, Mama's sister and her husband, had been taken by a fever that had carried them both off within days of each other. Thankfully, their children were spared, and Papa had at once gone to fetch them and bring them home. That had been over a year ago, and Clementine could hardly imagine what life would be like without the two little children in their midst.

Not that it had been easy, especially the extra expense of a nanny for them, for Papa refused to touch a penny of the money their parents had left upon their deaths. That would be kept safe for Caspar's education and Daisy's dowry, not that it was enough to cover either of those things with any comfort. Still, Mrs Mabbs had been a godsend, even if she did bicker with Mrs Adie occasionally. The running of the household, over which Clementine had long ago taken control, had become increasingly challenging when their finances were so stretched, but she did not mind, especially when the children were such a joy to them all. Clementine had decided not to marry, for how would Papa go on without her? This way, she assured herself, it felt like she had been blessed with children, even if they were not her own.

Mrs Adie was about to place a fresh rack of toast on the table when a blood-curdling scream reached their ears from the kitchens. Mrs Adie jumped in shock, sending the toast flying in all directions, one piece landing on the reverend's scrawled notes and another hitting Bea in the eye.

"Lord preserve us!" Mrs Adie cried, one hand pressed to her capacious bosom as she turned to Clementine in exasperation. "It's that dratted girl again! I tell you, she's driving me distracted, she is. Lawks, what has the harum-scarum creature been up to now?"

Clementine groaned inwardly but got to her feet, hurrying after Mrs Adie, who looked ready to do murder to their new maid of all work. Polly was a sweet girl, but even Clementine had to admit she wasn't the shiniest pebble on the beach.

Mrs Adie burst into the kitchen ahead of Clementine and then screamed herself, moving with astonishing speed as she leapt onto a chair, and then onto the table beside a quivering Polly.

"It went that way!" Polly shrieked, clutching at Mrs Adie, who had buried her face in her apron.

"Oh, good heavens, Mrs Adie!" Clementine said with a sigh. "It's only a mouse."

"Not a mouse, *mice!*" Polly squealed. "I saw two of the little devils. Them traps you put down ain't caught a single one. The cheese you put with 'em is all gone too. They're clever and sly and they'll be in the pantry and eating everything if you don't kill the lot of 'em."

"Rats," Clementine said, dejected now.

"Rats!" Mrs Adie exclaimed, her complexion ashen now. "I ain't staying in no house with rats!"

"I beg your pardon, Adie, a poor choice of words," Clementine said, cursing herself. "But I really don't think there is any need to stand on the table. The little creatures must be more afraid of you and all that noise than you are of them."

"Oh, but where there's two, there's more. Hundreds of 'em, you mark my words," Polly said, groaning and hiding her face in her apron.

Clementine muttered a bad word under her breath but could not fault Polly's reasoning. "Very well," she said. "There's nothing for it. If the traps don't work, I must get a cat, a good mouser, and the problem will be solved in a trice."

"A cat?" Mrs Adie objected, scowling at the idea. "In *my* kitchen?"

"It's either a cat or mice," Clementine said firmly. "You may take your choice."

Mrs Adie looked somewhat mutinous, her jaw tight, but she nodded, which was good enough for Clementine. Hurrying to fetch her bonnet and spencer, she informed her sisters she was going out on an errand, kissed her father, who didn't notice, and bustled to the front door.

Clementine let out a breath and stood outside for a moment on the doorstep. The roses were in bloom, cascading around the porch, and the decadent scent surrounded her, the early morning sun warm on her face. A perfect day, she thought with a smile. Well, except for the dratted mouse. *Mice.* Never mind. It was a lovely day for a stroll, and the Misses Brumley would be pleased to see her.

Striding out, Clementine made her way through the front garden, making a mental note to ask the gardener to oil the squeaky gate, and then out onto the lane. She bade the occupants of the graveyard a good morning as she cut through, past her father's church and out onto the footpath that crossed the stream and led on towards Honeysuckle Cottage.

Poppies and cornflowers studded the fields and the frilly lace caps of wild carrot waved as she made her way along the narrow path. The pungent scent of wild garlic tickled Clementine's nose, and she wished she had thought to bring a basket with her. Still, she doubted that sharing a basket with a bundle of smelly weeds would endear her to the cat she intended to buy. She did not doubt that Miss Dotty would have a cat, for she had many feline friends, much to the despair of her sister, Edith, who was always trying to find suitable homes for them.

Honeysuckle Cottage made an adorable picture on a sunny summer morning, the thick thatched roof overhanging a sturdy little building of timber frame with whitewashed plaster infill. The front garden rioted in a mad display of flowers and herbs, the lazy drone of insects loud as Clementine made her way up the brick pathway. Butterflies rose around her, disturbed by her passage as her dress brushed against a lavender bush, and Clementine stopped as a sweet ginger face with beady yellow eyes peered at her, before darting out of sight again. Stooping on the path, Clementine called softly, enchanted as the little ball of fluff peeked out once more. Breaking off a lavender flower, she wriggled it back and forth on the brick path. A moment later, the kitten pounced, catching the flower between soft pink paws.

"Oh, you will be a fine mouser," she exclaimed, scooping up the kitten.

"Who's there?"

Clementine looked up and then straightened, carrying the kitten to the front door. "Good morning, Miss Dotty," she called cheerfully. "It's Miss Honeywell."

"Oh, good morning, my dear. Come in, come in. I've just made tea. Oh, and I see you have found a friend," she chuckled, bustling Clementine inside.

A few moments later and Miss Dotty had hustled Clementine into their bright breakfast parlour and supplied her with a cup of tea and a currant scone, while the kitten attacked the hem of her dress.

"Of course you can take Little Ginger, not that it's the poor dear's name. I haven't named this litter yet. It's so difficult to decide what suits them best," Dotty said thoughtfully.

"It's really not," her sister remarked, striding into the room. "Morning, Clementine. How do?"

"Very well, Miss Edith, thank you," Clementine remarked, smiling at Miss Edith, who was as tall and slender as her sister was short and plump. They were nothing alike, for Edith was a no-nonsense, practical woman with sharp features and a restless air about her. Dotty, by contrast, was all softness, a sweetly faded rose of a woman. Clementine thought she must have been a considerable beauty in her time. Now she was comfortably plump, with pink cheeks and pale blue eyes that sparkled with mischief.

"You're going to take one?" Edith asked, nodding at the ginger kitten that had since been joined by several siblings.

"Oh, but you can't take one," Dotty cried, looking appalled. "The poor darling will be lonely. No, no. You must take two."

Clementine frowned, wondering how Mrs Adie would react to two cats in her kitchen, but Edith, sensing weakness, went in for the kill.

"Two or none," she said briskly. "Dotty will plague me to death, making me check on the wretched thing every day if you don't take two."

Clementine laughed. "You drive a hard bargain. Very well, I shall take the ginger one and… and that black one, with the white spot on his cheek. Is it a he?" she asked.

Edith, who had just sat down, got up again, and lifted both kittens, peering at their bottoms.

"Edith!" Dotty cried, mortified, as she buried her face in her hands. "Don't shame the poor little creatures, oh, and at the breakfast table too!" she moaned, shaking her head in despair.

Clementine bit her lip to stifle a laugh as Edith rolled her eyes. “The ginger one is a boy; the black one is a girl. So, you’ll certainly have more soon enough.”

Clementine considered this. Though she was a very practical young woman and never let her heart rule her head, as she looked down at the little balls of fluff, she could not help herself. It was probably a terrible idea, but… oh, they were adorable, and Caspar and Daisy would love having kittens about the place.

“I’ll take them,” she said with a smile. “Only, I was expecting to carry one kitten home, not two.”

“No trouble. I’ll bring them in our picnic basket later today,” Edith said with ease, lavishly buttering half of a scone.

“Perfect, then I shall give you some jars of our honey, a nice ham, some of our goat cheese, and a large jar of Mrs Adie’s pickled onions in payment. They’re eye-watering, but delicious.”

“Splendid,” Dotty said, clapping her hands with delight, having recovered from her sister's appalling lack of conduct. “That’s very generous, dear.”

“It is, but I actually want something else, too,” Edith replied, and Clementine smiled. Edith was definitely the more practical of the two women and would never let the opportunity to negotiate a bargain slip past her.

“Go on,” Clementine said, interested to hear what came next.

“You know we rent out the little house on the seafront during the summer months?”

“Oh, Edith, I really don’t think—” Dotty began, only to be silenced by the impatient look Edith cast her. She sighed.

“Well, we have rented it out to a brother and sister, a Mr and Miss Marwick, for an entire year. They paid handsomely and they *seem* very respectable.”

“Oh, but they were charming,” Dotty protested.

Edith rolled her eyes. "I'm sure they are, dear, only—"

"Only?" Clementine asked, now thoroughly intrigued.

Edith threw up her hands. "Oh, Dotty is right, I'm certain. They were perfectly charming. Only—" She laughed and shook her head.

"Do you think they are not really brother and sister?" Clementine asked cautiously.

"Oh, no. I have no doubt of that. The resemblance is striking and, really, people are entitled to their secrets. I wouldn't care a fig if they were unmarried and calling themselves Mr and Mrs, so long as it did not reflect badly on us. Dotty would be devastated, you see, and—" Edith looked increasingly agitated, for she was not at all the kind to judge others, and this suspicion of hers, whatever it was, appeared to be upsetting her deeply.

"I quite understand," Clementine said soothingly. In a small-town, gossip flew from door to door at astonishing speed and could cause a good deal of damage whether or not it was true.

"It's just that we do not want any scandal attached to us. You do see?" Edith pressed.

"Of course I do," Clementine replied. "So, you would like me to make myself known to Mr and Miss Marwick and see what I make of them?" she asked, unsurprised by the demand.

She often found herself poking her nose into other people's affairs, having discovered the hard way that it was better she find out the truth than let the neighbourhood speculate and think up their own unfavourable answers. Somehow, she had become the person people turned to for advice, especially on how to deal with their neighbours if there was a dispute, or how to resolve a family squabble. She supposed it had come about because she so often helped her father, and people had become as used to speaking freely before her as they did the reverend. Clementine Honeywell was sensible and level-headed and could be relied upon not to make an inflammatory situation worse. Of course, her sister

Beatrice was known for being sweet-natured and beautiful, Clementine thought ruefully, but at least she was useful.

"Oh, would you?" Edith gave a heartfelt sigh. "I believe they will not arrive until the end of July, but it would put my mind at rest. You are such an excellent judge of character. Why, when everyone was accusing Steven Brown of having stolen money from old Mother Sendal, you were the only one who stood up for him. Well, he's such a moody and unsociable fellow, it was easy enough to believe. I'm afraid I myself was quite convinced he'd done it, but you proved otherwise," Edith said admiringly.

"Oh, yes, such a clever girl you are. I mean, who else would have thought to look down the back of the dresser? Mother Sendal is getting forgetful in her old age, sadly. I doubt she even noticed when it fell, so I suppose we cannot blame her for pointing the finger," Dotty said doubtfully.

Clementine smiled. "Well, you just let me know when they arrive and I shall welcome them to the village and invite them to tea. How's that? It's no more than I ought to do, and then Papa can meet them too."

"Oh, splendid," Edith said, looking relieved. "That's just the thing."

Clementine nodded, pleased to have put the woman's mind at rest, and finished her scone. Then she bade the two ladies a good day and walked back towards the village. As it was such a glorious morning, she detoured, taking a circular route so she could walk along the beach before heading home.

It was early yet, and few of the shops lining the main street that looked out to sea were open, but Clementine waved at Mrs Peacock, who ran the grocer's shop with her husband, and determinedly kept her gaze directed away from Madame Auguste's. They were fortunate indeed to have such a stylish and clever dressmaker as the elegant Frenchwoman in a small backwater town like Little Valentine, but no matter how much

Clementine coveted the glorious cobalt blue silk that had been cleverly draped over a dressmaker's dummy, she could not afford it. Any extra coins she might wrangle from the housekeeping, or from the sales of honey or goat cheese, she squirreled away for safekeeping, determined to hoard enough to give Beatrice a London season. Clementine had never possessed the necessary qualities nor desire for such an extravagance, but Beatrice, with her beauty and her sweetness, was a diamond who deserved to be seen and admired. She would make a splendid match, Clementine was certain, and she had determined her sister must have the opportunity. Yet as Bea was already twenty, she despaired of ever having funds enough to cover the costs.

Clementine took the stairs, making her way up from the beach to the road, and walked towards a series of smart seaside villas, the largest of which was an elegant hotel named The Mermaid's Tale. From there she intended to follow the path that wended through Winsham Woods, not yet ready to return to the bustle and chaos of the vicarage. Lost in thoughts of selling embroidered handkerchiefs via Madame Auguste's and wondering who in their right mind would hand over hard-earned money for such ham-fisted efforts as she might produce, Clementine did not see the carriage until it was almost upon her. The elegant equipage swept around the corner, the four matched bays gleaming in the sunlight, and she barely had time to give a little shriek of exclamation before throwing herself out of the way.

"Steady there, gel!" exclaimed a man's voice, as hands steadied her.

Turning, Clementine stared at the man who had saved her.

"Major Hancock!" she said, breathless with relief as she stared up at him. He was an old soldier, perhaps sixty years of age, but still hale and hearty, as attested by the ease with which he had caught her.

"Should watch where you are going," he told her sternly, but there was more concern than condemnation in his eyes. "And you, sir!" he shouted, turning his glare upon the driver of the splendid carriage, which Clementine could now see was embellished with a brightly painted coat of arms.

The coachman leapt down from his perch as the postillion took hold of the horses and a groom ran from the hotel to see to the magnificent beasts.

"Beggin' your pardon, sir, madam. Only his lordship was took ill, and I was told to get him here quick sharp like," he said apologetically, swiping the hat from his head as he addressed Clementine.

Before either she or the major could respond, the carriage door was flung open.

"Don't do that, ye daft bugger!" shouted an angry voice from the dark confines of the carriage, but whoever it was giving instructions was ignored, and a shock of blond hair emerged first before the rest of the man fell out. He landed awkwardly on his hands and knees, gave a heartfelt groan, and vomited over Clementine's boots.

Clementine gasped, clapping a hand over her mouth in disgust as the major bellowed in horror.

"Good God! Show a little respect, you blackguard. How dare you arrive here in such a vile state of inebriation?"

As he spoke, a bull of a man climbed out the carriage. Hulking across the shoulders, he had a thick neck and a nose that had surely been broken on multiple occasions.

"S'cuse me," he said, his expression forbidding as he hauled the groaning heap from the ground and dragged him bodily into the hotel. It was no mean feat either, for though the bull-headed fellow was undoubtedly the largest man Clementine had ever seen, his golden-haired companion was no lightweight either. She watched, appalled and astonished, as the two men disappeared without so much as a murmur of apology.

"My dear Miss Honeywell," the major said, looking much discomforted by the situation. "I would invite you into my home and have Drummond clean your boots, but without a maid or one of your sisters—"

He trailed off uncomfortably and Clementine shook her head.

"It's of no matter," she said, managing a grim smile. "I'll take a paddle in the sea. That should rid me of the worst of it."

"I'm so sorry," the major said, looking dreadfully put out.

Touched by his concern, Clementine smiled a little more warmly. "It was not at all your fault. Indeed, you saved me from a nasty tumble, and I thank you for your gallantry, sir."

The major coloured a little at her praise. "Think nothing of it, a pleasure. At your service," he said, gratification at her thanks gleaming in his eyes.

Clementine did not linger, too eager to wash the disgusting mess from her boots. Keeping the hem of her gown high, she hurried down to the beach and walked for several yards through the frothing waves until she was certain her boots were vomit-free. Feeling queasy and annoyed, Clementine reflected that, if not for an invasion of mice in the vicarage kitchen, such an objectionable scene might have been avoided, and her best boots not entirely ruined. Such were the vagaries of fate. Then, with her feet squishing unpleasantly, she squelched the rest of the way home.

Chapter 2

A Godforsaken backwater full to the hilt with bumpkins.

The Mermaid's Tale, Little Valentine, South-East Coast of England, 1st June 1815.

"Go to the devil, you two-faced sly boots!"

Kirby did not bother to duck as his master took hold of a once immaculate Hessian boot and attempted to fling it at him. His strength was all gone, and the boot slipped from his grasp, landing with a dull thud beside the bed.

"There's no need to sweet-talk me, my lord," Kirby replied amiably. "I know you feel indebted to me for saving your sorry arse, but I don't need your thanks."

"I don't thank you, damn your eyes," the sweating heap that had been an elegant nobleman not so many hours earlier cried in despairing tones. "Where the hell are we? I thought you were taking me to Bath?"

"Little Valentine, my lord."

Sylvester Cavendish, the Earl of Beaumarsh, known to the fashionable upper ten thousand as Beau, gazed at his valet in horrified disbelief.

"Little what now?"

"Valentine," Kirby replied. "Like the saint."

"I've never heard of Little Valentine," Beau replied, the dread in his voice deepening. "What am I doing in a place I've never even heard of?"

"Well, so far as I can see, you're still breathing and squawking, so that's something," Kirby replied, unperturbed.

"Where am I?" Beau repeated, looking increasingly agitated. "And don't talk in riddles." Kirby sighed, noting the flush of colour on his lordship's alabaster skin and deciding it was not prudent to tease him. For a little while there, Kirby had truly believed the man was going to die, and he'd never been so damned scared in all his life. As it was, whatever poison his lordship had unwittingly ingested had, as far as Kirby was concerned, left him horribly weak and a long way from making sensible decisions.

"Little Valentine. It's a lot closer than Bath and I figured the journey was less likely to kill you. It's a small spa town in East Sussex on the south-east coast. Close to Rye."

Beau frowned, as if he was struggling to focus on Kirby. "Good God," he said, and passed out.

Kirby was uncertain whether it was the lingering effect of the poison or the idea of the exquisitely fashionable Lord Beaumont being caught in such a backwater that had caused him to lose consciousness again. It could be either. At least he wasn't being caught *dead*, Kirby thought sardonically, and set about unpacking his master's impressive wardrobe.

"He vomited… on your boots?" Izzy repeated, eyes wider than usual behind her spectacles as she digested this appalling information.

Clementine noted wryly that the information had shocked her sister so much she'd even put down the book she was reading.

"On my *best* half boots," Clementine corrected, determined this fact not be overlooked.

"Oh, dear." Izzy bit her lip as Clementine glared at her.

"It's not the least bit funny."

"Well, it is a little bit funny," Izzy said apologetically, getting to her feet to follow Clementine out into the garden.

"Not if you were wearing the boots," Clementine insisted, which Izzy conceded was true enough.

"But who is he?" she asked, as Clementine gathered her basket and a pair of pruning shears and headed towards the rose garden.

"I don't know. A nobleman, judging by the gaudy paintwork on the carriage and those flashy horses. We must hope he doesn't stay long, though what on earth the man is doing coming here in the first place, I cannot think," Clementine added with a shake of her head.

"Perhaps he was lost?" Izzy suggested.

It was the most likely explanation. Little Valentine was an elegant and prosperous place, but its visitors were middle class and elderly. Their town, charming as it was, had never been fashionable, unlike Bath or Harrogate. The county of Sussex, the last Anglo-Saxon kingdom to be Christianised, still felt somewhat removed from the rest of England, despite its proximity to London. Its geography kept it isolated, with the sea on its south side, marshes to the east and west, and terrible roads that made the journey ill-advised in bad weather. Yet in the summer months it became quietly busy, with the comfortably wealthy coming to spend a few days or a week by the sea and to take the famed waters.

Though Little Valentine had noble inhabitants, being inordinately proud of Hatherley Hall on its doorstep, a fine Elizabethan manor house that belonged to the Dowager Duchess of Hawkney, it could hardly boast of the connection. The family had not set foot in the place in close to thirty years, and Clementine could not conceive of what else would bring a fashionable nobleman to the place. He *must* have been lost. She reached over with the pruning knife and cut a dead head off a pale pink rosebush with a little too much satisfaction.

"Well, I imagine we shall find out soon enough," Izzy said with a shrug. "No one can sneeze around here without the entire town knowing about it. Nothing half so exciting has ever happened here that I can remember, so we are bound to hear the man's life story before the afternoon is out."

"I imagine we shall," Clementine said, glancing at her sister. "And if we do not, I shall discover the rest when I visit his lordship later today and demand he pay to replace my boots."

Izzy goggled at her sister, her mouth falling open. Clementine snorted at the sight, never having caused anyone to look so shocked in all her life. It was rather gratifying.

"You never would," Izzy said, just enough doubt in the words to suggest she wasn't entirely certain.

Whilst Clementine was just as well-behaved as her sisters, she had a stubborn streak and a sharp tongue that she sometimes struggled to rein in.

"Oh, wouldn't I?" Clementine repeated, snipping several dead roses with quiet savagery.

"Oh, but Clem, surely not? It's not *done*," Izzy said, aghast.

"What and vomiting on a lady's boots on a public street is?" she retorted crossly. "Those boots were a present from Aunt Susan. She gave them to me the Christmas before she died. Besides the sentimental value they held, I could never afford to buy anything half so stylish, and I have no means of replacing them. They're utterly ruined now, and I do not see why he ought not pay for the damage. Do you?"

Clementine gave her sister a challenging look, and Izzy considered her words.

"Well, when you put it like that, no, I do not. Yet it's bound to make people talk, and you know how much you hate being gossiped about."

"I doubt anyone enjoys it," Clementine remarked with a shrug. "But needs must."

"Oh, you're wrong, I think. The scandal sheets are full of people doing daft things that were bound to get them noticed and so, surely, they must have acted knowing that and inviting the scrutiny."

"Papa told you not to read those."

"Only because he thinks he *ought* to tell me not to," Izzy said, smiling fondly. "He doesn't really mind, or he would burn them after he's done, not leave them about his study."

"I suppose so," Clementine agreed, frowning at a rosebud with a nasty infestation of aphids. "I shall have to get George to look at this. He's bound to have some remedy."

"Yes, perhaps, but will you really demand this man pay for your boots, Clem? You can't go alone to call on him at the hotel, that's for certain."

"No, I shan't. You shall come with me," Clementine said, smiling at her sister.

Izzy's eyes widened at the prospect. *"Me?"* she squeaked in alarm.

"Yes. Well, I can't very well take Bea, can I?"

Izzy sighed, understanding at once why she could not. "No, I suppose not. The fellow would fall madly in love with her and make a nuisance of himself."

"Well, I doubt love would have anything to do with it, but he would certainly make a nuisance of himself," Clementine said dryly.

"Clem!" Izzy exclaimed. "The things you say."

Clementine laughed. “Oh, run along back to your book now. Only listen out for Miss Edith and the kittens and make sure Mrs Adie has prepared the things I promised them. We shall call on our mystery nobleman this afternoon. That should give him time to recover from his overindulgence.”

“Yes, Clem,” Izzy said with a sigh, and made her way back indoors.

“Oh, must we go?” Izzy said tragically, gazing at the kittens with longing as they played on the rug beside her several hours later.

“Yes. You can play with them when you get home,” Clementine said, trying to chivvy her sister up by making shooing motions.

“Where are you going?” Bea asked, lifting the little ginger cat up and kissing its nose.

Izzy and Clementine exchanged a quick glance. “Oh, just an errand to run. I’ll explain later,” Clementine said with a smile. Bea would be horrified both by the fate of Clementine’s best boots and her intention to demand money to replace them. “You had better stay and keep an eye on these little mischief-makers. Caspar and Daisy will wake from their naps shortly and you’ll need to supervise them.”

“Yes, all right,” Beatrice said easily, for Beatrice was the most compliant of the three sisters and rarely objected to being told what to do.

Hurrying Izzy out of the room before Bea could become curious about their errand, Clementine put on her bonnet and spencer and picked up a parcel wrapped in sacking.

“You’re bringing the boots?” Izzy asked, looking at the parcel with misgiving.

"Certainly," Clementine said as she waited for Izzy to finish tying her bonnet. "Otherwise, he only has my word for the damage he did."

"To be fair, Clem, walking in the sea probably did just as much damage," Izzy said reasonably.

Clementine, who did not feel like being reasonable, sent her a dark look and Izzy subsided.

"Well, I suppose you would not have paddled with them on unless the situation were dire," Izzy said, her tone conciliatory.

"Quite." Clementine nodded and strode briskly down the hill towards the seafront.

"Might we go to the haberdashery afterwards?" Izzy asked, surprising Clementine. Of the three sisters, Izzy cared the least for new gowns and pretty things, and Clementine wondered what had provoked the sudden desire to go to a place she normally only visited under duress.

Izzy coloured at the considering glance Clementine shot her. "I want to make collars for the kittens," she said, sounding a touch defensive.

Clementine laughed. That made a deal more sense. "Yes, of course we may," she said, linking her arm through her sister's as they walked.

"I shall never tire of that view," Izzy said as they turned a corner and the dazzling blue sea was suddenly before them, sparkling in the afternoon sunshine.

Clementine nodded, hardly able to disagree. She was fortunate enough to have a view of the sea from her bedroom, and she could stare at it for hours. It was one of the few things that never failed to calm her when she was vexed. "Yes, and I would love to find a quiet spot and have a paddle, without my boots," she added wryly. "But I must get this done before I lose my nerve."

"Would you?" Izzy asked, curiosity in her eyes.

Clementine glanced at her, frowning. "Would I what?"

"Lose your nerve. I've never known you back down before."

Clementine stood looking up at the jauntily painted sign that proclaimed The Mermaid's Tale and shrugged. "I've never confronted a nobleman in a hotel before," she replied, feeling a sudden stab of apprehension.

"We don't have to go in," Izzy reminded her gently. "We could explain the situation to Papa. I'm sure he'd know how to deal with it."

Clementine put her chin up, glaring at her sister. "Certainly not," she said briskly, and strode to the front door.

"I don't want it, damn you," Lord Beaumarsh replied wearily, pushing the suspicious-looking cup his valet offered out of his face. Reclining on a comfortable settee in the surprisingly elegant living room of the suite Kirby had secured for him, Beau contemplated how best to revenge himself on his cousin for his temerity. How the craven-hearted fribble had got up the nerve to slip poison into his glass, he could not imagine.

"I never asked if you wanted it. I said drink it," Kirby said, the implacable look on his face boding ill.

"I. Don't. Want it," Beau said again, a dangerous note to his voice. He glared at his valet, smoothed his hands over the heavily embroidered silk of his banyan, and closed his eyes. Perhaps if he took another nap, his head would stop feeling as though it was being repeatedly bashed against an anvil.

"Fine. Die. See if I care. It's nothing to me if you turn up your toes," Kirby muttered, setting the glass down and moving around the room, tidying things that did not require tidying. "It's not like I trudged for bleedin' miles up hill to fetch the water from the spa for you. Don't matter if I brought you here for that reason, just to make you better, does it? So, you trot along to kingdom come. I'll just be out of a job, won't I? Me old mum depends on me, but that's not your concern. I expect I'll find another job just as good what pays well enough to keep her in that nice little cottage. I mean, every nobleman wants to hire an ex-boxer with a criminal record, don't they? Shouldn't be no bother at all. It's not as if—"

"Oh, devil take you, Kirby, give me the damned stuff!" Beau snapped. Left to his own devices, Kirby would lead him through a protracted if imaginary history where he and his mother died in some rat-infested gutter of exposure and malnourishment. "Though I tell you now, this filthy stuff is more likely to have me pushing up daisies. A nice glass of claret would be better. I'll even take ale if you're going to get all mother-hennish on me."

"Water," Kirby said, handing him the water. "The doctor said five times a day. *Minimum,"* he added, drawing the word out as if daring Beau to argue.

Giving his valet a look that could have etched glass, Beau snatched the cup from him, sniffed it, and recoiled. "God's teeth!" he exclaimed, blinking. "Are you trying to cure me or finish me off?"

"It's just the sulphur," Kirby said, rolling his eyes. "That's the good bit."

"The good bit?" Beau repeated, incensed. *"The good bit?* What's the bad bit, pray tell? It reeks like rotten eggs."

"When did you ever take medicine that tasted of strawberries and sugar? If it's good for you, it's bound to be rank. Now stop bleating and carrying on and drink the stuff before I make you."

Beau fumed but was too weak to put up a proper fight. Kirby was not the sort of fellow one wished to argue with, but Beau was his employer and that probably meant he wouldn't *actually* lay hands on him. Probably. There again, he had scared the poor bastard half to death by almost dying on him. He'd been quite anxious himself come to that. Considering his own mortality had forced him to ask himself some rather uncomfortable questions about his life. Not that he had discovered any sensible answers.

Beau gazed down at the cup of water and contemplated swallowing the foul stuff. His stomach, having suffered enough, churned. A sudden knock at the door seemed like the answer to his prayers, and rather than tell whoever it was to go to the devil, as he certainly would have done two minutes earlier, he called for them to come in.

Kirby straightened, aghast at the idea of anyone seeing the exquisite Beau Beaumarsh looking anything less that his immaculate best, but it was too late. The door opened and the owner of the hotel, Mrs Adamson, a splendidly curvaceous woman with the most riotous red curls Beau had ever seen, strode in.

"My lord," she said, her voice apologetic though her expression was cool and businesslike. "It appears you have visitors. Now, this is a respectable establishment, and I do not allow unmarried female guests to visit gentlemen. However, as the circumstances are somewhat unusual, I have agreed to chaperone. Might I introduce your callers?"

Beau reclined, aware he ought to stand in the presence of ladies, but equally alive to the possibility that he might fall over if he made the attempt. Retreating behind the façade of the indolent nobleman—one he played to perfection—he waved a negligent hand in acceptance and looked bored.

His gaze, however, was drawn to the two young women who stood behind Mrs Adamson, remaining just out of his line of sight. Well, this was interesting, at least. Whatever did they want of him? If they had come to invite him to attend a god-awful assembly where the yokels could gape at him like some exotic species they'd never seen before, they were out of luck.

"My Lord Beaumarsh, may I present Miss Clementine Honeywell and her sister, Miss Isabelle Honeywell? Ladies, the Earl of Beaumarsh."

Beau watched as the two young women drew a little closer, regarding him exactly as if he were some strange and exotic species they had never seen before. The younger of the two looked fascinated, her blue eyes startled behind her spectacles. A quick appraisal of her form led him to suspect a splendid figure lay beneath her modest gown, which was certainly five years out of style, but she was far too young for his taste. Eighteen if she was a day, he thought, before turning his attention to her sister. He admitted himself disappointed, for though the younger sister wore glasses, she was certainly the prettier of the two. The elder girl was handsome enough, but nothing out of the ordinary. Well, if one discounted the contempt that glittered in her eyes. That, at least, was remarkable.

"Miss Honeywell, Miss Isabelle, a pleasure to meet you," he drawled, wondering if he ought to have just drunk the blasted water. No doubt Kirby would get on at him to do so the moment the door closed behind the ladies, and now he had guests to endure too. Damned fool idea.

"We've met," the elder Miss Honeywell said, holding his gaze.

Beau quirked an eyebrow, an expression that would have most people of his acquaintance scurrying away before he eviscerated them with some stinging comment. Miss Honeywell did not blink. "We have?" he asked sceptically.

"Yes," she said firmly. "You fell out of your carriage after your coachman almost ran me down and then vomited on my boots."

There were few occasions in Beau's life where he had felt truly embarrassed, experiencing the kind of toe-curling horror that woke one up in the middle of the night feeling just as excruciatingly mortified as the moment it had happened. The worst of those events had occurred when he was little more than a boy. His vile cousin was usually responsible for them.

Yet it was because of those events, and because he had sworn never to feel that way ever again, that *The Beau* existed at all. Still, brazen as he was these days, an unsettling sensation roiled in his guts that had nothing to do with poison, and a creeping sensation of heat that was as surprising as it was unwelcome burned the back of his neck. After a journey that had felt like a voyage to Dante's lesser known tenth circle of hell, where dwelt all indolent layabouts poisoned by jealous cousins, he had been exhausted and out of his head. A long sleep had given him hopes that he had climbed his way back to limbo, a place where he was not quite dead, but the jury was still out. The events of the hellish journey and the early morning had been erased from his memory, however.

Compelled to verify the woman's information, though sadly he doubted very much she had made it up, Beau glanced at Kirby, who nodded.

"You did, my lord."

"And did you offer the lady no compensation for the unpleasant occurrence?" Beau demanded, furious that Kirby had not dealt with the situation at once and saved him from this disagreeable interview.

"Seeing as how I was carrying you into the hotel and fearing you was about to turn up your toes from arsenic poisoning at any moment, I did not," Kirby said with dignity.

"I see," Beau replied with a heavy sigh. "Then pray do so at once,"

"I have brought them with me," Miss Honeywell said, unwrapping a parcel that seemed to have been packaged in a potato sack. "As you can see, they were a very fine pair of half-boots made of kid leather. They were a present from my aunt, who has since passed away, and I shall be unable to replace them easily."

Though he did not much relish the idea of looking at the mess, curiosity compelled Beau to glance at the boots she held up for his inspection. The young woman was very far from fashionable and, if the boots were so fine, he assumed they must have been a cherished possession. And from a dead aunt at that… he'd excelled himself this time. At a glance, his expert eye could see that though the half boots were sodden and stained, they had once been fine and had been made by a skilled craftsman.

Kirby, having made the same calculation, hurried to the bedroom and returned to place the sum of three pounds in the lady's hand. She looked startled by his prompt acquiescence, and Beau wondered if she had expected him to quibble, or to be less than generous.

"Thank you, my lord," she said, inclining her head.

Beau did likewise and hoped she would leave now. She looked to be on the verge of doing so, turning away from him, when she stopped, glancing back with an expression of curiosity.

"I beg your pardon," she said, addressing Kirby. "But did you say Lord Beaumarsh had been poisoned?"

"Damn you, Kirby!" Beau glared at his indiscreet valet.

"You were not simply inebriated?" she pressed, speaking to Beau directly now. Her eyes seemed alight with interest, though whether or not it was the thought of someone doing him a mischief that delighted her, he could not say.

"I was not," he replied crisply. "But I will thank you to keep that information to yourself."

"I shall, of course," she said at once, and her expression changed to one of concern. "But would you like me to summon a doctor? Surely if you have—"

"No, certainly not," he said with some force. "Kirby has already forced me to endure the prodding of an incompetent quack, and I'll not repeat the indignity. It because of the wretched fellow's advice that I'm here at all. I'll recover soon enough without the town's ghastly waters. I usually do."

"Usually?" she exclaimed, and Beau noted with interest that everything she felt was clearly expressed upon her face, judging from the scandalised shock he was looking at now. "You have been poisoned before?"

Beau felt his lip curl as he regarded her with well-earned world-weary cynicism. "My dear, I am a wealthy man with a title. My cousin is my sole heir, and he's so very eager to inherit. He is ten years older than I am and has been trying to end my life since I was a boy. Sadly, my health is shockingly robust, but he feels compelled to make these little attempts from time to time. Yet, I continue to breathe. Pray do not trouble yourself over it."

"But… But that is sheer wickedness!" she said, outrage shining in her eyes. Good Lord, but she was a virago. He'd bet anything that she ran this misbegotten town, for she was too bold and outspoken not to. "He must not be allowed to get away with it. Have you informed anyone? A magistrate?"

"Miss Honeywell," Mrs Adamson said in an undertone, but the young woman ignored the warning and Beau stared at her with interest before he replied.

"I have no desire for my family name to be dragged through the mud and to give the tattlemongers a field day."

"But you are always in the scandal sheets for one reason or another. What difference does it make?" she demanded, looking genuinely perplexed.

Irked by the question, Beau stiffened. "There is a good deal of difference between being remarked at a certain gathering in the company of a certain person, or for wearing something the ton finds remarkable, or for cutting a toadeater down to size with a few choice words. Personal family business ought to remain in the family."

"But surely you will do *something?"* she asked him, looking appalled by his sanguine acceptance of the situation.

"What do you suggest I do?" he replied, bored with this interview now. His guts felt most peculiar, his head throbbed like the very devil, and all he wanted to do was sleep. "Poison him in return?"

"Certainly not, but—"

"I think we had best leave his lordship to his recovery," Mrs Adamson said firmly, for which kindness Beau made a mental note to give the proprietress a generous tip. "It really isn't seemly for you to be here, Miss Honeywell, and I do not want your papa here preaching at me about the impropriety I have allowed in my establishment. It is hard enough to be a single female and run a respectable hotel. I cannot allow you to jeopardise my standing in the town."

Miss Honeywell looked vexed and frustrated by this observation but did not argue the point. Instead, she turned back to Beau and dipped a curtsy.

"Thank you, my lord, for your understanding. I hope you recover quickly."

Beau inclined his head and watched as Mrs Adamson escorted them to the door. She had almost ushered Miss Honeywell through when the woman stopped, opening her mouth to speak once more. What she might have said remained a mystery, however, as her younger sister gave her a firm shove and expelled her from the room.

Kirby gave a snort as the door closed behind them. "I like her. Got gumption," he observed with approval.

"Just because she thinks like you do, does not make her right," Beau grumbled, having heard enough from Kirby on the subject of how he ought to deal with his cousin.

"Yes, it does," Kirby replied, picking up the cup Beau had sincerely hoped he might have forgotten about. "Now drink your medicine like a good fellow."

Beau groaned.

Chapter 3

One cannot help but wonder who will drop dead first?

The Mermaid's Tale, Little Valentine, South-East Coast of England, 1st June 1815.

"I don't know what I was thinking, letting you visit that man in his rooms," Mrs Adamson said, shaking her head. "Your father will skin me alive."

Clementine laughed at this preposterous notion and Mrs Adamson smiled ruefully.

"Well, he *ought* to skin me alive. He's a deal too lax with you and your sisters, if you ask me," the lady added with some force.

"No one saw us, I'm sure," Clementine said soothingly. "And we'll go out through the kitchen and back through the woods."

Mrs Adamson looked sceptical, but she sighed and shook her head. "You two need to watch yourselves, especially around the likes of Lord Beaumarsh. You've got what you wanted from the meeting, now stay away from him."

"Oh, we shall," Isabelle said firmly, before darting a fierce look at her sister. "Won't we, Clemmie?"

"Hmm?" Clementine said, her mind still turning over the conversation with Lord Beaumarsh. Would he really allow his cousin to almost take his life and do nothing? Surely, he could not mean it. Catching Izzy's scowl, she started and returned to the conversation. "Oh, yes, of course," she said, hoping that was the correct answer.

Izzy raised her eyes to the heavens and sighed, and Mrs Adamson looked increasingly ill at ease. "His lordship's affairs are his own, Miss Honeywell. I know how it pains you when you cannot rearrange the world and everyone in it so everything falls into perfect order, but that man is not orderly and never will be. Be content with managing your family and all the lame ducks that fall into your path. Lord Beaumarsh is perfectly capable of looking after himself."

Clementine smiled and assured Mrs Adamson she had not the least intention of interfering. The lady looked relieved, if not entirely convinced, and bade them a good day.

"I overheard something the other day," Izzy said, lowering her voice as they made their way towards Winsham Woods. "About Mrs Adamson."

Clementine glanced at her. "Papa doesn't like us to gossip."

"I know that," Izzy said impatiently. "But everyone knows she was a rich man's mistress before she came here."

"Everyone *thinks* they know," Clementine corrected sternly.

"Yes, but I was in the haberdasher's buying some lace trim for Bea and I heard Madame Auguste talking to Mrs Doomsday, and they said she was mistress to the Marquess of Sheringham. They spoke as if it was common knowledge. Do you think that's really true? Can you imagine? A *marquess?"* Izzy shook her head in wonder.

Clementine shrugged, still aggravated by Lord Beaumarsh being so appallingly idle he couldn't bestir himself to save his own skin. "I don't know, nor do I care. Mrs Adamson is a lovely woman and a successful businesswoman who deserves our respect and friendship. The way some people in this town treat her is shameful. We do not know if there is a grain of truth in the rumours, and even if it is true, so what? We know nothing of her circumstances at that time in her life. She may have been in desperate straits and had no option but to accept an offer that was less than respectable. She has survived and made a success of herself in a world that is unkind to the female sex. I, for one, think she is admirable."

"Oh, so do I!" Izzy said hurriedly. "I was only curious. I mean, a *marquess.*" She breathed the word more than spoke it and Clementine laughed.

"A marquess!" Clementine repeated, throwing one hand out as if declaiming the word to the heavens. "You were not so impressed with an earl, I think."

Izzy grinned. "Well, I was a bit impressed. He looked terribly wicked and handsome lounging about like that, just like Childe Harold."

"Yes, a pretty fribble without a sensible thought in his head," Clementine said, the frustration in her voice clear. "Honestly, all that wealth and power and the fool can't even stop his family from trying to murder him. Oh, if only I were a man, the things I would achieve! Perhaps if I were, he'd listen to me, but you simply can't tell some people. Yet *someone* should make him see sense."

"Clementine," Izzy said, wagging a finger at her. "You may not interfere in his life. *No.*"

"Oh, I'm not going to," Clementine said crossly and picked up her pace, leaving her sister to scurry behind her.

The Vicarage, Little Valentine, South-East Coast of England. 2nd June 1815.

The following morning, Clementine threw herself into her daily tasks. She spent an hour developing her word square game, shared breakfast with her family and then began deciphering her father's horrible handwriting, reworking it into something legible. Yet in the back of her mind seethed a knot of irritation that would not let Lord Beaumarsh's imminent death by his cousin's hand alone.

She told herself it was none of her affair if he didn't care for his own wellbeing, but that had never stopped her from advising her neighbours when she saw a solution to their troubles. Clementine did not see why it ought to now, just because he was a stranger. Not that she was a busybody. Far from it. She was known for both her tact and her discretion, and loathed gossip as much as her father did. But people brought their troubles to her as often as they did Reverend Honeywell, knowing she was a sensible and educated woman with a good head on her shoulders. But just because they had invited her interference and Lord Beaumarsh had not, did not seem reason enough to at least *try* to help him.

Now she stood in the garden, wearing her oldest gown, helping Izzy pick fruit. She popped a raspberry in her mouth and chewed thoughtfully. The tart sweetness exploded on her tongue, but her mind was too occupied to fully appreciate the delicious treat. Still, she plucked another from the bush and ate that too.

"Clem."

Really, though, it was too vexing. How could that idiot man just leave his murderous cousin to go about attempting to finish him off and do nothing? Nothing! It was ludicrous. Not that she cared whether he lived or died. Well, no, that was not entirely true. Having been brought up to believe all life was sacred, she could not pretend indifference. But it would not matter if it were the Earl of Beaumarsh or Mr Bagot the butcher who was a grumpy curmudgeon, or some other fellow she didn't know from Adam. No one had the right to take another's life, and it annoyed her beyond bearing that the indolent fool of a nobleman was just going to let the matter rest. Clementine plucked another raspberry and was about to pop it in her mouth when her sister's voice penetrated her abstraction.

"Clementine!"

Clementine jumped guiltily and dropped the raspberry to discover Isabelle glaring at her.

"What?" she demanded.

"We're supposed to be picking raspberries, not eating them, and you've not heard a word I've said for the past ten minutes."

"I have!" Clementine retorted.

Isabelle raised an eyebrow and folded her arms. "Go on, then."

Clementine racked her brain for a likely topic, realising Izzy was right; she'd not heard a word.

"There, see?" Izzy said smugly. "You're mooning about the Earl of Beaumarsh. Don't deny it!" she warned, a devilish light in her eyes.

"I certainly shall deny it," Clementine said at once, appalled by the notion. "Daydreaming about that idle peacock? I should think not."

Izzy gave a disgruntled snort, challenging her sister with a hard stare. "Then it's worse than I feared."

"How could it be worse than daydreaming about a man of that ilk?" Clementine demanded, startled.

Hands on her hips, Izzy glared at her accusingly. "You're thinking up ways of thwarting his dastardly cousin."

Clementine opened her mouth to object and closed it again. "I was not thinking anything of the sort."

Izzy made a disbelieving sound and picked up the basket they were supposed to be filling, returning her attention to the raspberries. "If you are going to tell me fibs, I shan't talk to you," she said loftily.

"It's not a fib! I wasn't thinking of ways to thwart him. I was only thinking he ought to *be* thwarted. It's different," Clementine replied, scowling as Izzy rolled her eyes. "It is!"

"Clementine Honeywell, you love puzzles and rearranging people's lives for the better, and despite making out you cannot bear gossip, you delight in a bit of intrigue. On top of that, ever since you figured out Jem Smith was the one stealing our eggs, you've fancied yourself some manner of lady Bow Street Runner," Izzy said, shaking her head.

"That is a horrid thing to say and quite untrue," Clementine replied, irritated, not least because it was a little bit true. "I just cannot believe the man can be so lost to reason that he would allow his cousin to make another attempt. You cannot turn your back upon wickedness and pretend it away, or you allow it to flourish. Don't you remember that mangy dog that Joseph Bagot was beating for hanging around the butcher's shop? What did I do about that?"

"Snatched Captain Dearborn's whip from his gig where he'd left it and drove the fellow down the high street, asking how he liked it," Izzy replied, grinning at the memory. "I've never heard a man scream quite like he did. Still, old Mr Drury is so happy with his canine companion now. I must admit, you chose the perfect home for him once we'd fed the poor creature up a bit."

"Quite so, and you seem astonished that I would react differently when a man's life is at stake and not a dog's? It matters not whether he is a good man or a reprobate. No one may destroy a life. You saw Lord Beaumarsh, Izzy. He looked dreadful, so pale and hollow-eyed. His valet said himself he'd feared he might die."

"Hmm," Izzy replied with a sigh, affecting a nonchalant tone Clementine did not believe for a moment as she hurled raspberries into the basket. "Yes, he did. But such eyes he had, didn't he, Clem? I've never seen such a dark shade of blue. Would you call that azure or cobalt? And that hair, gold as a field of ripe barley. And those big shoulders clad in all that luxurious silk—"

"Izzy!" Clementine said, shocked by her sister's flight of fancy. "You cannot be serious! Do you know me so little as to think the sight of a pretty face should take me in and make me lose my wits?"

"No, of course not! I know he's not at all the type to make you act the fool, but you've just admitted you are considering meddling in his affairs, and that is bound to cause talk, if not trouble of the kind I tremble to consider. Can you imagine if it got about that you were entangled with the Earl of Beaumarsh? *Beau* Beaumarsh. Excitement of that kind would have half the population of the town drop dead with shock. They're just not used to it. This is a quiet place where nothing ever happens. Whilst that might be an appalling prospect, I'd rather it were not you who sets the cat among the pigeons."

"No, you'd rather do it yourself," Clementine said with a snort.

Izzy shrugged, unperturbed by the accusation. "When one spends such a lot of time reading about adventures and exotic travel, one cannot help but feel the desire to experience such things. However, I do know the difference between reality and fantasy, and I do not wish to see you ruined. I will not return to that hotel with you, Clem, and if you go alone, I shall never speak to you again."

"Oh, Izzy, don't be daft, as if I would," Clementine said with a sigh, immediately wondering how she might get word to his lordship when she figured out a workable plan.

His valet was her best option, for he was bound to go out and about the town on errands for his employer, or perhaps just to do a bit of exploring. Mrs Adamson, discreet as she was, had admitted they had come specifically to drink the waters, as most visitors did, though one would need to be determined or desperate for a cure to do so in Clementine's opinion, for they tasted utterly vile. That was if you could overcome the smell for long enough to swallow the horrid stuff. Still, people seemed to believe the worse something tasted the better it was for them, a principle Clementine was not about to challenge, even if she would never swallow the stuff herself.

She lifted her hand distractedly, about to eat another raspberry, but sensing her sister's gaze, stilled and, with a smile, made a great show of placing the berry carefully in the basket and picking another. Izzy scowled, and Clementine reflected that she would have to be careful and sly to thwart her sister's interest.

"You wish for me to ask you to come to the tea shop with me?"

Clementine gave Miss Clara Halfpenny a sheepish smile and nodded. "Yes, please."

Happily, Clara did not look at her as if she'd lost her wits, nor ask why on earth she was being manoeuvred. She simply nodded.

"Very well. Clementine, would you accompany me to the tea shop, please? Should we go at once?" Clara added in an undertone. "Is the alibi I am providing time sensitive? Or is there a specific hour when I should issue the demand?"

"Now would be perfect," Clementine admitted. "Providing your aunt won't notice your absence?" Clara's aunt was a mean-spirited virago of a woman and the last thing Clementine wished for was to get her into trouble with her relative.

"She's napping," Clara said, shaking her head. "Now suits me perfectly, so long as we are not away for more than an hour."

"No, an hour will do nicely, thank you, but aren't you going to ask me why I want you to ask me to go?" Clementine regarded Clara, wondering at her lack of curiosity.

"No, why should I?" Clara asked, getting to her feet. "It must be important, or you would not ask it of me, and I am too glad to have company for a while and to take tea with you to ask awkward questions."

Clementine felt a surge of guilt at this guileless answer and wished she had called upon Clara a bit more often. Not that she did not wish to, but calling too often could get Clara into trouble. Sometimes Clara would see her coming and come to the door, shaking her head and waving her away. Not for the first time, Clementine wished there was something she could do for Clara, who depended upon her aunt's miserly version of charity for her very existence.

"Does your aunt always nap at this hour?" Clementine asked quietly as they gathered their bonnets and spencers. Perhaps if the woman had a schedule now, she could time her visits to coincide.

Clara put a finger to her lips, and they tiptoed outside. Clementine thought perhaps Clara held her breath until she had successfully closed the front door and listened for her aunt's strident voice demanding to know where she was going. As all was silent, Clara let out a breath, and they hurried down the winding path to the front gate.

"She does often take a nap in the afternoons these days," Clara said, glancing over her shoulder as they opened the garden gate, still looking as if she believed her aunt would thwart the excursion. "Her health is not what it was, and she tires easily. But you cannot depend upon it, sadly. Just when one thinks she has a routine, she changes it and catches one sitting with one's feet up and reading a book she has expressly forbidden one from reading," she said with a rueful smile.

Clementine sent Clara a look of sincere concern, but Clara only smiled. "Don't look so horrified. It is not so bad, I assure you. I am grateful for my position here. The house is comfortable, and I do not go hungry. I enjoy the garden and walking and now and again my friend asks me to provide an alibi for her so she may get up to something nefarious," she said with a twinkle in her eye.

Clementine snorted. "It's not nefarious. Well, not exactly."

"Well, I am entirely reassured now," Clara said, darting her a look of mingled concern and interest.

"You've heard about the earl, I suppose?" Clementine asked, linking her arm through Clara's as they walked to the village."

"The earl?" Clara repeated.

Clementine looked at her in surprise before remembering how painfully shy Clara was when out in the world. Her visits to the shops were for necessities only and not society. She did not make friends easily, conversing with anyone was a trial to her, and her aunt crushed any attempt she made to create a life for herself. Many of the residents of Little Valentine, who heartily disliked her aunt, largely ignored Clara, and viewed her situation as a poor relation with indifferent contempt. Gaining anyone's attention for any reason was anathema to Clara and so she did nothing to change her position, despite Clementine's urging. The only reason they were friends at all was because of Reverend Honeywell. He had pitied Clara's miserable situation and had insisted her help in the church was not only indispensable but her Christian duty, something even her aunt could not gainsay, though she had tried. It had given Clara a small measure of freedom.

So, Clementine told Clara all about the earl's arrival in the town and their rather inauspicious meeting. To her delight, Clara crowed with laughter over the scene, which Clementine deliberately embellished to entertain her. Her laughter faded, however, when Clementine explained about the murderous cousin.

"The poor man," Clara said, her unremarkable features filled with pity. "How awful to know a member of your own family wishes you dead."

"I wouldn't pity him too much," Clementine remarked. "From all I know of him, he's a spoilt dandy with more hair than wit. Still, I think he ought to bestir himself to thwart his cousin and not just sit about looking decorative and waiting for him to make another attempt."

"Is he decorative?" Clara asked, interest shining in her eyes.

Clementine slanted her a look, startled by the question. "I suppose so, if you like that sort of thing," she said dismissively. Though the image of Lord Beaumarsh reclining in his silk banyan like some pampered pasha returned to her with some force, much to her consternation. He had looked like he was waiting for one of his wives, or many mistresses, to peel him a grape. Sinfully handsome and cynical to the core, it was no surprise he was the darling of the *beau monde*. She pushed the image away, disturbed by the odd frisson of awareness it sent prickling beneath her skin.

"What sort of thing?" Clara pressed, giving an impish grin at the look on Clementine's face. "Oh, come on, Clementine. I have very little excitement in my life and suddenly you've introduced this remarkable story, with murder and a handsome aristocrat. Give me some details, can't you? It's better than a Mrs Radcliffe so far, but I'm lacking vital information."

Clementine gave a short laugh, discovering herself unsettled at the demand, but complied all the same. "Well, Izzy said he had the bluest eyes she'd ever seen, though she could not decide between azure and cobalt, but she said his hair was the colour of ripe barley and that he had very broad shoulders."

"Never mind what Izzy said, though I grant you that is a fascinating description," Clara admitted. "What did you think? You were there too. You were the one who spoke to him, were you not?"

"Well, yes," Clementine said reluctantly.

"So?"

"I don't know!" Clementine replied, realising she sounded a little testy. "He is very handsome, I suppose. Too handsome. It's clearly not done him a whit of good, for he's idle and stupid and vain."

Clara stared, shocked by her words, and Clementine fought a blush. Her father would certainly have something to say about her judging a fellow creature so harshly when she did not know him at all, and rightly so.

"Goodness. He *did* make an impression on you."

"Vomiting on a lady's boots is unlikely to endear a fellow to her," she replied dryly, though a surge of guilt for her bitter words made her queasy.

"No," Clara said, regarding her with interest and making Clementine feel thoroughly unsettled. "I suppose it wouldn't."

"His lordship was also very sarcastic when I suggested he ought to do something about his cousin and demanded if he should poison him in retaliation. The wretched devil said it with such an air of bored indifference too, like he could barely be bothered to speak the words to me, for I was too far beneath his notice," Clementine said, still unnerved by how annoyed she sounded.

"He sounds insufferable," Clara admitted.

"Precisely," Clementine said with satisfaction, relieved her friend could appreciate what she had determined from the moment he had stumbled from his carriage. There, see? She was not being unreasonable.

"So, why are you determined to help him?" Clara asked.

It was not an unfair question, which made it even more galling when Clementine could find no ready answer.

Kirby did not slam the door as he left the earl's rooms, but it was a close-run thing. He did not appreciate gossip about his master, however, and was not about to add to it. Bad enough the great lummox had made a spectacle of himself the moment he'd arrived. He would not have people speculating about the quality of his valet. People did, of course, all the time, and would certainly do so in a place like this, for Kirby did not look like a valet. He looked precisely like what he was, an ex-con, ex-boxer, and a fellow who'd been born to swing at Tyburn. He would have done too, no doubt, if not for the earl.

As a young sprig of only seventeen, Beaumarsh had run with a fast set who got up to a fair amount of mischief. Discovering during this time that, whilst he could fight, he had not yet grown into his height and breadth, and was also too idle to exert himself overly, he had looked for a manservant who would act as a bodyguard. Why Beau had stepped in and saved him from the Watch that day, when they had wanted to take him up for starting a public disturbance, causing grievous bodily harm, and a deal of property damage, Kirby had never fathomed. Yet saved him, his lordship had.

Five years older than Beau, Kirby had been a prizefighter and had taken exception to discovering he was being cheated out of his rightful earnings. The ensuing fight had been violent and messy. Beau had paid for all the damage, smoothed things over with the magistrate, and given Kirby the first honest—mostly honest—employment he'd ever had. He'd even allowed him to learn on the job, for he had been a shocking valet in those early years. Somehow, however, the two of them had grown up together, and both appreciated their good fortune. Especially Kirby, who had discovered to his own great surprise he enjoyed his work and had a keen eye for colour and style.

All of which was why he owed the fellow his loyalty and would walk over hot coals if he must, despite wanting to break the devil's nose himself at regular intervals.

Still, the situation was what it was and no amount of bleating about it would change things. So, Kirby must go about the town and do a bit of damage limitation by throwing his master's money about and dropping a few interesting words in the right ears. It was amazingly easy to change people's perceptions of a situation if one had the right strategy.

Kirby began his day at the tobacconist, though Beaumarsh neither smoked nor took snuff, and spent a good deal of money whilst regaling the shopkeeper with one of the more amusing anecdotes about *the Beau*. By the time he left, Mr Garvis was chuckling appreciatively about the young man's ready wit and was well pleased with his patronage. He also gleaned some interesting information when asking about the best wine merchant to buy from. Garvis had readily supplied the name of a most respectable and long-established wine merchant, whilst asking some pertinent questions that led Kirby to understand that there was a healthy trade in smuggled goods that might be made available if someone was ready to make a significant purchase. Always alert to a good deal, and more than content to get one up on the taxman, Kirby gave the correct answers and was told someone would be in touch. Intrigued and pleased by this, Kirby went about his business.

He ate a hearty lunch at The Ship Inn, a respectable establishment where some of the clientele eyed him dubiously and then went for a drink at the less than respectable Dog and Duck. Here he stood the inhabitants several rounds of drinks, some of whom looked as if they'd not moved for several weeks, never mind hours. That the place was frequented by smugglers as well as fishermen, he did not doubt, but he certainly felt more welcome than he had at The Ship and whiled away a pleasant couple of hours. Still, the afternoon was upon him, and he knew he'd best return and check Beaumarsh hadn't, in fact, turned up his toes.

Whilst his master's constitution was indeed that of an ox, the arsenic had laid him low, and Kirby did not feel his concern undue despite the idiot's exasperation over his fussing. Kirby, suddenly anxious that his master's condition might have deteriorated during his absence, quickened his pace along the street. The tearoom door then flew open, startling him as Miss Honeywell rushed through. She stood directly before him and Kirby muttered an oath, skidding to a halt before he knocked the lady down. Beaumarsh had already made her suffer enough indignity, he did not wish to add to it.

"Good afternoon, Miss Honeywell," he said, raising his hat and giving a polite bow whilst wondering what she was about accosting him in the street. Kirby was well used to arranging assignations with ladies for the earl, whose handsome face and form was irresistible to certain women. His estimation of Miss Honeywell, however, had not been at all of that kind, and he'd been keenly aware of the ill-concealed contempt she had for his employer. That being the case, he was more than a little curious as to what she wanted.

"Mr Kirby," she replied, equally civil. "I would like a word, if it is not too much of an imposition."

Kirby looked at her in surprise. "I can spare a few minutes, I reckon, though I've been gone for some time and his lordship won't sleep forever. I was just hurrying back to check on him."

"Yes, you seemed to be in a rush. You are still concerned for his health, then?" she asked, her tone brusque.

Kirby nodded, appreciating her forthright manner. "I am, miss, but he won't see another doctor so you may as well save your breath."

She nodded her understanding. "It does not surprise me. He seemed a rather recalcitrant patient."

"Worse than a five-year-old, he is," Kirby said with a snort, and then felt his colour rise as he realised he'd been indiscreet. Years in the earl's employ, he was used to holding his tongue and keeping his master's secrets as close as his own. Yet two minutes speaking to Miss Honeywell and he'd been lured into speaking too candidly. Miss Honeywell did not seem to notice his discomfort, but merely nodded, apparently unsurprised by the description.

"And do you believe his cousin will try again?"

Kirby hesitated. He ought not say another word, yet he knew damn well Edwin would try again and, whilst the fellow was a snivelling little fop, even the most incompetent criminal got lucky occasionally and Edwin only needed to be lucky once. Moreover, no one else knew and his master refused to discuss the problem, believing Edwin was too incompetent and foolish to be an actual threat. Even having been made seriously ill, Beaumarsh just cited his continued ability to breathe as proof of his cousin's idiocy. He'd had the perfect opportunity, and he bungled it by underestimating the dose.

"I promise you I am the soul of discretion," Miss Honeywell said earnestly.

Kirby believed her. He had liked the young woman upon first meeting her, noticing the sparkle in her eyes and her disdain for Beau's indolent pose. Privately, he thought Beau could do with a bit of shaking up and could not help but wonder if Miss Honeywell might be just the thing.

As an interesting idea sparked into life, Kirby considered the young woman before him. She was not at all in his lordship's usual style, that was for certain. She was no highflyer, but neither was she bracket-faced nor bacon-brained. An intelligent, well-bred, handsome girl, she had a fine figure, striking blue eyes, and a peaches and cream complexion that glowed with vitality. There was a restlessness about her, and he suspected she was a woman who did not enjoy sitting about doing nothing. Well, why not confide in the girl, a bit at least, and see what she was made of?

"His cousin will try again," Kirby admitted, his tone grim. "He's up the River Tick without a paddle and, if things get much worse, he'll be forced to flee the country. He owes money to some fellows who are not kindly disposed towards people who can't pay their debts, and I reckon he's getting desperate. I'll be honest with you, miss, and admit I didn't give the previous attempts any more consideration than his lordship, for Edwin Cavendish is a fool and not up to his lordship's weight. But this last time has me thinking it's not so difficult to slip a dose of poison in someone's wine, and I can't be at his lordship's elbow at every moment of the day and night."

Miss Honeywell frowned, her nose crinkling charmingly as she considered this. "Then I was right to be concerned. Mr Kirby, I know I have not the least right to give you or your master advice, but the thing is, I feel certain I have a solution for dealing with Mr Cavendish, and think it is not only terribly simple, but almost certain to prosper. Yet, I suspect Lord Beaumarsh will dislike it very much and refuse to play along."

"You're right there, miss," Kirby said with a snort, intrigued to know what she was plotting. "He'll have my hide if he even suspects I've spoken to you about it."

Miss Honeywell nodded thoughtfully. "I presumed at much. Yet it really is a wonderfully simple plan," she said with a dejected sigh.

Kirby looked up, aware suddenly of the interest passers-by were giving them and realised it was not at all the thing for a fellow of his ilk to be seen chatting with a lady like Miss Honeywell. "I'd best be running along, miss," he said, jerking his head toward two women who had walked off looking scandalised. "Afore you set the whole town chattering. I'd be pleased to hear more about this plan of yours, though. If you'd be willing to share it with me."

Miss Honeywell brightened. "Well, of course I would. I have no interest in the matter other than seeing that a villain does not commit murder. If you can convince his lordship—" She broke off, noting as Kirby had that they were drawing rather too much interest. Brisk now, she spoke quickly. "I often walk on the beach early in the morning, Mr Kirby. I shall meet you there tomorrow at six am sharp."

With that, she gave him a curt nod and walked past him, disappearing back into the pretty little teashop. The door closed behind her with the jingling of a bell, and Kirby resumed walking, smiling a little as he considered Miss Honeywell and precisely how vexed his lordship would be when he discovered she had a plan.

Chapter 4

An assignation and a provoking peacock.

The Vicarage, Little Valentine, South-East Coast of England. 3rd June 1815.

Clementine padded silently down the stairs in stockinged feet, her oldest boots held in her hand. No one was awake yet, and the household was quiet except for the sonorous snoring from her father's room. Clementine spared a thought for her sister Isabelle, whose room was closer to her father's than her own, and wondered how the poor girl got any sleep.

Avoiding the third step from the bottom, which always creaked, Clementine made it downstairs without incident, stopped to put on her boots, and hurried outside, grabbing her bonnet with one hand and an apple in the other. Shoving the bonnet on her head, she did not bother to tie the ribbons and took a healthy bite of the apple, chewing contentedly as she strode across the garden and out into the lane. Avoiding the village, for there were plenty of early risers, she instead cut across and took the path through Winsham Woods. It was a little eerie at this early hour, for the woods was famous for being haunted, though Clementine set little store by such outlandish tales. But her father insisted ghosts were real, and he had far more experience with such things than she did. Instead of walking past The Mermaid's Tale, she headed directly down to the beach, which was deserted at this early hour. Farther along the coast, the fishermen would likely be busy, but here it was peaceful.

Feeling too conspicuous on the empty beach, Clementine walked to a rocky promontory that jutted out into the sea. The tide was a long way out at present and rockpools were plentiful around the big smooth rocks. It had been a favourite place for her and her sisters when they were children. They had spent many happy hours catching tiny crabs and darting shrimps. Clementine had to admit the place still held a certain fascination for her as she stared down into the pools of water that seemed to contain entire worlds all of their own.

She felt less visible with the rocks at her back, though, and she selected one that was smooth and dry and relatively free of seaweed before taking a perch and waiting for Mr Kirby to appear.

Beau had slept fitfully again, likely because he had done little else but sleep since he had arrived in this godforsaken backwater. He felt as shaky as a lamb, though, an image that made him smile despite himself. Him, a lamb? Hardly.

Rolling onto his back, he stared up at the ceiling and contemplated his life. Would anyone really notice any difference if Edwin had succeeded? Kirby would be bereft, that was certainly true. He seemed to view Beau as something between a recalcitrant pupil who wouldn't heed sensible advice and a saviour who could do no wrong. It was a somewhat confusing stance for them both, but they seemed to rub along merrily enough. His mother, of course, would mourn him. The poor dear had harboured such hopes of her only son, doing everything in her power to ensure he did not turn out like his benighted father.

When his sire had died, with Beau barely out of leading strings, she had been delighted with the turn of events, for it meant she could mould her son into exactly the kind of man she wanted him to be. So, as well as the obligatory classical education, Beau had been schooled in the art of looking beautiful, being a leader of fashion, and gaining the admiration of the entire ton. She had done a marvellous job too, doting on her only child and spoiling him beyond anything reasonable. Anything Beau wanted, Beau had been given. It had all been terribly easy.

And here he was, at the top of the tree. A leader of the fashionable world with everyone lower down the rungs of the ladder desperate to gain his attention, to ape his style and mannerisms. God, it was dull.

Of late he had harboured an intense desire to present himself to the ton wearing some outrageous costume, perhaps pink pantaloons festooned with embroidered giraffes and a purple-and-green spotted coat with a yellow waistcoat. Anything to break the monotony. Yet his innate sense of style would not allow him to do something so egregious. Knowing his luck, the style would catch on, and he would be forced to endure the sight of his peers decked out in such ludicrous getups. A horrifying thought.

So that was him. *The Beau.* The beautiful Earl of Beaumarsh. A fashionable fribble. No wonder his cousin wanted to kill him. Beau didn't blame him. Though the poor fool should not waste the effort, for Beau was convinced he'd die of boredom any day now. Certainly, he'd expire if he stayed in Tiny Sweeting for much longer, or whatever the blasted town was called. He did not know what Kirby had been thinking, bringing him to such a place. If he'd wanted to force those disgusting waters down his throat, the least he could have done was take him somewhere fashionable, like Bath.

Glumly, he wondered what his life might have been like if he'd been allowed to join the army as he had wanted to do. He might even now be preparing to fight Boney again, now that the devil had escaped his prison on Elba. Yet at the ripe old age of sixteen, when he had told his mother of his plans, she had thrown a hysterical tantrum, swearing that she would do something drastic rather than live the rest of her days waiting for news of her beloved son's death in some dreadful battle. Young as he'd been, he had not yet fully comprehended the ways in which she manipulated him and truly believed she might swallow an entire bottle of laudanum rather than endure the stress of not knowing whether he was alive or dead. All nonsense, of course. He knew better now, for though his mama truly was a kind and doting parent and could not be prouder of her son, she was as spoiled as he was and there was little, she would not do to get her own way. Still, he had retaliated by getting into some very dodgy situations until sense had prevailed and he'd hired Kirby to keep him alive.

Sighing, Beau wondered what mischief the dowager countess was up to now, and how much it would cost him to extricate her from it. Best not to think about that.

Thumping the pillow, Beau turned onto his side, reminding himself Kirby was unlikely to let him go home until he was properly well, and closed his eyes. Perhaps he could sleep a little longer if he tried.

He was just beginning to believe he could doze off again when the door to the adjoining room creaked. Ordinarily, Beau would not have stirred. Kirby often got up and went about his business when Beau was sleeping. Yet instead of his valet's usual competent and brisk movements about the room, whoever it was stopped, as though fearing the sound had woken him.

Instincts prickling, Beau instantly wondered if Edwin had tracked him down. A preposterous idea, for who in the name of everything holy would look for him here? Cracking one eye open, this scepticism was borne out as he saw Kirby tiptoeing across the floor, holding his boots in his hand.

Frowning, Beau wondered what on earth the devil was up to, creeping about the place. As he watched, Kirby padded on into the sitting room and Beau heard the door that led to the hotel's corridor opening and closing.

He sat up, wondering if Kirby had got lucky and found a willing woman to entertain him. But if that was the case, why was he sneaking out now, when he would be needed in an hour or so, when he might have had close to the entire night with her? He was up to something, but what? Hurrying from the bed and ignoring the curiously weak feeling in his legs, Beau ran to the window and pulled the curtain aside. The sitting room had a wonderful view, as the front of the property looked out onto the beach and a vast expanse of blue sea that glittered in the early morning sunlight. Beau ignored the lovely view, however, in favour of spying on his valet, watching until he appeared and headed out of the hotel, walking directly onto the beach.

His curiosity piqued, Beau did something he had never done in his entire life and dressed himself. As he needed to move fast if he wanted the slightest chance of finding out what Kirby was up to, he made a hash of it and did not dare look in the mirror. He did not wish to know what he looked like, unshaven and rumpled as he must be, and he hurried past the looking glass before his courage failed him and the idea of being seen in public in such a state of disarray forced him to remain imprisoned in his hotel suite.

Happily, it was early enough that there were few people out and about yet, and Beau slipped out of the hotel and down to the beach without anyone noticing him. The beach itself was deserted, though he could see tiny fishing boats bobbing about far out at sea. He looked right, and then left, and then right and left again, and had almost convinced himself he had lost his chance and should hurry back indoors before anyone saw him, when movement caught his eye. Staring harder at a long, low line of rocks that appeared as a dark, somewhat malevolent shape, he realised he had discovered his quarry, who was indeed speaking to a woman.

"Why, the old sly boots," Beau muttered, surprised, for he had never known Kirby to be much in the petticoat line himself. Though he liked a pretty wench as much as the next fellow, Kirby harboured fond, if unlikely, hopes of finding a sweet young lady and getting married, of having a home and a family. Beau did not like to disabuse him of the merits of the idea, nor to throw cold water on his valet's hopes and dreams with his own cynicism, but he did not believe the dream would prosper. The only marriages he had seen were financial transactions where two people wanted to gain something from the other. The ones that worked best seemed to be when the two joined together in holy matrimony led entirely separate lives.

He was about to return to the hotel and leave his valet to his assignation when Beau realised he recognised the young lady. And it was a young *lady.* More precisely, it was Miss Honeywell, the impertinent chit who had called on him demanding reimbursement for her boots. Not that he blamed her for doing so, only for staring at him with such a look of… of *revulsion.* As if his entire person offended her. Kirby had liked her at once though, that much Beau remembered. He had just not realised how much.

"Devil take you, Kirby, what are you playing at?" Beau exclaimed, darting a look around to see if anyone had noticed the couple, for he knew well enough what kind of stir it would cause if anyone got wind of his valet dangling after a well-bred young lady in a place like this. If Kirby looked less disreputable, it might not be such a problem, but people tended to take one look at him and assume the worst. That could sometimes be useful, but not right now.

Cursing under his breath, Beau realised he must intervene before either he or the young lady got too involved. Taking one last look around to be certain he was not observed, Beau hurried across the beach. Though it was a lovely summer morning, there was still a stiff breeze blowing across the beach, and the sound it made, combined with the distant shushing of the waves farther down the beach, disguised his footfalls until he was almost upon them.

Kirby looked up, startled, as he remarked Beau bearing down upon them.

"My lord!" he exclaimed, surprise turning to horror as he took in the Beau's rumpled appearance. "My *lord!*" he repeated, the appellation heavy with reproach this time.

"Don't you 'my lord' me," Beau said testily, glaring at his manservant with impatience. "You're the one who got me to drag my sorry behind out of my bed and dress in this unsightly fashion. You're the one keeping inappropriate assignations with young ladies who ought to know better," he added, giving Miss Honeywell a pointed look that should have made her blush scarlet. Indeed, her colour did rise, giving a pleasing pink tinge to her lovely complexion, but far from looking shamed or guilty, the girl only returned his glare with equal force.

"You really are the most ridiculous creature," she said with a huff. "I feel sure that if Mr Kirby had any romantic notions, he would have suggested we find a rather more intimate and comfortable meeting place than the beach. It is a trifle damp," she added tartly.

Kirby made a choked sound, and Beau swivelled his head to stare at his valet but, if that had been laughter, there was no evidence of it on his face now. Indeed, the wretch had adopted one of his best hangdog expressions, mingled with a healthy dose of reproach and hurt feelings.

"I'm here for your sake, my lord, and that's the God's honest truth," he said, all dignity and injured pride.

Beau narrowed his eyes at Kirby before regarding Miss Honeywell once more. "It's quite true," she said, holding his gaze. "We are here to discuss your continued wellbeing, and for no other reason, which I am certain must be apparent by now."

Damn, but she was a self-possessed female, so confident and sure of herself. Most women blushed, fluttered their eyelashes, and looked bashful when he turned his attention upon them. Well, apart from the knowing ones who were long past fluttering and pretending innocence. Not that he blamed them for using their charms to try to capture his interest, it was their assigned role, to pretend they had not a brain in their heads, just as it was his to play the indolent nobleman. This young woman clearly had not read her script with enough attention. Though, he supposed in such a countrified part of the world, the prescribed roles might not be held to so rigidly.

"My wellbeing," he repeated, bemused until he remembered her indignation at him letting his cousin off for his murder attempt with no reprisals. "Good Lord, Kirby, you don't mean to tell me you've indulged this foolish girl and allowed her to convince you I'm in mortal peril?"

Miss Honeywell's blue eyes flashed with a martial light that left him in no doubt of her opinion of him. "The only foolish person here is you, my lord, if you insist on believing you are in no danger. From what Mr Kirby has told me, it is only thanks to your resilient constitution that you survived this last attempt. If your cousin is as desperate as it appears, he will try again, and soon."

"My family and their somewhat dysfunctional method of showing their feelings is no one's business but our own," he said, his tone severe as Miss Honeywell gave a loud snort in answer to his words. Had she no notion of proper female behaviour? "I did not ask you to meddle in my affairs and, indeed, I asked you in no uncertain terms to leave them be. This is a private matter and—"

"It's a splendid idea," Kirby piped up, before Beau could finish his stinging set down.

Beau hesitated. His brain was still suffering the after-effects of being half dead for several days, and he lost his train of thought as he registered the excitement in his valet's eyes.

"It'll work. I know it will. Why not just hear her out, eh? No harm in that, is there?" Kirby wheedled.

"Isn't there?" Beau said darkly, eyeing Miss Honeywell with misgiving.

"Good heavens, Lord Beaumarsh. I do not see why you are getting so riled up when all I am attempting to do is to solve a problem for you," Miss Honeywell said, impatient at his apparently wilful refusal to hear her out.

"You must forgive me, my dear," Beau said, adopting his most condescending tone for the sheer pleasure of riling her. "But in my experience, ladies will do most anything for the chance of becoming the next Lady Beaumarsh. So, no matter what your scheme is, it will not prosper."

She gasped at that, the blush he had expected earlier staining her cheeks. This time it was not so attractive, a hectic splotch of red that was only outshone by the sheer fury blazing in her eyes.

"Why, you conceited, arrogant, vile—" She broke off, breathing heavily as she struggled to contain her temper. Having made what looked to be a truly heroic attempt to rein it in, she took a breath, her words measured and spoken with icy contempt. "Let me make one thing perfectly clear, my lord. My father is Reverend Honeywell, and, among other things, he has taught me the story of the Good Samaritan. I am doing this because it is my Christian duty to give help if I can, no matter how ill-deserving the person in question. The idea that I would ever lower my standards sufficiently to marry an idle peacock whose only concern appears to be whether his waistcoat is the precise colour of vibrant blue to match his eyes is an insult to my intelligence. I would not wed you if my life depended upon it, never mind my reputation. I trust I have made my position clear?"

Beau stared at her, admitting himself a little surprised by the attack and the precision with which she struck. It gave him a rather odd and most uncomfortable feeling to have a woman who ought to be beneath his notice call him out for all the things he despised in himself. He doubted whether he'd have cared a whit if anyone of his acquaintance had levelled the insult at him, for he would have put it down to jealousy. Miss Honeywell was not jealous. Oh, no. She was in earnest and meant every word, and he felt the cold sting of them as they pierced his usually elephantine hide.

"Crystal," he replied with a thin smile.

"Excellent," she said in return, the word accompanied by a bland expression that gave nothing more away. Having lost her temper once, she had retreated behind a mask of cool civility. He did not blame her and intended to do the exact same thing.

Kirby stood between them like a great ox, dithering. Beau sent him an impatient glare that promised retribution for this morning's work but held his temper firmly in check.

"Well, which one of you is going to outline this masterful plan? I have a day to idle away, wine to drink, and you might consider my position as a leader of fashion. Those waistcoats won't choose themselves, will they?" he said, trying to sound diverted by the idea but unable to keep the scathing tone from his voice.

Kirby glanced at Miss Honeywell, who seemed to have decided she had said enough for one day. Huzzah.

"Well, Miss Honeywell suggests we write to your cousin, telling him you are about to turn up your toes, and to come at once so you might give him details of your estates and financial dealings before you croak. Then, you enact a deathbed scene, where you get him to admit just how he administered the poison, assuring him you hold no hard feelings, and that you'd have done the same thing if your positions were switched."

"The devil I would!" Beau said hotly.

"Just to lull him into speaking plain," Kirby said, looking as though his patience was wearing thin. "So, you get him to confess, and once he has, Reverend Honeywell and the local justice of the peace come out from behind the curtains and bear witness to his confession. Then, if anything ever happens to you, nefarious-like, he knows he'll swing for it."

Beau opened his mouth to ridicule the plan and then closed it again. It was rather elegant in its simplicity, and he saw at once why Kirby liked it so much. It would work. Edwin would break his neck to get here and witness his nemesis' demise and would enjoy the opportunity to crow over his own cleverness. Though he wanted nothing more than to tell Miss Honeywell she was a silly chit with cobwebs for brains and bid her a curt goodbye, he could not.

“Fine,” he said, with a less than conciliatory manner, but he was cross and out of sorts and appearing before this woman who seemed to see him far too clearly in anything other than his precise best was making his skin itch. “You win. I’ll write to Edwin.”

With that, he turned on his heel and stalked back to the hotel.

Chapter 5

Sweet and Sour.

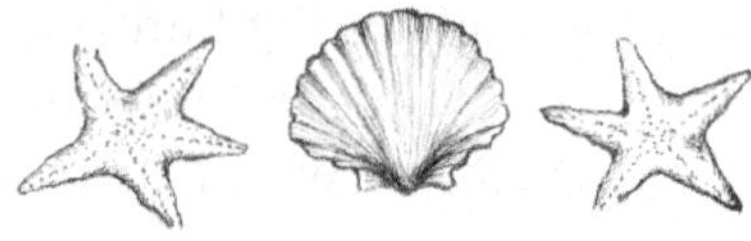

The Vicarage, Little Valentine, South-East Coast of England. 3rd June 1815.

Clementine seethed for the rest of the day, despite her best efforts. She kept busy, even forcing herself to perform tasks she usually avoided, like sorting the linens for mending, hoping to keep her mind from stewing over that… that *dreadful* man. How dare he! The gall of the arrogant peacock, implying she was only helping him as a ruse and was actually setting her cap at him. As if she would squander a moment of her time on such a… a waste of a man. Yes, she thought savagely. That was precisely what he was—a waste. He had been born to wealth and privilege, with good looks and robust health, and what was he doing with all the gifts bestowed upon him? Well, nothing useful, that was for good and certain. She ought to have left him to his fate and washed her hands of the entire matter.

"Whatever did that poor napkin do to vex you so?"

Clementine looked up at her father, who was regarding her with a fond mix of interest and concern. Glancing down at the napkins she had been arranging in the linen cupboard, she dropped the one she had been twisting in her hands and smoothed it out with little success.

"I hope that was not Lord Beaumarsh's neck you were wringing," he added with a wry smile.

Clementine sighed. Her father seemed to know everything that happened in Little Valentine, which, considering his well-known dislike of gossip, was quite remarkable.

"Mrs Adamson?" she guessed.

"I popped into The Mermaid's Tale to speak to Mr Cogger as he was not at Sunday service and I've been meaning to find out why. Mrs Adamson invited me to take tea with her whilst I was there and scolded me on my lackadaisical parenting. She is a lovely young woman. I cannot think what is wrong with the men in this town that she is not besieged with offers of marriage," he said, shaking his head in exasperation.

"She has offers of a different kind," Clementine said in disgust.

"Sadly, she does," her father agreed. "And yet she bears the indignity with such grace. I admire her, I do truly."

"As do I," Clementine agreed, closing the linen cupboard door and hoping to divert her father onto a different subject so he would forget the earl. "We really ought to do something to change people's perception of her and make her respectable. It is too bad that she is treated as though she's a scarlet woman by people who would call themselves Christians."

"Quite so, quite so," the reverend agreed. "But that does not answer my question. Was that Lord Beaumarsh's neck you were wringing with such enthusiasm?"

Clementine regarded her father, noting the mischief in his expression, and threw up her hands. "Yes, if you must know, it was indeed. Really, Papa, he is the most arrogant and vexatious man it has ever been my misfortune to meet. If that is what the nobility considers the cream of the crop, I can well understand why you decided to have nothing to do with it."

Her father returned a wry smile. "Well, that is kind, pet, but it is rather the ton that decided to have nothing to do with me. Or at least, my father decided for them."

"Yes, but you could have not married Mama, if it meant cutting ties with everything you knew," Clementine insisted.

The reverend laughed heartily at that. "Oh, no. No, indeed, I could not have done. One day, when you fall in love, you will realise how vital one person can be to your happiness. It was not even a choice. It simply never occurred to me not to marry her. The rest of the world could go hang for all I cared."

Clementine smiled, always delighted to hear her father speak of her mama. "You were both very lucky, I think."

"Undoubtedly," the reverend said with feeling. "But stop trying to divert me, you wicked child. I know your tricks, but I'm up to your weight, you see. We were speaking of the earl and his dastardly cousin's plot to murder him."

"You *did* have a nice chat," Clementine said wryly as her father followed her down the stairs to his study.

He closed the door behind them and went to pull the bell cord by the fireplace. "How could I fail to in such charming company?" he said, regarding her with a smile. "She thanked me again for all the help we gave her when that wretch Adderly was creating such a nuisance of himself making disrespectful offers, but I reminded her that was all your doing. Really, putting the word around that he was besotted and courting her with all the assiduousness of a lovesick puppy was just the thing to ensure she never saw the fellow again. If he'd continued to dog her steps, he would have looked entirely foolish. Your Machiavellian mind is a wonder to me," he said, without a trace of irony.

"That shouldn't be a compliment, Papa," Clementine observed, but her father simply shrugged. When Polly appeared, he asked her for a pot of tea and some biscuits before returning to their conversation.

"Well, it is a compliment when your skills are used entirely for the good of others, which brings me back to the earl. Mrs Adamson told me what his valet let slip and, of course, hearing that, I did not doubt you would be itching to come up with a plan to thwart his cousin in his endeavours. I take it you *have* a plan?" he asked, treating his daughter to a level look that was at once benign but dared her to pull the wool over his eyes.

Clementine nodded. "I do, and I fully intended to tell you, before you scold me for not doing so, for I shall need your help with it."

"Oh?" her father said, perking up, for he enjoyed being a part of her plots and schemes when he could.

Succinctly, Clementine outlined her plan for Edwin Cavendish, and her father sat back and chuckled, settling his hands on a rounded stomach that was rather plumper than it ought to be.

"Simple and easy to execute," he said with approval. "He shall be hoisted by his own petard. Well done, Clemmie, my dear."

Clementine smiled, basking in the light of her father's approval. "Thank you, Papa."

"No, no. I thank you," he said, grinning. "I have always wanted to hide behind a curtain and reveal my presence at a dramatic moment, and now I have the chance. How marvellous."

Clementine snorted and went over to her father, pressing a kiss to his whiskery cheek. "You are quite welcome, dearest Papa," she said, and left him to make a mess of her orderly desk.

The Mermaid's Tale, Little Valentine, South-East Coast of England. 5th June 1815.

"Not there, *there,"* Beau snapped, aware he was trying Kirby's patience.

He had been impossible for the past two days and it was a wonder the poor man hadn't landed him a facer. He knew he deserved it. No matter how many times he told himself he did not know why he was so vexed and out of sorts, he knew it was a lie. He could put it down to the remnants of poison in his system, or to the machinations of a man who was his own flesh and blood, or to being incarcerated in a place he would not be caught dead in usually, or simply to the usual ennui that seemed part and parcel of the life of a high-born gentleman.

It was none of those things.

Try as he might, he could not rid himself of Miss Honeywell's words, and more to the point, the scathing tone with which she had delivered them.

The idea that I would ever lower my standards sufficiently to marry an idle creature whose only concern appears to be whether his waistcoat is the precise colour of vibrant blue to match his eyes is an insult to my intelligence. I would not wed you if my life depended upon it, never mind my reputation. I trust I have made my position clear?

Beau felt his stomach clench as the words rang in his head again, and it definitely wasn't the arsenic or the wine. It was that dowdy young woman, wearing a gown years out of date, who seemed to have no notion of fashion and who ought to be far beneath his notice, who was twisting his guts into a knot. It was her cool appraisal of his character, the way she had called him out, pointing directly at everything he was feted for and yet hated most about himself. He had spent his whole life presenting himself to the ton as an indolent, cynical man of fashion, one who cared for nothing and no one, and he had succeeded beyond his wildest dreams. The ton thought him sophisticated and urbane, clever and witty, and the one man they must have at any gathering to ensure its social success. And Miss Honeywell had made him feel his entire life had been a colossal waste of time and effort. He could not understand how she had done it.

Miss Honeywell was not here, however, and Kirby was—the poor sod.

His increasingly aggravated valet gritted his teeth and moved the glass of wine one inch to the left.

“You ought to be drinking the waters, that’s what we came here for,” Kirby said stubbornly, not for the first time that morning.

“No, that's why you dragged my sorry carcass here. I had no say in the matter,” Beau grumbled, picking up the glass of wine before realising he couldn’t face it. His stomach twisted at the very idea. Frustrated, he set it back down with a clatter.

“No, that’s right, I should have left you to die in London and made no effort to help you. Don’t you worry, my lord, I’ll know better next time. Oh, but there won’t be a next time, ’cause that clever Miss Honeywell has come up with an idea to keep your cousin from causing anymore mischief,” he said with satisfaction.

Beau glowered and then gave up. He simply did not have the energy to continue being such a prick. “Kirby. I’m sorry. I know I’m being an unreasonable arse. Well, more than usual at any rate. I *am* grateful for what you did for me, truly.”

Kirby looked somewhat mollified by these words and shrugged. “S’alright,” he said gruffly. “You’re out of sorts, anyone can see that. Look, I tell you what, I’ll stop nagging you about drinking the water if you’ll get some air. It’s lovely down by the seafront. How about I find a blanket and a quiet corner, and you can get a bit of peace? I’ll even give you the local paper to read. That’s bound to keep you entertained,” he added with a grin.

Kirby looked so hopeful at this offer, Beau did not have the heart to reject it. The idea of bestirring himself from the chaise longue on which he was currently reclining did not appeal. Yet he remembered trips to the beach as a lad with his mother and they had been wonderful, with picnics and sea bathing and the building of sandcastles. Not that he was about to indulge in such childish pursuits, but it might be pleasant to sit and listen to the sea.

Still, it would not do for Kirby to think he had capitulated too easily, so he grumbled and protested some more before finally giving in.

Clementine stared down at the obstinate word square game and sighed. There were only two words and clues left to fit in to complete it, but her brain was refusing to cooperate. She sat in the garden, having come outside hoping that the fresh air might help, but her mind refused to settle and instead she watched her sisters playing with Caspar. Izzy was trying to teach him the rudiments of cricket and Bea was supposed to be helping but was laughing too hard at Caspar's antics to be much use. They persevered for another twenty minutes, with Caspar getting the hang of holding the bat, which was almost as big as he was, before he grew bored.

"I'm going to play with the kittens!" he announced, running off and abandoning the bat where it fell.

"Oh, me too! I'll get there first," Bea exclaimed, picking up her skirts and pretending to chase the little boy across the lawn.

They ran inside, Caspar squealing with laughter as he went. Izzy picked up the bat and hunted around in the shrubbery for the cricket ball, giving a little shout of triumph when she found it. She sauntered back to Clementine, the bat under her arm and her sunhat at a rakish angle.

"Any joy?" she asked, plonking herself down into the chair beside Clementine.

"No. My grey matter has shrivelled up and died," she said with a sigh. "I really must finish this one. You know how tetchy I get if I fall behind in my schedule."

"Well, why not go for a walk along the beach? That always clears your head."

Clementine perked up at the idea. She had not managed a walk since she had crossed swords with Lord Beaumarsh. "Yes, I shall do that. Will you come too?"

Izzy pulled a face. "Oh, no. Sorry, love. I'm too hot now. Besides, I've almost unpicked all the ribbon on my yellow muslin so Bea can put the lace on. She's been nagging me about it for days. You know how I detest sewing and furbishing but she insists it will give it a whole new lease of life," she added, rolling her eyes.

"Suit yourself."

Clementine gathered up her papers and put them away before fetching her bonnet and striding out of the house. As she had the morning she had met Mr Kirby, she took the winding footpath that led through the woods and went all the way to the beach. Well-hidden unless you knew to look for it, the path was rumoured to be used by smugglers at night, and only the locals were aware of it. Finding herself alone, she sat on the sand to take off her shoes and stockings. It was warm, even for June, and the idea of paddling in the cool water was too delicious to deny indulging herself.

As always, the mere sight of the sea soothed Clementine. No matter the time of year, no matter whether it was a placid blue or a seething riot of tossing grey waves, she felt better able to think, to breathe, when she was near it. Standing on the sand, the cool water frothing about her toes, and turning her face up to the sun, she felt entirely at peace. A short-lived situation as a drawling voice hailed her.

"Miss Honeywell, good afternoon to you."

Turning in surprise, Clementine started as she saw Lord Beaumarsh. He was lying on a rug, his long limbs arranged in their usual indolent sprawl that put her in mind of stories she had read of pampered pashas in their harems. As he was lounging in the shade of the trees that edged the beach, she had not noticed his presence. Now she wondered how she had missed him, for even in the shade his hair shone as bright as a newly minted guinea.

"Lord Beaumarsh," she replied stiffly, cursing herself for having removed her shoes and stockings and realising in horror he must have seen her do so. "You might have revealed your presence a little sooner," she remarked tartly, hoping she had not given him an indecent show.

"Sadly, I was dozing and did not notice you arrive. Nor did I see you remove your shoes and stockings, or I should have announced myself earlier. Do not tease yourself, though, for I do not expect you to believe that. Please, do go ahead and scold me for my disgusting behaviour." He waved a hand at her, as if encouraging her to get on with it.

Clementine looked at him with interest. There was such a scathing edge to the words, and something else too. Frustration? Though what he was frustrated about, she could not fathom. Perhaps being stuck in a place he obviously thought of as a rural backwater. Still, her instincts told her he was telling the truth and had not seen her arrive.

"If you did not know I was here, I cannot blame you for having said nothing," she said, her tone conciliatory.

"Thank you," he replied, then his eyes glittered, and she just knew he was going to make some off-colour remark.

"Don't," she warned, narrowing her eyes at him. "Don't spoil it."

He pressed his lips together, amusement in his expression, before giving her a slight nod. "I beg your pardon."

Despite herself, Clementine's lips twitched, and she wondered what he'd meant to say. "Did you write to your cousin?" she asked instead, steering the conversation to safer ground, though she knew she ought to leave. Standing here chatting with such a man with her legs and feet bare, even if they were mostly hidden from view, was quite shockingly improper of her.

"I did. Kirby would never have let me hear the end of it if I hadn't."

"I can believe that," Clementine replied, appreciating now that Mr Kirby was a most unlikely-looking valet. "He is a… a forceful character," she said diplomatically, realising he looked forceful enough to break a neck if he so chose.

The earl chuckled at this observation, and the sound was warm and inviting, disconcertingly so when she had felt so ill at ease in his company on the two previous occasions they had met.

"That's one way of putting it," he said mildly. "And yes, he is a rather unconventional manservant, for you are apparently quite desperate to ask me about him, but Kirby's secrets are his own. I will say that he is an excellent valet, if horribly bossy, and utterly devoted for reasons I cannot fathom. Though I suppose I do pay well," he added with a cynical curl of his lip.

Clementine digested this information with far more fascination than was good for her, but it revealed such a lot about the two men. More, perhaps, than his lordship intended to show her. Curious now, she could not help but delve a little deeper.

"He has been with you a long time."

It wasn't a question, for the rather disrespectful way Kirby spoke to his master illustrated something deeper than merely servant and employer. Why else would Beaumarsh put up with such treatment? Either they had been together since childhood days or were tied together by some shared experience that had formed a bond. Or perhaps they simply liked each other, she admitted, telling herself to stop trying to solve riddles where there were none.

"He has," Lord Beaumarsh agreed blandly, but offered no further information.

Understanding that the subject was off limits, Clementine nodded. She was a curious devil, it was true, but she had no desire to pry. Deciding she really must go before anyone saw them, she was about to bid him a good day when he asked,

"How long have you been setting the word games in the paper?"

Clementine froze and gaped at him, too astonished to deny it, or to react at all. Five years. For five years she had been setting the puzzle, and no one had ever figured out who the mysterious Mr Benedict Civil was. No one could have had told the earl, which meant he had figured it out.

Lord Beaumarsh grinned at her, a pleased, self-satisfied smile that lit up his face, making his eyes sparkle bluer and brighter than the sea at her back.

"Ah, not such a bottle-headed fribble after all," he murmured, delighted at having astounded her. Adjusting his position so he was lying on his side, his head supported on one arm, he said, *"The count is neither sad, nor sick, nor merry, nor well; but civil count, civil as an orange, and something of that jealous complexion."*

Despite herself, Clementine found she too was delighted by his cleverness, and, strangely, just as much by the smug satisfaction he took in showing her he was clever. Why it mattered to him that his deduction impressed her she could not fathom, but it did, and she was, and so she laughed. Beatrice's clever pun in Much Ado About Nothing compared Count John to a Seville orange, bitter and sour. From Mr Civil to Mr Seville, it was not such a leap to Clementine.

"Go on, admit it, you're impressed," he said, grinning now.

"I am," she confessed. "No one has ever worked it out. Indeed, Mr Civil is considered something of a phantom, and I have even heard of one fellow insinuating that *he* is Mr Civil, just to claim the glory," she added with feigned outrage.

"And were you never tempted to reveal the truth and give the fellow a terrific set down?" he asked, looking at her curiously.

"Good Lord, no," she said, shaking her head. "To what end? People would only despise me for thinking myself clever. My family knows and applauds my efforts and that is enough."

"And now I know too," he added, watching her with interest.

Clementine blushed. Inexplicably, her colour rose to such a pitch she wanted nothing more than to turn tail and run away. It was the way he had said the words, she decided, though there had been nothing suggestive or lewd in his tone, just the implication that they shared a secret, which she supposed they did. Yet it made her feel most peculiar, an odd squirming deep in her belly and such heat rushing beneath her skin it made her blush like the verriest ninny.

Unsettled, and cross with herself for being unsettled as much as with him for causing it, she stubbornly held her ground and did not look away nor flee, though the desire to do both was compelling. He continued to scrutinise her for what seemed an eternity before looking back at the puzzle.

"The word square itself was masterful too. How long did it take you to create it? I confess I was rather a dullard, and it took me a good ten minutes to complete, but my brain has not yet recovered, I fear."

"Ten minutes?" Clementine repeated, impressed. "You really did it so quickly?"

He gave her a wry look. "My, my, Miss Honeywell, you do think me a sorry specimen. Ten minutes is very much too long, and I truly am blaming my less than perfect health on slowing my mental faculties. I may be an idle creature whose only concern is the colour of his waistcoats, but I received a proper education like all gentlemen."

Clementine winced a little, recognising the words she had hurled at him in fury, but she refused to feel guilty for them. However, if he was being polite, she could do no less. "I beg your pardon. I ought not to have been so abominably rude, but then you provoked me by accusing me of trying to trap you into marriage, so really, I believe we are even."

He laughed at that and pushed himself into a sitting position. "I do believe you are correct. It was a most admirable set down, not least for being true, as all the best insults are. Mine, however, was mere fabrication, and for that I *am* sorry. I hope you can forgive me."

Clementine regarded him with interest, realising that the indolent, cynical façade he usually wore was absent and recognising his sincerity for what it was. "I do," she said with a nod. "I cannot blame you for being vexed with me. I must seem like the most appalling busybody poking my nose in where it does not belong."

"Oh no. Quite a delightful busybody," he said, lessening any discomfort she might feel at the rather flirtatious words by speaking them with a wry lilt as he got to his feet.

Clementine still felt awkward, however, and suddenly less certain of herself. Viewing Lord Beaumarsh from a distance, with his lordship lounging several feet away from her, felt safe. Rather like viewing a panther sleeping behind the bars of a cage. One could admire the beast and appreciate its beauty without being in the least bit of danger. Lord Beaumarsh, on his feet and standing over her, was quite a different prospect.

She felt suddenly petite and fragile, which was utter nonsense, for she was not especially small and very far from delicate. Yet he was broad and, despite his recent illness, exuded a sheer physical presence that was quite beyond anything she had ever experienced. So, this was a rogue, a libertine, she mused, intrigued by the sensation and realising this magnetic quality was what so many writers tried to evoke in the scandalous novels that Izzy hid under her mattress. Well, yes, she supposed she *could* see the appeal. For he was beautiful to behold, with the sunlight burnishing his golden hair, his blue eyes glittering, full of knowing and mischief and promises of things she did not yet understand, but would, if she allowed him to show her. Not that he was offering, but the possibility that he *might*, given the slightest encouragement, was inherent in his entire demeanour. Clementine studied him with fascination, drinking in the revelation of a creature she had only ever read about.

"Good Lord, the way you look at me," Beaumarsh said suddenly, taking a step back and breaking the spell.

Clementine blinked, wondering at his sudden retreat. He had not been *that* close, had not been overstepping any mark, not made a move or given any sign that he intended to act in a way unbecoming of a gentleman. Any sensation she had experienced had been nothing more than her instincts prickling, yet he was looking at her as if she had slapped him.

"My lord?" she said in confusion.

Beaumarsh stared at her and shook his head. "When you focus your attention on a fellow, it's like you might see directly into his head and poke about in his brain," he said peevishly.

Clementine laughed and then wondered if she ought to be insulted by his words. Honestly, she couldn't be bothered even if it had been an insult. She was too intrigued. "I assure you, I cannot do so," she told him gravely.

"Hmm." He looked unconvinced. "It's my belief you are lucky you were not born a few decades earlier."

"You mean I might have been burned for a witch?" she said with a snort. "Yes, I don't doubt. A handy method for getting rid of females with too much perspicacity or knowledge. I cannot help but observe, Lord Beaumarsh, that it is your *fear* of my knowing what is in your head that makes you ill at ease, for you know as well as I do, I cannot perceive that which you do not willingly share."

"Ah, but I don't believe that," he said, shaking his head and staring at her with an intensity that made her skin prickle. "What was it you gleaned about Kirby, about me, from the little I told you about him? There was a look in your eyes like I had revealed something of great interest that was most unsettling."

Clementine opened her mouth to deny it and then closed it again. Though she hated to admit it, she was rather enjoying their conversation and was loath to put an end to it just yet. So instead of doing the sensible thing and refusing to be drawn, bidding him a good day, she considered what she had inferred from his words.

"Mr Kirby treats you with what some might consider a lack of respect, and yet he is clearly devoted to you," she said, observing his face to see if his reaction confirmed her words. "There is a strong bond between you, one that runs deeper than employer and employee. That speaks of a long-standing relationship, or perhaps one forged in fire, by enduring an experience that shaped you both. But you refuse to acknowledge the sincerity of Mr Kirby's devotion, putting it down to the fact that you pay well. That speaks to me of a man who does not value his own consequence and feels he does not deserve such devotion. You do not like yourself very much, I think, my lord," she said gently, careful of his feelings and very aware she ought not to speak so intimately, and yet he had asked her to do so.

The coldly elegant, cynical lord she had first met at The Mermaid's Tale made a sudden and aggressive reappearance. His face shuttered, his bearing stiff where it had been relaxed. She felt the chill immediately. To her surprise, she deeply regretted having offended him, for whilst his good opinion was nothing to her, she had not meant to upset him and had clearly touched a nerve. That had been thoughtless of her and not well done. Just because the words might be true did not mean he wished to hear them spoken by a stranger.

"As I said, Miss Honeywell, a fellow does not enjoy having you poke about in his brain," he said curtly.

"My lord, I beg your pardon. That was dreadfully—"

"Think nothing of it. I invited you to speak your mind, did I not? Now, I believe I have had enough fresh air for one day. If you would excuse me."

"Of course," Clementine said, cursing her unruly tongue as she watched him snatch up the blanket he'd been sitting on and stride away. She wished he would allow her to apologise. What had she been thinking, saying such a thing? Yet it had seemed so obvious. Before her stood a man who had every advantage life offered, and yet he seemed not to value himself in the least. Why was that, she wondered? What had given him such a low opinion of himself?

"Not your business," she told herself sternly as she sat down on a rock, brushing the sand from her feet now they were dry. "You must stop interfering in other people's lives. Well, unless they specifically invite you to interfere," she amended, and then sighed.

She was a hopeless case.

Chapter 6

We few, we happy few, we band of brothers.

The Mermaid's Tale. Little Valentine, South-East Coast of England. 5th June 1815.

Beau strode back to the hotel, anger burning inside him. How dare she! How *dare* she? The words circled in his mind as he slammed through the doors of the hotel, making Mrs Adamson almost leap out of her skin at the sight of him. He startled her to such a degree, the lovely flower arrangement she was about to place on the table in the centre of the entrance hall almost slid from her grasp.

Beau leapt forward and steadied it, and between them they put it carefully down.

"I beg your pardon," he said, letting out a breath. "I did not mean to scare you."

Mrs Adamson smiled. It was a lovely smile, and she was a beautiful woman, yet the smile did not quite reach her eyes. It was not quite genuine. *She* was not quite genuine, as if she were playing a part. Unlike Miss Honeywell, who was most determinedly *exactly* what she appeared to be. An interfering little busybody, he thought crossly. Yet that was not true, nor fair. He had asked her, had he not, what it was she had gleaned from his words? Just because she was a deal too astute for his comfort was not her fault.

"You appear a trifle discomposed, Lord Beaumarsh," Mrs Adamson observed. "Why not come through to the terrace? Major Hancock and Captain Dearborn are already there, and Reverend

Honeywell. It is a lovely cool spot on a warm afternoon and overlooks the sea. I have a splendid Rhenish wine, chilled to perfection," she added enticingly.

Beau hesitated. He had fully intended to go upstairs and make a nuisance of himself to Kirby until he felt better, but he was far too curious not to meet the dreadful Miss Honeywell's father, and he thought perhaps his stomach might accept a little glass of white wine where it had baulked at the red.

"That sounds perfect," he said, and allowed Mrs Adamson to lead him up the stairs, through an elegant lounge area and towards large glass doors that opened onto the terrace.

Stepping outside, he discovered it was an enchanting spot. Large pots overflowing with red geraniums were set at intervals along the elaborate wrought-iron balustrade. The scarlet flowers seemed brighter still, set against the black painted fancy work of the railing. Along the wall of the house scrambled a lush climbing jasmine, the scent of its tiny white flowers quite intoxicating. Beau took a moment to appreciate the setting and the splendid view over the sea as Mrs Adamson led him to a table where three men were seated, sharing a bottle of wine. They looked up as Beau appeared, their expressions ranging from disapproving to welcoming.

"My Lord Beaumarsh, might I introduce you to Captain Dearborn, Major Hancock, and Reverend Honeywell? Gentlemen, this is the Earl of Beaumarsh."

The reverend leapt to his feet and grasped his hand, shaking it warmly. "Good day, good day to you, my lord. How delightful to meet you!"

Beau did not know what he had expected of Miss Honeywell's father, but he at once warmed to this jovial fellow with his twinkling blue eyes and toothy smile.

"A pleasure, my lord," Major Hancock said, his greeting more formal but no less cordial.

An old soldier, the major was perhaps on the high side of sixty, with iron grey hair and an upright bearing. His companion was younger, perhaps forty at most, his tanned, handsome face pleasingly weather-beaten. His eyes, however, were a deal colder, and he looked at Beau with obvious mistrust. Beau did not wonder at it. His title and his looks often set other men's backs up, making them feel they had something to prove even when they did not, and he ignored the man's offhand greeting, settling himself down at the table.

"Bring us another bottle, Anne, there's a good girl," the major requested of Mrs Adamson. The lady acknowledged the request, allowing the familiarity, which seemed fond rather than insinuating.

"I believe you have met my eldest daughter, my lord?" the reverend said, emptying the last of the bottle on the table into a fresh glass.

"I have had that pleasure, yes," Beau said, a little taken aback that the man would admit to it, for the circumstances of their meeting were rather improper.

"A lovely young woman," the major said approvingly. "But of course Lord Beaumarsh has met her. Vomited over her feet, didn't he?" he added, slapping his knee and giving a bark of laughter as if it were the funniest thing he'd ever heard.

Beau winced, and wished the fellow to the devil, but he could hardly pretend it wasn't true, as the major had witnessed the entire thing. "I believe she has forgiven me," he said, a little stiffly.

"Oh, no doubt. Never holds a grudge, does Miss Honeywell," the major added, wiping his eyes. "Must admit, I thought you a shabby devil for serving her such a trick, but her father here swears you really were taken ill, not drunk as a wheelbarrow as I had supposed. Nothing worse than a dicky tummy. I've had my fair share, you know. After the Battle of Seedaseer—that's in Mysore country, you understand—I had the worst attack of my life. Thought I would die in that infernal heat and—"

"Good God, Hancock, give it a rest," Captain Dearborn said, though not unkindly. "I'm as ready as any man to be impressed by your war stories, but leave out the unsavoury details, for heaven's sake. Beaumarsh here is not a military man and won't appreciate it."

The major blustered and apologised, though rather pedantically pointed out that he had given no unsavoury details yet. Beau simply smiled, very aware of the subtle rebuke the captain had offered him. The reason for his less than warm manner became obvious, however, as Mrs Adamson reappeared, and the captain's eyes lit up. He jumped to his feet, hurrying to take the tray she carried, laden with another bottle of wine and plates of sandwiches and small savoury tarts. As he moved, Beau perceived he limped badly and then noticed the walking stick propped on the back of the man's chair.

"Here, let me," the captain said, taking the tray from Mrs Adamson, who gently chided him, assuring him she was quite capable of managing without expiring of fatigue.

"That's beside the point," he said sternly, and placed the tray down on the table.

Giving Dearborn an impatient glance, Mrs Adamson returned her attention to the rest of them. "Do tuck in, gentlemen. Reverend, Mrs Fairway made the roast beef and horseradish sandwiches extra hot, just as you like them. The rest of you, consider yourselves warned," she added with a smile, before leaving them alone again.

The major watched Mrs Adamson leave the terrace, his eyes wistful as he followed the sway of her lush hips. "Ought to be married," he said, shaking his head sadly. "Not working her fingers to the bone in this place. If only I were twenty years younger."

"Indeed," the captain said, his tone a little snappish.

"Oh, I would certainly like to see her happily married with a family, but I rather think she enjoys running this place. She's made a terrific success of it, after all. A pity we don't have more customers of his lordship's rank to make it fashionable for her," the reverend said, surprising Beau, who might have thought a clergyman would believe a woman's job was as a wife and mother and nothing more. But then, he was Miss Honeywell's father, and she was hardly a conventional miss, was she?

Beau sipped his wine, discovering it was excellent, crisp and light with faint traces of honey and chamomile. Captain Dearborn changed the subject, turning the talk to Napoleon, which got Major Hancock so riled up that the reverend was forced to change it again and asked him about his roses. These were infested with aphids and so did little to soothe the old fellow. Still, the talk moved on to fishing, then to a rather fine French brandy that Honeywell had got his hands on, and then onto discussions about the eruption of Mount Tambora, which had caused so much devastation in the Dutch East Indies.

Before Beau knew it, the sun was going down, glowing gold and turning the entire sky the most extraordinary colour. He watched it slowly sinking, disappearing beneath the horizon as the men chattered and laughed, realising with some surprise that it had been a most enjoyable evening. Mrs Adamson had come and gone, lighting candles on the tables, and bringing more food, and several more bottles. Beau wondered how much they'd drunk between them, for he never seemed to have an empty glass, and regarded the reverend with dawning respect, for the fellow had kept up with them all and did not appear even a little disguised.

"Well, I'd best call it an evening. My little Penny will be waiting for me and wanting her supper," the Major said with a fond sigh.

The reverend caught Beau's eye and smiled. "His cat," he explained.

"I'll go with you," the captain said, unbending sufficiently to give Beau a polite nod and bid him a good evening as he followed the major, leaning heavily on the walking stick as he went.

"Excellent fellows," the reverend said with a smile, upending the last bottle into his own glass once Beau had refused it. "Jolly good company."

"They were," Beau admitted.

"You look surprised. You perhaps suspected such an out of the way town would be filled to the brim with provincial nitwits?" Honeywell observed, his keen eyes studying Beau.

Suddenly, Beau knew where Miss Honeywell had inherited her shrewdness from. Here was a fellow who missed nothing and was a good deal sharper than he made out. He could well imagine the unsuspecting inhabitants of Little Valentine lulled into thinking he was an amiable buffoon when the truth was quite different.

"Guilty as charged," Beau replied with a shrug.

The reverend chuckled. "Well, do not let me disabuse you of the notion. We *do* have a sufficiency of provincial nitwits, I assure you, but people will surprise you if you allow them to."

"Like your daughter," Beau replied with a trace of bitterness before he could think better of it.

"Precisely like Clementine," the reverend agreed, either not noticing the edge to his words or allowing them to pass without comment. "She is a remarkable girl. Do you know as many people in this town turn to her for help or advice as to me? They hold her in the highest esteem, and rightly so. I sometimes wonder how I created such remarkable daughters. I must give the credit to their mother, I believe. They are all quite extraordinary in their own ways, but Clementine is very much like her mama, God rest her soul. Such a clever and capable woman, she was, and such a capacity for love and compassion. She always knew just what to say when people were in distress. I miss her quite dreadfully," he added with a sigh that was so heartfelt, Beau felt a little uncomfortable at the emotion on display.

"I am sorry for your loss," Beau said diffidently, wishing they could go back to speaking about roses, despite his knowing nothing at all about the subject.

The reverend dragged out a large handkerchief and blew his nose with vigour before smiling at Beau. "Forgive me. It's the wine. Makes me maudlin. If I had a few more glasses, it would be another matter. Life and soul then, you know, but I've drunk just enough to be sentimental. It's a wondrous thing, though, to find a woman like my Mary. To share even a part of my life with her was the greatest good fortune and I shall never stop being grateful for that. And then to have my three girls to fuss over me," the reverend sighed and blew his nose again.

"You are fortunate indeed," Beau replied, though he was uncertain he meant it. It appeared the reverend had truly adored his wife, but she had died and left him to raise three children alone. How could that be fortunate? Added to that, his eldest daughter was Clementine Honeywell, which could not be a comfortable prospect for any father. Yet he seemed to bear God no ill will.

"Do you have no prospects in that regard?" the reverend asked thoughtfully. "I suppose you are young yet, but men of your ilk are usually under pressure to provide the requisite heir and spare, are they not?"

Beau stiffened at the question, which was none of the reverend's business. It was quite impolite of him to pry in such a way and yet, as Beau glared at the man, about to make a cutting reply, he did not see curiosity in the man's gaze. Instead, there was empathy and a genuine desire to… to do what Beau was not entirely certain. To help, he thought, though what on earth the reverend thought he could achieve, he did not know. Still, he relaxed his usually inflexible stance about discussing his personal life enough to reply. "My mother wishes me to marry and has done this past five years, but I confess the married state does not appeal to me."

"It doesn't?" the reverend asked, looking rather astounded by this. "Good heavens, my boy, why ever not? Why else were we put on this earth if not to find our soulmates and live our lives together with them?"

Beau laughed at this outrageously sentimental notion as much as at being called 'my boy,' which made him feel like a spotty youth. "You really have had a deal to drink, sir, if that is your opinion. I promise you, men of my class do not marry for love. They marry for wealth, power, connections and the promise of healthy sons to continue the line. It is a business transaction, nothing more."

The reverend shook his head sadly. "Yes, I know that is most often the case, but now and then a brave fellow bucks the trend, you know. You do not *have* to follow the herd. Indeed, I would most strongly urge you not to do so. No wonder you dread the married state so fiercely if that is all there is to look forward to. But what if you found a woman who was your equal, who entertained you and challenged you, and loved you with all the ferocity of a lioness? What if the sound of her voice made your heart sing, and the sight of her face each morning made you want to thank the good Lord for his beneficence? What then?"

"Then I should think I was as drunk as you are," Beau said agreeably, though the reverend's words resonated inside him like the clanging of a bell, exposing all the emptiness he knew was there but never dared to look at.

"Ha!" the reverend said, nodding. "A fair point, my lord. I think perhaps I might be a trifle foxed. Best be on my way, afore I say things I ought not."

"I think you passed that point half an hour ago, but we shan't worry about it," Beau said, chuckling as the reverend pushed up from his chair and sat down heavily again a second later.

"That Rhenish wine is tricky stuff. Makes out like it's an innocent little glassful when all the time it's hiding a wicked secret," Honeywell said, the words accompanied by a toothy grin that was most endearing.

"No, sir, you just drank a good deal," Beau replied, getting to his feet. "You may consider yourself lucky that my stomach would not allow me to drink as I do in town, for I am sober enough to see you home."

"Would you?" the reverend said, beaming at him as Beau helped him to his feet. "Ah, you are a good fellow. A jolly good fellow. Knew as soon as I met you. Bertie, I said, that is a jolly good fellow indeed."

Beau snorted and shook his head as he guided the slightly unsteady reverend towards the door and ensured he did not tip over the balcony. He ought not take a bit of notice of the words of a man who was clearly inebriated, and yet the notion that this agreeable fellow thought him a good man was touching.

Carefully, he accompanied the reverend down the stairs and out of the hotel before realising he had no notion where the fellow lived.

"Shortcut," Honeywell said, pointing away from the main street and towards the woods.

Beau nodded, the reverend was just tipsy enough to fall into a ditch, but hopefully not so cast away he would lead them in circles for hours. So, he walked beside Honeywell, who seemed to have found his feet now, and just pushed him gently back into the middle of the path when he veered off course. It was a pleasant stroll, a bright moon illuminating their way and the sound of the sea a peaceful backdrop as they made their way.

"'S'haunted. The woods, I mean," the reverend said, his teeth flashing white in the dim light as Beau glanced at him. "Though many of the ghosts are carrying brandy and French silk," he added with a chuckle.

"Ah, I see. Kirby mentioned something of the sort. I think he was hopeful we might find a supply of burgundy and brandy too. I don't suppose you know any of the fellows and could put in a word for him?"

"Oh, certainly. Easiest thing in the world," the reverend said, waving a hand, and somehow Beau was unsurprised to discover Honeywell knew the smugglers.

At this point, he wasn't certain it would surprise him to discover Honeywell *was* a smuggler. Still, the promise of the best French wine and brandy was certainly worth escorting the reverend home.

"You know," the reverend said, grinding to a halt and swaying a little as he focused his attention on Beau with some difficulty. "That's why you're so bored and unhappy."

"I beg your pardon?" Beau said in alarm.

"What I said earlier about finding the woman you love with all your heart. It's the most important thing you'll do in your life. Nothing else matters, my lord. You must find your other half, the bit of you that completes the circle and makes you whole. At the very least, you need love, and someone who makes you want to do better, who makes you better simply by loving you."

The loud belch that followed slightly undercut these sincere and spiritual words, but the reverend apologised for his rudeness and carried on walking. Beau stared after him for a long moment before following again, too surprised to say a word.

They arrived at the garden gate of the vicarage, which gave a violent squeak when the reverend leaned a little too heavily upon it to push it open. The sound must have alerted the inhabitants to their arrival, as a moment later the door flew open, and Miss Honeywell appeared. Lit by moonlight, she looked rather ghostly and ethereal, clad in her white nightgown and wrap. It was a modest ensemble, not in the least provocative, and yet she looked so wonderfully charming, with her blonde hair tied back in a loose plait, Beau's heart gave an odd sort of kick in his chest. He found it impossible not to stare, enchanted by the picture she made in the silver light, framed by the roses that scrambled around the porch.

"Papa!" she exclaimed. "You said you would be back by ten and its nearly midnight. I was about to search the woods. You might have sent word to tell me you'd be late."

"Mea culpa!" Honeywell said, standing with both hands pressed against his heart. "Forgive me, Clemmie darling. I was in the wrong but look who I found. We've had a splendid evening."

Clementine froze as she belatedly noticed Beau standing on the other side of the gate.

"Oh," she said, her posture suddenly alert as she drew her dressing gown tighter around her. Sadly, she did not realise how little this helped, as it did far more to reveal the lush curves hidden beneath the prim white cotton than to hide them. Beau did his best not to notice. It would not do him the least bit of good to go lusting over a girl of Miss Honeywell's stamp. Those were the kind that needed marrying. "I beg your pardon. I did not see you."

"It's of no matter. I'm sorry to have disturbed you, but I thought I had best escort your father home," Beau replied, remembering that they had not parted on the best of terms. She had been appallingly tactless, and he was furious with her. Yet, he could no longer summon the annoyance he'd felt earlier, especially when she looked so adorable in all her frilly white cotton. It made him want to smile. It also made him want to do dreadfully wicked things, but he pushed such thoughts aside because he was not lunatic enough to seduce a vicar's daughter.

"That was very good of you," she said, taking her father's arm and guiding him to the door. "Go straight up to bed now for you'll having a shocking headache in the morning, I fear. I will bring you a nice pot of coffee first thing, though."

"Ah, you're a good girl, Clemmie," Honeywell said, patting her cheek as she released her hold on him. "Night, night, pet.

Goodnight, Beaumarsh!" he called over his shoulder as he made his way indoors.

"Good night, sir."

Beau hesitated, knowing he ought to leave at once, but strangely reluctant to do so when he might continue looking at Miss Honeywell.

"My lord," she said, moving closer and stopping just the other side of the gate. "I wish you would allow me to apologise for my words earlier. I'm a tactless clodpole who sticks her nose in where it has no right being, I know it's true, and I ought never to have spoken so. Please forgive me."

Beau studied her, reading the sincerity in her expression. Moonlight fell upon her face, softening features that were often set in implacable lines, stubborn creature that she was. Why the devil was she even concerned about his difficulties? She had made it very clear she didn't give a farthing for him and was not interested in him as a man. Not as a husband, at least. Miss Honeywell had made that point most succinctly, and he did not doubt the veracity of her words. She would do far better than he when she took a husband. No doubt she would choose someone she considered worthy. A man of character, of high morals and unimpeachable honour. Perhaps the local schoolteacher was such a creature, though surely she could look higher than that. She did not care about social standing, though, that much was obvious.

"Oh dear. I *have* vexed you," she said with a sigh, as Beau realised he'd still not replied to her question. Worry made her brow furrow and, before he could think better of it, Beau reached out and touched the little crease in her forehead, as if he could smooth it away. It vanished as her expression shifted from concern to astonishment, colour flooding her cheeks, and Beau snatched his hand back, as shocked as she was.

"It seems I must apologise now," he said with an awkward laugh. "I believe I am a little foxed myself. Please do not trouble yourself, Miss Honeywell. There is nothing for you to apologise for. Now, I had best be going. Good night."

"Good night," she whispered, the words a little breathless.

They rang in Beau's ears as he hurried back the way the reverend had led him and prayed he would not get lost. Had she welcomed his touch, he wondered, despite reviling him for being a vain peacock? No, he had best not think of that. Far better that he got himself back to the hotel before Kirby fretted to death and convinced himself Edwin had kidnapped him.

With that happy thought quickening his steps, Beau hurried back to The Mermaid's Tale.

Chapter 7

Kedgeree, lace, and talkative seagulls.

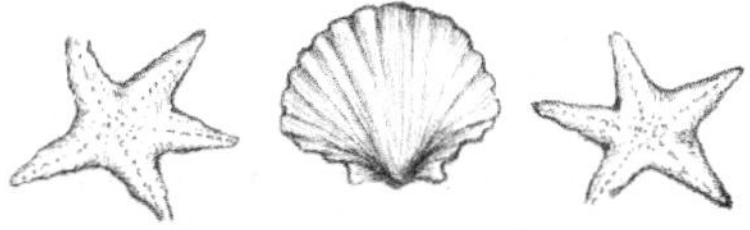

The Mermaid's Tale. Little Valentine, South-East Coast of England. 6th June 1815.

"You're looking quite the plump currant this morning, my lord," Kirby said with approval, as he handed Beau a pristine white cravat.

Though Beau would be the first to credit Kirby for turning him out in prime style, the cravat was his own domain and one he jealously guarded. Kirby took no affront, however, for Beau's hands were deft and sure and even the fussy valet would admit his efforts were to be applauded. Choosing the mathematical for its simplicity and style, Beau only needed one attempt before Kirby handed him a small gold pin with a sparkling sapphire at the top with which to fasten it.

"Yes, I feel rather better," Beau admitted, turning away from the looking glass.

"It's all that sea air, fresh, ain't it? Air in the city is so thick you can chew it," Kirby added with a grimace.

"That must be why I'm famished," Beau remarked, regarding Kirby with speculative interest. "But you cannot be implying that you would prefer to remove to the countryside?"

"Why not?" Kirby asked, not looking up as he rearranged his master's brushes and articles on the dressing table. "I like it here. Pretty, ain't it? Peaceful too, and it's not like there's no society. Reckon you had a fine time putting the world to rights with the reverend and his cronies."

Beau laughed and shook his head. “It was a very pleasant evening, I admit, but only because it was a novelty. You surely can’t see me retiring to such a spot? I’m not in my dotage.”

Kirby straightened and rolled his eyes. “Not retiring, and I ain’t speaking specifically of this town. But Cavendish House isn’t a million miles away, and it’s such a lovely place. Seems a shame to let it go to waste.”

“It isn’t ‘going to waste,’ it’s tended by an army of people and much enjoyed by my mother. It also supports itself and the staff, and is in excellent heart, I thank you,” Beau said testily.

“Reckon that’s true,” Kirby allowed. “But only your ma sees it. You’re never there. The place needs a family, kiddies running about and causing mischief and—”

“Good God, Kirby!” Beau exclaimed, exasperated. “What has got into you? You’re worse than my damned mother. Stop trying to get me leg shackled. Edwin ought to get that letter any moment, presuming he’s home, and he’ll be down here before we know it. Once that little scene has been enacted and I am safe to go about without employing someone to taste every morsel before I eat and drink, like some ancient Roman emperor, we shall be on our way.”

“Yes, sir,” Kirby said stiffly, gathering up his master’s dirty linens and stalking from the room.

Beau groaned. Now Kirby would sulk, and he really did not have the energy to jolly him out of it. Though he usually broke his fast in the privacy of his own room, today Beau decided escaping his huffy valet might be for the best and escaped downstairs.

Like the rest of the hotel, the breakfast parlour was bright and elegant. Large windows opened onto the front of the house, displaying the lovely blue sea sparkling in the sunshine. A soft breeze drifted in, bringing with it a salty tang and the soft rushing sound of waves upon the shore.

“Good morning, my lord.”

Beau looked up as Mrs Adamson walked into the room. She looked like a summer day in a lovely gown of white jaconet muslin. She wore her hair twisted with a simple bandeau and the cascading red curls were extraordinary against her fair skin and the white dress. He wondered what a woman of her looks was doing running a hotel of all things and speculated about Mr Adamson. Was she a widow perhaps, or was the 'Mrs' a social nicety? He suspected the latter but cared little either way. She was a delightful picture to rest his eyes upon, but she held no interest for him, and he wondered why.

"Good morning, Mrs Adamson. You are looking in prime twig, as my valet would say."

"Your valet *has* said so," she replied with a wry smile. "Now, what may I get you? Tea or coffee? The kippers are excellent but there is kedgeree or a nice sirloin, or you may have gammon and eggs."

"Oh, coffee, gammon and eggs, I think," Beau replied, looking up as Captain Dearborn came into the room.

"Very good, my lord. Good morning, Captain," Mrs Adamson said, turning to him. "Your usual table?"

Dearborn glanced at Beau and hesitated.

"Please, do join me," Beau offered, rather surprised at himself, for he could not endure company or conversation from anyone but Kirby in the morning until he'd had several cups of coffee.

Dearborn nodded and walked towards his table, carefully setting his walking stick on the back of his chair before sitting down rather heavily.

"Good morning, my lord."

"Oh, call me Beaumarsh, everyone does," he said, assuming the man would balk at calling him Beau.

Dearborn nodded and ordered the kedgeree and a pot of tea. "Will you be with us long?" he asked once Mrs Adamson had taken their orders.

Beau hesitated. He was of half a mind to tweak the fellow and pretend a long stay, but he shook his head. "No. I have a little business to conclude, and then I shall return to London."

"Business, in Little Valentine?" the captain said with a laugh. "Unless you are a smuggler or quack, I cannot imagine what your business might be."

Beau raised an eyebrow, wondering whether to give the fellow a set down, but couldn't be bothered. In London, he would have crushed such a comment, which showed too much interest in his personal affairs, but somehow it was different here, and he found he did not resent the captain's interest so much.

Still, Dearborn was not such a slow top as to not realise his error. He cleared his throat. "I say, I beg your pardon. None of my affair."

Waving this away, Beau shook his head. "It's of no consequence, but I can assure you I am neither a smuggler nor a physician."

"I never thought it," Dearborn replied dryly. "I supposed you came to drink the waters. If it is not prying to ask, why did you come here? I would have thought Bath more your touch."

"So would I," Beau said wryly. "But as I was out of my head, my valet made the decision. I believe my physician told him this was the closest spa town to the city, and that sold it. He's not much of a one for travel, especially in the company of a man who is as sick as a horse."

"Can't blame him for that," the captain remarked, falling silent as the coffee and his pot of tea arrived. A young maid set the tray down at the table, laying the items out along with a jug of milk, another of cream and a bowl of sugar, before bobbing a curtsey and scurrying away again.

"Did the reverend stay long after we left?"

"He did," Beau replied with a smile. "I walked him home, actually. I feared he might spend the night in a ditch otherwise."

"Oh, that was jolly decent of you," Dearborn said, looking so surprised Beau could not help but smile.

"It was. I can't think what came over me," he replied with a crooked smile.

The captain laughed at this sally and seemed to relax a degree, and when their breakfast arrived, they ate the splendid repast in amiable silence.

"Good morning, Miss Honeywell!" called a cheerful voice as Clementine made her way into the haberdasher's.

"Good day to you, Mrs Doomsday," Clementine replied, amused, as always, by the incongruity of the lady's name and nature. Her mother-in-law, old Mother Doomsday, more than made up for the disparity, but had long since retired from the shop, heaven be praised.

"What can I do for you today?" the lady asked, her eyes bright and alert with the prospect of a large order.

Sadly, the Honeywell family did not spend large sums upon fabric and furbishing, for whilst their home was a comfortable one and they were well provided for, fashion was rather beyond their reach. It had never bothered Clementine before, but that morning when she had slipped on her favourite sprigged muslin, she had noted how shabby it looked, the lace upon the short, puffed sleeves sadly threadbare, and the ribbon trim worn thin in places. Having noted the splendid job Bea had made of Izzy's yellow gown, she thought perhaps she might try to do the same herself.

There was no particular reason for the effort, she assured herself. A desire to have a few pretty things for the summer was perfectly natural. Yet the image of Lord Beaumont, handsome and unreachable in the moonlight, flickered in her mind's eye. Recalling the moment when he had reached out and softly traced a line over her brow with his fingertips still made her shiver.

Fool, she told herself sternly, and returned her attention to Mrs Doomsday, whose hopeful expression had fallen into one of resigned good cheer.

"Some blue ribbons, and perhaps a few yards of lace," Clementine said with a smile.

"Certainly."

A moment later a dozen or more reels of ribbon were presented to Clementine, in varying shades of blue, and different widths.

"This one is lovely," Mrs Doomsday said, sliding a thick cobalt blue length between her fingers. "Blue suits you, what with your fair colouring and those cornflower eyes of yours. Have you seen that lovely fabric in Madame Auguste's window? You'd look as pretty as a picture in that."

"And wear it on what occasion?" Clementine said with a laugh, well aware that Madame Auguste and Mrs Doomsday had an accord, where Madame bought all but her most exclusive fabrics from Mrs Doomsday, and Mrs Doomsday persuaded her clientele to go next door to Madame, instead of doing the work themselves.

"Well, to an assembly, or to catch the eye of a handsome lord. I hear you've met him. Is he splendid?" Mrs Doomsday asked eagerly, leaning closer to Clementine, the hope returning to her eyes at the prospect of a bit of gossip.

"You'd best ask my father. He spent the evening with him last night," Clementine replied, deflecting the question. "I shall take three yards of the blue. Can you show me the lace now, please? Just a narrow width for trim."

Mrs Doomsday sighed, aware that the Honeywell family did not indulge in idle gossip.

"You know, you're young yet, and pretty with it, Miss Honeywell," she said, sounding a tad frustrated. "Don't you go burying yourself in this little town of ours and cutting off your nose to spite your face. Take your courage in hand, my pet, that's my advice," the lady said, and then, blushing at her own temerity, hurried off to find the lace.

Clementine finished her purchases with Mrs Doomsday before popping into see Mr Muddel to order two pounds of cheddar and a smaller quantity of Stilton. Then to Mr Twyner to pay for their candle order. Her errands complete for the morning, she made her way down to the beach to make her way home, preferring this morning to walk beside the sea and then up through the woods than via the town. She told herself she was not in the mood to chatter with everyone who crossed her path today, for it would take her forever to make her way home if the world and his wife were out and about. But it was not true.

You just want to see Lord Beaumarsh again, you great hen wit, she chastised herself. It was nothing but the truth. Surely, his cousin would arrive in the town in the next day or two, and then the glamorous Beau Beaumarsh would be gone from their lives. Everything would go back to exactly how it had been before he had arrived, which, she told herself, was a good thing. She had been entirely content before he arrived. This was true enough. Sadly, she did not believe she would be perfectly content once he had gone.

Somehow, Lord Beaumarsh had stirred things up, stirred *her* up. He had reminded her that, whilst she might be on the shelf, she was only *just* on the shelf, and things she had not allowed herself to hope for suddenly nagged at her.

Sighing, Clementine turned to stare out to sea, watching the fishing boats on the horizon. Seagulls wheeled overhead, their raucous cries making her look up, watching them as they glided high above her. Suddenly she envied their freedom, their ability to just leave the ground behind and fly away, seeking adventure.

"Nonsense," she told herself, speaking aloud in the hopes she might pay attention this time. "All they are seeking is food and a mate. Stop this romantic babble at once. Else before you know it, you'll be writing poetry."

"Are you a poet?"

Clementine gave a little shriek and spun around, her heart beating wildly as the man who had unsettled her so since last night appeared like a genie before her.

He appeared entertained by her reaction and took a step back, holding out a hand in a peaceful gesture. "I mean you no harm, Miss Honeywell."

"Good heavens, but you made me jump," she said crossly, irritated by his coming upon her talking to herself, of all things. At least her annoyance reminded her she thought he was a pretty fribble and there was nothing to get all het up about. "It is very bad manners to creep up on a person, my lord."

"I did not creep," he said, his tone placating. "I swear I did not. Indeed, I called your name several times, but you were so intent on chatting with the seagulls that you did not hear me."

Clementine blushed, mortified. "I was not talking to the seagulls," she said defensively, and then wondered if that might actually be better than talking to herself. No matter. It was too late now.

"Who were you speaking to about writing poetry, then?" he asked curiously.

"I wasn't—oh, never mind," Clementine said with a shake of her head. "I know you are teasing me, and I shan't let you rile me, for I promised I would not be rude to you again. So there. You may do your worst, and I shall not rise to the bait," she added magnanimously.

His eyes shone, a hint of wickedness that made a tremor of unease stir in Clementine's belly. She ignored it and put up her chin, waiting.

"Was the poem for me, Miss Honeywell?" he asked slyly.

Well, drat the man. Of all the things to say! Though she had not actually been about to write an ode to the Earl of Beaumarsh—may God strike her dead if she ever considered such a dreadful thing—she blushed a horrible shade of scarlet. Cursing her fair skin, she just knew he would take it as confirmation of his suspicions and that made the situation entirely worse. She glared at him.

"Certainly not," she said coolly, wishing she could press her hands against her cheeks to stop them burning so.

His lips twitched, but he forced his features into a sombre expression and nodded. "No, of course not. I imagine your poems are reserved for more worthy suitors. Does your sweetheart live in the town? Let me guess, he's a schoolteacher, a fine man devoted to the education of young minds who spends all his spare time doing charitable deeds. No doubt he does not drink, nor smoke, nor gamble, nor does he take the Lord's name in vain. He is a pattern card of decency and honour and adored by one and all."

Clementine stared, appalled by the picture he painted. "He sounds a perfect prig," she said, startling a bark of laughter out of Lord Beaumarsh, who seemed delighted by her reply.

He continued to chuckle and, once again, the warmth of the sound struck her, though not as much as the effect it had on her. It was a wondrous thing to make the cynical Earl of Beaumarsh laugh with unaffected amusement and she was viscerally aware that the pleasure it gave her was a dangerous sensation, making her crave more.

Don't be foolish, Clementine scoffed inwardly. At four and twenty, she was not fresh from the schoolroom and was a long way from having her head turned by a handsome face. She knew this meant nothing to him beyond a momentary departure from the commonplace. *She* meant nothing to him. No more or less than a pleasant diversion for a few moments, in a rural town where there were none of the sophisticated delights of the city to be found. But all the same, why not enjoy it for what it was? She was not expecting a proposal of marriage, and he was not about to offer one. Yet he was handsome and witty, and he made her laugh, and could that not be enough?

Of course it could. So long as they did not overstep any boundaries of propriety, there was nothing stopping them being friends. They might be alone here, but they were not *alone.* There were plenty of people walking on the beach, and a group of children making sandcastles. Not to mention being in full view of the high street. Besides, he was friends with her father now, too.

"The poor young man," Beaumarsh said, returning her attention to their conversation. He emitted an overly sorrowful sigh. "He must be heartbroken."

"Hardly. He's in love with my sister," she said with a snort.

"Ah, the lovely Miss Isabelle?" he replied, grinning.

"Oh, no. He's aiming higher even than Izzy," Clementine replied. "He's holding out for Beatrice, but he shan't have her, I promise. You've not seen her yet or you would not be wasting your time here with me, I assure you."

Clementine had never in her life been jealous of her sister's beauty and was therefore startled to hear the faint tinge of bitterness that accompanied this statement. She glanced at Beaumarsh, wondering if he had heard it too, but he merely looked entertained, awaiting more information.

"Bea is a diamond of the first water," Clementine said gravely. "Incomparable. She is too good for this town, and I intend for her to have a season. She'll marry a duke, even without a vast dowry behind her, you mark my words."

"A duke?" Beaumarsh repeated, quirking one elegant eyebrow. "Well, no wonder I have failed to impress you when you have such ambitions."

"Oh, only for Bea, my lord, not for any of the rest of us," Clementine said, putting her hand to her heart and affecting a pious expression. "In all honesty, Bea would be quite content to spend the rest of her days in Little Valentine and marry a local lad, for she has no ambition in that regard nor any concept of her own beauty. I think she would live in a cottage with no modern conveniences and still find herself perfectly content."

"And you, Miss Honeywell, what would you settle for?" he asked, a teasing note to the question.

"Oh, I shan't marry," she said with a laugh. "I shall look after my father, for he will never be where he is supposed to be else, and I shall be a doting auntie to all my nieces and nephews."

She looked back at him, expecting him to make some playful comment about her lack of ambition when she might have the pious prig of a schoolteacher for the asking, but he did not. Instead, he looked vaguely annoyed, and she wondered if she had unwittingly offended him again. Clementine recalled her words, running through them to check she had said nothing that might put his back up, but found nothing.

Uncomfortable with the silence, she carried on talking, aware she ought to shut up but finding it impossible to do so.

"Mr Allenby is our schoolteacher, and I shall tell you a secret, if you promise not to breathe a word to anyone, but I do think him rather a prig. He's very well thought of, and seems to be good at his job, but he's so very stern. The poor boys never seem to have any fun, and fun is important for children, don't you think? I know that's not a very fashionable opinion, but my sisters and I had so much fun when we were children, well, until Mama died, but that's a different thing."

Clementine swallowed, cursing herself for rattling on. Well, it was a good thing she had never had a season, for she would clearly have wasted the opportunity. Flirting was obviously beyond her talent. Not that this came as a surprise, merely rather a disappointment. As the silence stretched on, Clementine felt increasingly foolish. No doubt he was cursing himself for having stopped to speak to her and was racking his brain for a polite way of leaving her again. She ought to say goodbye herself and put an end to the torture, but she was strangely reluctant to do so. Instead, she kept on talking, though each word made the situation worse.

"Papa is trying to raise funds for a girls' school, too. He believes women ought to be educated, as do I, though I imagine you can think of at least one excellent reason against the argument. I'm afraid I am that scandalous thing, a woman with a brain and a will of her own, which is why I shall never marry. No man would stand me questioning his good sense or listen to me explaining why my way of doing a thing is better. Well, apart from Papa, but someone must keep him in order. He'll turn up for Sunday service on a Wednesday afternoon without me to keep his appointments in order, you mark my words. But besides that, no one would have me, and I would never marry a man who thought I was chattel, his to do with as he pleased, or displeased, and so you see, I shall stay single.

"It is really not so terrible a fate, for Mama has left me a little nest egg, and Papa has also made provision too, so I shall do well enough. Also, though it might seem a strange thing to you, people here rather like me and welcome my interfering in their lives, though I cannot blame you for disliking it so, as you do not know me at all and—"

"If you will excuse me."

"What? Oh, yes, of course. I beg your pardon, I do not usually rattle on so, but hark at me, tongue enough for two sets of teeth this morning," Clementine said desperately, giving a nervous trill of laughter that was like no sound she had ever made in her life before.

"Forgive me, but I-I have things I must attend to. Good day to you, Miss Honeywell."

"Yes. Good day to you, Lord Beaumarsh," Clementine said jovially. She held herself together until she was sure he was out of earshot before turning and cursing out loud.

What in the name of everything holy had she been thinking? Utterly mortified, she wanted to do nothing more than curl up into a ball and will herself out of existence. However, she was not so weak-willed as all that, and so she decided she must make a virtue out of her appalling morning and entertain her friend with all the horrific details.

Chapter 8

Villains, victory and valedictory.

Willow Cottage. Little Valentine, South-East Coast of England. 6th June 1815.

"—and then I babbled on, telling him all the reasons I should never marry, but it was quite all right as Mama had left me a little nest egg and Papa had also made provision. As if he cared a fig about my plans. Honestly, Clara, I wanted to walk into the sea I was that horrified but I could *not* make myself stop," Clementine said in exasperation, feeling hot all over as she explained about her run-in with Lord Beaumarsh.

Clara regarded her over the rim of her teacup, clearly fascinated by her description.

"I'm sure it is not half so bad as you make out."

"He came upon me talking to *seagulls,"* Clementine repeated.

"Well, yes, I can see how that might have been somewhat mortifying," Clara admitted, struggling not to laugh.

"It's not funny," Clementine grumbled, though she could see very well why it was amusing to anyone who had not been at the centre of it.

"No. No, indeed." Clara made a heroic effort to rearrange her expression into something sympathetic, and Clementine was about to tell her she was a shocking friend when a strident voice sliced through the convivial atmosphere.

"Clara! *Clara!* Who is that you are talking to? I won't have visitors, girl. Have I not told you that you are not to spend my meagre savings on entertaining your friends? How selfish you are! Are you drinking my best tea? You had better not have used the best china!"

"No, Aunt," Clara called back, which was a blatant lie, for the pretty rose-patterned tea set was right before them, not that Clementine was about to mention the fact. "It is Miss Honeywell. Her father sent her to ask how you were," she added, giving Clementine a look that dared her to judge her for the falsehood.

Clementine merely nodded, having no intention of doing so. Miss Edna Holloway would make her niece's life a misery if Clara allowed her to, and Clementine admired Clara's minor rebellions and how she found contentment in a life so filled with restrictions.

"Ha! You may tell her I am beset with pain and suffering, and my wicked niece does not care a snap of her fingers about it."

"Yes, Aunt, I shall. Did you enjoy the crumpets I made for breakfast? There are more, and some more cherry jam if you would like," Clara replied placidly.

There followed a brief silence during which Clementine imagined Miss Holloway deliberating between the pleasure of refusing outright and giving her niece another scolding, and the pleasure of enjoying more crumpets.

"You may bring me two more crumpets, and another cup of tea, assuming you have not drunk it all," she said bitterly.

"Certainly, I shall," Clara replied before turning back to Clementine and lowering her voice. "I'm sorry. You had better go before she works herself up into a pelter."

Clementine nodded, not wanting to make Clara's life any more difficult. Her friend followed her to the door and Clementine stepped out, about to bid her a good day, when Clara spoke.

"Don't you wonder why Lord Beaumarsh makes you act like such a ninny? You are usually so sensible and very much in control. I have always very much admired and envied you your boldness and confidence," she said thoughtfully, and then smiled as she closed the door.

Clementine laughed as she walked back down the path to the gate, for Clara was not subtle. Indeed, she *had* wondered, not that it was a secret. Lord Beaumarsh was young and handsome and terribly eligible and, despite being eminently sensible and, in some people's minds, well beyond the age of forming a tendre for a fellow, Clementine was as human as the next girl and not above wishing for such a fine specimen to admire her.

"Foolish beyond permission," she said on a sigh, and then looked hurriedly around in case anyone else had spied her talking to herself. She'd suffered quite enough embarrassment for one day.

Beau, draped indolently over a well-padded chaise longue, pondered the sight of an endless blue sea that blended with the sky. Sighing, he lifted a glass of wine to his mouth and sipped. It was a pleasant spot with a fabulous view, and the wine was excellent, yet he itched to leave. Where was his ridiculous cousin? Surely the information that Beau was about to turn up his toes would have him careening over the countryside in his eagerness to witness the culmination of his dastardly plan? It was just like Edwin to be unreliable even in this.

Well, Beau would give him another day, no more. After that, he was done with Little Valentine. He was bored out of his mind, and he needed something to do, needed entertainment and more sophisticated company than could be found in this rural backwater. If he stayed here any longer, he might do something reprehensible just to break the tedium.

Despite promising himself he would not, his mind immediately turned to what kind of reprehensible thing he might do. Not that his wretched imagination needed much prodding. The sight of Miss Honeywell in her demure nightgown had burned itself into his mind and would not shift. There was something about that excess of prim white cotton that did terrible things to his equilibrium. The thought of putting his hands on it, of rumpling and tugging up all that smoothly ironed snowy fabric and feeling the warm body beneath it, made his libido surge.

Usually, the ladies he dallied with wore little scraps of silk and lace. Often the silk was damped down to cling, leaving far more on display than was hidden. Miss Honeywell was something new, something untried. Oh, yes. *Untried. As in not to be tried by the likes of you, Beaumarsh, you devil.*

Reviling himself more than usual, Beau took a larger swallow of wine and cursed his cousin anew. He was just contemplating opening another bottle and getting thoroughly foxed when Kirby burst into the room.

"Quick!" he exclaimed, puffing as if he'd just outrun the dogs of hell.

Beau sat up, alarmed. "What? What's wrong?"

"Edwin!" Kirby wheezed, bending double. "Just s-saw the blighter. Carriage will be here any moment."

"About bloody time!" Beau said with feeling. "Well, don't just stand there, help me out of these clothes. I can't enact a deathbed scene dressed like this."

Kirby wiped his face with his handkerchief and hurried over, still breathing hard. "I sent word to the reverend, and to Mr Chivers."

"Chivers?" Beau queried.

"The local justice of the peace. Honeywell said he'd arranged it, but we'll need to keep Edwin out of the way until they're here."

Beau flung his waistcoat to one side and began stripping off his shirt. "Well, I leave that to you, old man, but I reckon Mrs Adamson will play along if you ask her nicely."

"Reckon so," Kirby agreed, pulling a clean nightshirt out of the wardrobe and flinging it at his master.

Beau, not ready for the assault, glowered as it hit him in the face, before shaking it out and tugging it over his head. "Where's that rice powder you bought?"

"I'll fetch it," Kirby said, drawing the curtains so the room was plunged into gloom. "Best keep it dark, though, you look a damn sight too healthy now and the rice powder won't make you look overly sickly."

Beau nodded, but took the powder and covered his face with the stuff before giving an almighty sneeze.

Kirby rolled his eyes but drew back the bedcovers. "Hop in then. I'll send Honeywell and Mr Chivers up the back stairs once they're here. In the meantime, I'll tell Edwin you're sleeping, and you've had a dreadful night, so I won't wake you yet. He'll just have to kick his heels."

"Right you are," Beau said, eager for this farce to be over so he could get back to his life.

Climbing into the bed, he lay down with a sigh and stared up at the ceiling, trying to arrange himself in the pose of a man about to breathe his last. Uncertain what that might be, he figured it probably wasn't much different from a fellow passed out dead drunk, and he could pull that off without much difficulty.

Clementine glanced up from riddle she was working on just as her father rushed past the open door to the study. He looked to be in a terrible hurry.

"Papa?" she called, wondering if someone was dying, for that was the only thing that usually sent him out with such haste.

"Beaumarsh's cousin has arrived!" he called as he tugged the front door open.

"Oh! Wait for me," Clementine exclaimed, abandoning the word game without a second thought. Snatching her bonnet from hall stand where she had left it, she unhooked her spencer from the peg and ran after her father. Sticking the bonnet haphazardly on her head and shoving one arm into the coat as she ran, she turned to her father. "You can't be thinking of leaving me out of this. It was my plan!"

"Fine, fine, but we must make haste," the reverend said, moving with remarkable speed for a man of his years and generous girth.

By the time they reached The Mermaid's Tale, even Clementine was pink-cheeked as the afternoon sun made such strenuous effort hard work. Happily, Mr Kirby awaited them at the side entrance.

"Figured you'd be here too," he said sagely, not arguing about Clementine's presence and merely ushering them up the back stairs and into Beau's bedroom.

Clementine made haste at Kirby's urging but came to a grinding halt just inside the room as she got her first glimpse of the death-bed scene.

Beau lay with his head turned to one side, his eyes closed, arms laid carelessly upon the bedclothes as if moving them were too much effort. The room was dark, with only a chink of light from the not quite shut curtains illuminating his tableau. They moved in the breeze from an open window and, as the flickering shadows played with his finely chiselled features, he appeared pale and poetically tragic, a romantic figure of dissipation and a warning of the cost of licentiousness. The nightshirt he wore was open at the throat, showing a considerable expanse of hard, toned muscle and an intriguing scattering of dark golden hair.

Despite understanding the urgency of the situation, Clementine could not move, too fascinated by the scene before her. Beau Beaumarsh, dressed up in his immaculate best, was exciting and too handsome for his own good, but like this… like this he was some wicked god of wine and revelry, inviting her to sin with him. Heaven above, but he was beautiful.

Suddenly, as if feeling the weight of her gaze, Lord Beaumarsh's eyes flicked open, a dazzling flash of blue against the pallor of his skin. Clementine's breath caught as she gazed back at him, quite riveted and unable to look away. Beaumarsh did not so much as blink but held her gaze as her pulse rocketed. The situation was ridiculous, with her gazing down upon a man of his lordship's stamp, and him lying in such an abandoned pose upon his bed. She was uncertain if even the presence of her father and a justice of the peace would save her entirely if anyone heard of it.

She didn't care.

"Come, my dear," her father urged, taking her arm and tugging her towards the balcony.

Clementine went, unresisting, but did not look away from Beau until Mr Kirby closed the curtains on them with a snap. Finally free of whatever snare she had fallen into, she let out a shaky breath, coming back to her senses in time to realise she was sharing the tiny balcony not only with her father, but Mr Chivers.

"Good afternoon, sir," she said politely, only to be hushed by Chivers with some force.

She exchanged a glance with her father, whose lips twitched. Chivers had always been rather officious, and no doubt strongly disapproved of her presence. Still, he was an honourable fellow, and she believed she could trust him to hold his tongue about her being here. Certainly, he would do so for her father's sake.

The sun beat down upon them and Clementine wished she had brought a fan, belatedly looking around and realising their position put them in full view of the street below. Happily, no one was around for the moment, and she prayed it stayed that way and that Lord Beaumarsh's dreadful cousin would hurry.

Just as she'd had the thought, she heard the door open and close, and Kirby speaking in hushed tones.

"I must beg you not to fatigue him too greatly," Kirby said morosely. "He's not got much longer, I reckon, but I'll not have you upsetting him in his last hours."

"Yes, yes, fine," Mr Cavendish said, sounding all too impatient to step into his cousin's shoes.

Clementine gritted her teeth, deciding in that moment she loathed the man, and settled in to listen.

Beau heard his cousin's voice, snappish and irritable as always, and experienced a sudden surge of gratitude towards Miss Honeywell for forcing him to listen to her mad plan. As foolish as he felt, he knew it would be worth it the moment Edwin incriminated himself. Finally, he would be free of the man's insidious presence in his life, and the constant threat of sabotage to his carriage, or his horse, or having some noxious potion added to his wine.

His cousin had decided the title, the money, and the land were his when Beau was still a child. Yet things had changed, and where his previous attempts had been more opportunistic, this had been planned and executed with cold-blooded cunning. Edwin was getting desperate, and he would stop at nothing to get his hands on what he considered his due.

Beau kept still, forcing his breathing to remain shallow as he heard his cousin draw a chair up beside the bed.

"Sylvester?"

It took considerable effort to stop the cynical smile curving over Beau's mouth as Edwin addressed him. Edwin had never called him by his title, let alone Beau, for he envied his ownership of the honorific too deeply.

Beau allowed his eyes to flicker open and turned his head a fraction. "Edwin?" he rasped, his voice sounding frail and quavery. Really, he was rather good at this. Perhaps he should have tried his hand at acting in his misspent youth. Too late now, sadly, for it would be unbecoming for a man of his years. Still, this was an opportunity not to be missed.

"Yes, Cuz, it's me. Lord, but you look sick as a horse," he observed, sounding far too cheerful about it.

"Yes, Edwin. You have won, at last," Beau said, with a sad smile. Slowly, as though the effort cost him dearly, he moved his hand towards his cousin, palm up. "I'm ready to go. I have made peace with my demons and bear you no ill will, but I must know the truth before I leave this world."

"The truth?" Edwin said, an edge to his voice as he glanced over his shoulder. Happily, Kirby had made himself scarce, so it appeared they were alone. "I don't know what you mean."

Beau let out a breath of laughter, which he turned into a coughing fit he was rather proud of. "Come now, Edwin. You've been trying to do away with me for years now. Did you think I did not know it was you who cut the girth on my saddle, or perhaps you did not realise I understood your intention the time you encouraged me to swim the length of the lake at Cavendish House with you and then discovered you had turned back without telling me? I was over halfway before I realised. That was the first time, I think," he mused. "I was eight years old."

"Nonsense, just childish high jinks is all," Edwin blustered.

"Tell me the truth," Beau said, a thread of anger in his voice now. "You cannot deny the last request of a dying man. If you do not, I might discover I have just enough energy left to will all my unentailed goods to the nearest orphanage."

"Oh, I say!" Edwin said, indignation stiffening his spine. "That would be a shockingly ungentlemanly thing to do."

Beau laughed, unable to resist. "Yes, whilst murder is quite acceptable."

"It ain't murder," Edwin said testily. "The title ought to have been mine. I'm older than you. Just because my father wasn't the eldest, you got it. I deserved it more than you did. I would have made use of Cavendish House, for one thing. You never set foot in it!"

"So you *did* try, then?" Beau pressed, needing him to spell it out.

"Damned right I did," Edwin said in frustration. "But I swear you've got some guardian angel, for you always came out of every attempt without a scratch so there's no need to make out like I harmed you! You didn't so much as break a bone when you fell from your horse, and you swam to shore eventually, did you not? Though how you managed that, I still do not know, for you were all skin and bone in those days."

He sounded so ill-used, Beau struggled to hide his feelings. Still, he held himself in check, and simply gazed up at his cousin with soulful eyes. "Until now, Cuz. Finally, you have succeeded. Tell me how you did it. I should like to know how you finally bested me after all these years. Surely you can grant me that much. It's all yours now, after all. I cannot harm you."

Beau watched his cousin's face, watched the almost childish look of triumphant glee flicker behind his eyes and knew he had him. Edwin wanted to boast about how he had got the upper hand, for he had always been vain, and that would be his undoing.

"Well, all right, then. I suppose I owe you that much as you're giving everything over to me," he said, still managing to sound begrudging, even though he was clearly eager to display his cleverness. "It was simple, really. Once I settled on arsenic as the best method, I just had to figure out how best to dose you. I waited weeks, you know. Drove me half mad with impatience, but finally that patience was rewarded. Mrs Jenkins' ball was just the occasion I needed. The place is always a terrible crush, and you were with Stonehaven. He always leads you into trouble, so I knew you'd be half seas over well before the night was done. Then it was simple enough. I tipped the powder into a wineglass and switched your glass for the poisoned one. You never even knew I was there. I stayed in the background, watching, just to be sure you drank it and didn't spill the glass or something stupid, just in case I needed to give you more. I didn't want to give you so much you made a nasty scene and died on the spot, you see, better it happened when you got home, in private. I owed the family name that much, so the dosage was crucial. But you drained the glass like a good boy, and so I went to my club and played cards and made sure everyone knew I was there so I couldn't be viewed with suspicion. I'll admit it's taken far longer than I anticipated, but it worked in the end."

He looked so damned smug, so very pleased with himself. Rage bubbled up inside Beau at the notion that this entitled nothing of a man had almost ended him. Edwin had done nothing of note with his life, he never had a kind word for anyone, did no one a favour unless there was something in it for himself, he was ignorant and a bully and, on top of that, he had absolutely no fashion sense, and this man…this waste of space, had nearly killed him. *Him!*

"Why, you abhorrent little worm," Beau growled, and launched himself from the bed.

Clementine listened with growing horror as the two men spoke. The silence on the balcony was palpable as all three of them strained to hear the conversation. The words struck her like a blow, however, as she heard just what Beau had endured. His cousin, a fellow he had probably idolised as a child, had tried to end his life for no better reason than jealousy and avarice. She felt sick.

Eight years old. He had been just eight years old when Edwin Cavendish had encouraged him to swim out of his depth, too far from land. She could only imagine the terror Beau must have felt, and the sheer determination he must have had to keep going, to keep swimming, until he made it to the other side. To have to do so knowing that someone he had liked and admired, perhaps even loved, had tricked him… how that must have hurt. Her heart ached, and she realised this explained a good deal about Lord Beaumarsh, about his reluctance to take anything seriously or to show any genuine feeling, his desire to indulge in pleasure and turn his attention away from anything of true value.

"—you never even knew I was there," the wretched man crowed, making Clementine's blood boil. "I stayed in the background, watching, just to be sure you drank it and didn't spill the glass or something stupid, just in case I needed to give you more. I didn't want to give you so much you made a nasty scene and died on the spot, you see, better it happened when you got home, in private. I owed the family name that much, so the dosage was crucial. But you drained the glass like a good boy, and so I went to my club and played cards and made sure everyone knew I was there so I couldn't be viewed with suspicion. I'll admit it's taken far longer than I anticipated, but it worked in the end."

There was a taut silence, and Clementine looked to her father and Mr Chivers, hoping they had enough to convict the horrid man, because she wanted to throttle Edwin Cavendish with her bare hands. Both men nodded, but before they could make their presence known, they heard Beaumarsh's growl of fury.

"Why, you abhorrent little worm!"

There was a high-pitched scream and a heavy thud, and Clementine pushed through the curtain at the same time as her father and Mr Chivers, which meant none of them could pass and all three got tangled in the blasted fabric. By the time they were through, they found Beaumarsh standing over his cousin, who was sprawled on the floor and holding his nose as blood dripped through his fingers. He stared up at his lordship as if he'd risen from the dead. Clementine supposed he had, for all Edwin knew.

"Tell me you have heard enough," Lord Beaumont growled, staring down at his cousin, who was a thin man dressed in the most garish waistcoat of gold and purple stripes, which he had matched with yellow pantaloons and a green coat. No wonder Beaumarsh loathed him, Clementine thought irreverently.

"Enough to send the man to the gallows if you wish it, my lord," Mr Chivers said confidently.

Clementine glanced at Chivers, uncertain that were true as Mr Cavendish had failed in actually killing Beaumarsh, but the man was an earl, so perhaps multiple attempts were enough.

"What? What is happening?" Edwin said, the words coming out muffled as he pressed a handkerchief against his nose to staunch the bleeding. "You were supposed to be dying! You told me you were," he protested, as if Beaumarsh was not playing fair.

His lordship snorted. "No. I was supposed to be dead, but you failed again, you fool. This time, however, I've decided there will be no more attempts on my life. This is Reverend Honeywell, and Mr Chivers here is a justice of the peace. They've heard every word you just said and will attest to the fact that you have repeatedly tried to kill me. You've had your fun, Edwin, and now I'll have mine. Watching you swing *will* be great fun, won't it?" he asked snidely, his features set, a callous expression hardening his handsome face in a way she had never seen before.

Edwin gasped, all the colour leaving his face in a rush and for a moment, Clementine believed Beaumarsh would do it. She supposed she could not blame him. A man who ought to have been a brother to him had tried and tried to end his life. An eye for an eye. Yet the relief she felt when that savage light dimmed, replaced by one of sheer disgust, was more than she could account for.

"For God's sake," Beaumarsh said. "You really are the most unutterable fool, Edwin."

"You w-wouldn't see me hang, would you, Cuz?" the man pleaded, finally realising that he had been caught in a trap.

"No, damn your eyes. I wouldn't. More fool me. But don't think it's out of pity. I just can't stomach the scandal that would ensue. It would probably kill my mother. But you listen to me, Edwin. You'd better hope I live to be a very old man, for the moment I turn up my toes, if there is the least bit of suspicion, you'll be hunted down and tried for murder. Do I make myself clear?"

"C-Crystal," Edwin said, nodding vigorously. "But… But what shall I do? I'm rather desperate, old man. I owe some very shady fellows rather a lot of blunt, you see, and—"

"And if you had even an iota of decency, I would have bailed you out," Beaumarsh snapped. "But as it is, you can run away to France and hope old Boney doesn't have you hanged for a spy."

"Oh, but—" Edwin swallowed, silenced by the look in his cousin's eyes.

Clementine did not blame him, for Lord Beaumont looked like he wanted to murder the villain with his bare hands. An understandable impulse, she felt, which made his self-control even more remarkable.

"Kirby!" Beaumarsh bellowed.

"Yes, my lord," Kirby said, emerging from behind the door to the corridor where he had clearly been listening to every word.

"I believe Mr Chivers has a delightful cell for my cousin to kick his heels in until his voyage to France has been arranged. Do help ensure he gets there safely."

"With pleasure, Lord Beaumarsh," Kirby said, announcing the title with more precision and appreciation than Clementine had ever heard before. She smiled, aware whose benefit that was for, and wondered at the respect that the man had for his master. The proverb, no man is a hero to his valet, echoed in her mind, and she could not help but consider that, and wish she knew who Lord Beaumarsh really was, for the face he showed the world seemed to be a far cry from the man he was beneath.

Too late now, she thought, refusing to allow herself to feel regret for that fact. She had known he would leave as soon as this scene had been played out, and she would be a fool to lament that fact. It was only that he had brought excitement and glamour into her life, and she rather regretted having to lose it so quickly.

Kirby and Mr Chivers left with the prisoner, who Mrs Adamson agreed could be held in her wine cellar until after dark to avoid causing a scene. This left Clementine and her father alone with Beaumarsh, who excused himself to pull on another lavishly embroidered silk banyan. Clementine regarded it with true appreciation this time, admiring the heavy black silk and the gorgeous display of peacock feathers in variety of blue and green tones. They seemed to make his eyes appear an even more extraordinary shade.

Beaumarsh caught her gaze and returned a wry smile. “Yes, yes, showing my true colours at last, eh, Miss Honeywell? Do not deny it. I know you are thinking it, for it is written all over your face.”

Clementine bit her lip, struggling not to laugh. “I cannot think what you mean,” she managed, but the words were a little strangled.

His lordship’s eyes warmed with appreciation but, when he spoke, his voice was serious. “I must thank you, Miss Honeywell. I was appallingly rude to you when you first approached me with your plan, but it was simple and worked like a charm, just as you promised. You are a quite remarkable female, and I shall never forget the good turn you have done me. I am in your debt. If ever there is anything I might do to return the favour, I beg you will not hesitate to ask me.”

Clementine felt a sudden lurch in her stomach, a sense of regret that she had not had time to enjoy this man's friendship for a little longer. She knew that was all it was, all it would ever be, and she accepted that. Nevertheless, she would have liked to glimpse a little more of what else he hid beneath the mask he showed the world. His words were generous, though, more so because she knew he meant them, and though she knew she would never impose upon him, she was grateful for the offer.

"You are most kind, Lord Beaumarsh, but my reward is knowing you may live the rest of your days without looking over your shoulder. I wish you all the very best for your future."

Don't waste it, she added silently, willing him to do something with his life. She suspected he was far more than he would allow anyone to know and wished he would give himself more credit than he did.

Beaumarsh smiled and stepped forward to shake her father's hand. "You are a wise and generous man, Reverend, and it has been my pleasure to meet you."

"Likewise, my lord," her father replied, his tone warm. "But don't be a stranger. We are not so very far from London, certainly not from Kent. There will always be a welcome for you in Little Valentine, especially at the vicarage, so I hope you will not forget us entirely."

"As if I could," Beaumarsh said, his lips quirking as he turned to Clementine. "It has been an honour, Miss Honeywell."

As he spoke, his eyes twinkled, and he raised her hand to his lips, pressing a soft kiss upon her fingers. Clementine's breath hitched at the touch of his mouth, an odd fluttery sensation exploding in her belly. *He's just using his wiles, amusing himself, flirting with you, it means nothing at all*, she reminded herself. She knew it and was not silly enough to believe anything else. He was leaving, after all.

"You will leave at once?" she asked, refusing to feel regret for his answer, yet when he nodded, she felt she was losing a connection to someone who might have been dear to her, if only they'd had the chance. Foolishness, she knew.

"As soon as Kirby can get me in order. With luck, we shall be home sometime this evening."

He sounded cheerful, relieved to be going, so clearly, she was the only one who felt the loss. Hardly surprising. Lord Beaumarsh was popular and surrounded by friends in the city. His life was far larger than her own, which suddenly felt smaller than it ever had before. She must stop that at once, she decided. Her life was a full one, and she had many friends too, people who liked and respected her and sought her opinion. She did a lot of good in this small town and was appreciated for it. There was nothing to feel gloomy about. Nothing at all.

So, she smiled and wished Lord Beaumarsh a safe journey home and left without a second glance, chatting animatedly with her father about any subject she could grasp at, as they walked back home.

"Clara's aunt is so dreadful, Papa. I wish there was something we might do for her," she observed, having relayed the details of her recent visit.

"All we can do is to be kind and patient with her aunt, and hope that she softens. Sometimes people do not know how to be kind until they are shown kindness. We do not know what has made the woman so bitter and cantankerous, but it is she herself who is hurt most by it. Far more than Clara. Indeed, I find Clara a wonderfully wise young woman. She is a calm soul and does not allow her aunt's sharp tongue to wound her."

"It's difficult to be kind to a woman who cannot find a single nice thing to say about anything, let alone the niece who looks after her so well and whom she treats like a dog. Indeed, I should take issue with anyone treating a dog with such a lack of respect," she said hotly.

Her father smiled and patted her shoulder. "Don't fret, love. Clara is stronger than you think, and I believe Lord Beaumarsh will miss us more than he expects to."

Clementine started, staring at her father in shock. "I wasn't talking about Lord Beaumarsh," she said, bewildered.

"No. You weren't," he replied, a too knowing glint in his eyes.

Clementine huffed. Papa had too fine an understanding of human nature and was oddly omniscient at times. "I will not have you thinking that I am pining for the man, for I am not."

"I know," he said soothingly. "But he brought a bit of sparkle into our lives, did he not? I found him most interesting to talk to and wish I'd had the time to know him better, but he's not a happy fellow, I fear. He's searching for something, but he does not know it, and so he does not know what to look for."

Clementine said nothing, having had similar thoughts about the man herself.

"I would have liked to be his friend," she admitted.

"You are his friend, I think," the reverend said placidly, linking their arms together as they walked the rest of the way home.

Chapter 9

Town bronze and country mice.

62 Sloane Street, Kensington, London, 6th June 1815.

The carriage drew up outside Beau's town residence a little after eleven o'clock that evening. He jumped down, stretching out the cramps in his legs after too long confined in the carriage. He had allowed nothing but the briefest stops, too eager to be home. Yet now, as he looked up at his elegant townhouse, he was strangely reluctant to go in.

"I need a walk," he told Kirby, who had sulked for most of the journey, making known his displeasure at returning so quickly to London. "I think I'll visit my club and see who's around."

"Very good, my lord," Kirby said morosely.

Beau opened his mouth to take issue with his gloomy servant but thought better of it. Kirby would get over it soon enough and everything would go back to normal. There would be the usual rounds of parties and social events, and his life would be his own again. It was an oddly depressing thought.

He told himself it was only that London was so scarce of company in the summer. In a few weeks, most anyone with any sense would leave to escape the heat—and, more to the point, the smell—by retiring to their country residences. Beau toyed with the notion of a visit Cavendish House. He'd not been there for an age, and his mother would be delighted if he spent a little time with her too. Perhaps he would, he mused, as he pushed open the door to White's and looked around. It was quiet, making him wonder how many people had already left town.

“Beaumarsh!”

Beau looked around, raising a hand in greeting as he saw a familiar face.

“Stonehaven,” he said, nodding at the marquess, who had been a friend since his school days. “How do?”

“Well enough. This is an excellent claret, care to join me?”

Beau sat down and grimaced. “God, yes. I’ve spent the entire afternoon, and evening stuffed in a carriage with a sulking Kirby, and I’m tired and irritable. I’ll happily drink with you, but I need some food. Anything good on?”

“I had an excellent sirloin. I can heartily recommend it,” Stonehaven remarked, pouring out a glass for Beau.

Beau regarded his friend. He was a tall man, broad and powerfully built, with mid-brown hair and shrewd hazel eyes. They had been drinking companions and partners in crime since they were young lads sent away to school for the first time. Stonehaven liked to drink and to brawl far more than Beau, who feared breaking his nose, as Stonehaven had done more than once. Regardless of their differences, he was an excellent companion, yet Beau was aware he knew little about the fellow, despite having known him for so long. How odd, he thought suddenly, beset by the peculiar notion his childhood best friend was now a stranger to him.

“So, how are you? What have you been up to of late?” Beau asked with genuine interest, earning himself the quirk of an eyebrow.

“The usual,” Stonehaven replied, regarding Beau with curiosity.

“It wasn’t a trick question,” Beau said irritably, wondering *why* he was interested now when he’d been too idle or self-absorbed to ask the question in recent years. “I just wondered… I don't know. Are you well? Have you seen your family of late? Do you have plans for the summer? Read any interesting books?"

Stonehaven stared at him suspiciously. "Good God, Beau, I'd heard you'd been taken ill. Did it affect your brain? Do you actually want an intelligent conversation with *me?* I can prattle as well as any old biddy if you like, but it's not usually your brand of entertainment."

Beau glared at him, realising he had been a terrible friend and wondering why Stonehaven had endured his selfishness. "We talk." Didn't they? Did Beau never ask after his family, or discuss politics with him or… or the weather, heaven help him? Surely they did something other than discuss the latest *on-dits* and what entertainment they were attending that night.

"Oh, indeed," Stonehaven agreed with an amiable expression. "We say, 'look, old chap, the brunette is for me, you take the blonde,' or 'deal me in,' or 'did you hear about Peterson, he's up the River Tick and selling those fine greys.'"

"Fine, if you want to be an arse, I'll find more agreeable company." It was an unfair comment for Beau was now horribly aware *he* had been a complete arse, not Stonehaven.

Stonehaven chuckled, still good natured despite his friend's egocentric behaviour. "Fine, fine. Have it your way. I am in perfect health. I saw my family three days ago. All are still breathing and spending my money as fast as they can get their sticky paws on it. I recently read *Waverley*. It's rather hard going for the first few chapters, but overall, I rather enjoyed it. There. Does that satisfy your need for conversation?"

"You are an absolute pillock," Beau said, but without heat, too relieved to discover he had not done irreparable damage to a friendship that was almost as old as he was.

"Oh, very well. I'll indulge you and ask what you have been up to of late, does that make me a better friend?" Stonehaven asked, leaning across the table towards him, curiosity alight in his eyes.

"Marginally," Beau grumbled, making a show of his irritation so Stonehaven didn't think him entirely deranged, but still took the opportunity to talk. He had the sudden desire to tell someone about Little Valentine and, whilst Stonehaven would surely think he'd lost his mind, he needed to explain that the place was special in ways he could not articulate, and that the people too, had struck him as real in a way he did not quite understand. Except so much of his life was spent putting on a spectacle, presenting Beau Beaumarsh to his peers so they might admire him and ape his superior way of speaking, dressing and being his wry, cynical best. They did not know him at all, for he did not allow them to do so. Yet, in the brief time he'd been in Little Valentine, he'd been entirely himself.

"Little Valentine?" Stonehaven repeated sceptically. "Did you make that up?"

"No," Beau replied, irked. "It's quaint, I grant you, but the town is utterly charming. It's all winding cobbled streets and pretty cottages, and I swear the sea is as blue as any you'd see in the south of France or in Italy. The people, too, were most kind," he added, realising too late there had been a slightly wistful note to his voice.

"Oh, now I understand. There's a woman," Stonehaven said, smirking.

Beau scowled. "There is *not* a woman. I am trying to explain that it felt different, more honest than the life we lead in town! The people *cared* about each other," he exclaimed, throwing up his hands and then crossing his arms tightly across his chest.

Stonehaven looked at him, frowning with concern. "All right," he said slowly. "I'll quit ragging on you. Tell me about this little town. What was there about it that has you reevaluating your life? I take it that is what we are doing here?"

Beau continued to glare at him but could not keep it up. Instead, he sighed. "I suppose so," he admitted. "I've finally realised how shallow my existence is, not that I wasn't aware of it, but to realise how little it matters to anyone, myself even, is an uncomfortable feeling. Oh, ignore me. I've probably just enjoyed a little respite from the real world and now I'm feeling out of step with my old life."

"Probably," Stonehaven agreed amiably. "Tell me anyway."

So Beau did. He told him about Captain Dearborn and Major Hancock, about the Honeywell family, about the reverend and his daughters, about Miss Honeywell's plot to entrap Edwin and its satisfying denouement.

"The reverend is a wise old bird, you know," Beau said, watching as Stonehaven refilled his glass. "He seems to know what you are thinking, to know you when he doesn't know you at all. Isn't that strange?"

Stonehaven shrugged. "Not really. If anyone ought to understand and know human nature, one presumes it would be a man of the cloth."

"He said I was a good man," Beau mused.

"I take it back. Man's a fool."

"Arsehole."

Stonehaven grinned at him. "There, see? I rest my case."

"If you'd stop acting the halfwit for five minutes, you'd realise that the fellow made me think," Beau replied, still rather astonished that he was having this conversation at all. "He'd lost his wife, you know. Years ago. He raised his daughters single-handed. Yet he was so filled with gratitude for having had the woman in his life. Mary, her name was, and Reverend Honeywell loved her with every fibre of his being. I could tell that without him having to say so, though he did say it too. It shone from him."

Beau shook his head and raked a hand through his hair. What the devil had got into him?

"Sounds like an interesting fellow," Stonehaven said, his tone neutral.

"Yes, and you think I ought to go and have a nice lie down in a dark room until I'm feeling better," Beau said, his lip curling cynically.

Stonehaven chuckled and shook his head. "It might surprise you to learn I'm not as shallow as you might assume. I think the reverend sounds a fascinating fellow. Truly."

"He said I should find my soulmate and marry for love." Beau could have bitten his tongue off, for he wished the words unsaid the moment he'd uttered them. Glancing at Stonehaven, he expected to find disgust or, at the very least, mocking amusement in his expression. He did not.

Instead, Stonehaven looked interested. "Fellows like us don't do that."

"Well, obviously, but what if we did?" Beau asked. "Would the world implode? I mean, I do not need to marry for power or land, or financial reasons. I don't doubt my old man would have strongly disagreed with that, but he's long dead, so I need not heed his opinion. I'm plump enough in the pocket, so why not please myself? Why not find a woman who actually makes me happy, rather than some ornament to take out and flaunt to make other fellows jealous when I can't stand the sight of her? She'll only take lovers behind my back the moment it's turned. I don't want to live in a house where I'm at war with my wife, Stonehaven, I really do not."

"Your lovely wife, whom you married with your heart in your eyes, might also take lovers, Beau," Stonehaven remarked, returning to the cynical fellow Beau had known for such a long time.

Beau sighed. "Yes. Yes, I know that. I'm not entirely a fool, you know."

"Where would you even find such a paragon, supposing there's a woman fool enough to fall for your ugly mug?"

Beau rolled his eyes. "Just because I'm prettier than you are, there's no need to be snide."

Stonehaven laughed. "A fair point. However, my opinion is also one you ought to consider. So, do you think the candidate for your countess resides in Little Valentine? Perhaps I ought to visit myself, if the ladies are lovely enough to get you thinking of matrimony."

"I'm not thinking of matrimony, per se," Beau said, tutting with impatience as he tried to articulate the thoughts that had occupied his mind of late. "I'm just thinking that maybe the reverend is correct. I've been refusing to even contemplate the idea of marriage because I cannot stand the thought of a fashionable union, the kind we see all around us. It's just too depressing. Whilst I have not the least desire to experience such depths of love and devotion for the idea of suffering the loss of a woman who had become so very important to me is… well, horrifying, I want more than some hollow partnership. I am honest enough to know I do not have the courage for such a feat of bravery and foolishness as the reverend recommends. But, at the very least, I should like to be friends with my wife, I might even be fond of her."

"A novel idea," Stonehaven remarked, looking thoughtful. "Tell me about the ladies of this charming village. Should I like them too?"

"Certainly," Beau replied, and told him all about the Misses Honeywell, and about Mrs Adamson. "She's an absolute stunner. Far too beautiful to be hidden away in such a tiny place, though I think there's some scandal there. My guess is she's not a *Mrs* at all. It seems some of the locals treat her with less than her due of respect. A pity, for she was truly kind, and she runs a marvellous hotel. Even I approved of her taste in décor, and you know how seldom that happens."

"Oh, I do," Stonehaven replied, looking pained.

Beau ignored the underlying sarcasm to his friend's reply. "Still, to come down to breakfast every morning and see that fine figure dressed so splendidly and those tumbling red curls. Well, it's not an unpleasant start to a fellow's day, is it?"

"A redhead, was she?" Stonehaven asked mildly, interest flickering behind his eyes.

"Yes, said so, didn't I? Do pay attention," Beau said, shaking his head. "Mrs Anne Adamson. A shrewd businesswoman and a beautiful creature, too. But then, if Miss Honeywell is to be believed, I never even saw the diamond of Little Valentine. Apparently, the title goes to her sister, Beatrice. Miss Honeywell is determined that she shall marry a duke. I was not good enough for her, you'll note."

"A wise woman, your Miss Honeywell," Stonehaven said absently.

"She's not *my* Miss Honeywell," Beau snapped, irritated, but at that moment his dinner arrived, and so the conversation turned away from his sudden epiphanies about life and marriage and to far easier topics like horse racing, and how exactly Peterson had lost his fortune, and how much did he want for those splendid greys?

One month later…

The Vicarage, Little Valentine, South-East Coast of England. 9th July 1815

Clementine followed her sisters into the house, allowing their chatter to wash over her. Beatrice was promising Caspar she would take him out into the garden to play cricket after dinner, as he had been such a good boy and sat still and quiet throughout the reverend's sermon. Izzy was handing Daisy to Mrs Mabbs, who cooed over her charge.

"Come along, my ickle Daisykins," she said, hugging the child to her and carrying her towards the stairs. "Time for a nice little nap before your din-dins."

Mrs Adie bustled up, her face thunderous as Clementine laid her bonnet to one side. "Them wicked little beasts are at it again, miss," she said in an undertone.

"I beg your pardon?" Clementine stared at her in confusion.

"Mice," Mrs Adie whispered, looking over her shoulder as if she thought the entire town would find out if she said the word too loud. "There's... *evidence* on the pantry floor," she added, wrinkling her nose in disgust.

"Oh, I see. Yes, well, you may be sure I shall deal with it, Mrs Adie," Clementine said, though her heart wasn't in it.

The kittens were not yet quite the mousers she had promised, though she did not doubt they would be soon enough. They were trying, at least. Something must be done in the meantime, yet she could not bear the idea of setting traps herself, or even of demanding someone else do it. There had been enough killing of late.

Everyone went off about their business for the interval before they all gathered for dinner, but Clementine felt strangely restless. The sermon her father had given had been powerful and very moving. Well, she had known it would be, for she had helped him to write it, yet hearing her father speak the words aloud was a very different thing to reading them on paper. It was his sincerity and his empathy for all those who had suffered and died in the terrible conflict at Waterloo.

Though it had happened three weeks ago now, the stories were still coming through. The papers had been filled with the heroism of the mighty victory over France, and of Wellington's incredible leadership, but now the letters, from husbands, brothers, sons, or the friends of those fallen in battle were arriving and telling the true story. So much loss. So much devastation.

Her father had cried when he had told her of what Mrs Barham's son had written to her. The poor young man had been there on that fateful day and could not bring himself to come home. He felt he would sully his mother's house, for his hands and his soul were tainted with blood. The sweet, gentle boy who had gone away had changed beyond recognition, and Mrs Barham did not know if he would ever return to her.

Her father's sermon had touched upon loss, upon bravery, upon the need for all men and women to look at each other and see not a stranger, but part of a world in which they were all connected. If only there were more men like her papa, perhaps things would be different.

Clementine drifted out of the house, walked along the lane that took her through the woods, and down to the seashore. She stared out at the vast expanse of blue, her heart aching with sadness, and yet there was hope there too, for the war was over at last. Surely, there would be no more killing, and perhaps the cost of this terrible battle would teach the world a lesson.

Lord Beaumarsh's smile flickered in her mind's eye, a slightly cynical curl to his lip as he chided her for her naivety, and Clementine started in surprise. Though it had been harder than she liked to admit, she had refused to allow herself to think of him, to miss a friendship that had not really been a friendship at all. Not more than an acquaintance really, and yet at odd moments she would hear his voice in her ear and feel sure she knew what he might reply to her when she was about to say something far too bold.

"You cannot miss what you have never had," she said firmly, watching the seagulls as they danced in the breeze overhead. "Talking to the birds again, Miss Honeywell?" she added, and turned hopefully, half expecting to find him on the beach beside her. But of course he was not and never would be.

Cavendish House, Kent, 9th July 1815

Beau stood in his mother's rose garden, contemplating the sea of pink flowers. Whilst he had not precisely let her have free rein of the gardens at his home, he had given her leave to design certain areas as she pleased. In her opinion, the rose garden was her most splendid achievement. Though he found the pink a little overwhelming, Beau was disinclined to argue. It was a splendid sight, and the scent was quite intoxicating. Turning in a circle, he looked back at the building that came with his title, the one for which Edwin had been prepared to kill him.

A remarkably fine and vast fourteenth-century manor house, it was one of the jewels of the Kentish landscape. Its enormous Baron's Hall, which had a soaring sixty-foot-high beamed ceiling, was a sight to behold and had been built originally for the Lord Mayor of London before becoming King Henry VIII's hunting lodge. It had grown and grown over the centuries, with successive generations adding a wing here, more state rooms there, until it had become something sprawling and magnificent.

Beau hated it.

No, that was not true. He did not hate it. He admired it, appreciated its history and its beauty, and its stubborn determination to be as impressive as a bloody palace. Beau just did not enjoy living it in. It was too big, and he rattled about in it like a pea in a drum. The house made him feel isolated, which was ridiculous, because he was surrounded by a damned army of servants, not to mention his mother *and* Stonehaven, who had taken it upon himself to come for a visit. No doubt after their little *tête-à-tête,* Stonehaven feared for his sanity. Beau could not think what had come over him. Yet he had said nothing that was not true. That he had uttered the words out loud, however, was mortifying.

He turned his back on the house, instead walking through the rose garden, admiring the long rectangular fishpond at the centre. Gazing down at the fish, he saw instead his own reflection. He did not need to see to know that it mirrored the image of a handsome man, with golden hair, blue eyes, and a form any fellow would be proud to inhabit.

"You ridiculous creature," he said, shaking his head, hearing the words spoken in Miss Honeywell's clipped tones. Chuckling to himself, he adopted a higher-pitched tone and announced, "'The idea that I would ever lower my standards sufficiently to marry an idle creature whose only concern appears to be whether his waistcoat is the precise colour of vibrant blue to match his eyes is an insult to my intelligence!'"

"Well, my eyes are brown, and I don't remember asking, but there's no need to be rude," remarked a dry voice from behind him.

Beau started and spun around to see Stonehaven watching him curiously. Giving his waistcoat—which sadly *was* blue *and* the precise colour of his eyes—a sharp tug, he glowered at his friend. "Why must you go around sneaking up on a fellow?"

"I was doing nothing of the sort, and if you will go around talking to yourself—or was it the fish?—I do not know what to say to you," Stonehaven said, smirking and taking great enjoyment in his friend's discomfort.

"It's what Miss Honeywell said to me," Beau replied gruffly. "I accused her of setting her cap for me, when all she was trying to do was explain her plan to trap Edwin. I was appallingly rude, and she gave me the most magnificent set down. I am still recovering," he said with a rueful smile.

"Ah, I see. I must admit, I am curious to meet your Miss Honeywell after hearing so much about her."

Beau frowned. "She is not *my* Miss Honeywell, and if I've mentioned her twice in the past month, I would be astonished."

"Indeed, but it is the admiring tone you have when you do mention her," Stonehaven said.

Beau did not reply, well aware that his friend was trying to aggravate him.

"I think we should go for a visit. It's not far after all. Only three hours, I should think," Stonehaven remarked, a challenging note to his words.

Beau stared at him, astonished. "It's more like four, actually, and what the devil do you want to go to Little Valentine for?"

"Like I said," Stonehaven said with a shrug. "I'm curious. Both about Miss Honeywell, Reverend Honeywell, and this charming town that you insisted I really must see."

"I'm certain I insisted nothing of the sort," Beau said, yet the idea of returning to the place gave him an odd feeling. Not quite anticipation, but… surely not fear? Whatever was there to be afraid of? He shook off the sensation. Well, why not go? It might be fun to show Stonehaven around a bit.

"All right," Beau said grudgingly. "But we're not staying in the town. Austen Leigh has a place close to there. A hunting lodge. It's not much to write home about, but he says it's comfy enough. Else we'll set tongues wagging. Better if it's just a visit in passing."

"As you like, old man," Stonehaven said, a knowing look in his eyes that Beau refused to rise to. "As you like."

Chapter 10

Those wretched little beasts!

Little Valentine, South-East Coast of England. 10th July 1815

"Charming indeed," Stonehaven approved as the carriage navigated the narrow, cobbled streets.

Beau nodded, looking upon the cottages and winding streets that had lately become so familiar to him. He was glad to be back, he realised, and strangely eager to see Miss Honeywell again. Well, not *just* Miss Honeywell. Her father and her sister too, and of course he wished to meet the incomparable, naturally. He wondered if Miss Honeywell would be pleased to see him, wondered if she would blush and stammer. Perhaps she might read too much into the visit, he thought belatedly. What if she got some silly notion in her head and thought he had come to court her?

Miss Honeywell? a snide little voice said caustically in his head. *She wouldn't consider you if you were the last man on earth, so it matters little if she thinks you are courting her.*

Yet somehow it did matter, for if she was so set against the idea of him as a husband—which was perfectly fine and reasonable—he did not want her thinking he was trying to win her over. Suddenly, Beau felt anxious and out of sorts and wished he had not allowed Stonehaven to talk him into this. Well, he would just have to make it clear this was just a friendly visit, and she was not to read anything into it. He didn't wish for her to feel uncomfortable or… or obligated in any way. But there was no reason they could not be friends.

Reassured, he relaxed as the carriage bore them on towards the vicarage. Beau had instructed the driver to take them on a brief tour before they stopped, so Stonehaven could see the delights of the town.

"Shall we go to the pub?" Stonehaven said eagerly upon seeing The Ship Inn.

"Perhaps later. We can't go calling on the vicar and his family smelling like a brewery."

"You said the old fellow liked a tipple himself," Stonehaven pointed out.

"Yes, exactly. He'll be dreadfully miffed if we don't invite him to join us," Beau said reasonably.

Stonehaven laughed. "I like him already."

Beau regarded his friend with sudden concern. Whilst he was not classically handsome like Beau, he was appealing, with a roguish twinkle in his eyes and strong, masculine features. Belatedly, he wondered what effect the arrival of the marquess would have on the three young ladies. Good Lord.

"You will behave, won't you?" Beau said uneasily. "I mean, they're very young, and definitely innocent, and—"

"I do hope you are not impugning my honour, Beau," Stonehaven drawled.

"Oh, don't pretend you're offended," Beau said impatiently. "Just mind your manners."

"Yes, my Lord Beaumarsh," Stonehaven said, bowing slightly.

Beau shook his head in exasperation and turned back to the carriage window, just as the vicarage came into sight.

He jumped down before the carriage had fully stopped, too impatient to wait for the footman to open the door and regarded the vicarage with approval. It was an enchanting building, the garden riotous with roses and wisteria and flowers he had no names for, all thronged with butterflies and bees. This delightful bucolic scene was shattered a moment later, however, by a blood-curdling scream from inside.

Beau and Stonehaven exchanged a glance before running for the gate. Beau pushed through ahead of Stonehaven, just as a small furry creature shot across the path ahead of them. It was closely followed by a woman running pell mell, skirts hiked to her knees.

"Come back here, you little beast!" she cried, a second before she collided with Beau.

The Vicarage, Little Valentine, South-East Coast of England. 9th July 1815

It was a dream, Clementine decided. No. Strike that. *A nightmare.* That's what it was. Only in a nightmare would she run in such a hoydenish manner with her skirts bunched up, bellowing like a fishwife, and knock the Earl of Beaumarsh flat on his back in her front garden. If only George, their gardener, hadn't left the watering can in that precise spot, Beaumarsh might have recovered his balance. If, if, *if.*

It *wasn't* real, she assured herself.

Yet his chest felt remarkably solid as she pressed her hands against it and pushed in an effort to remove herself from his far too close proximity. Having never been so near to a male person of his lordship's kind before, she was at once scandalised and intrigued. He seemed so much bigger when pressed flat against him, and harder. *Stronger*. The knowledge of how much strength resided in the musculature of that broad chest made her heart skip. Heat rushed to all parts of her body and an odd sensation deep in her belly unsettled her further. She dared not look at him, could only imagine the horror with which he was regarding her, and yet her eyes were drawn inexorably to his. *Blue, blue, indigo blue* was all she could think for a moment. *Blue as the sea and the sky and…* and crinkling at the corners as his chest began to shake.

The devil!

He was laughing at her.

Horrified, Clementine recommenced her struggle to get upright and found herself hauled easily to her feet. Turning in surprise, she found a large man regarding her with a smile that was far too knowing for her comfort.

"Miss Honeywell, I presume?" he said, his voice deadpan.

Dreadfully flustered now, Clementine took a moment to smooth her skirts, lamenting the fact she was wearing her oldest and most faded gown. Well, yes, of course she would be. In what reality would she ever be prepared for the arrival of two handsome noblemen by wearing her best gown and being perfectly composed? None that she had ever lived in, that was for certain. She tried to rearrange her hair, which was a lost cause, as the man reached down to take his friend's hand and pulled Beaumarsh to his feet. The devil was still laughing, drat him, but she supposed it might be worse.

"I beg your pardon, my lord, I was not expecting you," she said, flushed with mortification.

"I d-dread to think what you might have done if you *had* been expecting me," Beaumarsh managed, wiping his eyes.

Clementine scowled at him, trying hard not to think about how it had felt to lie atop him, for that would not help in the least. "I did not do it on purpose. One of our kittens caught a mouse. I have been trying to train it to bring them to me alive, but so far, I have had little success."

"You wished for the cat to deliver the mouse to you *alive?"* the unknown man repeated, looking intrigued. "Whatever for?"

"So it is not dead," Clementine replied reasonably.

The fellow turned to Beaumarsh and grinned. *"Now* I see," he said, after which incomprehensible remark the earl's mirth vanished, and he sent his friend a warning look Clementine could not fathom.

"Have you come to visit my father?" Clementine asked, trying to get this nonsensical meeting onto a more reasonable footing, for she could not understand why else he might turn up out of the blue like this. Surely, he had not come to visit her? The thought made her spirits lift momentarily, though she knew it was foolish.

"Yes, actually," Lord Beaumarsh replied with a smile that reminded her of all the reasons she ought to keep her feet on the ground.

"And you and your charming sisters," his companion added before Beaumarsh could continue.

Clementine prayed she had in no way revealed her disappointment and glanced at him. He offered her a smile that was as wicked as it was appealing and, rather than feeling embarrassed, Clementine felt herself smile in response. He was not as handsome as Lord Beaumarsh, his features harsher and more rugged, but he was certainly attractive, and didn't he know it.

"Is your father home?" Beaumarsh asked, forcing her to turn away from his friend. A teasing smile played around his mouth and Clementine's stomach dropped. Was he aware of the outrageous thoughts she'd had when they'd been entangled so intimately? Oh, Lord. She hoped not. She looked away from him, unable to withstand the encouraging warmth she saw there, for surely she would blush and stammer like a ninny if he kept on. Instead, she kept her tone brusque and businesslike and avoided looking at him altogether.

"He is, and shall be most pleased to see you and…?" She trailed off, aware they still had not been introduced.

"My apologies," the earl said at once. "Miss Honeywell, may I present Lord Stonehaven? Stonehaven, Miss Honeywell."

“Charmed,” Stonehaven said, taking her hand and bowing over it.

“My lord,” Clementine said, dipping a curtsy. “Please, do come inside.”

Miss Honeywell left them in a cheerfully sunny parlour whilst she went to fetch her father. She could hardly look at him, and yet she couldn’t *not* look at him either. It was rather hard to keep the stupid grin from his face. Beau watched her go, still wishing he could have made their rather unorthodox meeting last a little longer. He’d been sorely tempted to put his arms around her, but he was too much of a gentleman to take advantage of the situation. Not too much of a gentleman to enjoy it, though.

It had been no hardship to feel her plastered against him. He hadn’t cared a fig for the fact there was a pebble digging into his hip, or that his immaculate person was likely covered in dust. He *had* cared that her lush breasts were pressed hard against him, and the feel of her hands pushing against his chest made him think of far more intimate situations where she might be in such a position. She had been so appalled, so terribly flustered, and yet he thought he had seen curiosity in her eyes, fascination even, and believed she had rather enjoyed the interlude herself, despite her embarrassment. He hoped so.

“I begin to see what you mean,” Stonehaven remarked, looking about the room with approval. Though the furnishing were a little worn, and the curtains faded at the edges, the room had a welcoming, homely air and Beau could well imagine many convivial afternoons and evenings spent in such a place.

“What does that mean?” Beau asked, praying he had not made a mistake in bringing Stonehaven here. He was an honourable fellow, but he could be the very devil when the mood took him.

"It's peaceful here. It seems to be a world away from London, almost another country, and yet it is not far at all."

Beau nodded, pleased that his friend understood the appeal. "It's a spa town, though the spa seems to be nothing but a thin trickle of water in a hidden spot, no fashionable pump room, and I should pay ten pounds to see you drink a glass of the vile stuff. I've never tasted worse," he said with a laugh. "No one seems to know about the place, charming as it is. The few visitors are mostly very old and middle class, from what I understand."

"Well, that will change soon enough, for I shall spread the word," Stonehaven said with a smile.

Beau opened his mouth to demand Stonehaven do no such thing. He did not wish for Little Valentine to change, but that was selfish, wasn't it? People needed to live and prosper, and how much easier it would be for those who lived here if their town became fashionable with the arrival of the *beau monde*.

He had no time to consider the matter further, however, as the reverend appeared.

"My Lord Beaumarsh!" the man exclaimed, his face lit with genuine pleasure. "How good of you to remember us and return to our little town. I told Clemmie you would not forget us, but she did not believe me."

Clemmie blushed and avoided Beau's gaze, which pleased him to no end. She had changed her gown and tidied herself, and looked pretty in a dress of sprigged muslin trimmed with blue ribbon. It was several years out of fashion, but suited her and showed her figure to advantage. Suddenly, Beau remembered the sight of her in her nightgown and found his gaze riveted to the way the material fit snugly over her bosom and then fell to skim her hips. There was a lovely little waist beneath that fabric, he thought with a smile. He glanced at Stonehaven and noticed with some irritation that he too was looking at her as if he was aware of how she looked in her nightclothes.

Beau turned his attention to the reverend and smiled. "We are only passing, but a friend of ours has a hunting lodge close to here. As we were on our way, and I had told Stonehaven about my stay here, he was fascinated and wished to meet you, sir."

"To meet me?" the reverend repeated, beaming at this information. "Why, you flatter me, my lord. I cannot think what possessed you, but I am most pleased. Most pleased indeed. Though I suspect my lovely daughters are more of a draw. Now, make yourselves at home, we do not stand on ceremony in this house. Clemmie darling, is tea coming?"

"Yes, Papa," Clementine said.

"And your sisters?"

"They were in the garden but shall be with us presently."

Beau looked at her as she sat and smoothed down her skirts. She had recovered her equanimity, for which he was a little sorry. Miss Honeywell in a fluster was terribly endearing, but now there was the sensible, no-nonsense creature he knew… somewhat, at least. Perhaps aware of his scrutiny, she glanced up, and this time held his gaze. He felt the determination behind the action, and it made him smile. There was something else too, as she refused to look away from him, a subtle pull, a flickering of interest, and the spark of curiosity that had been lit by their sudden proximity.

He had never exerted himself where Miss Honeywell was concerned. She had made her feelings about him so plain there had seemed little point in trying to flirt with her as he did with most women. He had simply relaxed in her company and been entirely himself, which had been a novelty. Now, however, he wondered how she would react if he used his wiles upon her. Give him a tremendous scold most likely, he thought with an inward chuckle, not finding the idea at all disheartening.

"I hope you are in good health, Lord Beaumarsh?" she asked politely.

"I am, thank you, and yourself?" he asked, wishing they could dispense with the small talk and feeling certain she was just as irked by the need for polite chatter. If only they had not had a witness earlier, perhaps he might have stolen a kiss. He wondered what she would have done if he had. The thought intrigued him more than he might have expected, and he found his gaze falling to her mouth as she answered.

"Quite well, thank you," she replied, gazing at him uncertainly. "You had a pleasant journey, I hope?"

"Yes, indeed we did, and returning here so soon was an unexpected pleasure. I am so very glad Stonehaven suggested it."

Beau knew his eyes were saying something else entirely as he stared at her, unblinking. Did she read his face, his words, correctly? And would she take him to task for it the moment they were alone? He rather hoped so. He bit back a laugh, but she clearly saw something in his expression, no matter how she interpreted it, for she stared back at him as if daring him to misbehave in company.

The door opened, and two young women walked in. Miss Isabelle, whom he had met before, was a lovely girl of perhaps eighteen years, and even the spectacles she wore could not diminish that fact. Indeed, they gave her face an interesting quality, a little owlish perhaps, but quite charming. Her sister, however, well, well. Miss Honeywell had been quite correct. Miss Beatrice could capture a duke, dowry or no. She was quite simply breathtaking.

"Ah, well, gentlemen, here are the lights of my life. Clementine, you have met, of course, but here is Miss Beatrice and Miss Isabelle," the reverend said, with obvious pride as the girls both made their curtsies.

Beau glanced at Stonehaven to see his expression of astonished delight at finding himself in the company of three such lovely creatures. Fair and blue-eyed, each was a step closer to perfection, with Miss Beatrice at the zenith. Part of what made her so lovely, he realised, as he watched the two young women sit themselves beside their older sister on the settee, was her complete lack of awareness of the effect she had on those around her.

London society would eat her alive, Beau thought with sudden concern and wondered if Miss Honeywell would be doing the girl the good turn she believed, if she gave her sister the season she desired for her.

The tea tray arrived, and, for a while, all was quiet whilst Clementine poured and prepared a cup to everyone's liking. There were cakes too, little vanilla sponges that were as light as clouds, and sugar biscuits, which Stonehaven devoured with unabashed pleasure.

"Have you just escaped the heat of the town, my lord?" Honeywell asked them with interest.

"No, sir. In fact, we have been staying at Cavendish House. My mother lives there much of the year and I am afraid I have rather neglected her. So we spent the past month there, which gave me time to catch up on some estate matters and to listen to my parent scold me for the various ways in which I have failed to be the perfect son," Beau said wryly.

"Ah, Cavendish House! A splendid prospect, I hear, though I have never seen it. In Kent?" he asked, wrinkling his brow.

"Yes, sir. It is very old and quite beautiful but, like all grand old ladies, it needs rather more attention than I can always give it."

The reverend chuckled appreciatively at this and nodded. "I don't doubt it. I should so much like to see it one day."

"Papa," Miss Honeywell said in an urgent undertone, obviously embarrassed by her parent's blatant angling for an invitation.

Her father regarded her with a frank smile, quite unrepentant. "Well, I would like to see it," he said, a little defensively. "And don't pretend you wouldn't, for I shan't believe you."

"That may be true, but I should not be so bold as to demand an invitation," Miss Honeywell replied, looking somewhat exasperated and darting an apologetic glance at Beau.

He chuckled at her consternation. "Please do not trouble yourself, Miss Honeywell, I should be glad to extend an invitation to you all. My mother loves entertaining and would be delighted to meet you, should you wish to stay for a few days. I will let her know that I have invited you."

"Oh, dear. Well, that is most kind," Miss Honeywell replied in resignation, looking increasingly mortified, much to Beau's amusement.

"How wonderful, and will you be there, my lord?" the reverend.

Beau hesitated. He was oddly tempted to show these kind people his home, yet it would not do. Such an invitation might lead Miss Honeywell to think… to hope…. "I'm rarely at home, I'm afraid," he said hurriedly, regretting the words as he saw the disappointment in the old fellow's eyes. He felt it himself, too. It would be fun to show Miss Honeywell around and tell her the history of the place. "But you never know," he added in a rush.

"Excellent." Honeywell beamed and Beau hid his smile, very aware of the fellow's machinations which had nothing on his doting mama's.

"I wonder, would the young ladies care to take a stroll to the beach with us," Stonehaven asked. "I should very much like to see a little more of the place before we leave."

"Of course they would!" Honeywell cried. "A capital notion. Run and fetch your bonnets, my dears, and show our guests the delights of Little Valentine."

Dutifully, and without a word of protest, the ladies hurried off.

The reverend rubbed his hands together, well pleased with this development. "Well, this has been a rare treat, my lord. I do hope you will call on us again if you are staying close by. I shan't join you on your walk, though, so don't fret. You young people enjoy a lovely stroll, and perhaps you should call in at The Mermaid's Tale for refreshments. They do the most marvellous ices. Bound to work up a thirst on such a hot day."

"We shall, sir, I thank you," Beau said, before shaking the man's hand and bidding him a good afternoon.

Beau and Stonehaven went to the front garden to await their companions, and Beau looked to his friend, awaiting what he might say.

"Certainly a duke," Stonehaven said with a grin. "She ought not to lower her sights to a mere marquess, and yet—"

"Behave," Beau said brusquely.

"As if I wouldn't," Stonehaven retorted indignantly, hand on heart.

Any reply Beau might have made, he stifled as the front door opened and the three ladies appeared. Stonehaven immediately took possession of Miss Beatrice and Miss Isabelle, demanding each take his arm and looking like the cock of the walk the moment they did. Beau shook his head and offered his arm to Miss Honeywell, who was regarding him with speculative interest. Awareness still thrummed between them, but Miss Honeywell had clearly got herself in hand and he knew she would do nothing to acknowledge it. Not unless he provoked her. It was a tempting thought, but one he resisted, at least for now.

Stonehaven and his new friends walked off, with Stonehaven chatting easily and doing his part to put the ladies at ease. Beau slanted a glance at his companion, her frank gaze as unsettling as always.

"You are trying to read my brain again, Miss Honeywell," he complained, startling a laugh from her, which pleased him.

"I am," she admitted. "I simply cannot fathom what you are doing here."

"I told you, we were en route to a friend's," he said, aware he sounded a trifle defensive.

"Yes, so you said," she replied, not sounding convinced. They walked on a little farther. "Stonehaven seems an amiable fellow."

Beau looked at her sharply, wondering if she had been beguiled so easily. Certainly, most women found Stonehaven to be a fascinating fellow, almost magnetic. Of course, his lofty title did not hurt, either. Beau studied her face, making her turn to look at him. She glanced away quickly, and he smiled, relieved he had not been trumped.

"He is," Beau agreed. They walked on a little further in silence.

After a while, he felt her studying his face, and allowed her to do so without comment, knowing she would ask whatever it was she wished to know shortly.

"How have you been? Have you truly recovered from your illness?"

Beau glanced back at her, rather touched by the sincerity of her question, which seemed more than simple politeness. "I have, thank you, and Cousin Edwin is coming to terms with life in France. At least now the war is over, he is in no danger of being accused of spying," he added wryly.

"Could a man who wears purple striped waistcoats with yellow pantaloons and a green coat be accused of spying?" she wondered idly. "He doesn't exactly escape one's notice."

Beau grinned at her. "A despicably clever one, perhaps."

"A double agent," she agreed, laughing.

"Good lord. Cousin Edwin, a spy," Beau said, his mind boggling at the idea. "Well, he's sly enough, I'll grant you. Just not terribly bright."

They walked in companionable silence for a while, enjoying the cooler temperatures beneath the shade of the trees, and made their way along the path to the beach. There were birds singing, and he wondered if he'd ever noticed such a thing in London. He must have done whilst at Cavendish House, and yet there was something very peaceful in this moment, as if the place had a magic of its own that cast a spell over one. It was pleasant too, he supposed, simply being away from the dirt and the noise of town life. Not that he'd admit that to Kirby for the world.

"How is Mr Kirby?" Miss Honeywell asked, and Beau looked at her, wondering if perhaps she could read his thoughts after all.

"Well, he's stopped sulking for the first time in over a month, so I count that as progress," Beau replied gravely.

"Oh, dear. Whatever is the matter with him?" she asked, a smile in her eyes that made his gaze rest upon her for a moment longer than it ought.

"He is most disappointed in me for returning to town. I believe he wishes me to establish myself in Little Valentine."

"Good heavens, what a distressing idea," she said with gleeful horror. "Imagine, such a pink of the ton, buried in a hole-in-the-wall town like this."

"You are mocking me, Miss Honeywell," he observed, remarking the delight shining in her eyes. He liked that she would poke fun at him; it was a novel experience. Though it saddened him to admit, most women were after him for his money and his title and flattered him at every turn. He had not understood quite how tired he had become of it. At least Miss Honeywell had never been impressed by his earldom, or anything about him, he thought ruefully.

"Oh, no, my lord, never that,"

"Lying through your teeth now!" he exclaimed with a bark of laughter. "You, madam, are beyond the pale."

"Oh, good. I've always wished to be reprehensible, but never quite had the stamina for it."

"You are a strange creature, Miss Honeywell," he said, with admiration behind the words. She was engaging in a way he was unfamiliar with, and he found he enjoyed her irreverence greatly.

"Ah, my secret is out," she lamented. "And now you know why I shall never find a husband."

Beau studied her curiously, not believing that for a moment. This woman was lovely and funny and kind and the sort to be relied upon. She had a splendid figure, and he suspected she was bold enough to be an entertaining lover. Yet she was also a capable creature who could run a household and raise children and keep anyone who crossed her path from falling into disaster or mischief. She would be a friend to her husband, and entirely loyal. She would certainly never have affairs behind his back.

He stopped in his tracks, remembering the things he had said to Stonehaven about wanting his wife to at least be his friend. A woman like Miss Honeywell would make a home for her husband, a home that was calm and peaceful like the vicarage. It would be orderly, and any children she was mother to would be sensible and quiet and kind like her. Funny, too, for she *was* funny. It would be good to laugh with the woman he married. His heart gave a terrified thump, and whilst a large part of him wanted to dissolve into hysterics at the idea, he could not deny that it made a good deal of sense. He believed they could be friends. Surely, they were already a good way towards *being* friends, and he had not the least problem with the way she looked, either. The sight of her in her nightgown had plagued him for weeks after, and he was not about to forget their recent accidental intimacy either, so the getting of heirs would be no hardship whatsoever. More importantly, Miss Honeywell would not betray him. She was decent to her bones, and utterly trustworthy. He was certain of that. This assurance seemed to quiet the hectic rhythm of his heart, and he let out a breath.

"My lord?" She watched him anxiously. "Is there aught amiss?"

"No." He shook his head, but she did not seem comforted.

"Are you quite certain you have recovered your health?" she asked, with the solicitous manner she no doubt reserved for old ladies. "It is rather hot. We might find somewhere to sit, if you prefer?"

Beau glanced ahead to see Stonehaven was some distance away from them and considered the merits of a quiet spot and a serious conversation. No, she would laugh her head off if he asked her such a thing out of the blue, and quite rightly. Then he remembered the forthright manner in which she had explained why she would never marry a man like him if her life depended on it.

Ah, yes. *That.*

Well, no matter. He could win her over. Besides, that had been bluster, surely provoked by his ill manners. He had seen fascination in her eyes, curiosity. *That* he could work with. Besides, now they were on more intimate and friendly terms, she had thawed a degree or two. Hadn't she?

"No, I'm quite well, I assure you. Let's carry on. Tell me, how have you been? Has life in Little Valentine kept you busy since I left?"

She looked at him oddly for a moment, as if deciding if he really wanted to know or was just going through the motions of polite conversation again.

"Yes, I have been well, and busy with keeping Papa in order, though I admit I have been a little bored of late. I believe I need a new challenge and have been considering starting a club for the ladies of Little Valentine. They need a place where they can meet and exchange news and perhaps do something for the benefit of the town."

She enjoyed organising people and events, which spoke well for someone taking on the role of countess, he noted with approval. "A fine notion. What would be your first project?"

Her expression grew troubled for a moment, and she opened her mouth and then closed it again. "Oh, I don't know. Perhaps we shall raise funds for the girls' school," she said with a smile. "It's about time someone helped Papa to make it happen."

Beau narrowed his eyes, watching her closely. He felt certain she was hiding something. "Admirable, of course, Miss Honeywell, but that was not what you had been going to say. Tell me what is really on your mind."

She stared at him, clearly startled by the observation. "Are you sure *you* cannot read *my* brain, my lord?" she demanded.

Beau laughed. "Certainly not, but I believe I am improving at reading your expressions. You have the most telling face, my dear. If I may give you a little advice, never play cards for money. You will lose."

She huffed but the corners of her mouth ticked up, so he felt certain he had not offended her. "I am troubled," she admitted. "And I do not know what to do."

He held her gaze as she looked back at him, her blue eyes searching his face as if weighing up his trustworthiness. "Tell me."

"You cannot tell a soul," she said, gazing at him with such ferocity he wondered what she might do if he broke her confidence. String him up by his nether parts, judging by that look.

"You have my word as a gentleman."

She nodded, satisfied, which surprised him a little. Her opinion of him when they had first met must have undergone a change, for he felt sure she had not trusted him an inch then.

"There is a lady in this town whose husband beats her. Everyone knows it, and no one will lift a finger to help her. To be honest, no one *can* help her, for she refuses all overtures from any of us. The appalling truth is that we are all helpless. She is his property in the eyes of the law and, unless he actually kills her, he may do as he pleases. My father has tried to intervene, but her husband has taken him in such dislike that I fear he will do Papa an injury if he continues, and to add to it, each time we help, or try to, I am certain his wife suffers worse consequences. I am at a loss, and it is driving me distracted."

"That is…" Beau began, a little startled to hear a young lady speak of such subjects, let alone wish to intervene and find a solution. "Horrifying," he said, unable to find another word for it.

"It is," she agreed with a sigh. "And I am so tired of noting how little power some women of this town wield. There are those who are capable and strong-willed and have carved out a place for themselves, but those are the fortunate ones. What of the others who have no power, no voice, and no way to make themselves heard should they try to do so? That must change."

Beau stared at her. Such radical ideas ought to shock him, for he had gone to school with boys whose parents had taught them that women were a foolish, fragile sex, to be looked after and not to be taken seriously. This way of thinking had been reinforced at school. Yet Beau's mother was neither fragile nor foolish, despite her sometimes frivolous ways, so experience had tempered his opinion.

"I have shocked you," she said, her voice cool now.

Beau shook his head, not wanting her to believe him the kind of man who thought women ought to be treated as children. "No. Well, yes, a little, but not in the way you think. I am afraid I have simply never considered such ideas before. An arrogant devil, am I not?" he added, before she could do so.

Her expression softened, and she smiled at him, which was a relief. "I cannot blame you for that. You are a man of wealth and title. Very few of your ilk would give such matters a second thought. But to unmarried ladies of a certain age, these considerations have rather greater significance. I am most fortunate, for my family have made provision for me, but if not I might be forced to live with an unwelcoming relative, unwanted and at risk of being cast out at any moment if I do not do precisely as I am told. It happens all the time, you know."

The idea of Miss Honeywell being at the mercy of some cruel relative made Beau's stomach cramp with distress. That would not happen to her, whether or not she agreed to his proposal, he reminded himself. She had financial security; she had said so. Yet an uneasy sensation remained squirming in his gut.

"So, a ladies' club, no doubt created under the guise of making corn dollies or knitting for charity, yet at heart seething with revolutionary ideas? Is that about the gist of it?" he asked, smiling.

She grinned at him, such a delighted expression that her nose crinkled, and Beau was arrested by how lovely she looked in the dappled sunshine beneath the trees.

"Quite so," she agreed. "We shall write pamphlets full of seditious ideas, calling for women all over the country to march on parliament and demolish this domineering male society once and for all."

"You terrify me, Miss Honeywell, for I believe if anyone could do it, that person is you," he said, hearing the admiration in his voice again and wondering at it. Surely he should mock her, not adopt this note of teasing approbation, for she was only funning. Yet he meant it, and he knew there had been a note of sincerity behind her fantastical words too.

Miss Honeywell must have noted the depth of his regard, for she blushed, staring at him as if he had turned into someone she had never seen before. Beau smiled and she looked away, clearly unsettled. He regretted having spooked her and changed the conversation back to more serious matters to return it to safer ground.

"And how will this club help the unfortunate woman you spoke of?" he asked with genuine interest.

"I don't know," she admitted. "I don't know if there *is* any way we can help her. Perhaps we could raise enough money for her to run away and start a new life, but she was born and raised here, so I doubt she would take it."

There was such frustration in her voice, he realised it truly pained her to be unable to fix the problem, to make the hateful husband mend his ways, or to go away.

"You cannot be responsible for everyone's happiness," he told her gently.

She laughed at that. "Now you sound like my sisters. You know I live in fear of becoming that terribly nosy old lady who will always stick her oar in. Yet sometimes I truly cannot help myself. If I can see a way of making a situation better, I *must* intervene. It's a curse, I'm afraid," she said with a sigh. "And one you are very well aware of."

"One I believe you are much admired for," he replied gently.

"Oh-ho! You have been speaking to my father," she said, the sparkle returning to her eyes as she dared to poke fun at him. "For I know you did not hold such a favourable opinion. If I remember correctly, I was asked in no uncertain terms to refrain from meddling in your affairs."

Beau shrugged, pleased to see she had regained her good humour. "And yet you meddled with such delightful efficiency, Miss Honeywell. If you remember, I thanked you very prettily and admitted I was in your debt. I think it most unkind of you to remind me of words I said in the heat of irritation, when I did not yet understand the depths of your cleverness and the workings of your diabolical mind."

She regarded him for a long moment with frank admiration. “Do you know, I cannot tell if that was a compliment, or a set down? Well done, my lord.”

“Wretched girl,” he snorted, making her laugh in return as they emerged from the trees and followed the path down to the shore.

Chapter 11

An afternoon at the seaside with delicious ices, and such lovely muscles.

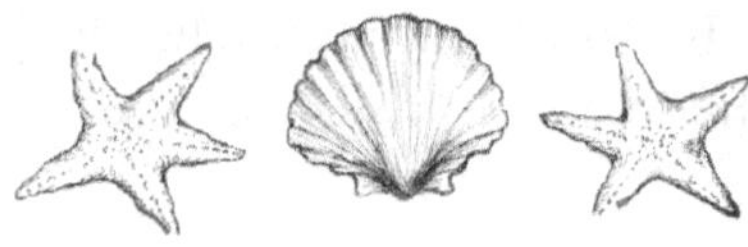

Little Valentine, South-East Coast of England. 10thJuly 1815

Clementine detached herself from Lord Beaumarsh once they reached the shore, needing to put distance between them. The feeling of his muscular arm beneath her fingers was doing strange things to her equilibrium, though acting like a girl just out of the schoolroom was something that made her cringe inwardly. Never in her life had she blushed and become so het up and flustered over a man as she had today, not even when she *had* been fresh out of the schoolroom. Yet her heart gave an odd little jolt in her chest whenever he looked at her and she knew it would not do.

Why he was regarding her with such admiration, or taking such an interest in her, she could not fathom, but it must just be a passing fancy. His friend had no doubt heard about the eccentric Honeywell family and Beau had indulged him by arranging this visit. Likely, they were just enjoying a pleasant interlude on the way to their friend's hunting lodge and would not give them all a second thought once they had gone. The idea dispirited her, and to such a degree it was horribly clear just how much trouble she was in.

She had only ever wished to be his friend, nothing more, but that had been before she had spent those bone melting moments sprawled on top of him and felt… felt such a rush of heat and attraction. Yes, attraction. There was no point in beating about the bush. One must call a spade a spade. She was attracted to Lord Beaumarsh. Well, it was hardly shocking. Half the beau monde were attracted to him, from all she'd heard and read.

She had spent the past month since he had gone determinedly not thinking of him. Now she knew why it had been so difficult, why he would creep in her thoughts at odd moments despite her best efforts. She had simply refused to notice him that way before. She had been on her guard, and rightly so. But now the scales had been pulled from her eyes, and she could not *unsee* him. He was right there, all golden good looks and dancing blue eyes. The Earl of Beaumarsh was beautiful. She had known it from the first, yet now it was a problem. Drat the man. Why had he come back today and stirred everything up again? She might have forgotten him if he had not, but now…

Honestly, was there ever such a fool?

"What do you think, Miss Honeywell?"

Clementine looked up with a start. "I beg your pardon?" she said, belatedly realising Lord Stonehaven was addressing her.

He smiled, and she suspected he was well aware of how his friend was flustering her as he repeated the question. "I am told The Mermaid's Tale serves the most delightful ices and I, for one, could do with something refreshing. It's dreadfully hot and I should be pleased to indulge us all with a cool treat."

"That sounds a splendid idea," Clementine said, though she glanced at her sisters to see them both looking at Lord Stonehaven with frank admiration. How funny, she thought, wondering how they could admire him so when Lord Beaumarsh was present. Stonehaven was certainly a magnetic presence among them, his sheer vitality and masculinity impossible to overlook, but he was the dark to Lord Beaumarsh's light. For the life of her, she could not understand why they would turn to the night sky when Beaumarsh's smile made you feel you were bathed in sunlight.

Oh, dear heaven, Clementine thought in disgust. This must stop at once. Somehow, she had to put an end to this visit and get the man firmly out of her mind.

Beau did not insist that Clementine take his arm as they made their way to the elegant hotel. He was aware he had unsettled her and did not wish to provoke further alarm. So, he kept his distance and instead tried to draw Beatrice into conversation. She was far shyer than either of her sisters; Isabelle was chatting animatedly to Stonehaven, who seemed to be enjoying himself enormously.

"I understand your sister is determined you will enjoy a London season?" Beau said with a smile, immediately regretting his words as the girl's rosy glow disappeared, leaving her pale, her blue eyes startling against her fair skin.

"Oh," she said, a frown tugging at her blonde brows. "That is just a fancy of Clementine's. She is a darling, always wanting the best of everything for everyone, and she has this notion that I can make a brilliant match, but it will come to nothing, I'm sure."

"How can you be certain?" Beau asked, relieved she had rallied enough to make an answer. "Miss Honeywell seems to be a very determined female."

She smiled fondly at that, and once again Beau realised Miss Honeywell was correct. The curve of Miss Beatrice's lush mouth might scatter a man's wits to the four winds with no effort whatsoever. He, however, was not so afflicted. He wondered at that.

"That much is true," Miss Beatrice admitted. "Clementine is an extraordinary person. Sometimes I am quite certain she keeps the entire town from falling into the sea. I confess, I often wish I had even a fraction of her intelligence and wit. Still, even she cannot turn pebbles into guineas," she said, with obvious relief.

Beau laughed at that, and she returned a shy glance that was still alight with mischief. He suspected perhaps there was more to

Miss Beatrice than just a pretty face, if a fellow had patience enough to draw her out.

The Mermaid's Tale was quiet today as they presented themselves at the desk and rang the bell. A moment later, Mrs Adamson appeared. Once again, she looked ravishing in an apple-green gown that complemented her riotous red curls.

"Lord Beaumarsh," she said, smiling with genuine warmth. "Why, I did not expect to see you again, but how delightful! How may I—" She broke off, the pleasure in her expression replaced at once by a look of chilly annoyance. "Oh. I see you have company. My Lord Stonehaven. How do you do?"

She performed a negligent curtsy, and Beau watched with interest as his friend smiled at her with far more warmth.

"Mrs Adamson!" he exclaimed, the words said in a way that implied something Beau could not put his finger on. Certainly, they knew each other. The devil. Who was she to Stonehaven, and had he known all along he could find her here? "It is a pleasure to see you again, and looking so well."

Mrs Adamson gave a slight incline of her head but otherwise did not react, instead returning her attention to Beau. "How may I help you, my lord?"

"I believe we and our charming company would like to enjoy some of your ices. They are very good, I'm told," he added, earning himself a pleased smile as the woman determinedly ignored Stonehaven. What an interesting turn of events.

"Well, we may not be Gunter's, and our selection is limited, for keeping the ice is rather a challenge, but they are indeed extremely good. If you would care to take a seat, I shall bring you the menu," she said, leading them up onto the terrace and ensuring they were comfortably settled before she hurried off again.

"You know Mrs Adamson?"

Of course, Miss Honeywell would be the one to question Stonehaven.

"A little," Stonehaven agreed. "Our families live very close to one another."

Miss Honeywell nodded, and was far too well-mannered to press for further information, though Beau suspected she was dying to know more.

Mrs Adamson returned with a maid in tow and the menus, handing them all to Beau so he might give them out, and did not acknowledge Stonehaven.

"If you would excuse me, I have business to attend to, but Martha here will take your orders and look after you. Good afternoon, Lord Beaumarsh, Stonehaven, ladies." With that, she curtsied again, without looking at Stonehaven, and left them with the maid.

Martha smiled at them brightly. A pretty girl of perhaps twenty, she waited with an expectant air as they perused the menu. As Mrs Adamson had explained, there was not a huge choice, but rose, lavender, raspberry, strawberry, and blackcurrant were all available.

Stonehaven chose the blackcurrant with very little deliberation, whilst Miss Beatrice said raspberry was her favourite. Miss Honeywell seconded this, with Miss Isabelle choosing the rose flavour. Beau plumped for strawberry and Martha noted down their orders and hurried away.

As they waited, the ladies got up to stand at the rail, looking out at the expanse of blue sea and the stretch of pretty buildings that followed the seafront. Beau hesitated, noticing that Miss Honeywell was standing alone. He went to stand beside her.

"Well, that was intriguing," he said in an undertone.

She glanced up at him, her lips quirking. "Don't," she warned. "Yes, I am desperately curious, but I am not yet that nosy old lady

I fear becoming. I *do* respect people's privacy and, unless the situation was dire, I would not dream of interfering."

"I know," he replied mildly. "But isn't it devilishly hard not to ask?"

"Not for me," she replied, laughing. "Happily, I do not know Lord Stonehaven enough to be so dreadfully bold, and I respect Mrs Adamson far too much to pry into her affairs."

"Whereas I have known Stonehaven since we were boys and can be as bold and provoking as I like. But if you are not interested, I shall not tell you if I discover anything."

"Oh! Why, you—!" she exclaimed, outraged and entertained all at once.

Beau grinned at her. "Go on, ask me to write and let you know. I shan't think any less of you."

"Never in million years," she said, looking back out to sea, her chin up.

"Stubborn creature," he murmured, finding himself captivated by her profile, by a long, straight nose and thick lashes a deeper shade of blonde than her hair.

"You have no idea," she said darkly, making him laugh.

"Oh, I think I am beginning to see you quite clearly, Miss Honeywell," he remarked, and made an immediate retreat before she could run scared from him once again.

Clementine moved to the open window of her bedroom. She could see a bright stretch of blue sea from her vantage point, and she sat down to brush out her loose hair. The scent of night-scented stocks drifted up to her, a perfume so entangled with memories of her childhood and summer and her mama that she felt nostalgic for a time when life had seemed far simpler.

She had believed herself content with her lot. Her life was a busy one, and rich in interest. Living in this beautiful town, surrounded by people she had known all her life, seemed a blessing beyond anything she could imagine. The people here liked and respected her, and she had envisioned herself growing old here, keeping her father company in his twilight years, and then moving to one of the little rented houses along the seafront. No doubt her sisters would be happily married by then, and she would spend a good deal of time with them and their children too and be a favourite auntie.

Suddenly, that prospect was not as appealing as it had once been, and she felt a surge of irritation towards Lord Beaumarsh, for which she immediately berated herself. She had wanted to be his friend, had she not? Here the man was, trying to be just that, and she was cross with him because she could not keep her growing attraction to him under control. That was her fault, not his, and she must do better.

Of course, she likely would not see him again, and so the point was moot. But then she had not expected to see him today and be taken out for ices. It had been a delightful afternoon, full of laughter and interest and… how she wished he were not so handsome. If he looked like Lord Stonehaven, she would not be so afflicted by the sight of his smile, or by his deep blue eyes that seemed to reflect the ocean back at her, and the way they crinkled at the corners when she said something to entertain him.

A soft knock at the door returned her attention to the present.

"Come in."

Beatrice stuck her head around the door. "I'm not disturbing you?"

"As if you could," Clementine replied with a smile, making room on the window seat for her lovely sister.

Even with her hair tied in rags and a nightgown that had seen better days, Beatrice looked like an earthbound angel. She wasn't.

Oh, she was kind and sweet and good natured and quite the nicest person in the world, but she was also quietly stubborn, surprisingly brave when the occasion merited it, and had a lively sense of humour. Clementine knew it irked her when people, especially men, looked at her and saw only her beauty, and it was this that made her shy and not wish to put herself forward.

"Did you have a nice day?" she asked as Bea settled herself on the seat.

"Oh, yes. A wonderful day," Bea replied, and Clementine noted the glow in her eyes with sudden disquiet. "I never expected such a treat, and out of the blue. I shall never forget it."

"It was only ices at The Mermaid's Tale," Clementine teased her uneasily.

Bea shrugged, looking out of the window, a faraway look in her eyes. "I know."

Clementine waited, wondering if she would say more. She felt like Bea wanted to talk, but sometimes you had to wait and give her the time to order her thoughts. Her patience was rewarded some minutes later.

"Lord Stonehaven was very kind, was he not?"

And there it was, Clementine thought with a sigh.

"I had such a lovely time talking to him. Raspberry ice and the company of such an… an interesting and charming man. It was more than I ever expected when I woke up this morning," Bea said, her eyes sparkling.

Well, of all the mismatched couples, Clementine thought with a groan. Stonehaven seemed aggressively masculine, rather overpowering, and certainly far too harsh a fellow for her gentle sister. He would crush her, literally and figuratively. Yet somehow he had captured Bea's attention. And then there was that business with Mrs Adamson. She was a sensible woman and if she held the man in such dislike, which she clearly did, there must be a reason for it. Yet, Clementine dared not say anything of the sort to Bea. Human nature being what it was, she would only like him even more if anyone said a word against him.

"It was a very pleasant afternoon, and Lord Stonehaven was most entertaining," Clementine replied cautiously. "It was so strange, however. Just think, we go for years and years without seeing a nobleman and then two turn up at once. Still, I doubt we shall see them again," she said confidently, as much for her own benefit as for her sister's.

"Oh, I do not know about that," Bea said, with more assurance than Clementine was prepared for. "I think we shall certainly see Lord Beaumarsh again soon. So perhaps his friend will accompany him."

Clementine turned to look at her sharply. "Why should we?" she asked, her heart performing a complicated series of beats in her chest that made her feel quite winded.

Bea laughed, pulling her knees up to her chest as she regarded Clementine. "Oh, Clemmie, you are far cleverer than I, but sometimes I swear you cannot see the nose on your face."

"Whatever does that mean?" Clementine said, staring at Bea and wondering what on earth it was she had missed.

"There is obviously something between you and the earl. I could sense it all afternoon. You could hardly look at him one moment and the next you could not look away."

Clementine blushed, horrified by the notion she might have behaved so blatantly.

Bea grinned at her, a mischievous look that few people got to see. "Oh, don't look so appalled. I'm sure no one else noticed, but I did."

"You misunderstand," Clementine said hurriedly. "Yes, there was… something, but it's not what you think. It's only that we had a bit of an… an accident. It made us both feel rather foolish. Well, it made me feel foolish, and very aware of Lord Beaumarsh, who obviously delighted in making me even more flustered whenever he looked at me. It's silly really. Nothing at all to get worked up over, so don't read anything into it," she begged.

Bea, however, only looked increasingly intrigued. "What kind of accident?"

"The kind where I knocked him flat and found myself lying on top of him," Clementine said with some heat. "One of the wretched kittens finally caught a mouse, and I was chasing it, and then there he was, on the garden path. I couldn't stop in time."

Bea's eyes grew very large and very round. *"Clementine!"* she exclaimed, and pressed her hands to her mouth to stifle her mirth. "O-Oh, Cle-Clementine," she sputtered, before dissolving entirely.

"Yes, well," Clementine said with what dignity remained to her. "Now you see. It was nothing romantic in the least. Simply… Simply…."

"Animal spirits," Bea wheezed, before going off into another peal of laughter.

Clementine sighed and waited for her sister to regain her wits. It took a good few minutes but finally, Bea sat meekly beside her, pink-cheeked, her blue eyes shining.

"I beg your pardon," she said gravely.

"Hmph." Clementine shook her head. "Do not go getting any silly notions about me and Lord Beaumarsh. I will admit, the incident was shocking, and it made me feel—" Clementine searched for the right words, words that would not incite another round of hysteria. "Very… aware of him. As a man, I mean. He was just so *big*, up close. Strong, too. So *robust.* All that hard muscle and…"

Clementine swallowed, the memory too vivid for her to dare another word on the subject.

“Oh, Clemmie,” Bea said, her voice laced with a mixture of pity and exasperation.

“Oh, go to bed, you vexing creature,” Clementine said, shooing her sister out of the room with good-natured little pushes. “And don’t you dare tell Isabelle. I cannot endure both of you teasing me!”

With that, she shut the door on her sister and went to bed, determined not to give Lord Beaumarsh another thought.

Chapter 12

New beginnings, high hopes, and cakes - obviously.

Marley House, Battle, South-East Coast of England. 15th July 1815

Beau swung down from his horse and handed his reins over to the waiting groom. Stonehaven had returned to the Lodge earlier, but Beau had felt restless still, his mind filled with possibilities, with doubts and questions and uncertainties. Even if it was the right decision, there was no saying how Miss Honeywell would react to it. Laughing in his face or giving him the most terrific set-down both seemed equally likely. Worse, she might be kind. She might thank him for his offer and tell him how honoured she was and still turn him down flat.

He told himself she was a spinster, firmly on the shelf and, given her family's situation, with no possibility of getting herself off it. She ought to be grateful for an offer from a man who was considered a prize of the marriage mart. God, what an insufferable bastard he was! She ought to send him away with a flea in his ear if he voiced so appalling a notion in her hearing.

Did she not wish to change her life for the better, though? Indeed, she seemed to have no inclination to do so. But surely, she wished for her own home, for children. Feeling irritable and out of sorts, he stalked inside.

Marley House, as with Cavendish House, was a hunting lodge and very ancient, but there the similarities ended. It was far smaller, built of red brick and with many leaded light windows, and was rumoured to have been visited by Henry the Eighth when he was courting Anne Boleyn, for its proximity to Hever Castle was notable. Likely in Beau's opinion, as old Henry had loved hunting and chasing women in equal measure.

Mr Heath Austen-Leigh, who owned the place, had clearly not visited any time recently, however, as it needed a thorough clean and a good deal of renovation. He kept on only a minimal staff, who were not much inclined to do more than the bare minimum. None of this improved Beau's temper, used as he was to the finer things in life. Kirby was not much impressed either.

"We could go back to The Mermaid's Tale," he said the moment Beau opened the bedroom door.

"Oh, let me get a foot inside before you begin nagging me again," Beau said crossly. "We are not going back there."

"Why not? Clean sheets, and good food, that splendid view, and people who would welcome the sight of you again," Kirby said with growing enthusiasm. "Here we've got leaky roofs, damp bedding, and I keep finding spiders in your unmentionables."

Beau stared at him in horror. "You made that up," he said accusingly.

Kirby shrugged. "Well, maybe the bit about the spiders, but it's only a matter of time. Place is alive with them."

Beau shook his head and sat down on the bed. "It hasn't rained since we got here so you cannot know the roof leaks either. Now, get these boots off me. It's too damned hot."

Kirby did as he was asked, and Beau regarded the top of his head whilst he eased off the tight-fitting boots.

"Who would welcome the sight of me?" "Miss Honeywell, I reckon. Leastways, after what Stonehaven said about her sprawling all over you—"

"The devil!" Beau exclaimed, incensed. He might give his valet a good deal of leeway, but his friend had no business gossiping with him like an old woman.

"Well, it ain't like I hadn't remarked it myself," Kirby said, unruffled by his lordship's reaction. "You like her, I reckon. Sparky you are, the two of you. Bickering like you do. Reckon it means something."

Despite himself, Beau could not help but ask, "What *does* it mean?"

Kirby snorted and straightened, having won the battle of the boots. "Bleedin' hell. You're the one for the ladies, my lord. Reckon you know a good deal better than I do. I could draw you a picture, maybe," he added brazenly, though he immediately realised he'd pushed his luck too far and beat a hasty retreat, muttering about polishing his lordship's boots.

Beau harrumphed. He ought to know better by now than to ask Kirby such daft questions. He changed out of his riding attire and made his way downstairs to find Stonehaven sitting on the terrace at the back of the house. It was a lovely spot, with far-reaching views over the countryside, and blessedly shady. The afternoon had grown hot and humid.

"Where do you leave off gossiping with my valet?" Beau demanded as he poured himself a glass of wine. Stonehaven had placed the bottle in a bucket of iced water to keep it cold, and it was mercifully chilled. He took a mouthful, savouring the fresh, grassy taste, and sat down beside his friend.

"Well, who else is there to gossip with around here? Besides, Kirby is the soul of discretion." Stonehaven sipped his wine and regarded Beau. "What is it I've been gossiping about?"

"About my little collision with Miss Honeywell."

Stonehaven chuckled. "Ah, yes. I've heard of fellows being struck by love like a thunderbolt, but never seen anything remotely close to it."

"Don't be an arse," Beau replied, knowing Stonehaven too well not to recognise a lure. He would not rise to the bait.

"You like her, though," the man observed nonchalantly.

"I do. She's funny and capable and… and surprising," Beau admitted.

Stonehaven nodded but said nothing.

"What?" Beau said.

Stonehaven returned a bland look. "I'm sorry? I didn't say anything, did I?"

"I know," Beau said with a sigh. "But I can hear you thinking."

"No, you just have something *to* say, but you are hoping I will say it for you, so you don't have to," Stonehaven replied placidly.

"I hate you sometimes," Beau grumbled, for at times his friend was too clever for his own good. "I tell you what. You tell me about Mrs Adamson, and I'll tell you what's on my mind."

"No dice," Stonehaven said, looking remarkably pleased with himself.

"Why not?" Beau said in frustration. "It's a fair deal."

"Perhaps, but I do not need to unburden my soul, and you do. You'll tell me anyway, whether or not I say anything."

Beau glowered. "I hate you more when you're right, damn you."

Stonehaven chuckled. "It's a curse."

Beau considered the vista before him, trying to decide if confiding in his friend was a good idea. Until their recent conversation, sparked by his meeting with Reverend Honeywell, it simply had not been the way their relationship worked. Yet, Stonehaven, despite a bit of ribbing, had not mocked him or ridiculed him overly for baring his soul a little. So, why not? It was either that or return to Cavendish House and confide in his mother.

Well, that decided it.

"I'm thinking of offering for Miss Honeywell."

Stonehaven nodded, evidencing not an iota of surprise.

"Oh, come on," Beau said crossly. "Don't sit there all inscrutable and act like you knew all along, damn you."

Stonehaven laughed. "I didn't, and I'm not, I swear it. But in light of what you said recently about being friends with your wife, it makes a good deal of sense. She'll not plague you endlessly for jewellery and parties; she won't fly up into the boughs over little slights, real or imagined. She's a sensible girl. A damned pretty one too, I noticed. She and Miss Isabelle are just cast into the shade by the incomparable."

Beau nodded, but felt somehow unsatisfied by Stonehaven's remarks, which seemed to diminish Miss Honeywell rather unfairly. She was a good deal more than sensible or pretty. Even damned pretty. Still, his friend's approval eased his mind somewhat. One more thing yet bothered him, however.

Though it near choked him to get the words out, Beau forced himself to say them aloud. "Think she'll have me?"

Stonehaven's eyes widened, and he stared at Beau in astonishment. "Good God! What is this? Lord Beaumarsh doubting his own desirability? I never thought I would live to see the day."

"Oh, stow it," Beau said, having had quite enough of Stonehaven's antics for one day.

Snatching the bottle from its watery haven, he took his glass and stalked off to find a quiet place to finish it alone.

"A club?" Clara said doubtfully.

"I think it is an excellent idea, and you are welcome to hold the meetings here when the place is quiet," Mrs Adamson said, passing another plate of cakes around the assembled company. They had already laid waste to the first lot.

The ladies were sitting on the terrace of The Mermaid's Tale, a delightfully cool breeze drifting from the sea and keeping the temperatures bearable. A pretty posy of roses and lavender adorned the table alongside a large jug of lemonade, and the atmosphere was relaxed and friendly.

"Well, if you let them know you will provide cakes like these, I don't think you'll have any trouble with getting the women to come," Clara said ruefully, taking her second cake from the assortment on offer. "We might all need to let out our gowns by the end of the year, mind," she added, sinking her teeth into the delicious sweet and giving a little moan of delight.

Clementine wondered how often she enjoyed such a treat and decided cakes were definitely something she would insist on having at their meetings.

"Well, I hope it helps," Clementine said, helping herself to another, for they were too delicious not to indulge. Thoughtfully, she added, "Perhaps we should add walking to the list of activities to keep ourselves fit. Seriously, though, how should we organise it? And what form ought it to take? Also, we shall need a name."

"The Ladies of Little Valentine," Bea said promptly.

Clementine pulled a face. "Well, it's very accurate, but I was hoping for something a little more inspiring."

"The Inspiring Ladies of Little Valentine," Bea replied with a grin.

Clementine laughed. "Keep working on it, love."

"You need a reason for the ladies to gather, for the first few times certainly," Mrs Adamson said, frowning. "Perhaps we should just offer tea and cakes to anyone who will come. If we meet once a month to begin with, it might mean even the ladies who work could find a way to come. Perhaps if it was at lunchtime? Then we could do other things, like offering a free painting lesson, Bea could do that, couldn't she?"

"Oh," Bea blushed, looking taken aback. "Well, I suppose so, but there's probably a lady with more talent than I have in the town."

"Nonsense, you'll be splendid. You're wonderfully patient and so encouraging, everyone will feel delighted with their achievements," Clementine said, pleased with the idea. "And Izzy and some of the other ladies could do a piano recital. We'd all appreciate that, and the likes of Polly and some of the other ladies might never have had the chance to enjoy such a thing. Perhaps we could do a dancing class too?"

Mrs Adamson nodded. "If we got the ladies talking, about the paintings they've done, or the music they've listened to, perhaps they will relax and make friends a little easier. Dancing should be a lot of fun too, with those that can teaching those that can't. Perhaps in time, we could invite guest speakers too, interesting ladies who have done something out of the ordinary."

"Authors, or painters," Bea suggested, delighted by the idea. "I should love to hear a proper artist speak about her work."

They spent a lovely afternoon taking notes and making plans, and drawing up a list of all the women in the town. They would put up posters too, but it seemed prudent to address a note to each lady, so they felt they had been personally invited to join. Being noticed, valued, and wanted was the point of the exercise, after all.

"The Misses Brumley will be certain to join, and I know Martha will want to," Mrs Adamson said. "Cook too, I'm sure. Mrs Fairway will love hearing everyone praise her cakes," she observed with a smile.

"Mrs Mabbs and Mrs Adie will come. Polly, too," Bea agreed.

"I do hope you are not expecting my Aunt Edna to join," Clara said suddenly, her face the picture of horror.

"No, love," Clementine said at once. "She doesn't leave the house anyway, does she?"

Clara relaxed and shook her head. "No, and she'll stop me leaving it too if she gets wind of such a thing as a ladies' club. Especially if there are cooks and maids among the members. She'll think it vulgar and shocking. Anything that's fun or diverting is vulgar or shocking."

"You don't think anyone would tell her?" Bea asked anxiously, looking concerned on Clara's behalf.

"Oh, no. I'm safe on that point at least. No one ever visits her. Other than Reverend Honeywell."

"That's so sad," Bea said, frowning. "I hadn't realised. I shall call on her tomorrow with a bouquet from the garden."

"Oh," Clara said anxiously, suddenly tongue-tied, despite usually being at ease with the Honeywell sisters. It had taken all her courage to force herself to converse in front of Mrs Adamson, Clementine knew, and she had marvelled at how well she had done. But Bea's sudden kindness towards her aunt had thrown her into confusion. "Oh, d-dear."

"It's all right, Clara. Bea won't hold it against you if your aunt is less than welcoming. Will you, Bea?"

"Of course not," Bea replied, smiling warmly at Clara. "Don't worry. She can be as mean and hateful as she desires, and I won't bat an eyelid. People like that are usually deeply unhappy, and we can only pity them. She won't hurt or offend me, I promise you."

Clara let out a breath, the anxiety leaving her body in such a rush her shoulders dropped a full inch. She nodded but turned her attention to the cake on her plate and added nothing further to the conversation.

"Clara has made a good point," Mrs Adamson said, looking concerned. "There will be ladies who consider themselves a cut above, who won't lower themselves to join a club that welcomes the lower orders. I am afraid even my presence might hinder your progress. Perhaps I ought not to be a part of it."

"Nonsense!" All three sisters spoke at once, and even Clara shook her head.

"The club is for anyone female," Clementine said, her voice firm. "No matter what their circumstances. It is a place for solidarity of spirit, for lifting each other up. Friendships will be made because of our similarities. Our differences will merely add interest to the conversation."

"I agree, Clemmie," Izzy said hesitantly. "But Mrs Adamson is right. It will probably stop some of the top-lofty women from joining."

Clementine nodded.

"To begin with, certainly. But if the club becomes what we hope it will be, if it is a safe place to speak your mind, and offers support and comfort and does good within the town, then they will demand entrance. Perhaps we should have a numbers cap," she added, grinning now as the idea occurred to her. "Then we can tell the ladies who refuse that it is a good thing, as we had not enough space for them anyhow. You know how people always want what they can't have."

"Clementine Honeywell," Mrs Adamson said, her tone filled with admiration. "You wicked, wicked girl."

Clementine carried the empty tray down to the kitchens of The Mermaid's Tale, where the cook, Mrs Fairway, snatched it from her with a little cry of distress.

"Miss Honeywell! What are you thinking? You are a guest here, not paid labour. Martha would have done that."

Clementine laughed, brushing a loose lock of hair from her eyes. "It's no trouble at all, Mrs Fairway. I don't think carrying an empty tray is going to do me any harm, and I wanted to thank you for the excellent cakes. They were quite divine."

Mrs Fairway beamed, her narrow frame seeming to grow with the compliment. "Well, thank you, miss. I suppose Mrs Adie has a light hand with pastry, but cakes and biscuits are my particular specialty," she said with pride.

Clementine hid a grin, aware of the rivalry between the two women. "They were quite delicious," she said diplomatically, refusing to be drawn on Mrs Adie's strengths and weaknesses in the kitchen.

"There you are," Mrs Adamson called, coming down the stairs to find Clementine in the kitchen. "Your sisters said they would meet you back at the vicarage. Clara has gone too, afraid her wretched aunt will be kicking up merry hell, I don't doubt."

Clementine pulled a face. "That is certainly one situation I wish to change with our efforts, though I do not know how we shall manage it."

"Well, a very wise reverend has told me that miracles do happen," Mrs Adamson said with a wry smile. "So, we shall go forward with the highest expectations, Miss Honeywell."

"Indeed, we shall, and thank you for everything, Mrs Adamson. I believe you will be critical to our success."

Rather to Clementine's surprise, the lady's cheeks grew pink with pleasure at her words.

"Thank you," Mrs Adamson said, her tone sincere. "You and your father and sisters welcomed me from the moment I arrived, and I am so grateful. It is for that reason that I hope you will heed my words carefully and believe I mean them for the best."

"Of course," Clementine said, wondering to what on earth she was referring.

"Have a care with Stonehaven. He can be remarkably charming, and it would be far too easy for a naive girl to form a *tendre* for him, but he is not the marrying kind. I would not like to see either of your sisters hurt by a man who does not comprehend what tenderness is."

Clementine nodded, her own concerns only underscored by the woman's warning. "Thank you, Mrs Adamson. I confess I had come to the same conclusion, but I doubt we shall see the marquess again anytime soon."

Mrs Adamson smiled, but did not look confident. "I hope you may be right, but Lord Stonehaven is used to having everything his own way, and to getting what he wants. Take care of your sisters, Miss Honeywell."

Clementine agreed she would certainly do so and walked out of the hotel, intending to go down to the beach. As she did so, she saw a young woman walking down the hill. Clementine had never seen her before and was suddenly reminded of Miss Edith's request that she make herself known to Miss Marwick, who would be renting one of the seafront cottages.

"Good day to you!" she called.

The woman paused at hearing her voice, and for a moment Clementine thought she saw a glimmer of irritation, but it vanished so quickly, replaced by a bright smile, that she felt certain she must have imagined it.

"You must be Miss Marwick," Clementine said, holding out her hand to the woman as they drew near.

"I am," she said, and Clementine realised she was very young, perhaps twenty years of age.

"Forgive me for waylaying you. I am Miss Honeywell. My father is Reverend Honeywell, of All Saints' Church. I shan't keep you, for I can see you are busy, but I wished to welcome you and your brother to the town, and to invite you both to tea. My father loves meeting new people," she added with a warm smile.

"You are too kind, Miss Honeywell. My brother travels a good deal, I'm afraid, and is away from home for the time being. Perhaps when he returns. Things are so topsy-turvy with only me and two maids to get everything put to rights. You know what men are for rushing off when there is housework to do," she added ruefully.

Clementine nodded reassuringly. "Of course. But please know that we would very much welcome a visit when the time is right."

"Thank you. That is so very kind of you. I shall be pleased to do so very soon."

Clementine smiled and bade her goodbye, reassured that there was nothing nefarious about the girl, and glad that she could put Miss Edith's mind to rest. Watching as Miss Marwick waved a friendly goodbye, she turned away and carried on down to the beach.

The breeze was cooler down on the sand and Clementine welcomed the faint prickle of sea spray as the waves frothed and bubbled upon the shore. She stood for a long time, watching the rush and foam, the tumble of shells and pull of sand as each wave drew back, taking and giving with each new back and forth. It was calming, somewhat hypnotising, and allowed her to put Mrs Adamson's disquieting words into perspective.

In the first place, Bea was a sensible girl, and no marquess in his right mind was going to seduce a vicar's daughter in a hole–in-the-wall town like Little Valentine. Bea was beloved by all, and the scandal would be appalling. The man would be a fool to consider it. But would he offer marriage, and ought Clementine to stand in her way if he did? She wanted her sister to marry well, did she not? Well, yes. But for love. She might believe Bea capable of snaring a duke, but Clementine would never force her into such a marriage if it did not make her happy.

"Good lord!" she said out loud, raising her head and staring up at the sky where the seagulls wheeled far above her, astonished that she'd had her sister both seduced by and married to the brute in the space of a few minutes. "Clementine Honeywell, what on earth are you thinking?"

"Ah, that is the eternal question, is it not? How I should like to know the answer."

Clementine gave a little shriek of alarm and turned to find the Earl of Beaumarsh's laughing blue eyes gazing down at her. She stared, disbelieving.

"Talking to the birds again, Miss Honeywell?" he asked, his slightly mocking tone softened by the warmth of the smile that accompanied it.

"Oh, drat you!" she said with a huff. "How is it you are always coming upon me in the most embarrassing situations? Are you *trying* to mortify me?"

He laughed at that and shook his head. "I promise I am not, and I find your desire to talk to wildlife most endearing, so please, do not feel even a twinge of discomfort on my behalf. I talk to my horse all the time. He is one of my most trusted advisors," he added gravely.

"I'm sure that's not the same thing at all, and I was not talking to the birds, but to myself," she added, uncertain whether that made matters better or worse.

"Oh, that's definitely worse," he said, his eyes twinkling with mirth as he answered the question she had not voiced.

Clementine rolled her eyes. "How has someone not shot you in a duel? Are you this provoking to all your acquaintances?"

"Oh no. Only my very dear friends."

Clementine started. She was his very dear friend? Her breath hitched, and it took considerable effort to speak easily.

"We ought not linger alone here, tongues will wag," she replied, finding herself back in the position of being unable to meet his gaze. How she wanted to look into his eyes and see if that had been a careless remark, or if he had meant it. Would she even know? Could she tell if he were in earnest, or was it just something men like him said to young ladies? Men like him *and* Lord Stonehaven. Mrs Adamson had not mentioned Lord Beaumarsh, and Clementine supposed she did not know him, but the two men were long-time friends. Were they also birds of a feather?

He nodded and held out his arm to her. After a second's hesitation, Clementine took it, annoyed with herself for the pleasure she found in feeling his strength beneath her hand once more.

"So, what on earth *were* you thinking?" he asked, quirking one blond eyebrow at her.

She levelled a look at him. "Mind your own business, my lord. You'll just have to keep trying to read my mind."

"Oh, I shall," he replied, making her increasingly vexed with him.

What was he playing at?

"Why are you here?" she demanded, unable to keep the words from sounding like an interrogation.

His lips quirked. "Ah, that inquiring mind of yours, Miss Honeywell. It cannot stand a mystery, can it? Well, why don't you work it out? I know how clever you are, I am certain you can unravel the inner workings of an idle peacock like me."

Clementine blushed scarlet as he repeated the harsh words she had flung at him in a temper. "I-I never meant… I ought not…"

"Oh, no," he said, wagging his finger at her, a delighted grin quirking his lips. "No, no. Don't take it back. You were quite correct, I'm afraid. I *am* an idle peacock. It has taken me a good deal of time to understand that is why I have been so damned bored and unhappy of late. But I believe the penny has finally dropped. There now, I cannot give you a greater clue than that without spelling it out for you."

Clementine stared at him. "I cannot make you out at all."

"Well, that's probably not a bad thing," he allowed. "I should hate it if you found *me* boring."

"Oh no," she murmured faintly. "Not boring."

Beaumarsh grinned again, and the expression made her stomach flutter. *Stop acting like a ninny*, she told herself severely, but it made no difference. He looked so ridiculously pleased with himself, and his eyes…oh, his eyes were so blue. She could never miss the sea if he was beside her, for there it was, endless blue.

Clementine groaned, appalled at her own sentimentality.

"Are you unwell?" the earl enquired in concern.

"Probably," she muttered, before shaking her head. "No. Quite well, only… I do not have the slightest notion why you are here, and I would not know where to begin in working it out."

He tutted impatiently. "Don't underestimate yourself. You can do it." Clementine squelched the desire to tell him he was the most maddening man she had ever met, temporarily at least, and took a deep breath.

"Very well. You came to tell me what you have discovered about Stonehaven and Mrs Adamson."

"I'm afraid not," he said apologetically. "Stonehaven was not in the least forthcoming and would not tell me a thing."

Clementine nodded, relieved that the man had some redeeming qualities and would not gossip… or was it only that the story reflected so badly on him he'd not repeat it?

"Then you have come to speak to my father," she said, for her father seemed to hold the earl in high regard, and the feeling appeared mutual.

"That is certainly part of it." Clementine frowned up at him. "I can only assume it is a private matter, then, and I would not dream of interfering."

"It is," he agreed, and there was that disquieting twinkle again. "But I would not dislike your interfering in the least."

She opened her mouth, then closed it again, his cryptic comments too confusing for comment. The odd fluttering in her stomach had become something far more unsettling, and she did not know what to make of it, or of him. Best her father speak to him. He was a sensible man, at least, and would know how to deal with the earl if he started talking in riddles.

"I would not do so for the world," she said firmly. "Come, Papa will be home by now and settling down for a cup of tea. It is the perfect time."

With that, she picked up her pace, practically marching the earl back to the vicarage in the hopes her father would know what to do with him, for she was at a loss.

Chapter 13

To have one's cake, and eat it too…

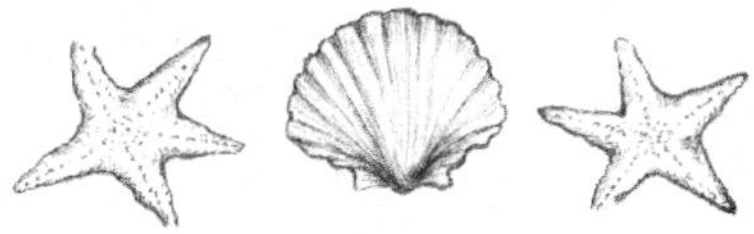

The Vicarage, Little Valentine, South-East Coast of England. 15th July 1815

Clementine sat in the parlour with her sisters, wondering why the two of them were staring at her with such peculiar intensity.

"What?" she demanded, folding her arms. "Do I have a horrid spot on my nose? Or spinach in my teeth? Or have I grown a second head? Why are you both looking at me like that?"

Izzy and Bea exchanged glances, then Bea leaned forward, her lovely expression gentle. "You said Lord Beaumarsh asked you to guess why he was here," she repeated.

"I did," Clementine confirmed, wondering if the entire town had been afflicted with some dread disease that made them ask pointless questions.

"And that he had come to *speak to Papa,"* Izzy added, almost sounding out the words.

"Yes, what of it?"

"She's hopeless," Bea said with a sigh, shaking her head.

"A lost cause," Izzy agreed. "There she is, wanting to marry you off to a duke, and she can't tell when she's landed an earl."

Clementine stared at them, bewildered. "Landed an earl? He's not a fish. A peacock, possibly, but definitely not a fish, and—"

She gazed at them as their meaning filtered through the turmoil in her brain. It did not help matters.

"Ah, there it is," Bea said cheerfully. "She's finally figured it out."

"Just to be certain, let me spell it out in words of few syllables. Clemmie, dearest, the earl has come to ask Papa if he can marry you," Izzy said, speaking in the same tones she might use on an elderly halfwit with hearing deficiencies.

Clementine shot to her feet. "No!" She shook her head, gave a hysterical bark of laughter, marched to the window, and then marched back again. Standing in front of her sisters and gazing down at them, she regarded them with fond exasperation. "You poor little hen-wits—" she began, just as the door opened.

"Ah, Clemmie, my dearest," her father said, bubbling with excitement. "There you are! I told you she'd be with her sisters, my lord. Now, girls, you must leave Clementine alone for a moment, for the earl has something most important he wishes to say to her."

Slanting 'I told you so' glances at her, Izzy and Bea rushed from the room, their muffled laughter and squeals of delight only too audible. Clementine, by contrast, stood frozen in place, shocked to her core.

She did not move, even as her father winked at her and closed the door, leaving her alone with the Earl of Beaumarsh.

"Ah," he said dryly. "I see you hadn't figured it out after all."

Clementine stared at him. Her heart was beating a hectic tattoo in her chest, and she did not know whether to laugh or to cry. Perhaps both. Yes, both at once were distinct possibilities. Hysteria seemed to her a perfectly reasonable response to an offer of marriage from an earl. From *this* earl.

"Is this a joke?" she managed, startled by the faint quality of her voice.

He shook his head, his expression gentle. "I'm afraid not. You'll have to take me seriously. And please remember that, whilst

I *am* an idle peacock, I do have feelings. Please take a moment to reflect before you laugh in my face or run away screaming. Or run and then laugh. I'm certain you are contemplating something of the sort."

A strangled giggle escaped her, his words touching so close to the truth she couldn't help herself.

His lips quirked, and that endearing smile made her stomach lurch again. "I thought as much." He gestured to the settee, moving slowly, as if afraid to spook her. "Might we sit down?"

Clementine nodded, but seemed unable to make her legs work. Apparently accustomed to dealing with hysterical females—was that reassuring?—Lord Beaumarsh took her arm and guided her to the settee. Clementine sat, put her hands in her lap and stared at them, wondering how she had got here. It had started out as a perfectly agreeable but quite unremarkable day. What had happened to it?

"Now, then, I'm sure this has all come as a most unpleasant shock to you," he said, his tone perfectly reasonable. "And you are wondering what on earth I am playing at. Well, if you will bear with me, I shall explain. Or attempt to. You will note that I am not quite comfortable with this situation myself," he added ruefully.

Clementine glanced up at him again. *He's nervous.* The realisation was startling. Why on earth was *he* nervous? The Earl of Beaumarsh was a catch, one of the prizes of the marriage mart. What had he to be nervous about? Any girl in her right mind would snap his hand off if he proposed marriage. Well, apart from her, obviously. She wouldn't. Would she?

She pushed the question aside. Obviously, she would refuse him, because… because this was insane. He'd obviously lost his mind. He could have any woman he crooked his finger at. What on earth would induce him to offer for her?

"Why?" she demanded, finally having got a hold of her wits. "Why me? We hardly know each other. You didn't even like me when we first met."

"You liked me less," he retorted.

"True, but that's by the by," she replied briskly, unsettled by the delighted smile he returned when she agreed with him.

"No, it isn't, it's entirely the point. I don't dislike you the least bit now. Indeed, I like you very well."

Clementine snorted. "Well, that is reassuring. I am heartened to discover you do not go about proposing marriage to females you dislike."

He grinned. "Not usually. Indeed, this is my first proposal, so I beg you will forgive me if I am making a mess of it."

"Oh, certainly. If you are using me as an exercise to improve your chances with another lady, this makes a great deal more sense," she said with growing agitation.

She started as he reached out and took her hand. Her gaze flew to his, her heart picking up speed again. The poor thing would run out of steam soon if it kept up this pace. Perhaps that was the best thing. If she fainted, she would miss the rest of his speech. But Clementine was far too sensible to faint and instead got lost in his sea-blue eyes again. Drat them for being so pretty.

"Miss Honeywell," he said softly. "Clementine."

Her breath hitched. His deep voice speaking her given name gave her chills, and the feel of his hand, oh, his *hand*, so strong and warm, clasping hers, made her flush. He had removed his gloves, and his bare skin against hers was an intimacy for which she was unprepared. Suddenly she was hot and cold all at once and her insides trembled with… with *something*.

"No," she said, and surged to her feet, pulling free of his hold. She shook her head and paced away to stare out of the window, her arms wrapped around her body as if to hold herself together. "No, I cannot allow you to do this, to say another word. I cannot imagine what maggot has got into your head, but this is sheer folly. I am on the shelf, with no dowry worth mentioning, as well as being far too independent and outspoken and… and a meddling busybody. I am a nobody from a town no one has ever heard of, and you would be a fool to ask for my hand when you might have a beautiful, well-behaved young woman with a fortune and…and… what are you smiling at, drat you?"

"I had a horrible feeling you were about to tell me you could not marry me because you cannot stand the sight of me," he admitted with a shrug. "Because I am a shallow fribble not worth your time. But you said only that *you* are not worthy of *me,* which only proves how badly I have upset your equilibrium. Do come and sit down again, my dear. Perhaps a glass of brandy would restore your spirits? You'll have to do better than that, you know, if you truly wish to be rid of me."

Clementine did not know what she wanted, but a glass of brandy did not seem a terrible idea. "Brandy," she agreed, putting a hand to her temples, which had commenced a dull throbbing.

Beaumarsh got up and walked to the decanter her father kept on a small side table for guests in need of a bracer. He poured her a surprisingly generous measure, and one for himself, before sitting down again.

"Are you trying to addle my brain with alcohol?" she asked, regarding the glass sceptically.

"Would it work?"

"Possibly."

"Excellent."

He sat down beside her, and they sipped their drinks for a few moments in silence.

"Clementine?"

His caressing voice sent little darts of pleasure rushing beneath her skin, and she closed her eyes, fighting the desire to run from the room. She had not realised how very dangerous he was. Not until now, when it was too late, and she had no defences ready to wield against this unforeseen attack on her emotions.

"Please let me explain."

She nodded, knowing she must listen, no matter how afraid she was.

"Your father is a wise man, Clementine, and he has helped me more than I realised until I had time to reflect upon his words. You see, I had always viewed marriage as a transaction, for that is what it often is for men of my class. I offer a title and wealth, and the woman offers herself, and her dowry and connections, or land. It matters little if the two people even like each other, only that they increase the value of the earldom. Yet my parents lived that way, two strangers who despised each other, sharing a house. I see it all the time: the bickering, the tit for tat and one-upmanship. It is a wretched way to live, and I do not wish for it."

Clementine swallowed, horribly afraid of what he might say next.

"Your father said I ought to find my soulmate, but I'm afraid I am too old and too cynical to believe such things exist, at least for me. A good-hearted man like your father, a man who works tirelessly for the benefit of others, a man like that might deserve such things, but not me. And even if I did, I think I might run from it, for fear of how I should feel if it were taken from me."

"I can understand that," Clementine said, finding in this at least, something she could comprehend. "Losing Mama nearly destroyed him. All of us, actually."

"I am not brave enough for such heartbreak," he admitted. "But all the same, I should like my wife to be my friend, to be someone I like and might share a home with, might raise children with. But she would need to be a rare sort of person. For a start, she would need to be cleverer than me, and sharp-witted, so she might keep me in line when I am getting too top-lofty. It happens, you know," he added with a wry smile. "When you have a title and everyone agrees with everything you say."

"You don't say," she managed, which made him laugh. Oh, and that laugh, deep and rumbling… it resonated inside her, and the little rushes of sensation seemed to light fires that burned away reason and all her good intentions.

"She must also be interesting, and out of the ordinary, with a mind that will keep fascinating me and keep me on my toes."

She quirked an eyebrow, but he carried on.

"A managing sort of female, who can entrap murderers, and stave off toadies, and keep my household in order. And me too, no doubt."

"No doubt," she replied, sipping her brandy and wondering why his words, rather than the contents of her glass, seemed to be making her feel intoxicated.

He shifted closer, lowering his voice. His brandy-scented breath fluttered against her neck, making her shiver. "She must be beautiful, for I am a vain peacock, you know, and I could not wed a woman I did not desire."

Clementine swallowed and closed her eyes against the tears that prickled there. It wasn't fair. He wasn't playing fair. No one had ever said such lovely things to her, things she had not realised how much she craved hearing. She was a sensible girl, not the kind to be swayed by romantic nonsense and sentimental words, and he knew that, so he had demolished any argument she might make before she could make it. And oh, how she wanted to say yes, but if she said yes, she would be married to a man who would not love her, and who she very much feared would consume her heart as her mother had done her father's. Then what?

"I've just begun our ladies' club," she said, her voice quavering.

She felt his gaze on her face, his attention absolute.

"Which is important to you."

"It is. My sisters are perfectly capable of running it with Mrs Adamson, I know. I am not indispensable, yet—"

"You are indispensable to me," he said, and she turned to stare at him, surprised by the sincerity of his words. "As the Countess of Beaumarsh, you will have far more power to change things for women than you do as Miss Honeywell, you know. The club will do wonderful things in Little Valentine, and you can still be a patron, still be a part of their plans, and donate as much money as you desire to their causes. I will give you a generous allowance and I will not question what use you put it to. That will be your own affair. I will also see to Caspar's education and settle a dowry on both Daisy and your sisters. You'll be able to give Beatrice the splendid season you so want for her. Izzy too, if she wishes for it."

Clementine gasped. She had not even considered what this would mean for her family, let alone the town. How selfish she was! "That's a dirty trick," she observed, realising now that he would not give her any reason to refuse him.

He laughed. "It is, and I shall use every weapon in my arsenal, my dear, for I do not wish for you to turn me down. I give you my solemn promise, however, that I will do everything in my power to ensure you never have cause to regret it. I have many more arguments lined up if you would like to hear them."

She already knew what she would say, for she could not refuse him. No matter her regret over the club, no matter her fear over how much he might come to mean to her, she could not run away, not when her marriage would bring such good fortune to everyone she loved. Clementine Honeywell was many things, but she was *not* a coward.

She turned her head, her heart thudding in her ears.

"Ask me, then," she said, her voice sounding strange and far off.

He gazed at her, searching her eyes for a long moment before setting down his glass and taking hers too. He slid from the settee in a smooth move that took him to one knee and, as he took her hand in hers, he was smiling. Clementine wondered how many times he would break her heart in the years to come but knew there would be compensations. Her family would be secure, no matter what. They would send Caspar to an excellent school and fund his education, and Beatrice would have her chance to shine. There would be a fine home and all the challenges that would bring. She would have security and, if she were lucky, there would be children to love. She had never allowed herself to mourn the fact that she would be childless, but now that she was to be given the chance of having them, she realised she wanted that chance. She wanted it badly enough to risk her heart by putting it in this man's keeping.

Her father said he was a good man, she reminded herself, and her father was the best judge of character she had ever known.

"Clementine Honeywell, would you do me the very great honour of becoming my wife?"

Clementine stared at him, felt her heart give an agitated thud in her chest, and took a deep breath. "I will."

Chapter 14

Seagulls, upside down or otherwise.

The Vicarage, Little Valentine, South-East Coast of England. 15th July 1815

Beau watched his fiancée carefully as the house erupted in chaos around her. Shouts and exclamations of surprise and joy rang out and the children ran about madly, not understanding the commotion but reacting to it all the same. Throughout everything, Clementine remained composed, smiling and receiving hugs and kisses, and thanking everyone for their words of congratulations. He suppressed a twinge of anxiety, knowing she was still in shock, that he had overwhelmed her and nigh on blackmailed her. He had held out the carrot of his wealth and position to secure not only her sister's happiness and that of her family, but the female population of the entire town. It *had* been a dirty trick, but he had needed her to say yes. He had not realised how much he had needed a positive answer until he'd been making his case, then it had become imperative that she agreed for reasons that he was disinclined to wonder about.

He smiled as the nanny and the cook and the maid of all work came rushing up from various parts of the house, chattering with excitement. They were all included in their celebrating, and he felt the warmth and love that lived in this house wrap about him. It was almost tangible, and he realised what a responsibility he had taken on. He would remove Clementine from the home where she was a beloved and cherished presence, and take her to his own. If he did not do things correctly, she would not flourish there, and all the colour and sparkle that he delighted in when in her company would wither and die. He could not allow that to happen. No matter what he had to do, he would ensure her happiness, first and foremost. He had made a promise that she would never regret giving him this chance, and he had meant it. He would not let her down. The realisation that he had something, some*one*, to live up to now might once have irritated him, or concerned him, but it was strangely satisfying to know he had a reason to do better.

"Congratulations, my lord," Reverend Honeywell said, beaming at him and shaking his hand vigorously. "Or may I call you 'son?'" he added, a merry twinkle in his eye.

Beau laughed, relieved and bolstered to know her father seemed to hold none of the reservations that he did. "You may. Or Sylvester, if you prefer."

"Sylvester," the man repeated, as if trying it out. "I like that. A good, strong name. Mind, you'll need to be strong and adaptable to keep that girl of mine out of trouble. Headstrong, she is, and clever with it, but you know that."

"I believe I do, sir," Beau replied, smiling as he watched Clementine across the room.

She looked up then, perhaps feeling the weight of his gaze and colour flooded her cheeks. The sight made heat rush beneath his skin, the knowledge that she would be his now giving him a strangely possessive feeling he had never known before. It settled in his chest, a warm sensation that grounded him as he realised he belonged to her too. They would be joined together, a partnership of a kind he had never expected to have. She would celebrate his successes with him, as he would celebrate hers, and if he behaved like an arse, she would have something to say about it too. The thought was both shocking and reassuring.

He'd never been accountable to anyone, not since he'd reached his majority… or even before that, given he'd become the earl when he was just a boy. His mother counted, perhaps, up to a point, but she had spoiled and indulged him to such a degree her scoldings had only ever been superficial, and she had delighted in his scandalous reputation. Her words been no more than lip service, she simply didn't mean them. Clementine would mean them. Every word.

"It's an excellent match," the reverend said, and Beau assumed he meant for Clementine, for her future security, but as he turned and met the man's eyes, he realised he was a fool to think it. "You'll be the making of each other," he told Beau, his voice quavering a little.

Startled, Beau watched as the reverend fumbled for his handkerchief and wiped his eyes before giving his nose a vigorous blow. Beau opened his mouth to say something, but found himself at a loss.

"You'll be as happy as I was with her mother," the reverend added, misty-eyed. "I can see that you will."

Once again, Beau tried to speak, a denial ready to burst from him. *No.* Certainly, they would be content, but not that… that terrifying depth of feeling. No. Not that. Yet, he could not say it. Not to this man. So he simply swallowed the anxiety the reverend's words gave him and smiled blandly.

"Excuse me. I believe I should like to steal my fiancée away for a while. If you have no objection."

"Goodness, no. Of course, you must. Take her for a walk. There's no rush. Young people in love must have their privacy," the fellow said, beaming as he called for Clementine to fetch her bonnet so that Sylvester could take her for a walk.

A few minutes later, Beau walked out of the vicarage garden with Clementine on his arm. They promenaded in complete silence for a few moments before she glanced up at him.

"Well, this is awkward."

Beau laughed. "And here I was racking my brain for ways not to draw attention to that fact. I ought to know better."

"You really should. If we are to be married— Goodness, but I still cannot believe I am saying that out loud," she said in bewilderment. "But *if* we are, you must understand that I am not the kind to beat around the bush. If a thing needs saying, I shall say it, whether you like it or not, I'm afraid. So, if you wish to cry off, now is your chance." She slanted an expectant glance at him and Beau grinned at her.

"Sorry, love. I'm not letting you off the hook that easily. You'll have to try a good deal harder to dissuade me."

She sighed and shook her head. "You poor fool. I do not think you have the slightest notion what you have done."

"Yes, I do. I've done the only sensible thing in a life filled with inanity and foolishness."

"I cannot abide inanity," she warned him, though her eyes danced with mirth. "I am very fond of the ridiculous, and I believe I have a lively sense of humour, but I have no patience for foolishness."

"Nor for fools, yet here we are," he remarked dryly.

She tutted at that and rolled her eyes. "You are no fool, my Lord Beaumarsh. The face you show the world might be that of a shallow fribble, but the truth is far different. I have learned that much of you, else we would not be having this conversation."

"I am glad you think so," he said, covering her hand where it rested upon his sleeve. "I shall try to make you proud of me." She looked so startled by this remark that he frowned. "Do you not think I can do it?"

Clementine shook her head and for a moment his breath caught until she said, "I *am* proud of you!"

He waved this away. "Yes, yes, for being an earl, for having a handsome face and form, I know *that*, but those things were given to me. I didn't earn them. I should like to earn your respect."

"You already have it, my lord," she replied, her voice soft, curiosity alive in her eyes.

"No," he said impatiently. "You do not understand. But you shall, I promise."

She smiled then, a sweet smile that stole his breath and shifted in his chest. "I am certain I shall," she said, a quality to her gaze he had never seen before.

Was that trust? He hoped so, but if it was not, he would earn that too.

"When will you be married?" Izzy asked, a combination of excitement and sadness in her voice that touched Clementine deeply.

It was late, past midnight, and yet none of them were ready to sleep, too overwhelmed by the events of the day. They sat cross-legged on her bed like they had often done as children, a plate of biscuits between them.

"Papa must read the banns, so in two weeks, after the third Sunday. Lord Beaumarsh does not wish for a long engagement," Clementine said self-consciously.

Bea smothered a giggle, and Clementine elbowed her.

"It's all happening rather quickly," she admitted with a bewildered laugh. "And I feel utterly wretched about the club. What on earth is to be done about Mrs Jenner and her vile husband? I can't forget about her and leave her to her fate. I have responsibilities, and then there's the everyday things, what about the word games and riddles for the paper? Who will do those?"

"Oh, Clemmie, don't be daft," Bea said at once. "This is your future! You cannot give it up for anyone. We will not forget Mrs Jenner and will find a way to help her, so do not insult us by believing otherwise. If you still want to do the word games, you can always send them. You're going to Kent, not Timbuktu, and think of all the good you will do as the Countess of Beaumarsh."

"That's what he said," Clementine replied wryly. "You should have heard him listing all the reasons I ought to marry him for the good of the family *and* the women of England, never mind Little Valentine. He's far craftier than I gave him credit for."

"It's true, though," Izzy agreed. "You can be our patron."

Clementine nodded slowly. She was still coming to terms with the fact that she would be a wealthy woman with money of her own. "He said he would give me a generous income and not question what I do with it."

"Goodness," Izzy said in wonder. "What else did he say, Clemmie? Does he love you?"

"Don't be silly," Clementine said at once. "It's not that sort of marriage."

"Isn't it?" Bea asked, watching Clementine with too much attention. Her sister was so lovely, those who did not know her often thought she must not be terribly clever, but Clementine was very aware she had an insightful nature. Bea comprehended a good deal more about what people really meant when they spoke than Clementine was comfortable with. "Don't you love him?"

Clementine opened her mouth to say she did not, but found the words stuck in her throat. "I-I don't know," she said instead. "I'm not certain how to tell. I like him very much. I enjoy his company, and he makes me laugh. He also—"

She blushed. Her sisters leaned closer.

"Well, don't stop there!" Izzy said impatiently. "He also *what?*"

Clementine covered her face with her hands and took a deep breath. "Oh, I don't know. It's silly, only, when he holds my hand or… or looks at me a certain way, it's like my entire body lights up."

Bea sighed, clutching her arms around her. "Yes," she said simply.

Clementine gave her a sharp glance, recalled to her senses and her job as the eldest sister.

"Bea," she said sternly. "Whilst we are on the subject of the dangers of men, Mrs Adamson told me I must warn you, and you, Izzy, about Lord Stonehaven. She says you must be on your guard around him. As he will no doubt be attending the wedding, you will be bound to see him again. She told me to tell you that you must not form any romantic notions about him. He's not the marrying kind and does not know what tenderness means. He may be friends with Lord Beaumarsh, but they are different men. Mrs Adamson seems to know him well, and she does not trust him. Neither do I. You must not encourage him, Bea. Is that understood?"

"Yes, Clemmie, of course," Bea said with a placid smile.

Clementine narrowed her eyes, a niggle of doubt still lingering. Bea could be surprisingly stubborn when the mood took her. "Well, good," she said, still watching her sister, who returned her gaze, her expression guileless.

Izzy reached for a biscuit and took a bite, chewing thoughtfully. "I can't believe you won't live here anymore in a few weeks. We shall all miss you terribly."

"And I-I shall m-miss you all too," Clementine managed, then burst into tears.

"Oh, love. Don't worry," Izzy said, as both she and Bea enveloped her in a hug. "It's going to be splendid. We both like Lord Beaumarsh very much, and you're going to be terribly happy."

"You will be," Bea agreed with certainty.

"But if you are not, we shall come and rescue you," Izzy said firmly. "I promise you, Clementine. Just give us a signal. Like… Like saying you saw a seagull flying upside down. If you say or write that, we shall know at once you are in trouble, and we shall storm Cavendish House and run away with you!" Clementine, already choked with tears, sputtered at her sister's outlandish imagination and the fierceness of her promise, and the three women fell about laughing.

Marley House, Battle, South-East Coast of England. 31st July 1815

"You, my lord, are a coward."

Beau regarded Stonehaven blearily across several empty wine bottles and shrugged. "I never denied it. The less time I spend in Little Valentine before the wedding, the less chance there is she will come to her senses and call the whole thing off. I'm not entirely stupid, you know." He smirked, though his guts were in a knot. He had almost gone to visit Clementine a dozen or more times over the past weeks, but had only seen her on Sundays in church, when her father had read the banns. There had been too many curious gazes, too much interest from the town, agog with the news of their nuptials, to get a moment alone. Beau still wasn't certain if he was relieved by that or not.

He wanted to see her, he realised, to ask her how she felt, to discover how plans were coming along for the wedding celebrations, and to tell her about Cavendish House, about his plans for it, and for their future. It could wait, he assured himself. They had the rest of their lives, but he had to get her to the altar first. Though he knew she was a sensible girl and would do the right thing for her family, and for her precious town, the possibility that she might marry him for those reasons alone made him feel a little sick. He wanted to ask her if she would marry him anyway, if those things did not come with the deal, but he didn't dare. She was too honest, too forthright, and there was a high chance he would not like her answer. Best not to discuss it at all.

"Craven," Stonehaven slurred, shaking his head. "That's what it is. I shall not run away and hide when *I* get engaged."

Beau snorted. "And who is the lucky lady?" he asked dryly.

"Mrs Adamson," the marquess replied, startling Beau so much he almost dropped his glass.

"I beg your pardon?"

Stonehaven grinned at him, his eyes glassy with drink. "Surprise!" he said merrily. "Didn't expect that, did you? But you're not the only one who can do something seni—senibal—*sensible*, you know."

"But the woman won't even speak to you," Beau protested.

Stonehaven tapped the side of his nose. "You don't know. Don't understand. Be fine. You'll see," he replied confidently.

Beau frowned and hoped Stonehaven's wits returned to him when he sobered up. He had no interest or energy to consider his friend's odd start, however, for his own marriage would happen tomorrow and, whilst the best man might have the hangover from hell for the occasion, Beau would not join him. He would not mess this up. Not if he could help it.

Chapter 15

The new Countess of Beaumarsh makes a promise.

The Vicarage, Little Valentine, South-East Coast of England, 1st August 1815.

Two weeks had disappeared with such speed Clementine felt her feet had not touched the ground since the day Lord Beaumarsh had proposed to her. She had hardly seen him since and cynically wondered if he were keeping his distance to ensure he did not do or say something to make her change her mind. She had not been bored, however. Dress fittings, constant visitors to the house bearing felicitations, and meetings to complete the plans for the ladies' club had all kept her constantly busy, and now the big day was finally upon her. Yet still she fretted over all the things she would do tomorrow if she were not marrying Lord Beaumarsh. Organising Papa and helping him manage his flock, getting her ladies' club up and running… No. Not *her* club.

Mrs Adamson had agreed to take over the management of the club, with Clementine as patron. She had not had the nerve to ask Beau how much money she would actually be able to call her own, but with her sisters help had agreed her first donation would be a generous sum, but not so much that would cause her husband to blanch if their estimations of 'generous' did not align. She could always make another donation in the following months. For now, this would be more than enough to pay for tea and cakes for many meetings and to get things started. She hoped she would be able to provide them with a piano, but this was such an outrageous expense she would need to ask Beaumarsh about that after they were married. Mrs Adamson had told her she would keep proper accounts, so Clementine could see exactly where the money was going.

At least the persistent stream of well-wishers to the vicarage had given Clementine the opportunity to tell her guests about the club, news which had been received with varying degrees of interest and warmth. It would be a success, she assured herself. Her sisters and Mrs Adamson and Clara would make certain of it. Would her marriage be such a success too? She wondered, for she would be on her own with *that*. Well, no. That was precisely the point. She would not be on her own. She would be married, joined such that no man might put asunder.

Her stomach twisted.

"Oh, Clementine!"

She turned from the window as her sisters came into the room. They both looked ravishing in new gowns paid for by her husband-to-be.

"Oh, you look so… so *beautiful!"* Izzy said, her voice thick with emotion. "Even Bea can't hold a candle to you today, I swear it."

Clementine laughed at his nonsense. "What a plumper. Good heavens, no one will cast a look in my direction with Beatrice looking like an angel fallen from the skies."

"Oh, do stop," Bea said impatiently. "Izzy is right, so stop trying to deflect the compliment. You look utterly perfect. Lord Beaumarsh will not be able to take his eyes from you."

Clementine turned back to the looking glass, considering the silvery blue gown. It shimmered in the sunlight as she moved, and she admitted she had never looked better. Nervously, she touched a finger to the daunting row of diamonds and sapphires that encircled her throat. More diamonds and sapphires adorned her wrists and ears, and sparkled in her hair. She must get used to such things, she supposed, but to wear the Cavendish diamonds was a responsibility for which she had not accounted.

She turned away again, suddenly worrying about her father and all the things he needed to do. "Has Papa got everything ready? Has he remembered to pick up the order of service, and to—"

"He has everything in hand," Izzy said firmly. "I went through everything with him again first thing this morning and put everything he needs in a leather satchel on his desk. I will ensure he does not leave without it, do not fret. I can do this, Clementine."

"Of course you can," Clementine replied, chastened. "I beg your pardon."

"Oh, don't be ridiculous," Izzy said at once, grinning at her. "Just stop worrying. Everything will be perfect."

Clementine hugged her father one last time as Izzy pressed another clean handkerchief into his hand. He'd been terribly emotional for the past few days and now, seeing his daughter in all her finery, it had become too much.

"I'm sorry," he sniffed, making use of the hanky. "It's just I so wish your mama could see you. Which is foolish, for of course she is looking down at us and shaking her head at me for turning into a watering pot, but really, Mary, look at her," he said, raising his eyes to the heavens.

Clementine swallowed down the lump in her throat, but was saved from having to find a sensible reply to such a lovely sentiment, because there was a sharp rap at the front door.

"Oh, who can that be? Devil take them!" Izzy said crossly.

"Language, Izzy," her father scolded with a fond smile. "All are welcome on this joyous occasion."

"Not if they make the bride late for her wedding, they're not," Izzy grumbled, going to the parlour door to see who it was, but Polly had already run to open it.

"Mind out, child. Don't keep an old lady standing on the doorstep. Don't you know your manners?"

Poor Polly stared in shock as the grand old lady barged in.

"You there," the woman said, pointing at Izzy. "Stop gawking and fetch the reverend for me."

"I'm here, my lady," their father said hurriedly, bustling past Izzy and into the hallway.

"That is 'your grace,'" the woman said, with all the *hauteur* only many centuries of breeding could give. "I am the Dowager Duchess of Hawkney."

"I beg your pardon, your grace," the reverend said, not in the least perturbed whilst his children all gaped at the woman in astonishment. "I had not heard that Hatherley Hall was once more occupied."

The woman, who was tall and slender, seemed to Clementine to be all angles and pointy corners, with high cheekbones and sharply defined features. She was dressed superbly, with a large emerald ring on her right hand that flashed in the sunlight. Her hair shone pure white, and she bore an unmistakable air of authority and power. She scoffed at their father's observation.

"If you ask me, it is occupied by vermin and fools," she said scathingly. "But that is why I am here. I need staff. If you would be so good as to give me a list of local people you recommend as being nice in their habits and trustworthy, I should be grateful. Also, I should like you to call upon me during the week. I have not been in residence here for many years, and I should like to reacquaint myself with the goings-on. You will attend me on Wednesday at eleven a.m.. Do not be late. I cannot abide tardiness."

"Yes, your grace," the reverend agreed easily.

Clementine opened her mouth to remind her sister of the appointments book, but Izzy had already scurried away to write down the date, knowing he would not remember it otherwise.

"Very good. Now then, what's this? A wedding?" she asked, her pale grey-blue eyes sharp with interest.

"Yes. My daughter, Miss Honeywell, is to be wed this day to the Earl of Beaumarsh," the reverend said with obvious pride, drawing Clementine forward to make her curtsy.

"Beaumarsh?" the dowager said with a snort. "A pretty fribble. Amusing, though, and certainly plump in the pocket. Quite a catch for *you*, miss," she said, leaning on her ebony walking stick and regarding Clementine with narrow-eyed interest. "You're no spring chicken, are you? At least four and twenty unless I miss my guess. How d'you manage it, eh?"

Clementine blushed, torn between irritation and delight at her outrageous manners. Perhaps she would emulate this kind of audacity when she was old and cantankerous.

"I could not say, your grace," she replied evenly.

"Hmmm." The dowager eyed her dubiously, and the reverend hurried to fill the gap before either Clementine or she could say something shocking.

"This young lady is my middle daughter, Miss Beatrice, your grace, and—"

"Here, Papa," Izzy said breathlessly, sketching a haphazard bob as she returned.

"And this is Miss Isabelle," he finished with relief.

"Hmph," the dowager said, regarding Izzy dubiously before turning her attention back to Bea. "My, you're an incomparable if ever there was one. You may visit me when your father comes… and *you,"* she added as an afterthought, regarding Izzy. She looked back at Bea once more, a calculating look in her eyes. "Why ain't you the one marrying an earl?"

Bea turned pink to the tips of her ears and took a step back.

"Because she does not have an ounce of cunning, unlike her elder sister," Clementine said tartly, moving forward and taking the dowager by the arm. "Thank you so much for calling upon us, we appreciate you taking the time. My father will call upon you, my sisters too, but if you will excuse me, I am to be married shortly, and the earl would be dismayed were his bride not to arrive at the altar at the arranged hour. I'm sure you understand. Good day to you."

With that, she hustled the woman back outside and closed the door. Letting out a breath, she turned to see her family regarding her in astonishment.

"Everything will be perfect, hmmm?" she said, giving Izzy the benefit of a sceptical expression.

Izzy pulled a face and shrugged. "The dowager duchess must be the exception that proves the rule."

Bells rang and the congregation cheered as Beaumarsh emerged from the dimly lit church into dazzling sunlight. Rice rained down all around them, with people he did not know coming up and shaking his hand, wishing him well and smiling.

Finally, he saw a familiar face as his valet darted forward to grasp his hand. "Well done, my lord. Never been so proud of you in all my days. God's honest truth," Kirby said, sniffing fiercely before rushing off again.

Beau felt utterly disoriented, like a mole emerging from velvety darkness into the glare of a summer sun. The entire service had gone past in a blur and he could only pray he had said the right thing at the right time. Well, Honeywell had pronounced them man and wife so he must have done something right, and Stonehaven hadn't fallen over laughing either.

Well, that was it then. He was married. His stomach, which had been knotted in a tangle of apprehension since the moment he'd woken at four a.m. after a restless night, twisted harder.

Cautiously, he turned his head to look at his bride. God, but she was lovely.

He had known it, obviously. He had eyes, after all, but something about the gown, about the way she had done her hair, the glow in her eyes and her pink cheeks, about knowing she was his… that changed everything. She was *beautiful.*

Feeling his gaze upon her, she looked up at him. Happiness shone in her eyes. Trepidation was there too, shyness and anxiety, but *that* was definitely happiness. The knot in his guts unravelled. He could do this.

"Countess," he said, smiling at her as he led her from the church.

"My lord," she replied, the words somewhat breathless.

It was only a short walk to the vicarage, where the wedding breakfast awaited them. It was to be a simple affair, much to his mother's disappointment, for she had wanted him to wait until the season was in full swing again and marry at St George's in Hanover Square. Even had his wife-to-be not been violently opposed to the idea, he would still never have agreed. So, his mama, quite correctly deducing her august presence would overwhelm the paltry affair they'd chosen, had informed him she would expect her first glimpse of his wife at Cavendish House, where she would make her welcome.

His wife, he thought with a grin.

"What are you smirking about?"

He turned to see Clementine regarding him curiously.

"My *wife*," he said out loud. "I am feeling smug and pleased with myself, for I have stolen a march on all those other fellows that do not yet know this delightful town exists, and stolen away its treasure before they got the chance."

She shook her head sadly. "You are a ridiculous person," she said soberly.

"It's too late to change your mind now," he told her, his voice severe. "So you may as well come to terms with it."

"Oh, I knew you were ridiculous from the beginning. I believe I told you as much when you accused me of arranging a romantic liaison with Mr Kirby."

Beau nodded, remembering. "Ah, yes. So you did. Well, it's your own fault, then."

"Entirely," she agreed, gazing up at him.

"Don't do that," he said, suddenly hit with the urgent desire to haul her off into a shady corner and show her what it meant to be married to the Earl of Beaumarsh.

"I beg your pardon?" She looked adorably confused, bless her.

"Don't look at me like that. Not yet, anyway," he added. "You can look at me like that later all you want. Indeed, I insist that you do. It's most… invigorating."

She turned pink, which delighted him to no end, but did not stop him from wishing the wedding breakfast was over and done with.

Clementine wished the wedding breakfast would go on a good deal longer. The reality of being married to the Earl of Beaumarsh was finally sinking in. Moreover, their wedding night, which had hardly been something she had failed to consider, was approaching all too rapidly.

Not being a complete ninny, she had worked many of the details out for herself but had approached Mrs Mabbs to confirm her suspicions. Though the children's nanny had outlived two husbands, the conversation mortified her, and she would only confirm or deny Clementine's questions, but she supposed it was likely still more information than many women had on their wedding night. She would just have to leave things up to Beaumarsh, a circumstance that bothered her somewhat as she did not like it when she did not know exactly what to expect.

If she were honest, which she always was—with herself, at least—she had been overwhelmed with pride to walk from the church to the vicarage on her husband's arm. Whilst she did not care a whit for his title, she could not deny how splendid he looked, how very handsome and commanding, every inch a nobleman, and she knew just how much all the other young ladies envied her. She was only human, after all, and had never been envied before, to her knowledge. Plus, discovering that he was still the same person and had not suddenly turned into some unknown tyrant she must fear angering, was also reassuring. The nonsensical conversation they had conducted on their short walk to her family home had gone a long way to calming her riotous nerves, but now they were making themselves known once more.

"You going away now?" Caspar said, running up to her, his little face crinkling with concern.

Clementine, grasping his sticky fingers before he plastered them all over her silk skirts, leaned in, pressing a kiss to his soft cheek.

"Not just yet, but soon," she said, feeling her stomach flutter with nerves.

"See you again, though?" he asked earnestly.

"Of course you will," she said, wiping his hands with a napkin before hauling him into her lap. "Beaumarsh has said you may all come and stay with me in the autumn, for as long as you wish.

Isn't that lovely? And I'm not very far away, so I can come back and visit you too, very often." The words calmed her, for they were true. Beaumarsh had been generous in all things, and so very kind.

Caspar nodded. "Bea and Izzy not going, though?"

"No. And you still have Uncle Bertie," she said, the name by which the children called her father. "And Nanny Mabbs, and Mrs Adie and Polly. So many people love you. Aren't you lucky?"

Caspar nodded. "More cake?" he asked thoughtfully.

Clementine nodded and set him down again. "Yes, there's more wedding cake if you'd like. Ask Nanny Mabbs. She'll fetch you some, darling."

Caspar ran off before she could give him a last kiss, but she smiled as she watched him run across the room to find his nanny.

"Well, my lady," said a deep voice from over her shoulder. "I believe we should depart, or we will not reach Cavendish House until late."

Clementine looked around, seeing her husband looking down at her. "Oh. *My lady.* That's me," she said inanely, but he laughed and held out his hand to her.

"It is, unless I did something very wrong this afternoon?"

"Oh, no. It will just take a little getting used to. I suppose I had better change, then. I cannot be travelling in this," Clementine said with some regret, though she had a few lovely new things thanks to Madame Auguste, including an evening gown in the exquisite blue silk she'd been sighing over for weeks.

"It is a pity," Beaumarsh agreed, a look in his eyes that made her stomach flutter and her heart do an agitated little dance behind her ribs.

"Well, I shall be two shakes of a lamb's tail," she said, and then regretted it, for surely that was not the sort of thing a countess would say. Oh, well. This countess would say it, and a good deal more besides. Best he get accustomed to the notion now.

Far from being appalled by her cant remark, Beaumarsh's smile widened, and Clementine hurried off.

Less than forty minutes later and her new husband was handing her up into his carriage. Four splendid bay horses stood waiting patiently, coats gleaming in the sunlight. Beaumarsh climbed in after her and they waved as her family and friends cheered and threw more rice.

Clementine felt her throat grow tight as her sisters wept, hugging each other as her father blew her kisses and Caspar ran beside the carriage until Mrs Mabbs caught him. Polly held little Daisy, the two of them smiling and waving, and Clementine felt a tear slide down her cheek as she left Little Valentine and everything she had known behind.

"Here."

She looked up as Beaumarsh handed her a handkerchief.

"I'm sorry," she said, her voice thick. "I promise you have not married a watering pot, only—"

"Only you have married a man who is little more than a stranger and put yourself entirely in his hands, and now he is taking you away from your friends and family. Indeed, you are quite an extraordinary creature to feel even a little perturbed by such an everyday occurrence," he said, deadpan.

Clementine gave a choked laugh and returned a watery smile. "Well, who would have thought it? Lord Beaumarsh knowing exactly the right thing to say."

"Oh, don't get used to it. It's a rare occurrence," he said with a crooked smile.

Clementine sighed. She turned away from the sight of the town that had been her entire life, and regarded the man who would occupy her future. "I'm not sure I believe that. But I admit, I suddenly feel rather… rather shy."

"We have seen little of each other the past few weeks," he agreed, a rather sheepish look in his eyes that confirmed her suspicions.

"Oh, you *were* avoiding me!" she exclaimed crossly.

He shrugged, not bothering to deny it. "I thought it might be prudent, in case I put my foot in it and you decided you'd made a horrible mistake. I didn't want to risk your calling off the wedding."

She ought to have been appalled, but instead Clementine laughed. She laughed long and hard until she had to clutch at her stomach and finally subsided.

"Better?" he asked, regarding her with satisfaction.

"I think so," she agreed.

"Are you hungry?" he asked, gesturing to a basket on the seat opposite. "I thought you might be too nervous to eat, and so I asked Mrs Adie to prepare a picnic for us."

"Oh, how thoughtful," Clementine said. "I am hungry, yes."

He looked surprisingly pleased by her words and opened the hamper. "There are slices of pie, chicken and ham, and game, I think. Also, chicken drumsticks, several cheeses, some apples, oh, and wedding cake."

"Cake!" Clementine said at once. "I didn't get to have any, and it looked delicious."

"Cake it is," he said with a grin. "Oh, there's wine too. What an excellent woman Mrs Adie is. She's even uncorked it ready for us," he said, raising the bottle enquiringly towards her.

Clementine shook her head, watching as he poured a glass for himself. "She is a treasure," she agreed, breaking off a piece of the rich fruitcake and putting it in her mouth. She gave a little sigh of pleasure at the sweetness of the cake and chewed happily. "Oh, that is divine," she said, breaking off another bit. Try some," she added, turning to offer some to Beaumarsh, only to discover him watching her. He had an intent expression, like a cat waiting for its prey, and Clementine swallowed awkwardly, belatedly aware of their proximity, of the confines of the carriage, and the fact they were married, and alone. She watched as he raised the wineglass to his lips and drank, noticing the strong column of his throat working as he swallowed. He licked his lips and Clementine's breath caught and she wondered with growing agitation how those lips would feel against hers.

Still, she forced herself to be brave and lifted the morsel of cake to his lips. He held her gaze as he opened his mouth and she had the sudden, strange and forceful image of feeding an enormous cat with smiling jaws and strong teeth, teeth that might devour her if she wasn't careful. Shaking off the sensation, she popped the piece of cake into his mouth, her fingers unwittingly brushing his lips as she did so. A shiver ran down her arm at the contact, fizzing in her belly and lower still, a confusion of sensations she did not know what to do with.

So, instead, she turned her attention to practical matters.

"H-How far is it to Cavendish House? I am certain I have asked that several times before, but suddenly I cannot remember."

"Around four hours, I'm afraid," he said, his gaze still lingering on her face. "We'll stop for an early supper at The Bell in Ticehurst, and then make the rest of the journey, if that suits you?"

"Perfectly," Clementine agreed. Her nerves, which he had calmed so nicely, were jittering all over again.

His expression changed to one of concern, his brows drawing together.

"Clementine, don't be afraid of me," he said, watching her still. "I know this isn't a love match, but I hope we are friends, are we not? I want you to be happy, and I would do nothing to make you unhappy. Certainly not on purpose, but if I do so accidentally, I would have your promise that you will tell me."

"Of course we are friends," Clementine agreed briskly, though for reasons she did not understand, her heart sank at his words. Well, of course it wasn't a love match. She knew that perfectly well and there was no reason to feel despondent about it. "Though we don't yet know each other well. As for telling you, of course I shall. I'm afraid that was never in doubt," she said apologetically.

He smiled at that. "Good. Have you finished your cake?"

Clementine picked up the last piece and ate it, handing him the plate, which he put back in the hamper alongside his empty wineglass.

"In that case, come here." He sat back and held one arm out, inviting her to move closer.

Clementine told herself she was a sensible girl and would not swoon if her husband put his arm around her. All the same, her insides trembled, and her heart sped as she did as he asked.

"There, now. That isn't so terrible, is it?" he asked, glancing down at her, his blue eyes dancing.

"Don't mock me," she warned him tartly. "You have all the experience and I none, which, I might add, is exactly how men have arranged things. So don't go teasing me for being an ignorant ninny."

"Good lord, Clementine, as if I would," he retorted, though amusement still lurked in his eyes. "And I cannot believe you ignorant."

"Not about the mechanics of the thing," she admitted. "Just the… the technique."

There was a tense silence. "The mechanics and the t-technique," he repeated, but she heard the quaver in his voice and elbowed him in the ribs.

"Wretch!" she exclaimed, though she was laughing now. "How else should I put it?"

"Oh, n-no, my dear. I think that explains the situation perfectly," he said, before giving a snort and bursting out laughing.

"One day, I shall make you pay for that," she grumbled, finding she did not mind in the least, for it was delightful to watch him laugh with such abandon, and to be the one who had given such mirth, albeit unintentionally.

"I never doubted it," he said, regaining his equilibrium and pulling her closer.

He looked down at her, his expression surprisingly tender as he leaned in, moving slowly so as not to startle her. Clementine held her breath, her heart thundering, watching. Ought she to close her eyes? She wondered but did not want to miss anything. This was her first kiss, after all.

He had not kissed her when he had proposed, for which she had been relieved at the time, but now she thought she regretted that. At least then she might have been a little prepared for… for…

His lips were surprisingly soft, plush and warm, and gentle as they brushed lightly over hers. A shiver ran over her skin and then he did it again, increasing the pressure a little. He kissed the corner of her mouth, and then moved, giving dozens of butterfly-soft kisses that made her mind feel hazy at the edges. Though she had wanted to watch, to experience this kiss, these kisses, with every sense, she found her eyes closing, unable to keep them open. She needed to savour, to focus her mind on the feel of his mouth caressing hers. It was…

Oh.

It was good. Very good indeed. Warmth curled through her, warmth that seemed to build with every press of his mouth upon hers. His hand was a sensual weight at her waist, and she wished he would move it, that he would slide it down to her hip, or up to her breast, which suddenly felt heavy and desperate for his touch.

Well, *now* she understood why people made such a fuss about men and women never being left alone together. If this was what temptation felt like, it was no wonder people got themselves into such trouble.

He did not hurry her or seem inclined to do anything more but continue in the same fashion, but as the kiss went on, one touch of lips melting into another, Clementine grew increasingly impatient. Boldly, she lifted her hand and rested it on his shoulder, thinking that perhaps it might encourage him to take them a little farther down this path.

It didn't.

Well, she was not a silly chit straight out of the schoolroom, she reminded herself. She would try something else. Her hand moved, sliding over the fine material of his coat, feeling the strength of the shoulder beneath and discovering there was not a bit of padding there. It was all Beaumarsh. Delighted by this information, she lifted her hand, touching his jaw. She would have liked to curve her palm around his neck, but his cravat had been folded so intricately she found the prospect of disordering it too intimidating and decided it was best avoided. His jaw, however, was firm and there was a slight rasp as she ran her fingers over his skin. This morning he had been clean shaven, but now, late in the afternoon, the first golden hint of beard was making an appearance. Encouraged when he made no objection to her exploration, she allowed her hand to move back, sinking into the warmth of his hair. The dark gold locks were silky, sliding through her fingers, and Beaumarsh sighed.

Clementine stilled, entranced by the soft sound of pleasure. She wished to make him sigh again, and perhaps make other sounds that would signal his approval of her touch but, just as she was considering her next move, he drew back.

"Enough," he said.

Clementine looked at him in shock, though somewhat mollified by the heat in his eyes, which had darkened considerably, the pupil wide and inky black, leaving only a thin sliver of blue visible. “Enough?” she repeated breathlessly. “I should think not.”

He grinned at her, so smug and pleased with her words she almost laughed. “Oh, just for now, love. But I promise you, your wedding night will be one to remember, and not because it happened in a carriage.”

Frowning, Clementine considered him with frustration. “Well, surely we can just carry on as we were and—”

“No,” he said, laughing. “That’s not the way it works. You’ll just have to trust me, because if we don’t stop now, neither of us will be inclined to stop at all. I would never do anything you didn’t want, Clementine, but if you keep encouraging me, we might find ourselves in a tangle on the floor by the time we reach our next stop,” he grinned as he spoke, looking as though he was ready to be persuaded if she really insisted.

“Really?” she said, fascinated despite knowing she ought not be curious about such things.

“Cross my heart and hope to die,” he said, settling himself back beside her. He slanted a glance at her and reached over, pressing a kiss to the top of her head. “But I am more than pleased that you wish to. I promise you, if I could make this blasted carriage move any faster, I would do so. I am counting the moments until we are finally home.”

“Well, that’s all right, then,” she allowed, glad she was not the only one afflicted by this sudden agitation and impatience for more.

“Come here,” he said, and she leaned into him, resting her head on his shoulder, feeling his arm curving around her shoulders. “Comfy?

Clementine nodded, though it was not entirely true. Her body was fizzing, alive with sensation, like a champagne bottle that had been handled too roughly. Her blood seemed to rush through her veins, hotter than usual, and her skin was oversensitive. Suddenly she was very aware of her clothes, of the places where they were tight, and of the too many layers between her and her husband. She fidgeted, conscious of the silk stockings and the garters that held them up. Madame Auguste had been a wonderful help to her with her trousseau and persuaded her to buy all sorts of things she would never have dared to consider before. But she was to be a married lady now, Madame had argued, and her husband would appreciate such things. The garters were embroidered with little roses and ornamented with tiny pink silk ribbons. They were the most frivolous and shocking thing Clementine had ever worn in her life, but she had seen them and wanted them, and now the knowledge they were there, hidden beneath her skirts, made her restless.

"Is something wrong?"

Clementine considered replying honestly, but discovered she was not that brave. "No. Not a thing," she said, avoiding his gaze.

Beaumarsh shifted in his seat, so he was gazing directly at her. "Clementine?"

She huffed and shook her head. "I said there was nothing wrong."

"Yes, and most unconvincing it was too. Are you uncomfortable?"

"Yes," she admitted.

"Would you like to stop the carriage and stretch your legs?"

"No!"

He gave her a quizzical glance, and Clementine shook her head. "I'm fine. Truly."

"Hmm."

"Don't keep looking at me like that," she said torn between laughter and exasperation, and then when he wouldn't stop, she added, "Well, it's your fault. What were you thinking, going and kissing me like that and then… then *stopping,* drat you! Aren't you famous for your many mistresses? Is that the sort of thing you would do with them?"

For a moment he looked shocked, then his lips quirked. "Well, mistresses tend to have rather more experience than newly married ladies, and so it's not at all the same thing. But I do apologise. What an ignorant brute I am not to have realised. I beg you will forgive me, my lady."

She pursed her lips, attempting to look annoyed which was impossible when he was looking so pleased with himself. "I don't see why I should," she grumbled, which only made the corners of his mouth tug upwards another notch.

"Do I need to beg your forgiveness some more?" he asked, sounding serious but mirth danced in his eyes. "I could get on my knees if you like." There was something about the way he said it that made her pulse quicken again. He knew it too, drat him.

Clementine huffed at his amusement. She ought to have known he'd delight in teasing her. Well may he find it funny, the wicked man. And then, an idea occurred to her. She moved suddenly, changing to the seat opposite his so she might face him.

"Clementine?" Beaumarsh said, a suspicious note as he spoke her name. "What are you thinking?" He did not sound displeased, quite the reverse, but she felt certain she would take the wind out of his sails.

"Only that I have something to show you. I bought them for my trousseau, so it only seems right you should see them," she said, her tone guileless as she reached down and grasped the fabric of her skirts and pulled them up to the tops of her shins in one swift movement. Then she lingered as the fabric exposed her knees, the soft slide of her silk gown quiet, but the rustle of her petticoat just audible in the rocking carriage. Beaumarsh's expression underwent a series of subtle changes as he realised her intention. Delight shifted to intense concentration, and then he went entirely still, once again putting her in mind of that big cat in the moment before it pounced.

Deliberately, though her heart thundered, she drew the expensive fabrics further up over her knees, along her thighs, until her garters were on show. *Good God, Clementine, what are you doing*, an internal voice shrieked, but whatever impulse had made her enact such a bold scene had taken control and there was no backing down now. She would simply have to brazen it out.

Staring at him, heat suffusing every pore of her body, she was relieved to see a slight tinge of colour crest his high cheekbones. Well, good. She was glad it wasn't only her feeling so hot and bothered.

"You see, my garters are embroidered with pink roses, and there are pink silk ribbons too. Here, and here," she added as she raised her leg, resting one foot on the seat beside him and turning her leg.

She pointed her finger at the tiny bow, watching his face. His attention was riveted to the place where she touched the silk ribbon. He swallowed, his Adam's apple bobbing.

"You are a very, very bad girl, Clementine, and I feel it only right to warn you that there will be retribution for this. Really, I cannot allow such a… a deliberate flouting of my authority."

His voice was a deep growl, which seemed to light a fire beneath her skin, but his words only delighted her as she realised it was all part of the game. Yet when he reached over and his ungloved hands took hold of her ankle and slid the shoe from her foot, her nerve almost failed her. The urge to pull her foot back out of his grasp was tantalising, but she was not faint-hearted, and would not back down now, just when things were getting interesting.

"You must do as you see fit, my lord," she said, her breath catching at the darkly amused glint in his eyes as his hand continued its path up her leg and he slid to the floor. Clementine held her breath, suddenly wondering if she had bitten off more than she could chew, but it was too late now. He pushed her knees further apart, making space for himself, one hand curved around each calf as it slid up her silk-clad leg and lingered beneath her knees. Then he lowered his head and kissed her right garter, pressing his mouth to each little pink ribbon, then to each tiny, embroidered rose.

Clementine's heart raced, picking up speed as she felt the touch of his lips through the silk of her stockings and wondered how they might feel against her bare legs. She did not have long to ponder the question, for he shifted his attention to her left garter, and kissed the bows there too, and each delicate rose, before pressing his mouth to the place where her stocking ended, above the garter.

She gasped at the warmth of his mouth, and then again as he moved higher, his breath tickling the inside of her thighs. Suddenly terribly aware of the private place hidden beneath her rucked-up skirts, she was torn between wishing she had never begun this ridiculous scene, and desperately wondering what he would do next. His hands continued their path, pushing her skirts higher still as she watched, frozen, too shocked and intrigued to say a word.

He looked up then, his blue eyes blazing, yet the heat was softened by tenderness, and any fear she might have felt was gone. Beaumarsh held her gaze before lowering his head and kissing along and up one thigh, before repeating the action on her left.

"Well, Mrs Mabbs never said *anything* about this!" she exclaimed, the words startled from her as she felt his hot breath stir the place between her thighs.

There was a muffled snort, and his shoulders shook for a moment before he pressed his mouth there, and Clementine closed her eyes with a little squeak of surprise. Sensation rocked through her, scandalous pleasure and disbelief and delight all melded together as he did the most wicked things with his mouth and tongue. She felt as though he was unpicking all the tidy little seams that held her together, that made her who she was, and everything that was unruly and wild and unpredictable came tumbling out. Abandoned to desire, she slid forward on the seat and sank her hands into his hair, holding on as if to anchor herself to a world that seemed suddenly very far away. He took her higher and higher, far away from who she was and the place she knew, to somewhere at once bright and dark, until stars burst behind her eyes and a burst of heat and sensation rushed through her.

He drew back and Clementine knew he was watching her but could not bring herself to open her eyes. She was still floating somewhere between the place he had taken her to and this world and she did not wish to return just yet. Nor did she wish to look him in the eyes, suddenly afraid he might think her too bold. Women were not supposed to enjoy such things, yet why else had he done what he had, if not to bring her joy?

Finding her courage, Clementine cracked first one eye, relieved to discover he was not staring at her in disgust. Rather, there was a look in his eyes that she could not quite read, but it seemed to be one of surprise and wonder, and he did not seem in the least bit displeased. Indeed, he looked rather smug.

Still, her cheeks, already pink from exertion, burned as she met his eyes. He grinned then, such a boyish, pleased expression that it tickled her, and she laughed. As that only made his grin wider still, she laughed harder and did not stop until he had rearranged her skirts and pulled her back beside him.

"Now, you dreadful creature, will you please sit still and behave yourself until we get home? You have done terrible things to my equilibrium, not to mention other places, and now I shall suffer until we get to Cavendish House. I hope you are proud of yourself?"

The way he said the words made her realise she was indeed proud of herself. She had surprised him, and, in a way, he was clearly delighted with. In that moment, Clementine promised herself she would always be brave with him, and perhaps if she was, she might encourage him to be more than just her friend. For she wanted that, she realised, as her heart gave an uneven thud. She wanted her husband to be everything to her, and to be everything to him in return, and she did not wish to settle for less.

It was foolish of her, when he had been very clear with what he was offering her, but Clementine was ready for the fight. She was stubborn and clever, and more than a bit devious. She would do everything she could to induce him to love her and, if he could not, she must find a way to live with that, for it was obvious to her now that she was falling in love with the man she had married, and she did not wish to be in love all on her own.

Perhaps sensing the turmoil of her thoughts, Beaumarsh frowned and lifted a hand to her cheek. "Clementine? Are you well? I did not shock you too badly, I hope?"

She smiled at the concern in his eyes and turned her face into his palm, covering it with her own as she pressed a kiss there. He looked far more startled by the tender gesture than she had been at his shocking intimacy. Tension sang through him, and he seemed not to know what to say.

"You did shock me, quite delightfully," she admitted with a smile. "I hope you will continue to do so."

The sudden tautness in him relaxed a degree, and his lips twitched. "Oh, I will do my best, love. You have my word."

Before he could continue, the carriage lurched into a pothole, and he closed his eyes.

"Oh, this is going to be the very devil of a journey," he said, sounding at once entertained and appalled.

Clementine's gaze shifted, and she suddenly noticed why he was so uncomfortable.

Ah. Yes. *That.*

Curious, she reached to touch him. “Is there anything I can—?”

“You’ve done quite enough damage, I thank you,” he said, snatching hold of her wrist before she could get any closer. He kept hold of her, lacing their fingers together and resting them on her knee. “Just wait until I get you home,” he added, squeezing her fingers and looking at her with such a twinkle in his eyes Clementine could only settle back and feel exceedingly pleased with herself.

The journey could not go fast enough.

Chapter 16

Mama dearest…

Cavendish House, Kent. 1st August 1815.

They stopped at The Bell in Ticehurst as promised, to change horses and stretch their legs. Though they were not hungry, having recently finished the contents of the picnic, Clementine enjoyed a pot of tea and some freshly baked biscuits, whilst Beaumarsh drank a pint of ale.

"It's very good," he said, licking his lips with relish. "Try some."

Clementine regarded the dark amber liquid dubiously but, having decided in the carriage she would be bold, she took the heavy glass from him and raised it to her lips.

"Ugh!" She pulled a face and set the glass down, hastening to pick up her tea and take a sip. "How can you drink that? It's so bitter!" He laughed. "That's what makes it good. Refreshing," he added, taking a large swallow.

"I will content myself with tea and biscuits. Now, if you have champagne or wine, I might reconsider sharing," she added, taking another biscuit from the plate and smacking his hand when he went to take one himself.

"Ah, but what's yours is mine, my lady," he said with a wink, and snatched one, stuffing it in his mouth whole as she rolled her eyes at him.

"Such a child."

He grinned, still chewing, and Clementine laughed.

The rest of the journey seemed to go on forever, as the day waned and the sun dropped ever lower. Yet, though she felt they had been travelling for days, it was barely seven in the evening when Beaumarsh announced they were approaching his home.

"I hope you like it," he said, and she noticed the way his brow furrowed and realised he was a little anxious.

"I'm certain I shall, if you do," she said with a smile, but this did not seem to soothe him. "You *do* like it here?" she asked, suddenly filled with trepidation.

He shifted in his seat, looking ill at ease. "It's a beautiful building, impressive and with an astonishing history. The gardens are splendid, in large part because of Mother, but… but it has never been my home. Never *felt* like home, at least," he amended with a frown. "I didn't really know what a home was, how it ought to be, until I spent time at the vicarage. There is a feeling about your home, something unseen and yet tangible that makes it welcoming and a place one where wishes to remain. I'm afraid Cavendish House is nothing like that, but perhaps in time and with your help, we might change it, so that it is?"

The words were a little diffident—perhaps he thought he was giving her a mountain to climb before she'd even set foot through the door—but Clementine could not have been more touched by his hopes for the place they would share as man and wife.

"Oh." She said, gazing at him. This information cast more light upon the man she had married, for how could he ever settle himself, be at ease and content, if he did not have a place where he could be comfortable, no matter what? Everyone needed a haven where they could close the door upon the world and be safe and loved. She had been luckier than she could ever express, and she was determined her husband should know that feeling too. Whether their marriage was the success she now wished it to be, or if they were only ever dear friends, she would give him that much. "I should like that very much. But, your mother…." she said, suddenly comprehending something she had been too preoccupied to consider as deeply as she ought.

His mother.

Heavens above. She was about to step into a house that Beaumarsh himself had declared he wished to change, a house his mother had enjoyed dominion over for decades.

"Clementine? My poor darling, you've gone white as a sheet," he said in concern, reaching for her hand. "I'm sorry. I ought not to have broached the subject like that, it's only that you asked. But do not worry about Mama. She is a dear creature, if somewhat vexing, but not half so frivolous as she makes out, and she is quite content to move into the dower house, I promise. Indeed, she immediately set about having the entire place redecorated, which she will enjoy enormously, I may assure you. I have been very generous to her, and she is eager to hand over the reins of Cavendish House to you, for it is quite a responsibility and—" He broke off, immediately realising he had inadvertently made things worse.

"Oh! My word!" Clementine exclaimed, as she saw exactly why his mother was eager to get rid of the responsibility. The place was on a palatial scale.

Her father had mentioned that he had read a description of the property, describing it as being one of the best examples of a fortified medieval manor house in England, but that had in no way prepared her. There were turrets everywhere, and towers, dozens of them, acres of roof tops, and an incalculable variety of mullioned windows that glinted in the sunshine. It was vast and terribly intimidating to think that she was now mistress of such a place.

"Did your father not explain to you what manner of property it was?" he asked, his voice gentle.

"No, he omitted that little detail," Clementine replied faintly, and then told herself to buck up. No, she had not been trained since birth to run such a grand and intimidating house, but she could learn. It was daunting certainly, but that did not mean she wasn't up to the task.

"It isn't actually as grand as it appears."

Clementine quirked a scathing eyebrow at this soothing comment. "Oh? Because it looks like a small town."

He laughed. "I know, love, but it's an illusion. A deliberate one, actually, to impress and make visitors feel small and insignificant."

"It's working," she replied, her tone rueful.

"There are dozens of halls and passageways that open onto courtyards, but whilst it is sprawling, in many places the house is only one room deep. Yes, it *is* large. There is no escaping that fact, but not as overwhelming as it makes out."

She returned a sceptical glance, and he smiled and took her hand in his, giving it a reassuring squeeze.

"Courage, love. You'll be fine, and I will help as much as I can. Mrs Abbott is housekeeper here, and you will like her very much, I know you will. She has the place running like clockwork. So, you'll be able to do as much or as little as you like, and the place will still run, I promise. If you wish to sit in the library and read all day, you can. The house won't fall down. But I know you won't be satisfied with that, and Mama makes work for herself because she likes to entertain a good deal, and she's particular about details."

Clementine nodded and steeled her spine. For hours, she had longed to get here, but she had failed to properly consider the ordeal she had to endure before she could be alone with her husband as she wished.

Much to her dismay, as the carriage drew closer to a building that—illusion or no—appeared as if it could encompass the entirety of Little Valentine, she saw a vast army of servants awaiting her arrival.

"You can do this," Beaumarsh said, seeing her eyes widen further in alarm. "I know how brave you are, and how capable. I'm proud of you, Clementine. Be proud of yourself."

Clementine turned away from the intimidating scene and stared at him, astonished by his words. She had not expected them, but they sank beneath her skin, warming her. She smiled and put up her chin.

"That's my girl," he said, his voice soft and approving, and the pride in his eyes seemed entirely genuine.

Baffled by his manner and his tenderness, Clementine had no time to ponder what it meant from a man who had offered only friendship, for her staff, and her mother-in-law, awaited her.

Beaumarsh felt sick. He should have warned her and explained more about his home, but he'd feared she might be frightened off. No matter how many times he'd assured himself Clementine was the bravest person he had ever known, it had still seemed safer to say nothing. Now he'd prepared her. He hated seeing the anxiety in her eyes and, worse, he feared she might already be regretting her hasty decision to marry him.

He knew she had done it for her family's sake more than her own, for the title and his wealth did not signify to her as it might to other young ladies. But the fear she might be as lonely here as he had always been, that she might not carve out a life for herself from the thick walls and endless acres of land, made his heart shrivel in his chest.

Still, she had rallied, and he felt a glow of pride as he introduced the elegant woman beside him to his staff. She really was lovelier than he had ever imagined. How had he not noticed that at once? And the way she had teased him in the carriage, bold and determined to have her own way, had made his blood sing and burn in equal measure. She had surprised him. No, not surprised, she had *stunned* him, revealing his wife to be a creature far more fascinating than he had even realised, and he had figured out how special she was some time ago. He was a lucky dog and, if he was to keep any of the other fellows from sniffing around and stealing her from under his nose, he would need to be on his guard. Whilst there was a code of honour regarding men's wives before they had delivered their heir and spare, not everyone could be trusted to keep to that. A woman like Clementine would be catnip to some unscrupulous fellow, and bored and unhappy wives were notoriously easy to seduce.

A chill went through him, and he shook himself. Christ almighty. They'd been married a few hours, and he was already predicting disaster. In the first place, Clementine was not the sort to betray a fellow, no matter how unhappy she was. Hadn't that been the reason he'd married her in the first place? She was honest to her core and, besides all that, he was damned if he would give her a reason to need to take a lover. Having had a taste of what was now his—oh, and what a glorious taste it had been—he was eager to show her all the delights that a married woman could indulge in with her husband.

"My lord?"

"Eh?"

Beau started as he realised his countess was regarding him expectantly, as were the staff.

"Ah. Yes. Very good. Thank you all, and you may go. Where is my mother, Jefferson?" he asked the butler, who was regarding Clementine with a steely eye that *might* have been approval. The man was damnably difficult to read.

"In the red parlour, my lord," Jefferson replied, without so much as batting an eyelid as he dropped the little bombshell.

"Very good. Come, my lady," he said, taking Clementine's hand and putting it on his sleeve. Damn his mother. She *would* choose the red room. It would likely give his new bride a migraine in short order and ruin his wedding night. His mother's idea of a joke, he did not doubt. He glanced at Clementine, noting her wide eyes as she entered the Baron's Hall with its vast ceiling. Cavendish ancestors glared at them from every wall and Beau suppressed a shudder. "Perhaps we should run away to Italy or France. Probably pick a lovely place up in France for mere pennies at the moment," he quipped.

Clementine levelled a look at him which suggested she did not find this funny, but then he saw her lips twitch, and he relaxed a degree. "That is in very poor taste, my lord, and were you not just now assuring me that everything would be fine?"

"Yes, but that was before Mother decided to greet you in the red parlour. I mean, it really is *red,* Clementine. It's like being dipped in bull's blood and then rolled in scarlet satin. It's… it's appalling. I must tell you it was my grandmother's favourite room. My father loathed it, which obviously meant that Mama insisted no one ever change a thing, even after they were both long dead." He sighed and shook his head. "Just don't hold it against me."

Clementine snorted and he noted the sudden glimmer of mirth in her eyes. "Perhaps I shall decorate it a lurid fuchsia pink, just to make my mark on the place."

He grinned, relieved she had not lost her sense of humour.

"You are quite wonderful, you know. I'm so glad I married you." The words were out before he could think about them, and she stopped in her tracks. He stopped too, wondering if he ought not to have said it. She had married him for her family's sake and—

She kissed him.

Right there and then, where any passing servant might see them, she pressed her mouth to his. Sensation rioted through him, a sense of rightness and of… of coming home, that he had never known before. He pulled her roughly into his arms and she went willingly as he held her close, her arms sliding around his neck and grasping tightly. She kissed him and kissed him, and he kissed her back until he was giddy with it, desire and yearning bursting through his veins like liquid fire, setting his skin alight. How strange, he thought, that she was the virgin and he the one with all the experience, yet he felt as if everything was new, that every touch was one he had never experienced before.

She pulled back, eyes shining, cheeks flushed, and he regretted the need to go to the ugly red room and face his mother when they might go straight to bed. He longed to do just that, but she stepped back, out of his arms.

“We’d best get it over with,” she said regretfully.

Beau lingered for a moment, reaching out to touch her cheek; so soft, the skin like satin beneath his fingers. “You are quite the loveliest thing I have ever seen.”

Her cheeks grew pinker still and her entire being seemed to glow at his words. “Are you flirting with me, my lord?” she asked, looking as if she was uncertain whether to believe him.

“No. I’m speaking the truth, nothing more,” he assured her, and then grasped her hand, towing her on towards the red room. The sooner this was over, the sooner they could be alone together, and that could not happen quickly enough.

Well, he had not been exaggerating. The room was red. It was not only red, it was aggressively scarlet, with hints of crimson and ruby. Every inch of wall, even the ceiling between the beams; every soft furnishing, and the carpets, which were layered four or five deep, blared a differing shade of cherry or burgundy, often with a lurid pattern adorning the fabric. It was perfectly hideous and quite overwhelming.

The Dowager Countess, however, was a dainty woman who did not look old enough to have sired a man of Beaumarsh's age, let alone size, for she was slender and waiflike. She was beautiful still, and it was easy to see from where her son had inherited his golden good looks. In the garish room, she was the only lovely thing one's gaze could rest upon, and Clementine did not doubt she knew it.

"Mama, you wretch. Of all the rooms you had to choose from, why in blazes greet us in this monstrosity? Are you hoping to send my wife screaming from the place before she has even sat down?"

"Oh, silly boy, as if I would," the woman said placidly, inclining her head so her son might kiss her cheek. "And I am certain your bride is made of sterner stuff than that," she added, looking Clementine up and down, her gaze frank and considering.

Dressed all in pale gold, with her tumbling yellow curls and deep blue eyes, she looked at first glance more like his sister than his mama. Yet as Clementine grew closer, she saw the tell-tale lines around her mouth and eyes that gave the game away.

"My lady. It is an honour to meet you."

She smiled, and the expression lit her face, turning her from merely lovely to exquisite. "I am so happy that Beau has married at last. I have been longing for grandchildren for an age, you know. I was sorry not to have more babies myself, but they are utterly ruinous to one's figure. At least, to one like mine," she added, smoothing a hand over the side of her tiny waist. "You appear to be built on far more robust lines, I think, so I don't suppose it will trouble you in the least," she remarked, smiling widely.

"Indeed, it will not," Clementine said, startled by the sudden attack and wondering how to react to it. Her instinct was to ignore the unkind comment, yet a glance at her husband revealed his obvious anger and that there was about to be an appalling scene if she did not do *something*. Taking a breath, she said the only thing she could think of. "Happily, I am not some poor creature who puts on pounds if I so much as glance at a sugar cube, nor one so vain I should prefer staring into a looking-glass to having a family, so I hope I might provide you with the grandchildren you long for."

There was a taut silence, and then the countess burst out laughing. "Oh, you are perfect. Well done. I was so afraid Beau would marry some frightful milk-and-water miss who would burst into tears at the first provocation, and it would have been such a trial to bring her up to scratch. But I see I have not a thing to worry about. Congratulations, you wicked boy. It seems, by some miracle, you have not made an appalling choice."

"Thank you, Mama," Beaumarsh said dryly as Clementine let out a breath she had not been aware of holding. "You are a horrid creature, and I ought to send you away for six months as punishment."

"Yes, yes. I know. Never mind. Now, don't fret, I know you are wishing me to perdition, so I shall not stay. I wished only to greet your lovely bride," she said cheerily, getting to her feet as she spoke. "I have been in such a dither over what manner of woman a vicar's daughter might be, and fretting that the ton would eat her alive, but I believe all will be well. You *might* even be happy," she added with an impish grin, before blowing them a kiss and heading for the door.

"That's it? You're going?" Beaumarsh said, incredulous, though not displeased if Clementine was any judge.

"Yes, of course I am going!" she exclaimed. "I do not wish to be here anymore than you wish me to remain. I'll see you in… shall we say three weeks? You might endure an entire conversation with me by then without dragging your bride off by the hair. Have fun, my darlings," she called over her shoulder, and closed the door behind her.

Clementine laughed as Beaumarsh covered his face with his hand. "Sorry," he said apologetically. "She's dreadful."

"She's delightful. I like her very much," Clementine said, trying not to laugh at his mortification.

Beaumarsh shook his head and walked over to her, taking her hands in his. "You are very kind and forgiving, and you do not know how grateful I am for that."

"You are kind too, my lord, and patient, and I am grateful for that. I promise I will try my best to be a good countess, one you can be proud of, but I shall certainly be a good wife, that much I know," she replied, gazing into eyes that immediately reminded her of the seaside at Little Valentine and made her feel entirely at home despite her surroundings.

"My name is Sylvester," he reminded her, his voice soft. "You do not need to 'my lord' me when we are in private. Or ever, if you do not wish to."

She smiled, a little ruefully. "I know, I… I'm just struggling to call you that, but I shall try, Sylvester."

He smiled and let out a breath. "Would you allow me to take you to our chambers now? Mrs Abbott will have prepared your bath, and then we can have a bite of supper if you wish and… and then—" He broke off, gazing into her eyes.

"And then?" she repeated, suddenly breathless.

He flashed a crooked grin, boyish and charming and utterly beguiling. "And then, we shall see," he teased, pulling her towards the door. "Come along, lady wife. Duty has been done to the staff and my parent. Now we can please ourselves, and I fully intend to."

He tugged her out and through a dizzying parade of rooms, each more fascinating than the last, but spared not a moment to allow her to look around. "You've got years and years to explore the house," he said, laughing. "If you think I'm giving you a tour now, you are out of your mind."

Up a vast, grand staircase and along a panelled corridor, Clementine hurried after him, almost running to keep up. She thought she heard giggling and turned her head to see a maid disappear behind a hidden door in the wainscoting, clearly hiding a servants' staircase. Oh yes, she would certainly enjoy exploring, but not now.

Finally, he opened a set of double doors that led them into a luxurious living room. It was a lovely space, with large windows that would allow light to flood in but now showed the last traces of a glorious sunset, with the sky streaked with great swathes of orange and pink.

"What a beautiful room," she said, looking around in delight.

Beaumarsh—*Sylvester*—looked pleased at her words. "I'm glad. Now, come and see your rooms. They're extraordinarily pretty, as everything Mama has a hand in is, but you must feel free to make them your own. She won't be offended, I promise. Indeed, if you want to make her happy, ask her for her opinion on colours or wall hangings. She'll be thrilled."

Clementine agreed she would and then gasped as saw the room that would be hers.

"Good gracious. I never saw anything so lovely in all my days. I wouldn't change a thing!" she exclaimed, regarding a chamber that was entirely feminine. Done in shades of yellow and pale green, it was a sanctuary more than a room, a place that seemed to hug you the moment you stepped through the door. Clementine let out a breath. Thick, luxurious fabrics covered the furniture, and pillows and cushions were piled high on the bed and sofa.

Sylvester stood in the doorway, watching her. "My rooms are through that door," he said, pointing across the living room to a door that mirrored her own. "But I would like it very much if we did not sleep in separate bedrooms. At least whilst we are still getting to know each other," he added quickly, as if he believed she might not like the notion.

Clementine hid a smile, for she had no intention of having a separate room to her husband if she could help it. The idea seemed strange to her, though it was how the upper orders lived.

"I think that is an excellent idea," she replied, crossing the room and going through another door. This chamber was smaller, and despite the warm weather, a fire burned in the hearth as steam rose from a large copper bath. The scent of roses pervaded the humid air, and Clementine gaped, overwhelmed by the sheer indulgence of having a bathing room for herself alone, and a bath awaiting her, brimming with hot water.

"Your dressing room is through that door," he explained, pointing, "and your maid will attend you the moment you pull the bell. Mama chose her for you, but if she does not suit, you can find someone who does. I want you to be happy here, Clementine, so if there is anything that does not please you, I beg you will tell me at once."

Clementine's lips quirked despite the sincerity of his words. "I believe I am quite beside myself and can find fault with nothing at all. A strange circumstance, I assure you. I will do better tomorrow."

He reached out and tweaked her chin before placing a kiss on her nose. "Wretch. Now, take your bath. I will order our supper for… an hour's time?" he asked cautiously, though he did not look terribly sanguine about the delay.

"Half an hour," Clementine amended, pleased when he let out a breath.

"Excellent. Half an hour it is," he said with relief. "I'll be ready in ten minutes. Just so you know," he added with a wink, and hurried to his own rooms.

Chapter 17

The heart of a lioness.

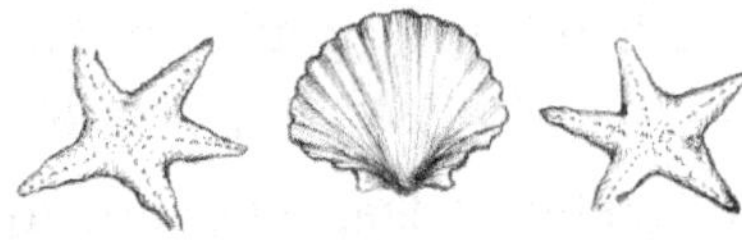

Cavendish House, Kent. 1st August 1815.

"Oh, it's ever so pretty, my lady!"

Susan, the new lady's maid, gazed reverentially at the fine linen and lace ensemble Clementine had put on after indulging in the most decadent bath of her life. It was all so strange, this new way of being. She had her own maid to attend to her every need, and a bath scented with expensive oils. Moreover, there was no one calling through the door, demanding to know where this or that was or how long she would be.

It was heavenly.

And now, standing before a full-length looking glass, she regarded herself in one of the items Madame Auguste had provided for her hastily put together trousseau. The nightgown was of the finest linen, so delicate it was nigh on sheer, and gossamer lace adorned the neck, cuffs, and hem. The wrap was likewise exquisite, and Clementine felt almost naked as she thanked the maid for her help and bade her goodnight.

"Yes, my lady. Shall I wake you in the morning? Do you like a cup of chocolate, or—"

"Not tomorrow morning, perhaps," Clementine suggested gently, watching as the eager maid turned scarlet.

"Oh! No, indeed. Goodnight, my lady." Susan bobbed a hasty curtsy and then fled, leaving Clementine to take one last look at herself.

Her blonde hair cascaded down her back, over her shoulders, and she wondered what Beau—what *Sylvester*—would think of his bride. He had seemed more than pleased so far. She only hoped that might continue.

Glancing at the clock, she realised she had been more than half an hour, and hurried to the door. She stepped out into the living room, which had been illuminated with two lamps, but was otherwise dark and still. Padding across to the door her husband had indicated was his, she gathered her courage and knocked.

The moment she did, the door flew open, and Sylvester stood before her.

"Thank God! I feared you'd got cold feet!" he exclaimed.

Clementine heard the frustration in his words as she stared at him and her lips curved upwards. *Dear me*. The poor man had got himself into quite a lather.

"I beg your pardon. I was enjoying the novelty of a bath with no interruptions and with hot water that was deeper than my ankles."

Sylvester sighed and held the door open for her. "No, it's I who should apologise. What a brute I am, barking at you for taking a little time for yourself on your wedding night. It's only that I've driven myself mad waiting for you, wondering—" He shook his head. "Never mind. Come and eat something. You must be famished by now. That picnic was ages ago."

"Wondering what?" Clementine asked as he led her to a small round table laid for two.

The room was as stylish and masculine as the man who owned it, painted in shades of deep blue, with rich fabrics and elegant furnishings.

"It doesn't matter. Come, sit down," he insisted.

Clementine gave him a curious glance but let the matter rest. There was time enough to discover what was troubling him.

Intuitively, she felt it was something significant if it could make a man who was generally so sophisticated and sure of himself so uneasy.

Instead, she admired her husband, whose attire seemed to be nothing more than a heavy silk banyan. Idly she wondered how many he owned, for this one was a rich forest green, with black silk fern leaves embroidered around the lapels. His feet were bare, and she glimpsed strong calves dusted with blond hair before she sat down and he took his place beside her. Still, she could see that intriguing triangle of skin at his chest and throat and longed to reach out and touch the wiry copper-gold hair. Sylvester handed her a napkin, and she tore her gaze away, hoping he had not noticed her gawking.

The food prepared for them was delicious and just what she would have desired if she'd thought about it. There were a dozen little dishes, with both sweet and savoury pastries so delicate they were like little puffs of air. There was a smoked salmon salad with fresh dill cream, a selection of cheeses, and grapes and peaches and raspberries, and a large bowl of jewel-like strawberries beside a dish of thick white cream.

Sylvester poured champagne for them both and raised his glass. "To my beautiful wife, the Countess of Beaumarsh, and to me, the lucky devil who married her."

Clementine laughed at his irreverent toast and clinked her glass to his, and they ate, picking at this and that as the tension between them grew.

"Have you eaten enough?" he asked a short while later, his voice low as Clementine toyed with a strawberry she did not really want.

She glanced up, rivetingly aware of the quality of his voice, and noted the look his eyes. Their blue had turned an intriguing shade in the dimly lit room, like a midnight sky. Finding her voice suddenly unavailable, Clementine simply nodded as her heart picked up speed. How strange to have been so keen for this moment so many hours ago, and now to feel all on edge. Determinedly, she told herself not to be such a ninny. She would not give her husband the impression she was a silly little nitwit by getting all shy on him after what she'd done in the carriage. It was too ridiculous.

"Come, then," he said, getting to his feet and offering her his hand.

Clementine took it, reassured by the warmth and strength in his grip, which held her hand securely but did not overwhelm her. He had already shown himself to be tender and considerate; she had nothing to fear.

He led her to stand beside the bed, an imposing four-poster that looked to be as ancient as the house itself. Smiling, he stood back to regard her.

"I have thought often of you like this," he murmured, his eyes twinkling. "Ever since that night I brought your father home and you came out to scold him, so worried you forgot you were wearing nothing but your nightclothes. How the sight of you tormented me! All that innocent white cotton. It was enough to drive me distracted, I hope you know."

Clementine gazed at him in wonder. "It was?" she said, confounded and delighted by this revelation. "I had no idea."

"I know, and I was too much of a gentleman to explain it to you," he said ruefully. "But it has plagued me and plagued me, and now I shall ease my mind by doing as I have longed to do for what seems like forever."

He stepped closer and Clementine found she could not breathe as he tugged at the first ribbon tie. It came undone with ease, and so he proceeded to the next, and the next, until the wrap slid from her shoulders. It glided to the floor soundlessly, barely stirring the air. Next, he reached for the ribbon tie that kept the neck of her nightgown closed and gently pulled the bow. Opening the neck gathers wide, he let go. The fabric fell, brushing her skin as it went, sliding over her hips with a whisper of sensation, making her shiver.

Clementine closed her eyes, suddenly unable to look at him, but she heard his swift intake of breath and hoped that was a good sign. Certainly, it could not be horror, for whilst she was not in league with an incomparable like Beatrice, she knew her figure was pleasing.

"Clementine, look at me."

Clementine gathered her courage and did as he asked and found herself gazing into her husband's eyes. His expression made her heart skip, for it was filled with tenderness and something very much like adoration.

"My beautiful girl, my darling, how lovely you are," he told her, and pulled her into his arms.

Clementine went willingly, overwhelmed by the depth of emotion she saw in him, so raw and so unexpected. When his arms went around her and his lips found hers, she knew at once she would have everything she had dreamed of. Perhaps he did not realise it yet, but Sylvester would give her the marriage she wanted, because he wanted it too.

The touch of his skin against hers was a delicious shock, heat and silk and the press of a body that was like and so unlike hers. He intrigued her, and her hands moved restlessly, exploring, wanting to discover everything all at once.

Laughing softly, Sylvester caught hold of her hands. "It's not a race," he told her, before lifting her into his arms.

Clementine clutched at his shoulders, panicked for a moment until she realised how very strong he was, for he lifted as if she weighed nothing, when she was very aware she was no lightweight.

"I've got you," he said, amusement in his voice as he carried her to the bed and laid her down upon the mattress.

Clementine immediately sat up, not wanting to miss a thing as she saw him untying the silk belt on his banyan. He let it fall, exposing all she had wished to see, but he did not allow her the time to gaze at him in rapt admiration as she certainly could have done given the chance. Instead, he climbed onto the bed, pushing her down as his mouth captured hers again, and she reached for him, relishing the heat and the weight of him as he pressed closer. Yet, she did not wish to have her chance taken from her, and she pushed him back, not hard, yet he moved away as if she'd shoved him.

"Is something wrong?" he asked, his brows tugging together in concern.

"Yes, I want to look," she said, struggling to get to her knees on the soft mattress. His lips quirked at that, his worry disappearing.

"I am at your disposal, my lady," he said gravely.

Clementine hid her smile and gave a brisk nod. "Good."

Still, it took her a moment to gather her courage. He watched as she reached out, until she almost touched his shoulders, and then he closed his eyes as she traced a path over his skin, lightly at first, her fingertips skimming his collarbone. Eager now, she flattened both hands against him and smoothed her palms over his chest, delighting in the scattering of wiry hair that gleamed bronze in the lamplight. Finding the intriguing little flat disk of his nipple, her thumb rubbed back and forth. He gasped, and so she did it again. His eyes flicked open, watching as she became increasingly fascinated at the way the tiny nub of flesh grew taut beneath her touch.

"Turnabout is fair play," he said, giving her the benefit of a devilish grin as he reached for her.

Clementine gasped, then closed her eyes as he gently pinched and tugged, his thumbs gently pinching the tight little peaks. The sensation was riveting, sending delicious darts of electricity shooting through her, and it was not until she felt the tickle of his hair against her skin that she realised he had moved nearer. She opened her eyes just as he closed his mouth over her breast, moaning against her skin as he suckled her.

The moment was sweet and dark as molasses and suddenly her hands were in his hair, pulling him closer still as her breathing grew ever more erratic. It seemed her husband was similarly affected, as his mouth moved over her, his hands doing likewise, his touch no longer so leisurely, but filled with an urgency that she wholeheartedly supported.

"Lay down," he rasped, and the sound of his voice, so low and husky, thrilled her to her core, for it revealed the desperation he felt, that she felt too, and the sharing of that need seemed to tug them together, not only physically, but in all ways.

"Tell me to slow down," he said, raising his head to look in her eyes as he moved over her, settling between her thighs. "Tell me to stop being such an impatient brute and take my time."

Clementine only laughed and shook her head. "Hurry!" she exclaimed. "Before I go mad."

"Oh, God," he moaned the words as her skin met his. "Oh, love." He slid between her legs and Clementine refused to feel shame as he discovered her skin slick with desire. Certainly, the revelation seemed to inflame him as he growled against her ear. "I need to be inside you."

Despite the urgency of his words, he slowed his touch, and when he pushed forward he did so gently, with the tenderness she had known he would show her, and yet she felt the trembling in his limbs, the restraint required to give her these moments to adjust to the sudden invasion.

"Sylvester," she said, not wanting him to slow down despite knowing that he knew best, and she pulled her legs up, grasping at him as she tugged him close.

She made a sharp sound, half protest, half surprise, as he groaned and thrust deeper. Panting as he continued to move, Clementine forced her tense muscles to relax, to give way, and then his mouth found hers and he kissed her and suddenly it was easy, as natural as breathing and, oh, the feel of him, of this. She was lost, overwhelmed, and from the way he touched her, with such reverence, murmuring sweet words and reassurances, he felt the same way.

As his movements became more rhythmic, her hands roved over him, stroking him, her touch gentle and loving, wondering if he could understand what it was she was trying to tell him, to show him. Though her heart trembled at the possibility he might close the door on an even greater level of intimacy, he opened his eyes, and she lost herself in his expression. He gazed down at her with wonder, warmth and desire coalescing into something she could not only see but feel in her heart. Time hung suspended as he loved her, nothing of the outside world able to reach them here, as they learned the shape and feel of each other, and of the future they would share.

Clementine's breath caught anew as his hand slid between them, and he shifted slightly, finding the tiny nub of flesh that he had pleasured so exquisitely before. Impatient now, aware of the shining pinnacle before her, she abandoned herself to his touch, hearing the rasp of her own breath echoing his, the tension growing within her just as it did in him.

He cried out when her body tightened beneath him, around him, her hands clutching at his shoulders, her cry of surprise and pleasure bursting from her lips. Together they tumbled headlong into the decadence of release and allowed bliss to overwhelm them.

"Don't forget the strawberries and cream! Oh, and those little lemon tart things."

Beau, who already had his hands full with the champagne bottle, glasses, and a plate of savoury tarts, looked at his wife with a wry expression. "And where do you propose I put them?"

"Well, I don't know. I seem to remember someone promising to keep me in sickness and in health mere hours ago, but if you can't even feed me properly, it seems I have struck a very bad bargain."

She sat in bed, as regal as a queen, surrounded by pillows. Her hair was a mess of billowy blonde tresses that fell over her naked breasts, and Beau was finding it increasingly hard to keep his wits intact. She was just so… so splendid, and bold, and funny and kind and… and he was in a very, very bad way.

He wasn't even certain he cared, except there was a tense little knot inside him, one that feared what would happen if he let go and loved her the way he knew he could, the way he now knew he must, if she was to be happy with him.

Returning to her, he arranged the plate of savoury tarts on the bed, poured her a glass of champagne and handed it over before going back to the table. "Strawberries, cream, and…"

"The lemon tarts, they were divine. Oh, but the raspberry ones were delicious too. Best bring them along as well," she called.

Beau glanced over his shoulder and shook his head at her. Deciding to play it safe, he upended all the sweet tarts onto one plate, and brought the entire lot back, as well as the strawberries and cream.

"A feast," she declared, her eyes sparkling as she leaned over and kissed him. "Thank you, my lord, you have provided for your wife. Well done."

Though he knew perfectly well it was all nonsense, and she was only funning, Beau had the absurd desire to preen. Not for having provided food that had been little over twenty feet away, but for having pleased her, and made her laugh, and not least for having made her lose her wits so delightfully as she had abandoned herself to his touch.

Best not think of that, he realised as his body stirred anew. The poor girl was hungry, not to mention she'd likely be sore and not wish to repeat the act so soon.

So they ate, uncaring about crumbs in the bed—for now at least—and feeding each other, and drinking champagne, and laughing, and it was all so easy. How was it possible for it all to be this easy?

Soulmates.

The words rang in his mind as her father's question came back to him like the clanging of a bell.

But what if you found a woman who was your equal, who entertained you and challenged you, and loved you with all the ferocity of a lioness? What if the sound of her voice made your heart sing, and the sight of her face each morning made you want to thank the good Lord for his beneficence? What then?

"What then?" he repeated, his heart pounding.

"I'm sorry?"

Beau started as he realised he'd spoken aloud. "Nothing," he said with a swift grin to cover his confusion. "Woolgathering. Have another lemon tart."

She took the sweet treat from him, popped it in her mouth and chewed with obvious pleasure, but her gaze remained steadfast upon him, and he felt the sudden and urgent desire to change the subject. He opened his mouth, but not fast enough.

"What were you wondering?"

Frowning, he pretended ignorance, though he knew very well what she was asking. He ought to have realised she would not let it rest. She was too perspicacious not to unravel his every thought. Good God, he was doomed.

"When I so unkindly kept you waiting, you said that you'd driven yourself mad waiting for me, *wondering.* What were you wondering?"

Beau tried avoiding her gaze as he racked his brain for some flippant comment, but he knew it wouldn't wash. He couldn't fight whatever this was, not when he wanted it just as much as it scared him. So, he looked his wife in the eyes and answered honestly, allowing her to see the parts of him no one else ever saw, or even knew existed.

"You married me for the sake of your sisters, for Caspar and Daisy, for the women of Little Valentine, far more than you did for your own sake, and… and I just wondered if you had spent the extra time steeling yourself to come to me. If perhaps it had suddenly come home to you that you had tied yourself to a vain peacock for all eternity, and the realisation was not a happy one."

He prayed she would not be kind, for that would humiliate him. Equally, he could not bear it if she lied to him and pretended feelings that were not real. *They were real*, his mind insisted. *Remember the way she touched you, the way you touched her…* But that was passion, lust, it wasn't—

"Idiot," she said succinctly. "How can you be so adept at seducing women and being the toast of the ton and all that nonsense, and not know when a female is utterly infatuated with you? Well, I mean I *was* infatuated with you. I'm afraid the situation is far worse than that now. I'm quite besotted, unreasonably adoring. It's quite sickening actually, or perhaps I've had too many lemon tarts," she added, licking her fingers with a thoughtful expression.

Beau stared at her, a delighted smile curving his lips. "Unreasonably adoring?" he repeated, charmed beyond reason by this description.

"Mm-hmm," she replied, apparently having decided the lemon tarts were not at fault as she reached for the last one.

Beau lunged, upsetting the strawberries, which careened over the mattress and dropped onto the floor to destinations unknown. Plates clattered and Clementine squealed as he pushed her onto her back, though she somehow kept hold of the lemon tart.

"It's mine," she said, apparently serious, though laughter danced in her eyes.

"But you love me," he reminded her, taking hold of her wrist so she could not devour it. "You are besotted. You said so. Unreasonably adoring."

"It's true," she lamented, putting her free hand to her forehead. "However shall I endure it?"

"How about we survive the madness together?" he suggested, his heart thudding so hard he wondered it did not escape his ribcage.

She stilled, staring up at him. "Together?"

He nodded, and she watched as he leaned in and took a bite of the tart, leaving half of it behind. "I am *not* infatuated, Clementine. I am all the other things, though. Besotted, adoring, devoted, amorous, passionate and quite ridiculously in love with you. I didn't see it coming, so I had no defence ready for it, and now it's too late. Whatever shall I do?"

"Well, firstly, you may give me the rest of my tart," she replied.

Beau let go of her hand and she ate it, her gaze watchful. Then she flung her arms around his neck and kissed him hard on the mouth. She tasted of sweets and lemon and laughter, and of things he had no name for but hungered for desperately. "Secondly," she said, breathless now. "You may love me for so long as we both shall live, and perhaps for a very long time after that too. I will if you will," she added softly, and for the first time he glimpsed the vulnerability in her eyes alongside the strength he had always known was there.

"I will," he said, discovering this vow was just as solemn as the ones he'd made in church, and that it was one he would not struggle for a moment to keep.

And so she kissed him again, and Beau loved her with everything he had, and she returned everything he gave her with her whole heart.

Sometime later, sweaty and breathless and ready to sleep in each other's arms, they decided they would sleep in her bed that night, for his was rather a mess.

Epilogue

The birth of the venturesome ladies.

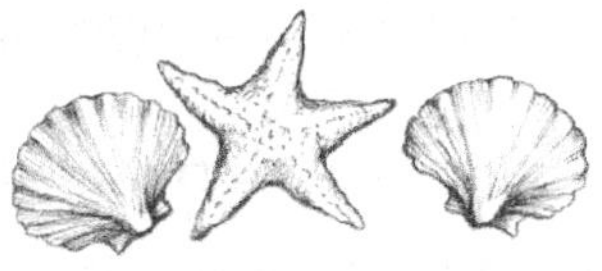

The Vicarage, Little Valentine, South-East Coast of England. 18th August 1815.

"It's perfect!" Clementine exclaimed, regarding the flyer Beatrice had designed with approval. "*The Venturesome Ladies of Little Valentine*. Who could resist being part of such a group?"

"Well, quite a few people, actually," Mrs Adamson said with a sigh. "There are some ladies in the town who think it is an appalling idea, and they do not hesitate to say so."

"Stuff them," Izzy said, earning a reproving look from Bea, who covered Caspar's ears.

The little boy was sprawled on the parlour floor, drawing a picture for Sylvester, who could now do absolutely no wrong in his eyes, having taken Caspar up on his horse and trotted all over town. The horse didn't even belong to him, but rather Stonehaven, who—for reasons Sylvester had promised to explain later—was still here. However, he'd seen the way Caspar looked at the big black stallion and purloined the creature before his friend's very eyes. If Clementine hadn't already been unreasonably in love with the man before now, that would have done it.

"Well, I cannot help but agree with Izzy. This club must be something special, for women who are ready to make changes, for themselves and for others. But in time, perhaps we shall prove ourselves to those who think it vulgar or improper to make friends with those of other classes. We shall bring them around, and one day, they will clamour to join us. Perhaps there will be clubs just like this one all over England," Clementine added, never one to hesitate to reach for the stars.

"All over Europe," offered a voice from the doorway.

Clementine glanced up, her chest tightening at the sight of her husband. He watched her as though she held his heart in her hands. She did, she knew that, but it was all right. He had hers too.

He had confided in her that he did not know how her father had survived when her mother had been taken from him, and she knew just what he meant. But she refused to allow either of them to hold back or to fear the future. The only thing they could do was to live and to love every day as fully as they could. Fate would take care of itself.

"Why not?" she agreed, grinning at him.

"Well, let's just start with Little Valentine, yes?" Izzy said, looking between them with interest. She turned to Bea, mischief alight in her eyes. "I don't think we're going to be seeing any of those upside-down seagulls, Bea. We can cancel our plans for invasion."

Clementine bit her lip as Sylvester looked at her sisters and then at her. "Upside down seagulls?" he repeated, bewildered. "Invasion? What invasion?"

Bea and Izzy dissolved into giggles, only adding to his confusion.

"I'll explain later, love," she told him as he sat down beside her.

His eyes warmed at the word 'later,' which made her heart quicken. How strange that this place, her childhood home, had been all she'd known for so long, and yet now everything had changed. Little Valentine would always be dear to her, a place to which she would relish returning whenever she could, but now she had another home… and it wasn't a place, but a person.

The man beside her meant home to her now and, finally, he had found the place he had been searching for too, with her.

Coming next in The Venturesome Ladies of Little Valentine

The Song of the Siren

The Venturesome Ladies of Little Valentine
Book 2

The beautiful young widow, Mrs Anne Adamson, is not exactly thrilled when the eligible Marquess of Stonehaven proposes marriage. Once upon a time, she might have thought all her dreams had come true, but that was a lifetime ago, when she still believed in heroes and foolish romantic imaginings. Now, she relishes her independence, her own financial security, and her new life, running the successful Mermaid's Tale Hotel in Little Valentine.

Miss Beatrice Honeywell, by contrast, can think of nothing more delightful than a life spent in the company of the charming Marquess. She cares little for his title, nor even his wealth, but something about the man calls to her, making her believe in soul mates, love at first sight, and daring her to risk too much. Yet despite her much-vaunted beauty, the maddening man never looks her way.

Indignant and insulted at having his proposal so summarily refused, Stonehaven comes up with a plan to get back into Anne's good books. They were close friends once, after all, surely, he can bring her around again.

But the events of one summer evening alter the future for all concerned when a brutal attack leaves Stonehaven blinded. Suddenly, everything he thought he knew about himself and about the women in his life has changed. Yet the Marquess of Stonehaven is not a man to sink under the weight of challenge, and despite the trials ahead, he faces the future with courage.

With varying degrees of guilt and love and hope driving them on, neither Anne nor Beatrice will turn their backs on the brave marquess, doing what they think best for his future, and theirs, no matter the hazard to their hearts.

Turn the page to read a sneak peek.

Chapter 1

The beginning is always today.

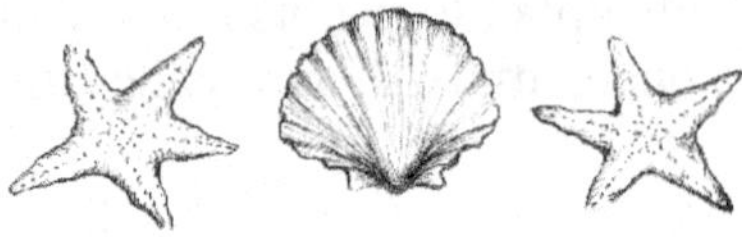

The Mermaid's Tale, Little Valentine, South-East Coast of England. 24th August 1815.

"There's fewer than I hoped," Miss Isabelle Honeywell observed, a small frown furrowing her brow.

Mrs Anne Adamson nodded, having been thinking the same thing herself. She had given over the dining room of her hotel, The Mermaid's Tale, to the very first gathering of The Venturesome Ladies of Little Valentine, and it was far from full.

"It's early days." Izzy's sister, Miss Beatrice Honeywell, smiled placidly, her blue eyes twinkling. "Honestly, you two have no patience. You cannot run before you can walk. This is the perfect first meeting."

"Hmmm," Izzy replied, apparently unconvinced.

"Well, come along. Let us mingle and get people talking, or the whole thing will be for naught," Anne said briskly, pasting a smile to her face. She knew very well why many of the ladies of the town had not come. In the first place, there were those who would be appalled at joining a club that admitted shopkeepers and cooks and maids to its ranks. In the second, it was because of her.

In the eyes of many of the inhabitants of Little Valentine, Mrs Anne Adamson was a thorn in the side of their lovely town. Her history, whilst unknown to most, was rumoured to be scandalous, and a breath of rumour was all it took to ruin a reputation. That much she knew better than most. Not that she was going to let those inhabitants, or anyone else, dictate how she ought to live her life. Once upon a time, she had been weak enough to expect a man to rescue her from circumstances beyond her control. That would not happen again. If there was any rescuing to be done, she'd do it herself.

"Miss Marwick, isn't it?"

The young woman stood at the very edge of the room, teacup in hand, looking as though she very much wanted to sneak out of the door. Anne was not about to let her escape when their numbers were so poor already.

Miss Marwick jumped a little at being addressed but turned to face Anne.

"That's right."

She was a new arrival to the town, her brother having recently bought Ocean View Villa. Her voice was pleasant, softly spoken and obviously educated, but there was a measuring look in her hazel eyes that made Anne wonder if Miss Marwick had heard the rumours already and was judging her unkindly. Not that she cared… much.

"Do come and meet Miss Halfpenny," Anne said, giving the woman a bright smile and taking her firmly by the arm. Poor Clara Halfpenny was so shy she'd not speak to anyone given the opportunity, but Miss Marwick did not look terribly threatening and would likely appreciate meeting such a well-bred young lady.

As she had expected, Anne found Miss Halfpenny trying to disappear behind a large potted fern. "There you are, dear. Poor Miss Marwick is new in town and doesn't know a soul. I just know you will take pity on her and tell her a little about our lovely home."

"O-Oh," Clara blinked, colour flooding her cheeks. "Umm."

To her relief, Miss Marwick instantly recognised the wide-eyed terror of the socially inept and leapt to the rescue. "Why, Miss Halfpenny, how kind of you. I'm afraid Mrs Adamson is quite right. I do not know a soul in town, save my brother. I would not have come at all if Miss Isabelle had not swept me up on her way here. I was just going for a walk and before I knew it, I had a cup of tea in my hand. I'm afraid I'm not very sociable," she added with an apologetic smile.

Anne let out a breath and sent Miss Marwick a grateful smile. Whether true or not, it had been the perfect thing to say.

"Izzy is rather str-strong willed," Clara replied hesitantly. "But lovely!" she exclaimed, glancing between Anne and Miss Marwick with horror in her eyes at the idea they might believe she were being critical.

"She is lovely," Anne said soothingly. "And impossible to say no to. As are the wonderful cakes Mrs Fairway has made for us," she said, speaking loudly enough that her cook overheard the remark.

Mrs Fairway, dressed in her Sunday best and looking very ill at ease, turned pink at the compliment as Anne swept up a plate of queen cakes and offered them to Clara and Miss Marwick. "Do try them."

The young women accepted, and both gave a sigh of pleasure as they chewed.

"Divine," Miss Marwick said, eyes still closed.

"Heavenly," Clara managed, before taking another hasty bite to avoid having to speak again.

"Well, thank you," Mrs Fairway said, unbending enough to come a little closer.

"I've tried and tried to make queen cakes, but mine are like lead," Miss Marwick said sadly.

"Air in the flour, that's the trick. You must sieve it from on high," Mrs Fairway said confidingly.

"Oh?"

"But before that, when you cream the butter, it must change colour before you add the sugar," Mrs Fairway continued, confidence growing as she noticed the rapt expression on Miss Marwick's face. Even Clara looked interested. "If you'd like to learn—"

Anne smiled, hoping their conversation was now on a firm footing, and looked around for her next victim. Movement out of the corner of her eye caught Anne's attention, and she glanced toward the windows. A face peered through the glass, and just as quickly turned away.

"Drat it," Anne muttered, and hurried out of the room, through the entrance hall, and tugged open the door. *"Mrs Jenner!"* she called, waving as the woman glanced back at her.

Mrs Jenner shook her head. "I can't," she said, looking around as if she feared someone might have spotted her. Without another word, she fled, hurrying away from the hotel.

"Oh, dear."

Anne turned to see Beatrice Honeywell standing in the open doorway. With the sunlight glinting on her blonde hair, she was quite the loveliest woman Anne had ever seen. More than half the young men in the town were head over ears in love with her, yet she seemed totally unaffected and utterly oblivious to their devotion. Bea was also kind to a fault, and the look in her eyes as she watched Mrs Jenner's retreat reflected Anne's own regret.

"Quite," she replied with a sigh.

"I'll take her some cakes and tell her about the meeting once we've finished," Bea said, her beautiful face determined.

"I'm not sure that's wise," Anne said cautiously.

Bea's father, Reverend Honeywell, was a very open-minded and rather too easy-going papa, in Anne's opinion, but surely he would not approve of his lovely daughter visiting Mrs Jenner. Not when her brute of a husband might find out and object. The reverend had narrowly avoided getting his own nose broken when Mr Jenner accused him of interfering in his marriage. Not that it had stopped him, but as help from the outside world often rebounded on Mrs Jenner, much care had to be taken.

"Nonsense," Bea said, a surprisingly mutinous look appearing on her face. "Mr Jenner works in the gardens at the Hall during the day, now that the duchess is back in residence. It will be quite safe."

With that, she turned and went back inside.

"Oh, if I were a man," Anne said under her breath, and not for the first time in her life.

She thought the Mr Jenners of the world were no better than a disease, a nasty infection that people hid from shame and fear of judgement when what they needed was curing. He was a gangrenous limb that ought to be cut off before he did any more damage.

"She is most *élégante*," Madame Auguste said with a nod as she watched Mrs Adamson move around the room. She lifted her teacup to her lips and took a delicate sip. "I adore creating for her, as she has such style, and she does not care what people say about her. I admire this."

Beatrice frowned a little as she offered the equally stylish Frenchwoman a sugar biscuit. "What *they* say about her?"

Madame shrugged. "People talk," she said with a nonchalant wave of the sugar biscuit, as if she were not one of those people herself. "I 'ear things."

"Well, I think people are most unkind in that case, and such talk ought not to be repeated." Bea met Madame's eyes, refusing to regret her rather disapproving tone.

Madame Auguste smiled, pleased and feline, as she regarded Bea. “Oh, the little mouse has sharp teeth. I am so glad. I feared the ton would eat you up when you leave us for your season. Per’aps you will survive, after all.” She grinned and snapped her pearly white teeth together. “But truly, I do not know why you English get so excited about *une petite affaire.* So, she had a liaison with a man. So what?”

Bea stiffened, increasingly vexed by the conversation. It was not in her nature to lose her temper, but if her friends or family were criticised, she had discovered she could come out fighting when the need arose. “In the first place, I will not have a season,” she said with a smile to soften the blow, knowing that this would take the wind out of Madame’s sails, for the woman had probably assumed all her new gowns would come from her shop. “In the second, Mrs Adamson is a respectable widow, and no one has any proof that she is anything else. Unless you hear such talk from her own lips, I think it would be best if you did not repeat it. In France, such *little affairs* might be acceptable, in England. they are ruinous, and I should hate to see someone I care about hurt by idle chatter.”

Madame Auguste stared at her, aghast. “Not have a season?” she repeated, having immediately lost interest in Mrs Adamson. “But… But… why not? Your brother-in-law is an earl, surely—”

“Lord Beaumarsh is most generous and would indeed pay for me to have as many seasons as I desire. However, I do not wish for one, so I shall not go. If you would excuse me.”

Bea left Madame Auguste with her mouth hanging open and let out a breath as she went to the refreshments table and poured a cup of tea.

“Very nice tea.”

Bea turned to see their family nanny, Mrs Mabbs, at her elbow. “Them cakes are delicious too. Not what I’ll say so to Mrs

Adie. More than my life's worth," she added with a confiding wink.

Bea laughed, well aware of the rivalry between Mrs Adie and The Mermaid's Tale's Mrs Fairway. Though the two women were friends, that did not stop them being fiercely competitive. Any fair or village affair where they both provided cakes could become fraught if you accidentally favoured one's creation over the other.

"Do you think I ought to go now?" Mrs Mabbs fretted. "Caspar is quite a handful and—"

"No." Bea patted Mrs Mabb's shoulder. "Mrs Adie is perfectly capable of looking after the children, and you made an agreement. She will come next time, and you will have the children and look after things at the vicarage. Today is your turn. Stop worrying and enjoy yourself. Look, there's Mrs Peacock. Her daughter Sarah had her baby boy last week. You remember how upset Mrs Peacock was when she moved to Rye after she got married, though it's not exactly far away. I'm sure she is simply bursting to tell you all about it. You might have some good advice for her, too."

Bea smiled as she saw this idea take hold.

"Well, Sarah always was a delicate little thing. It wouldn't surprise me if she needs some help. I'll see how she's getting along," Mrs Mabbs said with a nod, and bustled off.

Lifting her teacup to her lips, Bea watched as the women of Little Valentine took the first step towards making new friendships. She saw Mrs Marwick and Miss Halfpenny talking quietly and even laughing. Madame Auguste, who considered herself rather above the rest of the shopkeepers in the town, was chatting animatedly to Miss Doomsday, the haberdasher's daughter. She'd been noticed walking to church with Mr Twyner's son, and the entire town was now agog to see if there was a romance blossoming. Bea wondered if Madame had an eye on the wedding gown and trousseau that would be required and then scolded herself for being cynical.

Setting down her empty teacup, Bea helped herself to a cake and had just taken a bite when the door to the dining room swung open. She glanced up, sucked in a breath, and began to choke and splutter as a crumb hit the back of her throat. The woman in the doorway stood rigidly upright despite her advancing years, her keen gaze raking over the assembly with the sharp scrutiny of a bird of prey seeking its next meal. Utterly confounded, Bea put the cake back on her plate and hurried to the door.

"Your grace," she said, dipping into a low curtsey before the august personage of the Dowager Duchess of Hawkney.

"Is this the Adventurous Ladies Club?" the dowager demanded.

Bea stared at her for a moment. "The Venturesome Ladies Club," she corrected gently. "Yes, it is."

"Hmph," the dowager said with a sniff. "A pity. I'd rather join the Adventurous Ladies."

Bea opened her mouth and closed it again.

"Why was I not invited to join?" the dowager asked, narrowing her eyes at Bea and brandishing the small advertising pamphlet that they had given out in the town. "It says to *all the women* of Little Valentine. Well, I'm a female person, am I not?"

"Indeed, your grace," Bea replied, blushing at the realisation they had neglected to invite the most aristocratic woman in the town to join them. "In truth, we did not think our little club would interest you."

"Know me, do you?" the woman said, a mocking lilt to her voice as she quirked one elegant eyebrow.

"No, indeed, and I beg you will forgive us for making assumptions. That was very wrong of us. The principle of our club is that all women are included, from all walks of life. You are most welcome here and I would be delighted to make introductions, if you would allow me the honour."

The dowager nodded, still scrutinising Bea. "You're the incomparable, one of those Honeywell chits. Your pa and your sister came for a visit, but not you. Frightened, were you?"

"No, your grace," Bea replied placidly, too used to sharp-tongued old women to allow herself to be further discomforted. "Unfortunately, I was unable to come that day as I had a prior engagement. However, I should be delighted to call upon you at another time, should you like me to."

"Hmmm. I might, at that. Come when it suits you. I'm old and cantankerous so I don't get many visitors, and I don't go about like I once did. You'll find me at home."

Bea smiled. "Then I shall certainly come. Now, do let me make you known to our club. I'm afraid our numbers are not great yet, for this is our first meeting, but with such an esteemed member as yourself, I feel certain we shall be a great success."

"Oh, you do, do you? And how do you know I want to join your blasted club?"

"You are here, ma'am," Bea said, holding the woman's gaze.

The dowager snorted. "True enough," she said, and then gestured behind her. "Mabel! Come along. Don't dawdle."

A nondescript woman scuttled forward. "Here I am," she murmured, offering her arm to the dowager, who did not look as though she needed the support offered by either the woman or the ebony walking stick she held.

"Come along then, gel," she said, making shooing motions at Bea. "But I warn you, I can't abide toadies."

"Understood, your grace," Bea said, anxiously scanning the room for the woman most likely to entertain the dowager without being utterly terrified. "Mrs Adamson?"

Anne turned, the colour leaving her face as she noted the woman beside Bea. Still, she put up her chin and a polite smile curved over her full lips.

"Your grace," Anne said, sinking into an elegant curtsey. "You honour us."

"Who are you?" the dowager asked, narrowing her eyes at Anne. "Who are your people?"

"I am Mrs Adamson, proprietress of this hotel, and I am nobody in particular."

The dowager looked thoughtful. "Them green eyes and all that hair, dreadful colour of course, but striking. Don't see red of such a bright shade often. Unusual, I'd say."

"Not terribly, no. Half my family have the same colouring and many others too, I'm sure. Now, can I offer you a cup of tea and one of our splendid cakes, perhaps?"

"You may and find me a seat for heaven's sake. These old bones can't be doing with standing about for hours."

Within minutes, they had installed the dowager duchess in the centre of the dining room, a cup of tea on a small table beside her, and a plate with a variety of cakes and biscuits in her hand.

"These Ratafia biscuits are exceptional," she said with surprise, regarding the small biscuit she had just taken a bite of. "Who made them?"

Somehow, everything the dowager said seemed to be uttered as a demand or a command, and Mrs Fairway leapt forward, bobbed a haphazard curtsey and said, "Me, your grace."

"Excellent. You have a talent for sweet things. Might I have the recipe for my cook?"

Mrs Fairway opened her mouth to reply but was halted by the sudden sound of a throat clearing. She glanced at Miss Marwick, who stood beside her, gazing at the ceiling and appearing quite innocent, though Bea was certain it was she who had coughed.

Mrs Fairway blushed scarlet but held the dowager's gaze. "I'd be honoured to give you my recipe, your grace, but the thing is, we have a rule in the Venturesome Ladies. If you give a recipe, you get one in return."

Bea glanced at Anne beside her. "We do?" she whispered.

Anne shrugged. "We do now. Well done, Mrs Fairway."

For a moment the entire room held its breath as the dowager glared at Mrs Fairway, then a pleased smile curved her lips. "Certainly. I have an excellent recipe for lemon cream. It is tart and refreshing. How's that?"

Mrs Fairway looked like she'd just been given access to the crown jewels and was so overcome she ran forward and shook the dowager's hand. "Done," she said, and then blushed scarlet at her own behaviour. Cooks did not touch aristocrats under any circumstances, let alone negotiate with them, but the dowager looked entirely satisfied by the transaction.

"Excellent. I shall have my man send it around to you tomorrow, if you would have your recipe ready to give to him. I suspect I shall have guests arriving shortly and these delicious biscuits are just the thing to soothe prickly tempers."

"It will be my pleasure," Mrs Fairway said, turning to Miss Marwick and shaking her head. "Just think. My own recipe that is, and to be served by the dowager duchess too! Maybe the duke will eat them."

Miss Marwick returned a rueful smile. "Whilst it is certainly an impressive achievement, I fear not. The duke is a high stickler, and I doubt he would ever lower himself to visit Little Valentine."

"Well, she might take it to town with her," Mrs Fairway said, determined not to be downcast.

"Indeed, she might at that," Miss Marwick said with a laugh, meeting Bea's eye and smiling.

Chapter 2

Hail fellow, well met – or not.

The Mermaid's Tale, Little Valentine, South-East Coast of England. 24th August 1815.

Anne excused herself from the dining room, where the little gathering of women had arranged themselves into smaller groups. Some were chatting with more animation than others, but for the moment no one was being left out, and even the dowager duchess seemed to be enjoying herself. Or perhaps *especially* the dowager duchess, who was telling a rather racy story that Anne was not entirely certain ought to be shared with some of the unmarried ladies, but she was not about to put a stop to it. The way the dowager had looked at her had been unnerving, and she had no desire to pique the woman's interest further. The further away they kept from one another, the better she would like it.

Making her way to the kitchen, intending to take up the extra supplies of cakes and biscuits Mrs Fairway had left ready, Anne ground to a halt in shock at the sight before her.

"Devil take you!" she exclaimed as she looked across the kitchen to see the Marquess of Stonehaven sitting at the end of the kitchen table, chewing his way contentedly through one of the plates of biscuits.

"These are jolly good," he mumbled, pointing at the half empty plate.

Anne folded her arms, glaring at him. "What are you playing at, Stonehaven? Are you trying to get me ruined for a second time?"

Wiping his mouth with his hand and looking like a small boy caught stealing jam tarts, he returned a sheepish grin, which did not fool Anne for a moment.

"The first time wasn't my fault, Anne. Nothing to do with me."

"Oh, you made that very plain, I assure you," Anne said, surprised by how angry the words were, even after so many years had passed. "So have you decided you'll have a go now, to make up for it?"

"Good God, I'd forgotten what a termagant you can be," Stonehaven said, grinning at her. "Is that anyway to greet an old friend?"

"An ex-friend," Anne clarified. "And one I have no wish to reacquaint myself with."

"Harsh, Anne," he said, shaking his head. "Surely we can let bygones be bygones."

"Certainly, if you go at the same time," she said pleasantly, moving to the back door and yanking it open. "Goodbye, Stonehaven."

The marquess pushed to his feet, making her uncomfortably aware of how big he was, and how much room he took up. Somehow, with the passage of time, he had become smaller in her memory. Not in reality, however.

"Anne, be reasonable—"

"That's Mrs Adamson to you," she said crisply.

He snorted. *"Mrs Adamson.* Where on earth did you come up with that notion?"

"Are you going to make trouble, Stonehaven?" she demanded, deciding she had better have things out in the open. She was happy here, and she had made a success of herself, but if it was about to come crashing down about her ears, she'd rather be prepared.

His good humour slipped away, his temper flaring as it did all too often. Not that she was any better. "Curse you, Anne, as if I would! What the hell do you take me for?"

Anne regarded him frankly. Once upon a time he had been her best friend in all the world, and then he had been the man she had believed herself in love with. Happily, she had been wrong, for that would certainly have been a disaster, but the discovery he was not her knight in shining armour had been a blow all the same. "I don't know, my lord."

His mouth thinned. "Don't do that."

"Do what?"

"You know very well what. Christ, Anne, we've known each other since we were children. My name is Lawrence. Use it, damn you."

Anne took a breath and replied with great deliberation. "If there is nothing else, Lord Stonehaven, I'll bid you a good day."

Angry hazel eyes bore into her, his anger so palpable her skin prickled with it, but just as suddenly it vanished, and he let out a breath. "I had forgotten the ease with which you make me lose my mind," he said, shaking his head. "It's all coming back to me."

"The feeling is mutual," Anne grumbled, folding her arms. "Are you going to tell me what you want? Some of us work for a living, you know."

His expression clouded and Anne became increasingly apprehensive as she noted the compassion in his eyes. Hell and the devil, was he *sorry* for her?

"I have come to ask your forgiveness, Anne. I want you to know I have long regretted our argument, and… and I know now that I behaved badly. I was a young fool, selfish and arrogant, and you were right to be furious with me. I looked for you for months after you left, I want you to know that. But you are too clever to be found when you have no desire to be found. I ought to have known that much."

Anne looked at him suspiciously. Stonehaven was never humble, and she had certainly never seen him contrite. He wanted something, surely? But what the devil did she have that he could possibly want?

"Fine, you're sorry. Apology accepted. The truth is you did me a favour. Marrying you would have been a disaster for both of us. Instead, you set me free. I have a new life, I'm independent and living exactly as I wish, with no one to answer to. That would not be the case if you had not refused to marry me."

"I didn't refuse," Stonehaven said, indignation glittering in his eyes.

Anne snorted. "No. You just made it very clear you did not wish to do so, which amounts to the same thing. You knew very well I would never force you to wed me."

"That's not how it happened, and what the hell do you mean it would have been a disaster? With hindsight, I think we would have dealt very nicely together."

Anne stared at him. Her heart gave a panicked thud. Surely… *Surely,* he could not be considering it. Had he lost what little sense he had? He glared at her, his stance rigidly upright, centuries of breeding visible in every uncompromising line.

Heaven have mercy, he meant to propose to her!

"Stonehaven," she said, struggling to keep her voice even. "Tell me you have not got some maggot in your brain. Tell me you are not thinking of offering for me?"

"And why not?" he demanded, resentment writ large on his face. "Are you too good for me? Am I unworthy of such a grand lady?"

"Oh, Stonehaven," she said, pinching the bridge of her nose. "I don't—I don't even know where to begin."

"Don't give me that exasperated look and make out like I'm the lunatic," he growled. "You're working for a living, Anne. *Working!* You were born a lady, you were supposed to—"

"Keep your voice down!" she hissed, furious with him.

His jaw snapped shut but she could feel rage burning off him, a wash of heat that seemed to fill the room. Anne took a deep breath. She had to be careful. She had to make her intentions crystal clear, for Stonehaven could be a dog with a bone, but she did not wish to injure his pride.

"I know you will find this hard to understand," she said, trying to reason with him. "But I do not need to marry a titled man to find happiness. Or any man, come to that. I *am* happy. My hotel is my pride and joy, and I love this town. It is my home now, and I am not about to turn my back on everything I have worked for. So, whilst I am aware of the honour you do me, I will not marry you, Stonehaven."

Stonehaven rolled his eyes. "Very nice. Very prettily said, and that's well enough for now. You are young and healthy, and no doubt besieged by admirers even if half the town believe you're a scarlet woman. What happens when you are old, Anne? What happens when you have no family and no one to look after you? What about children, about lineage and history, and all the things we were brought up to believe in?"

"To the devil with lineage," she said savagely, all her good intentions going out of the window at the mention of a word that had been thrust under her nose since she was old enough to understand its meaning and that both their father's believed hers was not good enough for Stonehaven. "And to the devil with you! I have tried to be polite, but as usual you are too pigheaded to heed me. I won't marry you, and I won't change my mind. Just because your friend has got himself leg-shackled, you think you ought to do the same. He's happy, and you think, oh yes, I'd like a bit of that. But you're a great clodpole, Stonehaven, because the thing is, Beaumarsh is *in love* with his wife, and she loves him. Whereas the sight of you makes me want to throw things and you've not given me a thought during the past six years!"

"Fine," Stonehaven retorted, biting the word out. "Rot here. See if I care. Just don't come running to me when everything goes to hell and you find yourself destitute."

"I would rather starve," she said, smiling sweetly at him.

He glared at her and then threw up his hands, stalking to the door. "Good day to you, *Mrs Adamson.*"

Anne closed it behind him and slid the bolt across.

Clara Halfpenny closed the door of The Mermaid's Tale and inhaled a deep breath. She'd done it. She had survived an entire hour in company without making a complete fool of herself. Miracles did happen.

Of course, that did not mean she had survived the day.

Having deliberately helped their maid of all work to cook a substantial breakfast followed thereafter by a hefty lunch for her irascible Aunt Edna, she had crept out of the cottage where she was considered an unwelcome guest, delighting in the sound of her aunt snoring. There was no telling how long the woman would sleep, however, and if Clara had the slightest bit of sense, she would run home as fast as she could. Yet sense was something she had less and less of recently. There was some small but determined little devil inside her that had reared its head over the past weeks, and she found herself rebelling in dozens of small ways.

To most people, using her aunt's best china when she had been told in no uncertain terms she might not, was probably not the most thrilling crime of the past century. To Clara, however, it was a break for freedom. So, whilst she knew it was in her own best interests to go directly home and enjoy her minor victory in peace, the sight of the sunshine glittering on a bright blue sea was too much to resist, and instead she walked down to the beach.

It was a glorious summer day. Whilst a little too hot for walking along the narrow lanes of the town, here on the beach, with the cool touch of sea spray kissing her cheeks and a delightful breeze tugging at her bonnet, it was perfection. Clara inhaled deeply, considering her somewhat one-sided conversation with Miss Marwick. At first glance, she had not expected the young woman to be kind, which she now realised was unfair. Miss Marwick was a stranger and therefore bound to be somewhat diffident, yet she had drawn Clara out little by little, and whilst it could not have been considered a scintillating conversation, it had been pleasant. Rather to her surprise, she believed Miss Marwick had thought so too.

Perhaps the club the Honeywell sisters had begun with Mrs Adamson was not such an ill-conceived notion. Clara had not wished to go to the meeting at all and had only done so because she had faithfully promised the eldest Miss Honeywell she would. Except she was no longer Miss Honeywell… Clementine was now the Countess of Beaumarsh and living an altogether different life with her husband in Kent. It was not so very far, and Clementine had promised to visit, and to invite Clara to stay, a prospect Clara found utterly terrifying. Yet Clara missed her friend. Perhaps Miss Marwick would be a new friend, though, if she could endure the looming shadow of Aunt Edna.

Sighing, Clara counselled herself not to borrow trouble. She had enjoyed a splendid afternoon—with cake—and a walk on the beach. Life was not so bad.

Indeed, as she walked farther along the shore, she smiled as she noticed a little dog, yapping and running back and forth, barking at the waves.

"Here, boy!" Clara called, delighted when the little fellow left his game to scramble over to her. He was only a puppy, and Clara looked about, wondering where he had come from.

There was no one around, and the puppy looked up at her expectantly.

"Well, don't look at me like that," she said, frowning at him. Well, drat. What was she to do now? She couldn't just abandon him.

"I'm sure your owner or your mama must be near," she said reassuringly. "Goodbye, now."

With that, she turned and walked along the beach, only to glance down and see the dog trotting merrily beside her. He was a scruffy little darling, mostly white with patches of grey, though some of that might have been dirt. Clara thought he looked rather bedraggled and on the skinny side and her heart went out to him.

"Oh, dear," she said, staring at the pup in consternation. "Aunt will not approve of you. Not one little—"

A smile curved her lips, and she bent down, scooping the little dog into her arms. The puppy wriggled and squirmed with delight, his whole body wagging along with his tail as he tried to lick Clara's face.

"Yes, yes, I am delighted to meet you too, sir. I am Miss Halfpenny, and who might you be? We must be properly introduced, you understand," she said, speaking gravely to the little dog.

As if quite understanding her meaning, the puppy yapped.

"Hmmm, she said, remembering the butler at her parents' house. He had heartily disliked small children and animals and had been a dreadful snob. Clara had been terrified of him. Whatever devil, or perhaps maggot, that had got into her brain of late, decided that this was the perfect name for this small, rather unkempt little dog. "Mr Bennet, how do you do?"

As she spoke, she shook the puppy's paw. He yapped again, apparently approving her choice.

"Excellent. I hope you will excuse me if we forgo formality in private. I shall call you Benny, and you may call me Clara," she said, and then burst out laughing at her own insanity. She set the puppy back on the sand. "Well, what a fine pair we shall make. Come, Benny. Shall we go home?"

He yapped once more and trotted merrily after her. Though she kept turning around, certain that the dog would lose interest, or find something more enticing to do, Benny kept following, only delaying from time to time when an exciting smell took his fancy.

Clara made her way back up the stairs to the high street, down the small lane that ran to the left of Madame Auguste's and took the safer, if longer, route home through the meadows over Summer Hill. The lane would have been quicker, but it led past the Dog and Duck, an inn that was not entirely respectable, and even during the day was sometimes frequented by men who were more than a little worse for wear. According to the gossip, half the smugglers in Sussex drank there, and whilst Clara was willing to believe this an exaggeration, she had no wish to meet one smuggler, let alone a gang of them.

Benny gambolled behind her, making her heart lift each time she turned and saw him. How she was going to keep him a secret from her aunt, she simply could not fathom, she only knew that she would. As they approached the crest of the hill, Clara turned to discover Benny had sat down, tongue lolling and as she watched, he sprawled in the long grass, panting.

"Oh, dear," she said, smothering a laugh. "It must be more like Summer Mountain with such short little legs. Poor darling," she cooed, bending down and reaching for the dog.

Perhaps if she had not been feeling quite so happy and at peace with the world, the sound and vibration of thundering hooves might have reached her sooner, but as it was, she stood and discovered a huge black stallion bearing down upon her. There was time enough to throw herself clear, but Clara stood frozen to the core, speechless as the horse reared, quite as terrified by her sudden appearance as she was by his.

Massive hooves flailed, flicking mud hither and yon and Clara had a brief glimpse of the rider, of furious blue eyes, as an obscene curse rent the air before he was unceremoniously unseated and thrown to the ground. There was a heavy thud, and she registered a grunt of pain while the horse danced about her, appearing to consider the merits of bolting for good measure.

Too shocked to speak, let alone move, Clara stood clutching Benny, who was trembling as hard as she was. She had once heard it said that at the moment before death, your entire life flashed before your eyes. Clara could not say if that were true, but she knew one thing: she had almost gone to her fate without a whimper, without a scream or a shout or a word of protest. It was the most depressing realisation of her entire life.

"Well, for God's sake, don't just stand there, grab his reins!"

She started, jolted out of her immobility by the imperious, and not to mention, irate voice. There was such command behind the instruction that she did not hesitate, despite being afraid of horses, and hurried to grab at the trailing reins of the enormous beast that was still huffing and stamping, as if he might eat Clara in one bite.

A second rider appeared suddenly, giving a whoop of delight at the scene before him. He cantered around them, grinning irrepressibly.

"Haha! Well, well, never thought I'd see the day you lost your seat, old man. Pride comes before a fall, I reckon. I'll have my winnings in hand this evening then, eh, Al?"

With another shout of laughter, he sprang his horse and galloped off. The man sprawled on the floor, cursed anew and leapt to his feet. He was an impressive sight, despite the rip in his coat sleeve and being covered in dust. His dark auburn hair glinted in the sunshine, his face rigid with fury as he turned to glare at her.

“Are you entirely witless, madam?” he said, reaching down to snatch up his hat from the long grass. “What in the name of everything holy were you thinking, leaping out in front of me like that? Did you mean to kill me?”

“No, sir,” Clara retorted, meeting the man’s eyes and thrusting the reins of his horse out for him to take. “I had merely bent to pick up my dog, who was fatigued by the climb, and the next moment a big brute, with as little sense as he has manners, tried to mow me down. Not that I should expect an apology for such vile treatment from a man who is clearly no gentleman.”

The man, who very clearly *was* a gentleman, and a fine one at that, gazed at her with appalled astonishment, but it was nothing compared to what Clara herself was feeling. Her legs trembled with fear, and she did not know how she was still standing, or from whose mouth those vitriolic words had issued, for surely it had not been hers. Too afraid of what she might say next, Clara clamped her mouth shut.

“I beg your pardon, madam, for any inconvenience I might have caused you,” the man said, though the words were gritted out and the look in his eyes made Clara heartily wish to take several steps back.

She did not, in part because she feared she might fall down, but also because she refused to let the devil cow her. She had spent too much of her life being bullied and she was damned if this ill-mannered lout was going to do it too.

Clara merely watched as the man took back the reins, steadied his horse, and climbed into the saddle with such athletic grace she could not help but notice. It was not until he had cantered off and was out of sight that she let out an unsteady breath and looked down at Benny.

The puppy made a small whimpering sound and wagged his tail apologetically. “Not your fault, sweetie,” Clara said, and kissed his nose.

"And then," Clara said, her eyes glowing with excitement, "he said, 'I beg your pardon, madam, for any inconvenience I might have caused you,' looking just as though he wanted to murder me on the spot."

Bea stared at her, wondering what on earth had got into Clara, who never said boo to a goose. "But weren't you terrified?"

Clara considered this as they stood in the front garden of her aunt's cottage. Bea had come to call upon her Aunt Edna—for no one else wanted to—and arrived to find Clara pottering in the garden. Before she had announced Bea's arrival, Clara had been full of her adventure the previous day, of finding Benny, who was asleep on the path at her feet, and her run in with the man on the black horse.

"Well, I was when the horse was about to trample me to death, or so I thought, anyway. But after that, no, not really. I was just furious that this… this big bully was ordering me about without a word for my welfare."

Bea bit her lip, rather amused. "Quite right too. He sounds perfectly dreadful and deserving of every word. I suppose if he took rather a tumble and lost a bet at the same time he was not at his best. Not to mention being embarrassed in front of his friend. That sort of thing is bound to put a fellow in a bad skin. His pride would have been bruised, if not other parts."

Clara covered her mouth to hide her smile. "Oh. Well yes, I suppose that is true, but at the time I was too… too…"

"Riled up?" Bea suggested.

Clara nodded. "Far too riled up to think rationally. Oh, dear. Do I owe the wretched man an apology?"

Bea considered this. "Certainly not. He earned his scolding by behaving like an ill-mannered brute. His horse, perhaps," she added devilishly, which made Clara grin.

"Clara! Clara! Where are you, you wretched girl? Where's my tea? I've been waiting this age!"

Clara turned back to the cottage and gazed forlornly at the upstairs bedroom window, from where the demand had come. She sighed. "Well, I hope you are ready to have your day ruined."

"Nonsense," Bea said, lifting the basket she'd brought with her. "I've brought flowers and some of our honey, and Mrs Adie baked some of her gingerbread. Ever since the dowager duchess asked for Mrs Fairway's biscuit recipe, she's been cooking up a storm, trying out new things. She's determined her recipe will be asked for too. Heaven help us if it isn't."

"Come along, then, if you are determined," Clara said with a smile. "You are too good, Bea, truly you are. Oh, but you won't mention Mr Bennet, will you?"

"Mr Bennet?" Bea repeated, confused, until Clara reached down and picked up the sleepy puppy.

"Oh, Benny. No, indeed, I will not."

Bea spent half an hour with Clara's Aunt Edna, which she had to admit was a rather fatiguing experience. Never had she met a woman so determined to be displeased with the world and everything in it. The beautiful flowers Bea had brought were bound to make her sneeze, the honey was too sweet, the tea Clara had supplied too strong, and the delicious biscuits Mrs Adie had baked, too gingery.

It had been all Bea could do not to laugh in the face of such stubborn ill temper, but in the end, she could only pity the poor woman and wonder what had befallen her to view life as such a battle. She only hoped Clara could continue to keep little Benny a secret, for she felt sure her aunt would threaten to turn her out if she discovered him. Bea secretly doubted that would ever happen. Edna would be lost without Clara, who did so much for her and was not paid a farthing for doing so. Without her, Edna would be forced to pay for extra help, and that she would not like. She was a miserly pinchpenny who begrudged every morsel of food or sip of tea poor Clara took.

Bea walked home, lost in thought, wondering if there was anything she could do to change the old woman's perspective on life when saw a figure approaching. Thoughts of Clara's grumpy Aunt Edna fled as she recognised the man walking towards her and her heart gave an excited and very foolish extra thud behind her ribs.

"Lord Stonehaven," she said, dipping a curtsey as they met on the path. "Good day to you."

"Miss Honeywell. It is indeed a wonderful day when I have such good fortune as to meet you."

He smiled, his words as charming as always, but Bea sensed he did not mean them. There was an air of distraction about him, of frustration and impatience, and she thought, as she had thought the first time she had met him, that he too was an unhappy soul. Not in the manner of Aunt Edna, perhaps, for the marquess appeared to be jovial and generous to those around him, but he was not a restful person. In part, Bea thought perhaps it was that restless energy that drew her to him, for his proximity made her entire frame thrum with awareness. From the very first moment he had stolen her breath and her wits, and she had been quite unable to think of anyone or anything else. It was a curse of sorts, and yet one from which she would not wish to be freed.

"My father was asking after you," she said, which was not entirely true. However, she knew her papa would welcome a visit and, being such a wise man, might have a calming effect on whatever upset the marquess was stewing over. “He hoped you might call upon him whilst you were still in town.”

This was an outright lie, for he had said nothing of the sort, but Bea knew her papa would forgive her when her intentions were good, if not entirely unselfish. But she assured herself that just because she wished to remain in his company for as long as possible, it did not make her wish to ease his mind any less sincere.

“He did, eh?” Stonehaven said, his dark eyebrows drawing together.

Bea struggled not to blush. As much as she delighted in seeing him, Lord Stonehaven was an intimidating prospect and one who made her feel rather gauche and shyer than usual. “Y-Yes, my lord. He misses Lord Beaumarsh’s company, I believe, and would welcome a visit from an educated man like yourself.”

The considering light in Stonehaven’s eyes made her wonder if he knew she was not being entirely honest. She dropped her gaze to the floor, too abashed to hold his gaze a moment longer. Yet it did not last, for she could not fight the need to dart another look at him, discovering a lazy grin curved over his lips, which made her insides feel most peculiar.

“A capital idea, Miss Honeywell. Is your father at home now?”

“Yes, he ought to be back by this time.”

“Very good. Then, if you would allow me?”

Turning direction to match her own, Stonehaven offered her his arm. Bea felt another blush burnishing her cheeks and stepped forward, putting a tentative hand upon his sleeve. Feeling giddy and foolish, she glanced up again and saw a mischievous twinkle in his eyes. He was enjoying the fact that he flustered her, the wretched man. Not that she begrudged him his enjoyment, for she was too pleased to walk beside him, to look up and admire the harsh planes of a face that was entirely masculine, all hard lines and an uncompromising jaw.

Stubborn devil, she thought with a smile, and walked with him back to the vicarage.

Stonehaven looked around the reverend's study with interest as the man himself poured two glasses of brandy. There were papers piled in haphazard stacks, alongside towers of books, others discarded still open and abandoned upon shelves and chairs, and even on the rug. The desk that dominated the room was relatively tidy, or at least, not such a muddle as every other surface, but Stonehaven wondered how he could find anything he needed without turning the entire place upside down.

"So good of you to take the time to call upon me," the reverend said, turning to grin toothily at him.

He held out a glass, which Stonehaven accepted with thanks, then the reverend plonked himself down in the chair opposite with obvious relief. They sat either side of the fireplace, which was unlit as the summer was still in full swing, and a prettily embroidered fireguard of poppies filled the space.

"It is my pleasure, sir. Beaumarsh spoke highly of you, and your daughter tells me you are missing his company. I am a poor substitute, I fear, but I hoped a visit would not be unwelcome."

"True, true. I miss them both. Darling Clemmie is such a comfort to me, you know, but they have invited me for a visit, which I shall enjoy, but not for a while. Newlyweds need their privacy, eh?" He winked at Stonehaven and took a large swallow of his brandy, smacking his lips with satisfaction.

Stonehaven drank too and regarded his glass with surprise.

"Aha, thought you'd like that. I gave you the good stuff," the reverend said with a chuckle.

"Good?" Stonehaven said, sniffing the amber liquid with appreciation. "That's spectacular. Wherever did you get it?"

"I couldn't possibly tell you," the reverend replied demurely.

"I see," Stonehaven regarded the clergyman with deepening interest. He'd known from what Beaumarsh had said that the reverend was not the average clergyman, and also that smuggling was rife in the area. All the same, he had not expected to be served contraband French brandy with such aplomb. "Could you get me some?"

"I might, for a price."

Stonehaven's eyebrows lifted. "And you, a man of the cloth," he said reproachfully, giving a sorrowful shake of his head.

Reverend Honeywell snorted. "It's all in a good cause, so the good lord will forgive me. I have it in mind to arrange a dance, said as much to the dowager duchess when I spoke to her last. She thought it was an excellent notion and agreed to lend her support. Still, there is rather a dearth of respectable men in the town, and—"

"Oh, no." Stonehaven shook his head. "I beg your pardon, reverend, but no brandy is that good. I'm not a high stickler, I hope, but I draw the line at parading myself at a country assembly for all to gawk at."

The reverend's face fell comically, and Stonehaven took another bracing swallow of the brandy. "No. No, it won't do," he said, his voice firm. "There's no point in giving me that soulful look. I'm a hard man and not the sort to— Dash it all! *No!* Look, I tell you what I'll do. I'll send word to town that there's a lot of pretty girls here and see if anyone takes the bait. If I'm here, a few of the younger fellows are bound to come down. For some reason they like to emulate me, God help them. I'm still at Austen-Leigh's hunting lodge. It's a bit of a ramshackle place, which they won't like one bit, but I can move to the Ship Inn, which looks tidy enough, and they can stay at the Mermaid's Tale. I can't pretend I want a lot of young puppies following me about, but I'll make sure they turn up and do the pretty with the locals. That's a fair exchange, isn't it?"

Stonehaven warmed to the idea as he spoke. Perhaps if he did Anne a good turn, she'd soften her stance a degree or two. It was worth a try. He was still smarting over their last run in. Though he could not fathom what she was playing at, the hotel was obviously doing well and seemed important to her. Well, if she was a marchioness, there was no reason she couldn't be an eccentric one who owned a hotel, was there? It couldn't hurt if he sent some fashionable and well-paying clients to her door. As for not being in love with her, or she with him, well, what did that matter? They'd been friends, good friends. Once upon a time she had looked at him as if he'd hung the moon, he thought a little wistfully. He wondered if he could get her to look at him that way again.

"You won't stay at the Mermaid?" Honeywell asked, and a deal too nonchalantly if Stonehaven was any judge.

"No," Stonehaven replied, refusing to be drawn.

"Well, that is certainly a start," the reverend replied placidly, stretching out his legs before him. "I shall just have to persuade you that attending is in your own best interest."

"Good luck with that," Stonehaven replied sardonically.

"I don't need luck," the reverend said, raising his eyes to heaven. "The good Lord is on my side."

"Hmm. You, sir, are a reprobate. It takes one to know one, and I know your sort. An innocent fellow who looks like butter wouldn't melt and the next thing you know, you've lost your entire fortune to him at Hazard."

"Ah, but I do not approve of gambling," the reverend replied gravely. "Well, that's not entirely true. A little flutter now and then does no one any harm, provided the expense is easily afforded. Indeed, it happens I had a stroke of good fortune myself last month…."

Entirely beguiled, Stonehaven settled into listen as the reverend chatted amiably about horseracing, cricket, the annual summer fair, and his approaching Sunday service. Before he knew it, Stonehaven had agreed to show his face at the fair and come for Sunday lunch—which naturally meant he had to appear in church too.

Shaking his head as he made his way back to the Ship Inn to collect his horse, Stonehaven decided any fellow who underestimated the Reverend Honeywell did so at his peril.

Click this link to pre-order now: The Song of the Siren

The Peculiar Ladies who started it all...

Girls Who Dare – The exciting series from Emma V Leech, the multi-award-winning, Amazon Top 10 romance writer behind the Rogues & Gentlemen series.

Inside every wallflower is the beating heart of a lioness, a passionate individual willing to risk all for their dream, if only they can find the courage to begin. When these overlooked girls make a pact to change their lives, anything can happen.

Twelve girls – Twelve dares in a hat. Twelve stories of passion. Who will dare to risk it all?

To Dare a Duke

Girls Who Dare Book 1

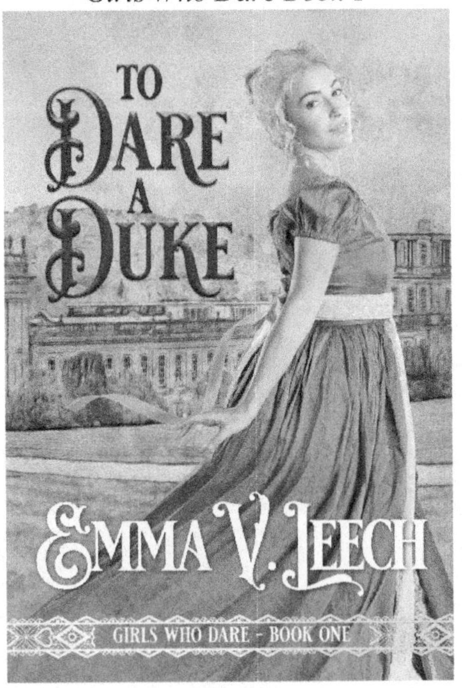

Dreams of true love and happy ever afters

Dreams of love are all well and good, but all Prunella Chuffington-Smythe wants is to publish her novel. Marriage at the price of her independence is something she will not consider. Having tasted success writing under a false name in The Lady's Weekly Review, her alter ego is attaining notoriety and fame and Prue rather likes it.

A Duty that must be endured

Robert Adolphus, The Duke of Bedwin, is in no hurry to marry, he's done it once and repeating that disaster is the last thing he desires. Yet, an heir is a necessary evil for a duke and one he cannot shirk. A dark reputation precedes him though, his first wife may have died young, but the scandals the beautiful, vivacious and spiteful creature supplied the ton have not. A wife must be found. A wife who is neither beautiful or vivacious but sweet and dull, and certain to stay out of trouble.

Dared to do something drastic

The sudden interest of a certain dastardly duke is as bewildering as it is unwelcome. She'll not throw her ambitions aside to marry a scoundrel just as her plans for self-sufficiency and freedom are coming to fruition. Surely showing the man she's not actually the meek little wallflower he is looking for should be enough to put paid to his intentions? When Prue is dared by her friends to do something drastic, it seems the perfect opportunity to kill two birds.

However, Prue cannot help being intrigued by the rogue who has inspired so many of her romances. Ordinarily, he plays the part of handsome rake, set on destroying her plucky heroine. But is he really the villain of the piece this time, or could he be the hero?

Finding out will be dangerous, but it just might inspire her greatest story yet.

To Dare a Duke

The stories of the **Peculiar Ladies Book Club** and their hatful of dares has become legend among their children. When the hat is rediscovered, dusty and forlorn, the remaining dares spark a series of events that will echo through all the families... and their **Daring Daughters**

Dare to be Wicked

Daring Daughters Book One

A Daring and Delicious Victorian Romance from Best Selling Author Emma V Leech

Art, rivalry, temptation, sisters, secrets, and one very distracting viscount.

Lady Elizabeth and Lady Charlotte Adolphus have never been the meek, swooning young ladies the Victorian era expects. Raised by an unconventional mother and a fiercely protective duke, the sisters crave adventure, independence, and a life far more thrilling than embroidery and polite conversation.

Enter Cassius Cadogan, Viscount Oakley — their gloriously handsome childhood friend, newly returned from two years studying art in France. Cassius has always adored both sisters, but now that they're grown, the air between them crackles with something far more dangerous than childhood affection.

And Cassius hasn't come home alone.

Two mysterious Frenchmen accompany him, each more intriguing than the last, and suddenly the Bedwin household becomes a simmering tangle of jealousy, secrets, and temptation. Elizabeth and Charlotte find themselves competing for Cassius's attention… and perhaps for something deeper. Meanwhile, Cassius is discovering that the girls he left behind have become women capable of turning his world upside down.

Passion, art, and hidden truths collide as the sisters navigate rivalry, desire, and the risk of losing not only Cassius — but each other.

One viscount.

Two daring daughters.

And a summer that will change everything.

Perfect for fans of Sarah MacLean, Evie Dunmore, and Joanna Shupe, this is a lush, emotional Victorian romance filled with sensual tension, artistic intrigue, and the dangerous thrill of first love

⭑ ⭑ ⭑ ⭑ ⭑ A wonderful book to launch the series ~ Amazon Customer

**** *Warning: This book contains all manner of bold adventures and daring ladies, some mild perspiration and perhaps even some rather descriptive sex scenes.*

Click here to get your copy: Dare to be Wicked

.

Please enjoy another foray into the world of Girls Who Dare and their offspring with this series about the sons of the Girls Who Dare, Wicked Sons.

Their mothers dared all for love.
Their daughters did the same.
Something wicked this way comes…

The Devil to Pay

Wicked Sons, Book 1

A Wicked Son…

Tall, dark and handsome, ridiculously wealthy, and the heir to a title. With so many blessings in his life, for this Wicked Son there is very little point in being anything more than ornamental. Or at least… that is what everyone believes, but this man has a secret. For a man in his position, if anyone discovered he is the mysterious author of *The Ghosts of Castle Madruzzo*, it would make him a figure of ridicule.

His first novel was a tremendous success, and though his sales are excellent, he is aware he has never quite recaptured the dynamism of that first book. His readers don't seem to care and clamour for more, yet a certain lady critic keeps plaguing him with bad reviews. Somehow, she has guessed he is a nobleman, and delights in finding fault with his less elevated characters.

A little time undercover should do the trick, to prove to himself, and the lady, that he is nothing if not committed to his art.

A lady to be reckoned with…

As the eldest–and only sensible sibling–in an overburdened family, Selina Davenport is holding onto sanity by a thread. The absolute last thing she needs is the presence in her life of an over privileged nob pretending to be something he's not. Like she can't tell at a glance that he is not the lowly gardener he is purporting to be. The nincompoop.

That's not to say she isn't prepared to have a little fun at his expense.

A game that gets out of hand…

But when an immovable object meets an irresistible challenge, sparks are bound to fly, but will they burn down everything around them?

Available now:

The Devil to Pay

Also check out the series that started Emma's first foray into regency romance, Rogues & Gentlemen. Available now!

The Rogue

Rogues & Gentlemen Book 1

A sensual, witty Regency Romance from Best Selling Author Emma V Leech

In the wild heart of Cornwall, danger and desire collide…

Henrietta Morton has always known to keep her head down in a world ruled by smugglers and secrets. But when a notorious pirate—infamous as The Rogue—bursts into her quiet life, Henrietta makes a reckless choice: she hides the dangerously handsome fugitive from the relentless Militia. Her reward? A searing kiss she can't forget—and a letter that could destroy them both.

When her father gambles away her future, forcing her into the arms of a cruel nobleman, Henrietta refuses to surrender. With nothing left to lose, she turns to the only man who can help: the pirate captain with secrets of his own. Blackmail, betrayal, and forbidden passion swirl as Henrietta risks everything for freedom—and for love.

Perfect for fans of:

- Regency romance with high emotional stakes
- Marriage of convenience and forbidden love
- Country house intrigue and windswept coastal adventures
- Scandalous earls and brooding, scarred heroes
- Runaway heiresses and courageous heroines
- Pirate captains, daring escapes, and romantic suspense
- Holiday love stories and happily ever afters
- Enemies to lovers, second chances, and swoon-worthy heroes

Flirty Warning:

This story contains scandalous earls, desperate heroines, and a pirate with a kiss worth risking everything for. Expect witty banter, daring escapades, and scenes that may cause mild swooning—or perhaps even a blush or two. Proceed with fan and fainting couch at the ready!

Free to read on *Kindle Unlimited*: The Rogue

Interested in a Regency Romance with a twist?

A Dog in a Doublet

The Regency Romance Mysteries Book 2

A witty and sensual Regency Romance Mystery by Best Selling Author Emma V Leech

Secrets built the Preston estate. Murder may bring it down.

Harry Browning has never believed in fate — but fate has very definite plans for him.

Born a motherless guttersnipe and raised in the shadows of London's poorest streets, Harry never expected his life to change. But the morning he rescues the elderly Alexander Preston, Viscount Stamford, from a sheer rock face, everything shifts. In a rare moment of gratitude — and even rarer charity — the miserly old lord takes Harry under his wing.

Suddenly Harry is thrust into a world of Regency privilege, taught to read, to manage a vast and crumbling estate, and to behave like a gentleman. But no amount of polish can erase the truth: he is a man with a past, and the past has sharp teeth.

As jealousy, ambition, and old grudges stir within the Preston family, Harry finds himself entangled in a dangerous web of revenge and hidden motives. And when those closest to the Prestons begin to die, suspicion spreads like wildfire.

Then there is Lady Clarinda Bow — lovely, spirited, and far too tempting. Clara threatens Harry's hard-won composure at every turn, drawing him toward a future he has no right to want. But when Lord Stamford's will reveals a shocking demand, Harry is offered a chance at everything he has ever desired… including Clara.

If he dares to take it.

And with danger closing in, Harry may not have a choice.

A self-made man.

A spirited lady.

A legacy steeped in secrets — and a killer who wants it buried.

Perfect for readers who love Regency romance, class-gap love stories, historical mystery, slow-burn tension, and heroes who rise from nothing only to risk everything.

⭐⭐⭐⭐⭐Unique and angsty HR that will keep you reading past your bedtime! Amazing read full of heart! -Amazon Customer

Warning: This book is liable to contain mild swearing and descriptive sex scenes!

Order your copy here. A Dog in a Doublet

Lose yourself in Emma's paranormal world with The French Vampire Legend series….

The Key to Erebus

The French Vampire Legend Book 1

An epic Fantasy Romance from Best Selling Author Emma V Leech

He's waited centuries for her. She's only just discovering what she is.

Jéhenne Corbeaux has always been drawn to the dark. She just never understood why.

When she returns to rural France to live with her eccentric grandmother, the sheltered young witch is thrust into a world she was never meant to remember — a world of vampires, shifters, Fae courts, and ancient magic that whispers her name. Protected, lied to, and hidden away since childhood, Jéhenne has no idea who to trust.

Her powerful grandmother, who knows far more than she admits.

Felix, the dangerously charming shifter who seems determined to protect her.

Or Corvus — the ancient vampire whose first instinct is to kill her… and whose second is far more complicated.

Corvus has waited centuries for her return.

Jéhenne has only just begun to understand her power.

As she's dragged deeper into a supernatural world filled with dark magic, forbidden desire, and deadly secrets, Jéhenne must rely on her instincts rather than the lies she was raised on. Every revelation brings her closer to the truth — and closer to Corvus, whose pull she cannot resist, no matter how many warnings she ignores.

But the truth is far more dangerous than she ever imagined.

And some secrets don't just change your life…

They can end it.

A witch awakening to her destiny.

A vampire bound by fate.

A legend that begins with blood.

Perfect for fans of dark paranormal romance, witches and vampires, found family, slow-burn desire, and dangerous, brooding immortals.

⭑ ⭑ ⭑ ⭑ ⭑ "I loved all the twists and unexpected turns, I feel like I knew the characters as friends. Very rare that a book does that for me." ~ Amazon customer

Now available at Amazon and Kindle Unlimited

The Key to Erebus

Check out Emma's exciting fantasy series with hailed by Kirkus Reviews as "*An enchanting fantasy with a likable heroine, romantic intrigue, and clever narrative flourishes.*"

The Dark Prince

The French Fae Legend Book 1

An epic Fantasy Romance from Best Selling Author Emma V Leech

Two Fae Princes. One human woman. And a destiny that could destroy them all.

Laen Braed, Prince of the Dark Fae, has a reputation as black as his eyes. Ruthless, volatile, and raised to despise the human race, he has no interest in the mortal world—until he's forced through the forbidden gates between realms to retrieve an ancient Fae artifact.

He returns home with far more than a relic.

He brings back a woman who will change everything.

Corin Albrecht, the most powerful Elven Prince ever born, is Laen's opposite in every way. His golden eyes are said to be a gift from the gods, and his love for the human world runs deep. But his friendship with Laen is fracturing under the weight of prejudice, prophecy, and a woman neither of them expected.

Océane DeBeauvoir is an artist and bookbinder whose imagination has always been her refuge. When a jewelled dagger is discovered in a museum—a relic rumoured to prove the existence of the Fae—Océane is inspired to create a work of art unlike anything she has ever attempted.

She has no idea her creation will draw the attention of two princes…

or that her quiet life is about to shatter.

With Laen and Corin vying for her trust—and something far more dangerous—Océane is thrust into a world of Fae courts, ancient magic, forbidden desire, and deadly secrets. Their rivalry threatens to ignite a war, and Océane must decide who to believe… and which of them is truly the Dark Prince.

A human woman with hidden power.

Two Fae princes bound by fate and rivalry.

A legend that begins with a single choice.

Perfect for readers who love Fae romance, enemies-to-lovers tension, love triangles, dark fantasy, court intrigue, and slow-burn, high-tension passion.

Available now to read at Amazon and Kindle Unlimited

The Dark Prince

Want more Emma?

If you enjoyed this book, please support this indie author and take a moment to leave a few words in a review. *Thank you!*

To be kept informed of special offers and free deals (which I do regularly) follow me on *https://www.bookbub.com/authors/emma-v-leech*

To find out more and to get news and sneak peeks of the first chapter of upcoming works, go to my website and sign up for the newsletter.
http://www.emmavleech.com/

Or follow me here......

http://viewauthor.at/EmmaVLeechAmazon

To see more of the amazing artwork from my talented sister and illustrator, Amanda Wood, follow her here:

Amanda Wood Art Instagram

Made in the USA
Las Vegas, NV
03 March 2026

42985768R00184